Trouble on Triton

Samuel R. Delany

TROUBLE
ON TRITON

An Ambiguous Heterotopia

Foreword by Kathy Acker

WESLEYAN UNIVERSITY PRESS

Middletown, Connecticut

for
   Isaac Asimov,
   Jean Marc Gawron,
and
   Howard, Barbara,
   David, Danny, Jeremy,
   and Juliet Wise

Wesleyan University Press
Middletown, CT 06459
www.wesleyan.edu/wespress
Copyright © 1976 by Samuel R. Delany
Foreword © 1996 by Kathy Acker
First published as *Triton* by Bantam Spectra Books, 1976
Wesleyan University Press paperback 1996
All rights reserved
Printed in the United States of America   10   9   8   7
ISBN-13: 978-0-8195-6298-2
CIP data appear at the end of the book

This edition originally produced in 1996 by Wesleyan/
University Press of New England, Hanover, NH 03755

The lyrics on pages 145–47 are by Bruce Cockburn,
from his album *Night Vision*, and are reprinted by permission.

The social body constrains the way the physical body is perceived. The physical experience of the body, always modified by the social categories through which it is known, sustains a particular view of the society. There is a continual exchange of meaning between the two kinds of bodily experience so that each reinforces the categories of the other. As a result of this interaction, the body itself is a highly restricted medium of expression . . . To be useful, the structural analysis of symbols has somehow to be related to a hypothesis about role structure. From here, the argument will go in two stages. First, the drive to achieve consonance in all levels of experience produces concordance among other means of expression, so that the use of the body is co-ordinated with other media. Second, controls exerted from the social system place limits on the use of the body as medium.

MARY DOUGLAS, *Natural Symbols*

Contents

On Delany the Magician

A Foreword
by Kathy Acker

On Naming

"I feel the science-fictional enterprise is richer than the enterprise of mundane fiction. It is richer through its extended repertoire of sentences, its consequent greater range of possible incident, and through its more varied field of rhetorical and syntagmic organization. I feel it is richer in much the same way atonal music is richer than tonal, or abstract painting is richer than realistic."

So speaks a man in the book that you are about to read. The man who is the author of the book. Written in 1976, *Trouble on Triton,* by use of the name or genre of sci-fi, carved in literary geography a pathway between novel-writing and poetry.

"I feel the science-fictional enterprise . . ." What is the necessity to name? Why does Delany need to name science-fiction and posit it against other fiction? And isn't there "other fiction" whose territories and strategies are neither minimal nor restricted by the outdated laws and regulations of bourgeois realism?

"Naming is always a metonymic process," Delany writes. That is, a name doesn't tell you what something is so much as it connects the phenomenon/idea to something else. Certainly to culture. In this sense, language is the accumulation of connections where there were no such connections. And so, to Delany, names such as "science-fiction" form a web:

> All the uses of the words "web," "weave," "net," "matrix," and more, by this circular "etymology," become entrance points into a *textus,* which is ordered from all language functions, and upon which the text itself is embedded.

Into the Web

It is this web, a web now named Triton, to which I want to introduce you. If you are Dante, I am Virgil: I am taking you down to the underworld. Into the world under, the worlds of language, words, the world in which there is a secret.

There must be a secret hidden in this book or else you wouldn't bother to read it.

Remember: it all comes down. One must go down to see. Down into language. Once upon a time there was a writer; his name was Orpheus. He was and is the only writer in the world because every author is Orpheus. He was searching for love.

For his love. For Eurydice.

Eurydice is secret, a secret. This is how Eurydice became secret: she was walking down by the river, always by water, and a man named Aristaeus tried to rape her. She escaped from him before he got to do anything, but in the process, she stepped on a snake. It bit her; she died.

So Orpheus couldn't see her anymore. Dead, she became secreted, secret. He wouldn't accept her death, death. Every poet is revolutionary. Orpheus started searching for Eurydice, for his secret. For all that was now unknown and, perhaps, unknowable. He journeyed, for he had no choice, into the land of death.

For the poet, the world is word. Words. Not that precisely. Precisely: the world and words fuck each other.

Delany is Orpheus searching for Eurydice by means of words. By going down into words. Into the book. As you read this, you will become Delany/Orpheus.

The book's protagonist, Bron Helstrom, looks for his Eurydice—who is totally unknown to him. Unknowable? Therein lies the narrative of *Trouble on Triton*: the trajectory from "unknown" to "unknowable." Here, also, is the mystery of the Orpheus myth.

Delany is going to take you to Triton. To a society to which you are a stranger. To all that is other, to the other-world or underworld. Bron Helstrom is also a stranger in this society: you and he will share problems. The book is not named *Triton*, but *Trouble on Triton*.

Every book, remember, is dead until a reader activates it by reading. Every time that you read, you are walking among the dead, and, if you are listening, you just might hear prophecies. Aeneas did. Odysseus did. Listen to Delany, a prophet.

You are about to enter a story or a land in which there is a mystery, a secret, a prophecy about you.

Bron, another appearance of Orpheus, is in the land that is strange to him, in Triton; he's searching for someone to love. Since that means that he's also searching for how to love, he's trying to find himself. Every search for the other, for Eurydice, is also the search for the self. Who, Bron will ask, do I desire? Who can I desire? What does my desire look like? Strange even to himself, Bron learns that he cannot find himself and so he begins to look more widely, more profoundly, and, as you see through his eyes, for he is your guide, you will begin to look. For Eurydice; for yourself. As soon as you find Eurydice, who lies in the center of this masterpiece by Delany, because she is the one who does not lie, *as soon as you see Eurydice's face,* you will know everything.

You shall see desire.

Delany has seen Eurydice's face, for he is also the constructor of Triton, he is the magician. Look at his language. Call it "poetic language." But "poetry" doesn't mean much anymore. This, his, is magic language. It is, as Delany says, not the language of the web so much as the language that makes webs. Delany the author entered into language until language made his desires/questions into a world. The last part of this creation process is you entering the same language by reading until the language shows you you. Delany, a magician.

Eurydice? Where is she? As another woman, Luce Irigaray, has asked: are there women anywhere?

In the utopia/distopia of Triton, women can become men and men, women. In 1976 Delany, magician, was prophesying or creating the San Francisco of 1996. But . . . what of Eurydice by herself?

According to Robert Graves in *The Greek Myths,* Eurydice, whose name means "wide justice," is the serpent-grasping ruler of the underworld. (Remember: she died because a snake bit her as she was running away from Aristaeus.) There in the underworld, she is offered humans who have been sacrificed by injecting them with snake venom.

Eurydice, then, whom Bron/Orpheus cannot find in Triton, in the underworld, becomes Eurydice whom Bron/Orpheus cannot bear to see. She becomes doubly unable-to-be-seen.

Bron, you will learn as you try to see him, is looking for a lover. He has already decided that he isn't homosexual. To find a female lover, he will have to find women, to see them, to understand them, their real sexualities. Increasingly desperate to find and to see love, he will become what he cannot see.

As if it's possible to become what one cannot be/see. For it is possible to change form, to become another form, for Bron to become female with regard to form, but it is not possible to have another history. To really become a woman, Bron must understand patriarchy and sexism, history that he has not experienced.

Orpheus cannot bear to see Eurydice.

As Bron/Orpheus's quest fails, turns on itself, it changes form. It becomes something other than quest, than story. It becomes Bron/Delany/Orpheus's meditation on gender, desire, and identity. Delany's story refuses to find an ending, to end. Rather it turns on itself like one of the snakes Eurydice handles when she's ruler of the underworld; it becomes a conversation. A conversation, not only about identity, desire, and gender, but also about democracy, liberalism, and otherness. And, perhaps more than anything, a conversation about societies that presume the possibilities of absolute knowledge and those societies whose ways of knowing are those of continuous unending searching and questioning . . .

Enter now into *Trouble on Triton:* enter into a conversation between you and Samuel Delany about the possibilities of being human. By choosing the novel as an arena for conversation, Delany is revealing himself as a great humanist.

—*San Francisco, 1996*

Trouble on Triton

Some Informal Remarks toward the Modular Calculus,
Part One

1. Der Satz

No two of us learn our language alike, nor, in a sense, does any finish learning it while he lives.   WILLARD VAN ORMAN QUINE, *Word and Object*

He had been living at the men's co-op (Serpent's House) six months now. This one had been working out well. So, at four o'clock, as he strolled from the hegemony lobby onto the crowded Plaza of Light (thirty-seventh day of the fifteenth paramonth of the second year$_N$, announced the lights around the Plaza—on Earth and Mars both they'd be calling it some day or other in Spring, 2112, as would a good number of official documents even out here, whatever the political nonsense said or read), he decided to walk home.

He thought: I am a reasonably happy man.

The sensory shield (he looked up:—Big as the city) swirled pink, orange, gold. Cut round, as if by a giant cookie-cutter, a preposterously turquoise Neptune was rising. Pleasant? Very. He ambled in the bolstered gravity, among ten thousand fellows. Tethys? (No, not Saturn's tiny moon—a research station now these hundred twenty-five years—but after which, yes, the city had been named.) Not a big one, when you thought about places that were; and he had lived in a couple.

He wondered suddenly: Is it just that I am, happily, reasonable?

And smiled, pushing through the crowd.

And wondered how different that made him from those around.

I can't (he stepped from the curb) look at *every* one to check.

Five then? There: that woman, a handsome sixty—or older if she'd had regeneration treatments—walking with one blue, high-heeled boot in the street; she's got blue lips, blue bangles on her breasts.

A young (fourteen? sixteen?) man pushed up beside her, seized her blue-nailed hand in his blue-nailed hand, grinned (bluely) at her.

1

Blinking blue lids in recognition, she smiled.

Really, breast-bangles on a man? (Even a very young man.) Just aesthetically: weren't breast-bangles more or less predicated on breasts that, a) protruded and, b) bobbed . . . ? But then hers didn't.

And she had both blue heels on the sidewalk. The young man walked with both his in the street. They pushed into parti-colored crowd.

And he had looked at two when he'd only meant to look at one.

There: By the transport-station kiosk, a tall man, in maroon coveralls, with a sort of cage over his head, shouldered out between several women. Apparent too as he neared were cages around his hands: through the wire you could see paint speckles; paint lined his nails; his knuckles were rough. Some powerful administrative executive, probably, with spare time and credit enough to indulge some menial hobby, like plumbing or carpentry.

Carpentry?

He humphed and stepped aside. A waste of wood and time.

Who else was there to look at in this crowd—

With tiny steps, on filthy feet, ten, fifteen—some two *dozen*—mumblers shuffled toward him. People moved back. It isn't, he thought, the dirt and the rags I mind; but the sores . . . Seven years ago, he'd actually attended meetings of the Poor Children of the Avestal Light and Changing Secret Name; over three instruction sessions he'd learned the first of the Ninety-Seven Sayable mantras/mumbles: *Mimimomomizolalilamialomuelamironoriminos* . . . After all this time he wasn't *that* sure of the thirteenth and the seventeenth syllables. But he almost remembered. And whenever the Poor Children passed, he found himself rehearsing it, listening for it in the dim thunder of labials and vowels. Among a dozen-plus mumblers, all mumbling different syllable chains (some took over an hour to recite through), you couldn't hope to pick out one. And what mumbler worth his salt would be using *the* most elementary sayable mumble in a public place anyway? (You had to know something like seventeen before they let you attend Supervised Unison Chanting at the Academy.) Still, he listened.

Mumblers with flickering lips and tight-closed lids swung grubby plastic begging-bowls—too fast, really, to drop anything in. As they passed, he noted a set of ancient keys in one, in another a Protyyn bar (wrapper torn), and a five-franq token. ("Use this till I report it stolen, or the bill gets too big," had been someone's mocking exhortation.) In the group's middle, some had soiled rags tied over their faces. Frayed ends flapped at an ill-shaved jaw. A woman to the side, with a cracked yellow bowl (she was almost pretty, but her hair was stringy enough to see through to her flaking scalp), stumbled, opened her eyes, and looked straight at him.

He smiled.

Eyes clamped again, she ducked her head and nudged someone beside her, who took up her bowl and her begging position, shuffling on with tight-clenched lids: she (yes, she was his fourth person) sidled and pushed among them, was absorbed by them—

Ahead, people laughed.

He looked.

That executive, standing free of the crowd, was waving his caged hands and calling good-naturedly: "Can't you see?" His voice was loud and boisterous. "Can't you *see*? Just look! I couldn't give you anything if I wanted to! I couldn't get my hands into my purse to get anything out. Just take a look!"

The executive was hoping to be mistaken for a member of some still severer, if rarer, sect that maimed both body and mind—till some mumbler opened eyes and learned the dupe was fashion, not faith. A mumbler who blinked (only newer members wore blindfolds, which barred them from the coveted, outside position of Divine Guide) had to give up the bowl and, as the woman had done, retire within. The man harangued; the Poor Children shuffled, mumbled.

Mumblers aimed to ignore such slights; they courted them, gloried in them: so he'd been instructed at the meetings seven years ago.

Still, he found the joke sour.

The mumblers, however laughable, *were* serious. (He had been serious, seven years ago. But he had also been lazy—which was why, he supposed, he was not a mumbler today but a designer of custom-styled, computer metalogics.) The man was probably not an executive, anyway; more likely some eccentric craftsman—someone who worked *for* those executives who did not have *quite* the spare time, or credit, to indulge a menial hobby. Executives didn't—no matter how good-naturedly—go around haranguing religious orders in the street.

But the crowd had closed around the Poor Children. Had the harasser given up? Or been successful? Footsteps, voices, the roar of people passing blended with, and blotted out, the gentle roar of prayer.

And he'd looked at, now . . . what?

Four out of five? Those four were not very good choices for a reasonable and happy man. And who for the fifth?

Six kaleidoscopically painted ego-booster booths ("KNOW YOUR PLACE IN SOCIETY," repeated six lintels) sided the transport kiosk.

Me? he thought. That's it. Me.

Something amusing *was* called for.

He started toward the booths, got bumped in the shoulder; then forty people came out of the kiosk and all decided to walk between him and the booth nearest. I will not be deterred, he thought. I'm *not* changing my mind: and shouldered someone hard as someone had shouldered him.

Finally, inelegantly, he grabbed a booth's edge. The canvas curtain (silver, purple, and yellow) swung. He pushed inside.

Twelve years ago some public channeler had made a great stir because the government had an average ten hours videotaped and otherwise recorded information on every citizen with a set of government credit tokens and/or government identity card.

Eleven years ago another public channeler had pointed out that ninety-nine point nine nine and several nines percent more of this information was, a) never reviewed by human eyes (it was taken, developed, and catalogued by machine), b) was of a perfectly innocuous nature, and, c) could quite easily be released to the public without the least threat to government security.

Ten years ago a statute was passed that any citizen had the right to demand a review of all government information on him or her. Some other public channeler had made a stir about getting the government simply to stop collecting such information; but such systems, once begun, insinuate themselves into the greater system in overdetermined ways: Jobs depended on them, space had been set aside for them, research was going on over how to do them more efficiently—such overdetermined systems, hard enough to revise, are even harder to abolish.

Eight years ago, someone whose name never got mentioned came up with the idea of ego-booster booths, to offer minor credit (and, hopefully, slightly more major psychological) support to the Government Information Retention Program:

Put a two-franq token into the slot (it used to be half a franq, but the tokens had been devalued again a year back), feed your government identity card into the slip and see, on the thirty-by-forty centimeter screen, three minutes' videotape of *you*, accompanied by three minutes of your recorded speech, selected at random from the government's own information files. Beside the screen (in this booth, someone had, bizarrely, spilled red syrup down it, some of which had been thumb-smudged away, some scraped off with a fingernail), the explanatory plaque explained: "The chances are ninety nine point nine nine and several nines percent more that no one but you has ever seen before what you are about to see. Or," as the plaque continued cheerily, "to put it another way, there is a greater chance that you will have a surprise heart attack as you step from this booth today than that this confidential material has ever been viewed by other human eyes than yours. Do not forget to retrieve your card and your token. Thank you."

He had, for several weeks, worked at the public channels (as a copy researcher, while, in the evenings, he had been taking his metalogical training course) and, eight years ago, had been appalled at the booths' institution. It was as if (he used to think, and had said a number of times, and had gotten a number of laughs when he said it) the Germans, during Earth's Second World War, had decided to make Dachau or Auschwitz a paying tourist proposition *before* the War was over. (He had never been to Earth. Though he'd known a few who had.) But he had not made a stir; it had simply become another of the several annoyances that, to live in the same world with, had to be reduced to amusements. For two years, while finding the booths derisively amusing in theory, he had never gone into one—as silent protest. He had kept it up till he realized practically no one he knew ever went into them either: they considered the millions of people who did, over all the inhabited Outer Satellites, common, unthinking, politically irresponsible, and dull—which made it depressingly easy to define the people who did *not* use them, if only by their prejudices, as a type. He hated being a type. ("My dear young man," Lawrence had said, "*every*one is a type. The true mark of social intelligence is how unusual we can make our particular behavior for the particular type we are when we are put under particular pressure.") So, finally (five years ago? No, six), he had entered one, put in his quarter-franq token (yes, it *had* been a quarter-franq back then) and his card, and watched three minutes of himself standing on a transport platform, occasionally taking a blue program folder from under his arm, obviously debating whether there was time to glance through it before the transport arrived, while his own voice, from what must have been a phone argument over his third credit-slot rerating, went back and forth from sullenness to insistence.

He had been amused.

And, oddly, reassured.

("Actually," he'd said to Lawrence, "as a matter of fact I *have* been in them, a number of times. I rather pride myself on occasionally doing things contrary to what *everyone* else does." To which Lawrence—who was seventy-four, homosexual, and unregenerate—had muttered at the vlet board, "That's a type too.")

He took his card from the pouch on his loose, rope belt, found his two-franq token, and, with his thumb, pushed it into the slot, then fed the card into the slip.

Across the top of the screen appeared his name:

Bron Helstrom

and below that his twenty-two digit government identity number.

The screen flickered—which it was not supposed to. A blur, filling the right half, rushed upward, froze a moment on the image of a door that someone (him?) was starting to open—then the blur rushed again, sliding (the heavy black border; the single bright line up the middle) across the screen; which meant the multitrack videotape had somehow lost sync. (When it happened on one of the public channel viewers at the co-op, it was quickly followed by a "We Regret That, Due to Technical Difficulties . . ." in quaint, 1980's computer type.)

Snap! from the speaker (which he assumed—though he had no reason to be sure—was a length of five-hundred micro-track video-tape, somewhere in an Information Retention storage bank, break-ing) turned the screen into colored confetti. The speaker grill hummed and chuckled, simultaneously and inanely.

Broken?

He looked at the card slip: How do I get my card out? he thought, a little panicky. Pry it out with my five-franq token? He couldn't get it with a fingernail. Was the fault possibly here in the booth and not in the storage bank . . . ?

Indecision storming, he leaned against the booth's back wall and watched storming dots. Once he bent and put his eye to the slip. A centimeter beyond the aluminum lips, the card edge, to some whirring timer, quivered like a nervous tongue.

He leaned back again.

After three minutes, the screen went gray; the speaker's burr ceased.

From the metal slip the card thrust (like a printed-over tongue, yes; with a picture of him in one corner). As he took it, thick wrists heavy with bracelets, that on a thinner wrist would have jangled

(Lawrence had said: "Thick wrists are just not considered attractive right through here," and sighed. Bron, finally, had smiled), he saw his reflection in the dead glass.

His face (syrup spilled his shoulder), under pale, curly hair, was distraught. One eyebrow (since age twenty-five it had grown constantly, so that he actually had to cut it) was rumpled: his other he'd had replaced, when he was seventeen, by a gold arc set in the skin. He could have had it removed, but he still enjoyed the tribute to a wilder adolescence (than he would care to admit) in the Goebels of Mars's Bellona. That gold arc? It had been a small if violent fad even then. Nobody today on Triton knew nor cared what it meant. Frankly, today, neither would most civilized Martians.

The leather collar he'd had his design-rental house put together, with brass buckle and studs—which was just nostalgia for last year's fashions. The irregular, colored web for his chest was an attempt at something original enough to preserve dignity, but not too far from this year's.

He was putting his card back into his purse when something clinked: his two-franq token had fallen into the return cup, reiterating what the booth itself had been placed there to proclaim: The government cared.

He forefingered up the token (with the machine broken, he would not know if the two franqs had or had not been charged against his labor credit till he got to his co-op computer) and fisted aside the curtain. He thought:

I haven't really looked at my final person. I—

The Plaza of Light was, of course, now almost deserted. Only a dozen people, over the concourse, wandered toward this or that side street. Really, there was just no crowd to pick a final person from.

Bron Helstrom frowned somewhere behind his face. Unhappily, he walked to the corner, trying to repicture the colored dots fading into his syrup-edged reflection.

The sensory shield ("It merely shields us from the reality of night;" again, Lawrence) flowed overhead, translating into visible light the radio-sky behind it.

Neptune (as was explained on various tourist posters frequently and, infrequently, in various flimsies and fiche-journals) would not be that intense a turquoise, even on the translation scale; but it was a nice color to have so much of up there.

Night?

Neriad? From Triton, the other moon of Neptune never looked larger than a star. Once he'd read, in a book with old, bright pictures, ". . . Neriad has a practically sausage-shaped orbit . . ." He knew the small moon's hugely oblate circuit, but had frequently wondered just *what* a sausage was.

He smiled at the pink pavement. (The frown still hung inside, worrying at muscles which had already set their expression for the crowd; there was no crowd . . .) At the corner, he turned toward the unlicensed sector.

It was not the direct way home; but, from time to time, since it was another thing his sort didn't do, he would wander a few blocks out of his way to amble home through the u-l.

At founding, each Outer Satellite city had set aside a city sector where no law officially held—since, as the Mars sociologist who first advocated it had pointed out, most cities develop, of necessity, such a neighborhood anyway. These sectors fulfilled a complex range of functions in the cities' psychological, political, and economic ecology. Problems a few conservative, Earth-bound thinkers feared must come, didn't: the interface between official law and official lawlessness produced some remarkably stable *un*official laws throughout the no-law sector. Minor criminals were not likely to retreat there: Enforcement agents could enter the u-l sector as could anyone else; and in the u-l there were no legal curbs on apprehension methods, use of weapons, or technological battery. Those major criminals whose crimes—through the contractual freedom of the place—existed mainly on paper found it convenient, while there, to keep life on the streets fairly safe and minor crimes at a minimum. Today it was something of a truism: "Most places in the unlicensed sector are statistically safer than the rest of the city." To which the truistic response was: "But not *all*."

Still, there was a definite and different feel to the u-l streets. Those who chose to live there—and many did—did so because, presumably, they liked that feel.

And those who chose only to walk? (Bron saw the arched underpass in the gray wall across the alley's end.) Those who chose to walk there only occasionally, when they felt their identity threatened by the redundant formality of the orderly, licensed world . . . ? Lawrence was probably right: They were a type too.

The wall right of the arch was blank and high. In their frame, green numbers and letters for the alley's coordinates glowed. Forty or fifty stories up, windows scattered irregularly. Level with him, someone had painted a slogan; someone else had painted it out. Still, the out-painting followed the letters enough to see it must have been seven . . . eight . . . ten words long: and the seventh was, probably, EARTH.

The wall to the left was scaly with war posters. "TRITON WITH THE SATELLITE ALLIANCE!" was the most frequent, fragmented injunction. Three, pretty much unmarred, demanded: "WHAT ON EARTH HAVE WE GOT TO WORRY ABOUT!?!" And another: "KEEP TRITON UP AND OUT!" That one should be peeled down pretty soon, by whoever concerned themselves with poster peeling; as, from the scraps and shreds adangle, somebody must.

The underpass was lit either side with cadaverous green light-strips. Bron entered. Those afraid of the u-l gave their claustrophobic fear of violence here (since statistics said you just wouldn't find it inside) as their excuse.

His reflection shimmered, greenly, along the tiles.

Asphalt ground, grittily, under his sandals.

An air convection suddenly stung his eyes and tossed paper bits (shreds from more posters) back along the passage.

A-squint in the dying breeze, he came out in near darkness. The sensory shield was masked here, in this oldest sector of the city. Braces of lights on high posts made the black ceiling blacker still. Snaking tracks converged in gleaming clutches near a lightpost base, then wormed into shadow.

A truck chunkered, a hundred yards away. Three people, shoulder to shoulder, crossed an overpass. Bron turned along the plated walkway. A few cinders scattered near the rail. He thought: Here anything may happen; and the only thing my apprehensiveness assures is that very little will . . .

The footsteps behind only punctured his hearing when a second set, heavier and duller, joined them.

He glanced back—because you were supposed to be more suspicious in the u-l.

A woman in dark slacks and boots, with gold nails and eyes and a short cape that did not cover her breasts, was hurrying after him. Perhaps twenty feet away, she waved at him, hurried faster—

Behind her, lumbering up into the circle of light from the walkway lamp, was a gorilla of a man.

He was filthy.

He was naked, except for fur strips bound around one muscular arm and one stocky thigh; chains swung from his neck before a furry, sunken chest. His hair was too fouled and matted to tell if it was dyed blue or green.

The woman was only six feet off when the man—she hadn't realized he was behind her . . . ?—overtook her, spun her back by the shoulder and socked her in the jaw. She clutched her face, staggered into the rail and, mostly to avoid the next blow that glanced off her ear, pitched to her knees, catching herself on her hands.

A-straddle her, the man bellowed, "You leave him—" jabbing at Bron with three, thick fingers, each with a black, metal ring—"alone, you hear? You just leave him alone, sister! Okay, brother—" which apparently meant Bron, though the man didn't really look away from the top of the woman's blonde head—"she won't bother you any more."

Bron said: "But she wasn't—"

The matted hair swung. His face glowered: the flesh high and to the left of his nose was so scarred, swollen, and dirty, Bron could not tell if the sunken spot glistening within was an eye or an open wound. The head shook slowly. "Okay, brother. I did my part. You're on your own, now . . ." Suddenly the man turned and lumbered away, bare feet thudding through the circle of light on the cindery plates.

The woman sat back on the walkway, rubbing her chin.

Bron thought: Sexual encounters *are* more frequent in the u-l. (Was the man part of some crazed, puritan sect?)

The woman scowled at Bron; then her eyes, scrunching tighter, moved away.

Bron asked: "I'm terribly sorry—but are you into prostitution?"

She looked at him again, sharply, started to say one thing, changed to another, finally settled on, "Oh, Jesus Christ," then went back to fingering her jaw.

Bron thought: The Christians aren't making *another* comeback . . . ? He asked: "Well, are you all right?"

She shook her head in a way that did not, he decided, mean specifically negation. (As her exclamation, he decided, did not specifically mean Christianity.) She stuck out a hand.

He looked at it a moment (it was a hand wide as his own, with pronounced ligaments, the skin around the gold nails rough as some craftsman's): she wanted help up.

He tugged her to her feet, noting as she came, unsteadily, erect that she was generally big-boned and rather awkward. Most people with frames like that—like himself—tended to cultivate large muscles (as he had done); she, however—common in people from the low-gravity Holds or the median-gravity Keeps—hadn't bothered.

She laughed.

He looked up from her hips to find her looking at him, still laughing. Something inside pulled back; she *was* laughing at him. But not like the craftsman at the mumblers. It was rather as if he had just told her a joke that had given her great pleasure. Wondering what it was, he asked:

"Does it hurt?"

She said, thickly, "Yes," and nodded, and kept laughing.

"I mean I thought you might be into prostitution," Bron said. "Rare as it is out here—" which meant the Outer Satellites—"it is more common *here*—" which meant, the u-l. He wondered if she understood the distinction.

Her laugh ended with a sigh. "No. I'm into history, actually." She blinked.

He thought: She disapproves of my question. And: I wish she would laugh again. And then: What did I do to make her *stop* laughing?

She asked: "Are *you* into prostitution?"

"Oh, not at . . ." He frowned. "Well, I guess—but do you mean buying or . . . selling?"

"Are you into either one?"

"Me? Oh, I . . ." He laughed now. "Well, actually, years ago, you see, I was—when I was just a teenager . . . um, selling—" Then he blurted: "But that was in Bellona. I grew up on Mars and . . ." His laugh became an embarrassed frown; "I'm into metalogics now—" I'm acting like I *live* here (which meant the u-l), he thought with distress; it was trying not to have it appear he lived outside. But why should he care about—? He asked: "But why should you care about—?"

"Metalogics," she said, saving him. "Are you reading Ashima Slade?" who was the Lux University mathematician/philosopher who, some twenty-five years ago, had first published (at some ridiculous age like nineteen) two very thick volumes outlining the mathematical foundations of the subject.

Bron laughed. "No. I'm afraid that's a little over my head." Once in the office library, he had actually browsed in the second volume of *Summa Metalogiae* (volume one was out on loan); the notation was different and more complicated (and clumsy) than that in use now; it was filled with dense and vaguely poetic meditations on life and language; also some of it was just wrong. "I'm in the purely practical end of the business."

"Oh," she said. "I see."

"I'm not into the history of things, really." He wondered where she'd heard of Ashima Slade, who was pretty esoteric, anyway. "I try to keep to the here and now. Were *you* ever into—"

"I'm sorry," she said. "I was just making polite noise." And while he wondered *why* she disapproved, she laughed again: "For a confused person, you're very straightforward."

He thought: I'm *not* confused. He said: "I like straightforwardness when I find it."

They smiled at each other. (She thinks *she's* not confused at all . . .) And enjoyed her smile anyway.

"What are you doing here?" Her new tone suggested she enjoyed it too. "You don't live in here with us mavericks . . . ?"

"Just taking a shortcut home." (Her raised eyebrow questioned.) "What were *you* doing? I mean, what was *he* doing . . . ?"

"Oh—" She made a face and shook her head. "That's their idea of excitement. Or morality. Or something."

"Who's 'they?'"

"The Rampant Order of Dumb Beasts. Another neo-Thomist sect."

"Oh?"

"They sprang up about six weeks back. If they keep sprung for another, I may move back into your side of town. Well, I suppose—" She shrugged—"they have their point." She swiveled her jaw from side to side, touched it with her fingertips.

"What are *they* into?"

"Putting an end to meaningless communication. Or is it meaningful . . . ? I can never remember. Most of them used to belong to a really strict, self-mortification and mutilation sect—you saw that eye? They disbanded when some of the shamans managed to do themselves in by particularly lingering and unpleasant means. They'd completely given up on verbal communication; and two of the leading-lady gurus—as well as one of the gentlemen—had their brains publicly burned out. It was pretty grim."

"Yes," he said, on the verge of giving a small, sympathetic shudder. But she didn't.

So he didn't.

"Apparently, some of the former members who survived—they

didn't even allow themselves a name, back then; just a number: a very long, random one, I believe—have gotten together again around more or less similar principles, but with a, I guess you could call it, more relaxed interpretation: The Order of Dumb Beasts . . ." She shook her head. "The fact that they do talk, you see, is supposed to be a very subtle sort of irony. It's the first time they've bothered me. They *are* a nuisance—next time, I just may nuisance back!"

"I can imagine," he said, searching for some point in the unpleasantness to take the conversation on.

He found none and floundered, silently.

She saved him again with: "Come walk with me," and smiled, beckoning with her head.

Smiling back, he ducked his in relief; and came.

Seconds later, she turned (on a turning he had often seen and never thought about), then glanced back at him again.

He said: "Have you noticed? To meet a new person here in Tethys is always like entering a new city . . . ?" He'd said that before, too.

In the narrow way, gray walls either side (under the black ceiling), she glanced at him, considering.

"At least, it's always been that way with me. A new friend, and they invariably have an appointment or another friend on some street you've never been on before. It makes the city—come alive."

Her new smile mocked slightly. "I would have thought to someone like you all places in the city looked alive," and she turned down an even narrower alley.

He glanced at the glowing, red (for the u-l) numbers of the street's coordinates up on the wall, following. Then the thought, But *why* am I following? overtook him. To dispel it, he overtook her.

The young man Bron had hardly noticed leave the archway ahead suddenly turned his back to them, crouched, then leaped, flinging his arms, and his hair, up and over; feet—red socks flashed between frayed cuffs and fringed shoes—swung through air and over, after hands: coppery hair swept the ground. Then he was right side up. Then another back-flip. Then another. Then he bounced, whirling, arms out for a brief bow. Shirtless, in tattered pants, panting a little, with hair hanging over his shoulders, straggling across his face, he (a lot cleaner than the gorilla Bron had just rescued her from) grinned.

And she, again, was smiling: "Oh, come on! Let's follow *him*!"

"Well, if you—" He still wondered why he was following *her.*

But she grasped his hand! He thought of it with the exclamation.

And thought, too, That's the first thing that's happened today that
deserves one! And *that* thought (he thought) was the second . . . !—
which began an infinite regress of pleasure, only interrupted as she
took his wrist now and pulled him around a corner: In the small
square, a refuse can blazed, flaking light over the dark-haired girl's
guitar; she turned, strumming slowly. The music (the acrobat pre-
ceding them did a final flip and, staggering and laughing, stood)
quickened.

Some man started singing.

Bron looked for him and saw the poster—mural rather—across
the back wall:

A winged beast with near-naked rider rose through thrashing
branches, the rider's expression ecstatic, flexed arms bound in
bronze. Reins of chain hung slack on the left, pulled taut on the
right, with the mount turned against them.

Someone had set up a hand-lamp, with a swivel beacon, on the
gravel; it put a bright pool over the rider's jackknifed thigh. The
beast's scales were tight where the creature's neck turned out, and
wrinkled where one of its legs bent.

A dozen people stood near the fire. One woman, seated on a crate,
suckled a baby: in the warm draft from the burning can, her chiffon
lifted and fell.

Bron saw the rope from the overhead black . . . swaying. He could
only follow it up some thirty odd feet; which meant it could have
been tied to a support hidden in darkness thirty-one feet above them,
or, indeed, one up three hundred. (From the swing's frequency, it was
more like thirty-five.) Someone was sliding, slowly, down: gold
chains hung from her toe-rings. At the end of each, small mirrors
spun in the firelight (fire dots sped over the mural); the rope slipped
and slid, around her calf, around her waist, around her overhead arm
as, descending into the glow, she watched the company. When she
halted—was she the model for the rider? Those bronze gauntlets,
that leathern skirt . . . ?—the highest head was some two feet below
the lowest mirror.

Some of the people were swaying to the unseen singer's song.

He'd just caught the last half-dozen words, when: "Look . . . !" he
whispered, pulling the woman to him. "Isn't that the man who
punched . . . ?"

His companion frowned toward where he'd nodded (her shoulders
moved beneath her short, gray cape) then looked back at Bron

(shoulders settling) and whispered: "Look again, when she sways into the firelight . . ."

He'd dismissed the "she" as a slip of the tongue, when the muscular creature with the fur-bound thigh and arm, matted hair and ulcerated eye, swaying among the dozen others swaying, shifted weight: Bron saw, across the hirsute pectorals, scars from what must have been an incredibly clumsy mastectomy. Someone in front stepped aside so that a wavering edged shadow fell away: Obviously from the same bestial sect, however naked and grubby, this *was* a woman—or a castrate with chest scars. Neither had been the case with the gorilla assailant.

The singing went on.

Now, how (Bron looked away so as not to be noticed staring) could I possibly have mistaken *her* for that other? (Others had joined the singing. And still others.) Her face was wider; underneath the dirt, her hair was brown, not blue; from her neck hung only a single, rusted chain.

The song she sang (among the dozen others singing) was beautiful.

The voices were rough; seven-odd stuck out, raucous, unsure, off-key. But *what* they sang—

Bron felt his hand squeezed.

—kept rising, and rising over itself, defining a chord that the next note, in suspension, beat with beautifully. His back and belly chilled. He breathed out, breathed in, trying to inhale the words, but catching only: ". . . all onyx and dove-blood crinkling . . ." to miss a phrase and catch another: ". . . love like an iced engine crackling . . ." which, in terms of the dozen words he'd first heard, was profound.

The woman on the rope began a high descant oversoaring the melody.

Chills encased him. His eyelids quivered.

The acrobat, legs braced wide, shoulders and long hair back, face up—sparse red beard scraggled just under his chin—sang too.

Voices interwove, spiring.

His ears and tongue felt carbonated.

His scalp crawled with joy.

Something exploded in the refuse can. Red sparks spattered over the rim, spilled on the gravel. Sparks, blue-white, shot up in a four-, a six-, a dozen-foot fountain.

Bron drew back.

"No, watch . . ." she whispered, pulling him forward. Her voice sounded as if it reverberated down from vaulted domes. Awed, he looked up.

The fountain was up over two dozen feet!

Sparks hit the shoulder of the woman on the rope. She was chanting something; he heard: ". . . point seven, one, eight, two, eight, one, four . . ." She paused, laughed, let go with one hand to brush sparks away. For a moment (as though she recited some mystical countdown) he thought her image on the mural would tear loose and, flapping, spiral the bright pillar into the holy dark.

The guitarist bent over her instrument, hammering on with her left hand and, with her right, flailing furious chords. People began to clap.

He raised his hands, clapped too—weakly: but it shook his whole body; he clapped again, wildly off-rhythm. Clapped again—had the song ended? There was only the quiet chanting of the woman on the rope, her voice measured, her eyes fixed on Bron's: ". . . five, nine . . . two . . . six . . . one . . . seven . . . five . . ." Bron clapped again, alone, and realized tears were rolling one cheek. (The sparks died.) His hands fell, swung, limp.

The red-haired acrobat started another flip—but stopped before he left the ground, grinned, and stood again. To which Bron's reaction was near nausea. Had the flip been completed (at the silence, the baby pulled from the woman's breast, looked around the square, blinked, then lurched again at the nipple and settled to sucking) Bron realized he would have vomited; and even the incomplete handspring seemed, somehow, incredibly *right*.

Bron swallowed, took a step, tried to bring himself back into himself: it seemed that fragments were scattered all around the square.

He was breathing very hard.

I must be incredibly overoxygenated! Purposely, he slowed his breath.

His body still tingled. Anyway, it *was* exciting! Exciting and . . . beautiful!—even to the point of nausea! He grinned, remembered his companion, looked for her—

She had moved over near the people at the smoking can, smiling at him.

Smiling back, he shook his head, a little bewildered, a little shaken. "Thank—" He coughed, shook his head again. "Thank you . . ." which was all there was to say. "Please . . . Thank you—"

Which was when he noticed that *all* of them—the girl with the guitar, the woman on the rope, the still panting acrobat, the woman sitting on the crate with the baby, the matted-haired woman with the scars and that eye, and the other dozen around the extinguished can (a sooty trickle of smoke put a second vertical up beside the rope)— were watching him.

The woman who had brought him glanced at the others, then back at Bron. "Thank *you!*" She raised both hands before her, nodded to him, and began to applaud.

So did the others. Half of them bowed, raggedly; some bowed again.

Still smiling, Bron said, "Hey, wait a minute . . ." Some negative emotion fought for ascendance.

As the woman stepped forward, he fought back and, for the moment, won. Confused, he reached for her hand.

She looked at his, a little puzzled, then said, "Oh . . ." and showed him the palm of hers (a small metallic circle stuck to the center) in explanation; perhaps because he didn't appear to understand, she frowned a little more, then said, "Oh—" again, but in a different tone, and, with her other hand, took his, clumsily; well, it was better than nothing. "This is a theatrical commune," she said. "We're operating on a Government Arts Endowment to produce micro-theater for unique audiences . . ."

Behind her, somebody picked up the lamp (the beam swung from the mural), turned it off. The woman with the mirrors hanging from her toes was climbing the rope, hauling herself back into the dark.

"I hope you've enjoyed it as much as we have." Again the gray-caped shoulders moved with gentle laughter. "Really, you're the most appreciative audience we've had in a while." She looked around. "I think we'll all agree to that—"

"He sure is!" a man, squatting before the refuse can, called up. He seized the can's rim, yanked. The can opened. The acrobat, on the other side, caught one half, pulled something, and—clank!—clash!—clunk!—the whole thing folded down into a shape the two of them lifted and carried off into an alleyway.

The rope climber was gone: the rope end, jerking angrily, went up, and up, and up into the black—

"I hope you didn't mind the drugs . . . ?"

—and disappeared.

She turned over her palm again with its metal circle. "It's only the mildest psychedelic—absorbed through the skin. And there's a built-in allergy check in case you're—"

"Oh, I didn't mind," he protested. "Cellusin, I'm quite familiar with it. I mean, I know what . . ."

She said: "It only lasts for seconds. It gives the audience better access to the aesthetic parameters around which we're—" Her look questioned—". . . working?"

He nodded in answer, though not sure what the question was. The hirsute, scarred woman took hold of one of the poles edging the mural and pulled it from the wall, walking across and rolling the loose, rattling canvas with great swings.

"Really . . ." Bron said. "It was . . . wonderful! I mean, I don't think I've ever . . ." which, because it didn't sound like what he'd intended to say, he let trail.

Behind the mural was a palimpsest of posters. The last of the canvas came away from "Look what *Earth* did to *their* Moon! We don't" The rest had been torn off:—*want them to do it to us*! he supplied mentally, annoyed he knew it but not from where. Like lyrics of a song, he thought, running through your head, that, basically, you didn't like.

The woman dropped his hand, nodded again, turned and walked across the square, stopping to look up after the rope.

Bron started to call, but coughed (she looked back) and completed: "—what's your name?"

She said, "My friends call me the Spike," as one of the men came up, put his arm around her shoulder, and whispered something that made her laugh.

The variety, he thought, that subsumes her face between mild doubt and joy!

"We'll be in this neighborhood for another day or so." (The man was walking away.) "By the way, the music for our production was written by our guitarist, Charo—"

The dark-haired girl, pulling up the cloth case around her instrument, paused, smiled at Bron, then zipped it closed.

"The backdrop and costumes were by Dian—"

Who was apparently the hairy woman lugging the rolled mural over her shoulder: before she turned off down the alley, she gave him a grotesque, one-eyed grin.

"Our special effects were all devised by our tumbler, Windy—but I think he's already getting set up at the next location. The solo voice that you first heard singing was recorded by Jon-Teshumi."

One of the women held up what he realized was a small playback recorder.

"The production was coordinated by our manager, Hatti."

"That's me too," the woman with the recorder said, then hurried after the others.

"And the entire production—" The guitarist (Charo?) spoke now, from the corner—"was conceived, written, produced, and directed by the Spike." The guitarist grinned.

The Spike grinned—"Thank you, again—" and, with an arm around the guitarist's shoulder, they were around the corner.

"It was great!" he called after them. "It was really—" He looked about the empty square, at the poster-splotched wall, at the other streets. Which way *had* he come? The emotion Bron had been fighting down suddenly surged. He did not shout out, No—! He lunged instead for the low archway and loped into the alley.

He had already turned at two intersections when his mind was wrenched away from what was going through it by the shambling figure that, thirty yards ahead, crossed from corner to corner, glanced at him—the eye; the chains; the sunken chest; the high coordinate lights made a red snarl of the hairy shoulder: This time it *was* the gorilla-ish man—and was gone.

At the corner, Bron looked but couldn't see him. Were the Dumb Beasts, he wondered suddenly, also part of the charade? Somehow, the possibility was appalling. Wander around the u-l until he found him? Or some other member of the sect? Or of the cast? But if the initial encounter *had* been theatrical prologue, how would he know the answer he got were not some equally theatrical coda? Meaningless communication? Meaningful . . . ? Which one had she said?

He turned, breathed deeply, and hurried left—sure he was going wrong; till he came out on the familiar, plated walkway, three intersections down from where he'd entered.

And what *had* been going through his mind?

Mimimomomizolalilamialomuelamironoriminos . . . And 'mu' and 'ro' *were* the thirteenth and seventeenth syllables! From out memory's detritus they had reachieved their places, fixed and certain.

Was it the brief drug? Or some resonance from the theater piece? Or simply chance? Walking slowly, strangely pensive, he reviewed the mumble again. In the swing between pleasantry and unpleasantness, the Spike's laugh returned, either as something that effected, or that was, the transition.

The mumble rolled about his mind.

Then Bron frowned.

The *third* syllable . . . and what about the ninth? With sure memory of the thirteenth and seventeenth, another came that he had not reviewed for years: The Instructor, at the last meeting of the Poor Children he had attended, had stood by his bench, correcting his pronunciation of those two syllables again and again and again and again and again and saying, finally, "You still don't have them right," and proceeded to the next novice. The class had recited the mumble, several more times, in unison: He *had* been able to hear that his own vowels, for those syllables, three and nine, were indeed, off. Finally, he had looked at his lap, slurred over the whole thing; and hadn't come to the next session. The truth, undercutting present pleasure— the new feeling (the Spike's face flickered a moment, in memory, laughing) was somehow part of the first negative one he had tried to suppress back at the little square (the *No*—! he hadn't shouted)— was that, having nothing to do with the thirteenth syllable, or the seventeenth, or the third, or the ninth, he had never, really, known the mantra.

All he had (once more the syllables began to play through) was something with which he could, as he had done with so much of his life, make do.

The realization (it wasn't the drug; it was just the way things were) shivered his vision with leftover tears that—no, *that* wasn't what she'd laughed at . . . ?—he blinked, confusedly, back.

2. Solvable Games

The death at the center of such discourse is extraordinary and begins to let us see our own condition.   ROBIN BLASER, *The Practice of Outside*

Bronze clasps, cast as clawing beasts, snapped back under Lawrence's wrinkled thumbs. Lawrence opened out the meter-wide case.

"What I mean," Bron said, as the case's wooden back, inlaid with ivory and walnut, clacked to the common-room's baize table, "is, how are you even supposed to know if you *like* something like that . . . ?" He gazed over the board: within the teak rim, in three dimensions, the landscape spread, mountains to the left, ocean to the right. The jungle between was cut here by a narrow, double-rutted road, there by a mazy river. A tongue of desert wound from behind the steeper crags, alongside the ragged quarry. Drifting in from the border, small waves inched the glassy sea till, near shore, they broke, foaming. Along the beach, wrinkling spume slid up and out, up and out. "Do you see?" Bron insisted. "I mean, you understand my point?" The river's silvers leaving the mountains, poured over a little waterfall, bright as falling mica. A darker green blush crossed the jungle: a micro-breeze, disturbing the tops of micro-trees. "There was this man, you see, from some sect she called the Dumb Beasts—I mean, if there *is* such a sect. But considering all that happened, how do you tell if any of it was real? *I* don't know how big their endowment was . . . and maybe the 'endowment' was part of the 'theater' too."

"Well, her *name* is certainly familiar—"

"Is it?" Bron asked in the quiet commons. "The Spike?"

"Very." Lawrence assembled the astral cube: The six six-by-six plastic squares, stacked on brass stilts, made a three dimensional, transparent playing space to the right of the main board, on which all

21

demonic, mythical, magical, and astral battles were enacted. "You don't follow such things. I do. I even think I've heard something about the Dumb Beasts—they're the fragments of some bizarre sect that used to go by just a very long number?"

"She told me some nonsense like that."

"I can't remember *where* I heard about them—that's not the sort of thing I do follow—so I can't swear to the validity of your beasts for you. But the Spike, at any rate, is quite real. I've always wanted to see one of her productions. I rather envy you—There: That's all together. Would you get the cards out of the side drawer, please?"

Bron looked around the side of the vlet case, pulled out the long, narrow drawer. He picked up the tooled leather dice-cup; the five dice clicked hollowly. Thrown, three would be black with white pips, one transparent with diamond pips, and the fifth, not cubic, but scarlet and icosahedral, had seven faces blank (usually benign in play, occasionally they could prove, if you threw one at the wrong time, disastrous); the others showed thirteen alien constellations, picked out in black and gold.

Bron set the cup down and fingered up the thick pack. He unwrapped the blue silk cloth from around it. Along the napkin's edge, gold threads embroidered:

$$\sum_{n=-\infty}^{\infty} \frac{1}{\pi} \log_2 \frac{\left| \int_{-A}^{A} M(\theta)\exp(i\frac{\pi n\theta}{A})d\theta \right|^2 + \left| \int_{-A}^{A} N(\theta)\exp(j\frac{\sin\theta}{A})d\theta \right|^3 + A_M^N}{A_M^N - \prod_{r=\pm n}^{\infty} \frac{1}{e}\log_\pi \left| \int_{-A}^{A} N(k\frac{\cos\theta}{A}d\theta \right|^3 - \prod_{r=A}^{\infty} \frac{1}{\pi}\log_e \left| \int_r^n M(i\frac{\pi n\theta}{nr})\,d\theta \right|^5}$$

—the rather difficult modulus by which the even more difficult scoring system (Lawrence had not taught him that yet; he knew only that θ was a measurement of strategic angles of attack [over different sorts of terrain N, M, and A] and that small ones netted more points than large ones) proceeded. As he pulled back the blue corner, two cards slid to the table. He picked them up—the Wizard of Rocks and the Child Empress—and squared them with the deck. "Lawrence, the point is, even if he wasn't a member of their company—I mean, there was a woman member of the sect who definitely *was* with them—unless that was just makeup too. It was as though, suddenly, I couldn't trust *anything* . . ."

Lawrence opened the drawer on the other side of the case and took out a handful of the small, mirrored and transparent screens (some etched with the same, alien constellations, some with different), set them upright beside the board, then reached back in for the playing pieces: carved foot soldiers, mounted men, model army-encampments; and, from this same drawer, two miniature cities, with their tiny streets, squares, and markets: one of these he put in its place in the mountains, the second he set by the shore. "I don't see why you're so busy dissecting all this—" Lawrence took up one red foot soldier, one green one, sat back in his chair, put the pieces behind his back—"when it seems to me all that's happened is, in an otherwise dull day, you've had—from the way you described it—something of an aesthetic experience." (Bron was thinking that seventy-four-year-olds should either get bodily regeneration treatments or not sit around the co-op common rooms stark naked—another thought he decided to suppress: it was Lawrence's right to dress or not dress any way he felt like. But why, he found himself wondering, was it so easy to suppress some negative thoughts while others just proliferated?—like all those that had been forming about that theater woman, the Spike: which, essentially, was what he had been avoiding talking about for the last quarter of an hour.) Lawrence said: "If you were asking for advice, which you're not, I'd say why don't you just leave it at that. If you don't mind comments, which I must assume you don't, because despite all my other comments, you're still talking to me and haven't merely wandered away—" Lawrence brought his fists together above the mountains—"I can only suspect that, because you *haven't* left it at that—the only logically tenable conclusion—there probably is more to it than that. At least as far as you're concerned. Choose—"

Bron tapped Lawrence's left fist.

The fist (Bron thought: Perhaps it's simply because Lawrence is my friend) turned over, opened: a scarlet foot soldier.

"That's you," Lawrence said.

Bron took the piece, looked around at the other side of the case, and began to pick the scarlet pieces from their green velvet drawer. He stopped with the piece called the Beast between his thumb and forefinger, regarded it: The miniature, hulking figure, with its metal claws and plastic eyes, was not particularly dumb: During certain gambits, the speaker grill beside the dice-cup drawer would yield up the creature's roar, as well as the terrified shouts of its attackers. Bron turned it in his fingers, pondering, smiling, wondering what else he might say to Lawrence other than "yes"—

"Freddie," Lawrence said to the naked ten-year-old, who had wandered up to the table to stare (his head was shaved; his eyes were blue, were wide; he wore myriad bright-stoned rings, three, four, and five to a finger; and he was sucking the fore and middle-ones; the skin at one corner of his mouth was bright with saliva), "*what* are you staring at?"

"That," Freddie said around his knuckles, nodding at the board.

"Why don't you guys go to a nice, mixed-sex co-op, where there may be a few other children and, maybe, other people to take care of you?"

"Flossie likes it here," Freddie said. His cheeks went back to their slow pulsing as Flossie (a head [also shaved] and a half taller, eyes as wide [and as blue], hands heavy with even more rings) came up to stand just behind Freddie's shoulders.

Flossie stared.

Freddie stared.

Then Flossie's brightly-ringed hand pulled Freddie's from his mouth. "Don't do that."

Freddie's hand went down long enough to scratch his stomach, then came back up: Two wet fingers, a near dozen rings between them, slid back into his mouth.

Six months ago, Bron had just assumed that the two, who lived in adjacent rooms at the end of his corridor, were lovers; later, he'd decided they were merely brothers. Lawrence, with his ability to ferret out the gossipy truth, had finally revealed the story: Flossie, who was twenty-three and Freddie's father, was severely mentally retarded. He had brought his ten-year-old son with him from a Callisto-Port commune because there was a very good training and medical institute for the mentally handicapped here in Tethys. (The gemstones in those rings were oveonic, crystalline memory units, which, while they did not completely compensate for Flossie's neurological defects, certainly helped; Flossie wore different rings for different situations. Freddie wore the rest. Bron had noticed Flossie often switched off with his son.) Who, or where, a mother was, neither seemed to care or know. From commune to co-op and back again, Flossie had raised Freddie since infancy. ("And *he's* rather bright," Lawrence had commented, "though, with that fingersucking, I think he suffers socially.") Their names had been Lawrence's idea ("An arcane literary reference as far beyond you as it is beyond them," Lawrence had explained when Bron had requested explanation), codified when the two had started using them themselves. All right, what *were* their real names, then? someone had asked. Save their twenty-two digit government identity numbers, no one (they explained), had ever bothered to suggest any before which they particularly liked ("Which," said Lawrence, "is merely a comment on the narrowness of the worldlets we live among").

"Now if you two want to watch," Lawrence said, "you go over *there* and sit down. Standing up close like that and leaning over our shoulders will just make me nervous."

Flossie put a glittering hand on Freddie's shoulder: They went, sat, and stared.

Looking back at the board, Bron tried to remember what it was he had been about to answer 'yes'—

"*No*—!"

Bron and Lawrence looked up.

"*Here* I am, running my *tail* off to get to this Snake Pit in time, and there *you* two are, already frozen in!" From the balcony, Sam leered hugely, jovially, and blackly over the rail. "Well! What can you do? Anybody winning?" Sam came down the narrow, iron steps, slapping the bannister with a broad, black hand. It rang across the common room.

Half a dozen men sitting about in reading cubicles, tape niches, or discussion corners looked up, smiled. Three called out greetings.

"Hey there . . . !" Sam nodded back to the others and swung around the newel. He had a large, magnificent body which he always wore (rather pretentiously, Bron thought) naked. "How've you been going along since I left?" He came over to stand at the table's edge and, with black fists on narrow, black hips, gazed down over the arrayed pieces.

Bron hated Sam.

At least, of the three people in the co-op he considered, from time to time, his friends, Sam was the one who annoyed him most.

"He's getting pretty good," Lawrence said. "Bron's got quite a feel for vlet, I think. You'll have to try some to catch up with him from where you were last time."

"I'm still not in the same league with Lawrence there." Bron had once actually traced the development of his dislike. Sam was handsome, expansive, friendly with everyone (including Bron), even though his work kept him away eleven days out of every two weeks. All that bluster and backslapping? Just a standard, annoying type,

Bron had decided; but it was mitigated somewhat because, after all, Sam *was* just your average hail-fellow-well-met, trying to get along (and, besides, he *was* friendly to Bron).

About a month and a half later—revelation came slowly because Sam was away so much—Bron began to realize Sam was *not* so average. Under all that joviality, there was a rather amazing mind. Bron had already noticed, from time to time, that Sam had a great deal of exact information about a range of subjects which, with each new example of it, had grown, imperceptibly, astonishing. Then once, when Bron had been absently complaining about one of the more tricky metalogical programs at work, Sam had made a rather quiet, rather brilliant suggestion. (Well, no—Bron reminded himself; it *wasn't* brilliant. But it was damned clever.) Bron had asked: Was Sam at one time into metalogics? Sam had explained: No, but he had known that Bron was, so a few weeks back he'd picked up a couple of tapes on the subject, a few books; and he'd found a programmed text in General Info that he'd flipped through a few frames of. That's all. Bron did *not* like that. But then, Sam was just a good-looking, friendly, intelligent guy doing his bit as some overworked salesman/consultant that took him racketing back and forth from Tethys to Lux on Titan to Lux on Iapetus to Callisto Port, or even to the seedy hotels and dormitories clustering on the cheaper sides of the city centers of Bellona, Port Luna, and Rio. Bron had once even *asked* Sam what he did; the answer, with a sad smile and a shaking head, had been: "I troubleshoot after some really *low*-grade crap." Sam, Bron had decided, was as oppressed by the system as anyone else. Bron had been saying something of the sort to Lawrence when Lawrence had explained that "oppressed by the system" was just *not* Sam at all: Sam was *the* head of the Political Liason Department between the Outer Satellite Diplomatic Corps and Outer Satellite Intelligence; and had all the privileges (and training) of both: He had governmental immunity in practically every political dominion of the inhabited Solar System. Far from being "oppressed" by the system, Sam had about as much power as a person could have, in anything short of an elected position. Indeed, he had a good deal more power than any number of elected officials; it came home the next time Sam did: Some outmoded zoning regulations had been plaguing the co-op and three others near them for more than a year (the mixed-sex co-ops, in which three-sevenths of the population lived, tended to get more reasonable treatment, someone had grumbled; someone else had grumbled that wasn't true), and the construction for the laying of some new private-channel cable suddenly brought the zoning plan to the fore. Threatened with eviction again? But Sam, apparently, had walked into some office, asked to see three files, and instructed them to throw away half the contents of one of them; and there went the contradictory parts of the zoning regulations. As Lawrence said, "It would have taken the rest of us a year of petitions, injunctions, trials and what-all to get those zoning codes—that were illegal anyway—straightened out." Bron didn't like *that* either. But even if Sam was jovial, handsome, brilliant, and powerful, Sam was *still* living in a nonspecified co-op (nonspecified as to sexual preferences: there was a gay male co-op on the corner; a straight one three blocks away; yes, just over two fifths of the population lived in mixed co-ops, male/female/straight/gay, and there were *three* of those ranged elegantly one street beyond that, and a heterosexual woman's co-op just behind them). If Sam had any strong sexual identifications, straight or gay, there would have been a dozen co-ops delighted to have him. The fact that Sam chose to live in an all-male nonspecific probably meant that, underneath the friendliness, the intelligence, the power, he was probably rotten with neurosis; behind him would be a string of shattered communal attempts and failed sexualizationships—like most men in their thirties who would choose such a place to live. *This* illusion lasted another month. No, one of the reasons that Sam was away for so long between visits (Sam explained one evening) was that he was part of a thriving family commune (the other fifth of the population) of five men, eight women, and nine children in Lux (on Iapetus), the larger of the two satellite cities to bear the name.

Sam would spend a week there, three days here on Triton, and four days various other places, which is how his fortnights were divided up. At that, Bron (they were all, Bron, Sam, and Lawrence, drinking in one of the common room conversation niches) had challenged Sam (rather drunkenly): "Then what are you hanging out with a bunch of deadbeats, neurotics, mental retards, and nonaffectives like us for, six days a month? Does it make you feel superior? Do we remind you how *wonderful* you are?" (Several others in the commons had looked over; two, Bron could tell, were staunchly *not* looking.) Sam said, perfectly deadpan, "In the one-gender nonspecified co-ops, people tend to be a lot less political-minded. On the job, I'm in the middle of the Outer Satellite/Inner Worlds confusions twenty-nine hours a day. At one of your quote normal unquote co-ops, straight, gay, mixed, or single, it would be war talk all day long and I'd never have a moment's peace." "You mean," Bron had countered, "here at Serpent's House we're too tied up in ourselves to care *what* goes on in the rest of the universe?" "You think so?" Sam asked, and considered "I always thought we had a pretty good bunch of guys here." And then, very wisely, Sam had excused himself from the argument—even Bron had to admit it was getting silly. And two hours later, Sam—in a way that didn't seem wise or winning or ingratiating or anything unpleasant that Bron could put his finger on—stuck his head in Bron's room, laughing, and said: "Have you seen that thing that Lawrence has down in the commons room?" (Which Bron, indeed, *had* already seen.) "You better get down there before it explodes or takes off or something!" Sam laughed again, and went off somewhere else. On his way back to the commons, Bron had wondered, uncomfortably, if one of the reasons he disliked Sam so much wasn't simply because Lawrence thought Sam was the Universe's gift to humanity. (Am I *really* jealous of a seventy-four-year-old homosexual who, once a month, gets falling-down drunk and tries to put the make on me? he asked himself at the commons room door. No, it was easier to be friendly to Sam three days every two weeks than to entertain that idea seriously.)

What Lawrence had laid out on the green baize table was the vlet game.

Sam said: "Can you play this one with the grid—" And lowered an eyebrow at Bron—"or are you beyond that now?"

Bron said: "Well, I don't know if—"

But Lawrence reached for one of the toggles in the card drawer. Across the landscape, pin-points of light picked out a squared pattern, thirty-three by thirty-three. "Bron could do with a few more gridded games I expect—" For advanced players (Lawrence had explained two weeks ago when Sam was last in) the grid was only used for the final scoring, to decide who had taken exactly what territory. In the actual play, however, elementary players found it helpful in judging those all-important θ's. Bron had been contemplating suggesting that they omit it this game. But there it was; and the cities had been placed, the encampments had been deployed. The plastic Sea Serpent had been put, bobbing, into the sea. The Beast leered from its lair; Lawrence's soldiers were set up along the river bank, his peasants in their fields, his royalty gathered behind the lines, his magicians in their caves.

Bron said: "Sam, why don't you play this one. I mean I've had the last two weeks to practice . . ."

"No," Sam said. "No, I want to watch. I've forgotten half the moves since Lawrence explained them to me anyway. Go on." He took a meditative step backward and moved around to view the board from Bron's side.

"Bron has been fretting over a new-found friend," Lawrence said. "That's why he's being so sullen."

"That's just it." Bron was annoyed at having his preoccupation labeled sullenness. "She didn't seem very friendly to *me* at all." He picked up the deck and shuffled, thinking: If that black bastard stands there staring over my shoulder the whole damn game—And resolved not to look up.

The hand Bron dealt himself was good. Carefully, he arranged the cards.

Lawrence rolled the dice out over the desert to begin play, bid five-royal, melded the Juggler with the Poet, discarded the three of Jewels and moved two of his cargo vessels out of the harbor into open waters.

Bron's own throw yielded him a double six, a diamond three, with the three-eyed visage of Yildrith showing on the icosahedron. He covered Lawrence's meld with the seven, eight, and nine of Storms, set the tiny mirrored screen, with the grinning face of Yildrith etched on it, four spaces ahead of Lawrence's lead cargo ship, bid seven-common to cover Lawrence's six-royal, discarded the Page of Dawn and took Lawrence's three of Jewels with the Ace of Flames; his own caravan began the trek upriver toward the mountain pass at the Vale of Kahesh, where, due to the presence of a green Witch, all points scored there would be doubled.

Twenty minutes into the play, the red Courier was trapped between two mirrored screens (with the horned head of Zamtyl, and the many-tongued Arkrol, reflected back and forth to infinity); the scarlet Hero offered some help but was, basically, blocked with a transparent screen. On the dice a diamond two glittered amidst black ones and fives, and Lawrence was a point away from his bid; which meant an astral battle.

As they turned their attention to the three-dimensional board which dominated higher decisions (and each of the seven markers which they played there bore the frowning face of a goddess), Bron decided it was silly to sit there fuming at Sam's standing behind him. He turned, to make some comment—

Sam was not at his shoulder.

Bron looked around.

Sam sat at one of the readers, in the niche with Freddie and Flossie, sorting through some microfiche cards. Bron sucked his teeth in disgust and turned back to Lawrence with a, "Really—"

—when the common room lamps dropped to quarter-brightness. (Lawrence's wrinkled chin, the tips of his fingers, and the base of the green Magician he was about to place, glowed above the vlet board's light.) A roaring grew overhead.

The lamps flickered once, then went out completely. Everyone looked up. Bron heard several men stand. Across the domed skylight, dark as the room, a light streaked.

Sam was standing too, now. The room lights were still out and the lights on all the room's readers were flickering in unison.

"What in the world—" someone who had the room next to Bron (and whose name, after six months, Bron still did not know) said.

"We're not *in* the world—" Lawrence said, sharply even for Lawrence.

As the room lights went on again, Bron realized with horror, excitement, or anticipation (he wasn't sure which), the skylight was still black. Outside, the sensory shield was off!

"You know," Sam said jovially—and loud enough for the others in the room to hear—"while you guys sit around playing war games, there *is* a war going on out there, that Triton is pretty close to getting involved in." The joviality fell away; he turned from his reader and spoke out across the commons: "There's nothing to worry about. But we've had to employ major, nonbelligerent defensive action. The blackout was a powercut while energy was diverted to our major force. Those streaks across the sky were ionized vapor trails from low-flying scouting equipment—"

"Ours or theirs?" someone asked.

A few people laughed. But not many.

"Could be either," Sam said. "The flickering here was our domestic emergency power coming in; and not quite making it—the generators need a couple of seconds to warm up. I would guess . . ." Sam glanced up—"that the sensory shield will be off over the city for another three or four minutes. If anyone wants to go out and see what the sky really looks like from Tethys, now's your chance. Probably not too many people will be out—"

Everyone (except three people in the corner), including Bron, rose and herded toward the double doors. Bron looked back among the voices growing around them. The three in the corner had changed their minds and were coming.

Coming out onto the dark roof, Bron saw that the roof beside theirs was already crowded. So was the roof across the way. As he glanced back, the service door on the roof behind them opened; dozens of women hurried out, heads back, eyes up.

Someone beside Bron said, "Lord, I'd forgotten there *were* stars!"

Around him, people craned at the night.

Neptune, visibly spherical, mottled, milky, and much duller than the striated turquoise extravaganza on the sensory shield, was fairly high. The sun, low and perhaps half a dozen times brighter than Sirius, looked about the size of the bottom of the vlet's dice cup. (On the sensory shield it would be a pinkish glow which, though its vermilion center was tiny, sent out pulsing waves across the entire sky.) The atmosphere above Tethys was only twenty-five hundred feet thick; a highly ionized, cold-plasma field cut it off sharply, just below the shield; with the shield extinguished, the stars were as ice-bright as from some naturally airless moon.

The dusty splatter of the Milky Way misted across the black. (On the shield, it was a band of green-shot silver.)

The sky looks smaller, Bron thought. It looks safe and close—like the roofed-over section of the u-l—yes, punctured by a star here and the sun there. But, though he knew those lights were millions of kilometers—millions of light-years away, they seemed no more than a kilometer distant. The shield's interpenetrating pastel mists, though they were less than a kilometer up, gave a true feel of infinity.

Another light-line shot overhead: It pulsed and diffused color across the dark like a molten rainbow.

"They're flying so low—" That was Sam, calling from near the roof's edge—"that their ion output is exciting a portion of the shield into random discharge: that's not really their trail you're seeing, just an image, below it, on the—"

Someone screamed.

And Bron felt suddenly light-headed; his next heartbeat reverberated in his skull, painful as a hammer. Then, at a sudden blow to the soles of his feet, his stomach turned over—no, he didn't vomit. But he staggered. And his knee hit someone who had fallen. Somewhere something crashed. Then there was a growing light. His ears ceased pounding. The wash of red dissolved from his eyes. And he was on his feet (Had he slipped to one knee? He wasn't even sure), gasping for breath.

He looked up. The shield's evening pastels, circled with a brilliant blue Neptune, were on again. People on his roof (and the roofs around) had fallen. People were helping each other up. His own hand, as he turned, was grasped; he pulled someone erect.

". . . back inside! Everybody get back inside!" (Still Sam; but the surety had left his voice. Its authority tingled with a slight, electric fear.) "Everything's under control now. But just get back in*side*—"

They herded into the slant corridor, spiraling down into the building; anxious converse broiled:

". . . cut the gravity . . ."

"No, they *can't* do . . ."

". . . if the power failed! Even for a few seconds. The whole atmosphere would bulge up like a balloon and we'd lose all our pressure for . . ."

"That's impossible. They *can't* cut the gravity . . ."

Back in the commons, the strain (if, indeed, the city's gravity had faltered for a second or so) had shattered one of the skylight's panes. No pieces had fallen (it was, apparently, "shatter-proof") but the glass, smithereened, sagged in its tesselations.

Chairs were overturned.

A reader had fallen, file drawers spilled; fiche cards scattered the orange carpet.

The astral cube had come loose from its holder and leaned askew, its god-faced markers fallen out onto the gaming board among scuttled ships and toppled soldiers.

Sam was saying to those who stood around them: "—no, this *doesn't* mean that Triton will have to enter the war between the Outer Satellites and the Inner Worlds. But the possibility's been a clear one for over a year. I doubt if the odds on it have changed one way or the other—at least I assume they haven't. Maybe this incident has just made the possibility a little more clear in *your* minds. Look, pull up some chairs—"

"Now you explain the gravity thing again," Freddie said, a little nervously. He sat cross-legged on the floor, one bright-ringed hand on his father's knee (Flossie sat in the chair behind him, both hands a-glitter in his naked lap): "You explain it *very* slowly, see? And very clearly. And very simply." Freddie glanced up, then around at the others. "You understand now how you have to do it?"

Someone else said: "Sam, that's terrifying. I mean, if it *had* been cut for even fifteen or twenty seconds, everyone in the city might be dead!"

Sam sighed, leaned forward with his elbows on his knees, and patted two sides of an imaginary question. "All right. I'll go over it once more for those of you who still don't understand. Think back to your old relativity model. As a particle's speed in a straight line approaches the speed of light, its volume decreases in the direction of the motion, its time processes relative to the observer slow down, its mass increases and so does its gravity. Now suppose the acceleration is in a curve. This all still holds true, only not at the rate governed by Fitzgerald's contraction; suppose it's in a very tight curve—say a curve as tight as an electron shell. Does it still hold true? It does. And suppose the curve is tighter still, say, so tight its diameter is smaller than that of the particle itself—essentially this is what we mean when we say the particle is 'spinning.' The relativity model still holds: it's just that the surface of the particle has a higher density, mass, and gravity than the center—a sort of relativistically-produced surface tension that keeps the Particle from flying apart in a cloud of neutrinos. Now by some very fancy technological maneuvering, involving ultrahigh frequency depolarized magnetism, superimposed magnetic waves, and alternate polarity/parity acceleration, we can cause all the charged nucleons—which is theoretically only protons but in actuality turns out to include a few neutrons as well—in certain, high-density, crystalline solids, starting with just their spin, to increase the diameter of their interpenetrating orbits to about the same size across as the nucleus of an atom of rhodium one-oh-three—which, for a variety of reasons, is taken to be, in this work, the standard unit of measurement—while still moving at speeds approaching that of light—"

"You said before, Sam, that they didn't really circle," someone else said, "but that they wobbled, like off-center tops."

"Yes," Sam said. "The wobble is what accounts for the unidirectionality of the resultant gravitic field. But I'm trying to explain it now for those who couldn't understand the *last* explanation. Actually, it isn't even a wobble; its a complex vertical gradient wave-shift—the thing to remember is that *all* of these terms, particle, spin, orbit, wobble *and* wave, are just highly physicalized metaphors for processes still best understood and most easily applied as a set of purely mathematical abstractions. Anyway, all the particles in a bunch of trilayer iridium/osmium crystalline sheets, spaced about under the city, are madly orbiting in tiny circles of one point seven two seven the diameter of a rhodium one-oh-three nucleus. The magnetic resonance keeps the crystals from collapsing in on themselves. The resultant mass, and the gravity set up, is increased several hundred million-fold—"

"—in one direction, because of the wobble," Flossie said, slowly.

"That's right, Floss." (Freddie, visibly relaxed, dropped his hand from his father's leg—and slid two glittering fingers into his mouth.) "The result is that anything above them is held neatly down. This, coupled with the natural gravity of Triton, gives street-level Tethys point nine six two Earth-normal, at-sea-level-on-the-magnetic-South-Pole, gravity."

"You *mean* Earth has one point oh three nine five the normal bolstered gravity of Tethys," someone said from the back of the room.

Sam's black brow wrinkled above a smile. "One point oh three nine five oh *one* . . . more or less." He glanced around the group. "The cold-plasma atmosphere-trap works by similar magnetic maneuvering, though it has nothing to do with the gravity. The thing to bear in mind, with all of those twelve hundred thousand trilayer crystal sheets, is that each group of ten has its own emergency power supply."

"Then they *couldn't* all go off at once," Lawrence said. "Even for a few seconds. Is that what you mean?"

"That's what I said." Sam put his chin on his dark knuckles, looking up at the men from under lowered brows. "What I suspect is far more likely: Some synchronous overtone in the magnetic resonance was induced—"

"Induced by *whom*?" someone asked.

Sam raised his chin about an inch from his knuckles. "—was induced in the magnetic resonance, that caused the gravity field—remember, the magnetic field that controls the particle's spin is alternating at literally billions of times a second—to list: all the wobbles wobbled to one side at once. Not even for a second; perhaps as much as a hundred-thousandth of a second, if that long. Yes, we got a sudden bulge in our atmosphere. But I doubt if we lost more than a pound or three's pressure, and it settled back in seconds. Sure, it was a big shock, but I don't think anything really serious—"

"What *was* it—!"

They turned to the balcony.

"What *happened*! I didn't . . ." Alfred (who was seventeen, had the room directly across from Bron, and was the third person in the co-op Bron, from time to time, thought of as a friend) stood naked at the rail. A blood bubble burst in one nostril. Blood ran down his neck, across his bony chest. He reached up with a hand, already smeared, and wiped more blood across a bloody cheek. "I was in my room, and then . . . I was scared to come out! I didn't hear anything. Except some screaming first. What . . . ?" A trickle crawled his belly, reached his genital hair, built there for three, silent breaths, then rolled on down his thigh. "Is everybody . . . ?" With terrified, green eyes, he blinked about the common room's assemblage.

Somehow, twenty minutes after that, the pieces had been rearranged on the vlet board; some dozen people were back at the various readers around the room, and several others (among them Sam) had taken Alfred to the console room where the co-op's outlet for the city information computer would give him a medical diagnosis and any necessary referrals. Then someone came back to report, with astonishment, that there would be a seven-to-ten-minute wait for processing of all medical programs due to a city overflow! "I guess a lot of people sprained a lot of ankles . . ." was someone's dubious comment. Bron decided to go down and see for himself. Downstairs, he crowded into a room with several others. Between two shoulders, he could see the screen flashing: "There will be a three-minute delay before we can . . ." Now that was unsettling. But other than a bloody nose and scared, Alfred seemed all right. While Bron was there, the delay sign was replaced with the usual: "Your diagnosis will begin in one minute. Please prepare to answer a few simple questions." So while Alfred, one knuckle pressed against his upper lip, was sitting down to the console, Bron and several others came back to the commons.

He lost the astral battle seven to one.

"What," Lawrence said, sitting back in his chair, "were you ever thinking of?"

Bron reached out and removed his own, overturned, scarlet Assassin and slid Lawrence's green Duchess into the square by the waterfall's bank, to threaten the caravan preparing to cross the river less than three squares to the East. With the piece still in his fist (he could feel its nubs and corners), he picked up his cards and surveyed his depleted points. "That woman." Only one meld was possible and he was three away from his most recent bid.

Lawrence laughed, sat back, and turned his own cards down on his bony knee. "You mean to tell me, in the middle of all this excitement, you're thinking about some woman? If you're *that* kind, what are you doing in *this* co-op? There're plenty of places set up for you oversexed, libidinous creatures. Most of them, in fact. Why do you want to come here and let your nasty id mess up our ascetic lives?"

"The first time I ever saw you," Bron said, "you lumbered into me in the upstairs corridor, drunk out of your mind, and demanded I screw you on the spot."

"I remember it well." Lawrence nodded deeply. "The next time I get drunk, I may do the same: There's life in the old pirate yet—the point, however, is that when you refused, saying that you just weren't (as you put it so diplomatically) all that turned on by men, I did *not* immediately drop you from my acquaintanceship; I did *not* snub you in the dining area next time we passed. I even, if I recall, said hello to you the next morning and volunteered to let the repairmen in to fix your channel circuit while you were out at work."

"What *is* the point, Lawrence?" Bron looked back at his cards. Several times in his life, people had pointed out to him that what friends he had tended to be people who had approached him for friendship, rather than people he'd approached. It meant that a goodly percentage of his male friends over the years had been homosexual, which, at this stage, was simply a familiar occurrence. "*You're* the libidinous one. I admit it, my relationships with women have never been the best—though, by the gods of any sect you name, sex itself never seemed to be the problem. But that's why I moved in here: to get away from women *and* sex."

"Oh, really! Alfred rushing his little girl friends in here after midnight and hustling them out again before dawn—it may be screwing, but it *isn't* sex. And anyway, it doesn't bother anyone, though I'm sure it would just destroy him if he found that out."

"Certainly doesn't bother me," Bron said. "Or you hustling your little boyfriends in and out—"

"Wishful thinking! Wishful thinking!" Lawrence closed his eyes lightly and raised his chin. "Ah, such wishful thinking."

"If I remember correctly," Bron said, "that evening in the corridor, when I said 'no,' you called me a faggot-hater and demanded to know what I was doing in an all-male co-op if I didn't like to go to bed with men—"

Lawrence's eyes opened; his chin came down. "—whereupon you politely informed me that there was a gay—you know, politically that has, from time to time, been a very nasty word, till that silly public-channel series denatured it once and for all back in the Seventies, the same one which reestablished 'into' into the language—men's co-op two streets away that might take me in for the night. Bastard!"

"You kept on insisting I screw you."

"And you kept on insisting that you didn't want to go to bed with *any*body, in between explaining to me, in the most sophomoric manner, that I couldn't expect *this* kind of commune to be more than twenty percent gay—where you got *that* dreadfully quaint statistic from, I'm sure I shall never know; *then* you went on to explain that, nevertheless, due to your current disinterest in women you felt yourself to be *politically* homosexual—"

"At which point you said you couldn't stand political homosexuals. Lawrence, what *is* the point?"

"And I *still* can't. The point is merely—" Lawrence returned his eyes to the board: In the Mountains of Narnis a situation had been developing for some time that Bron had hoped would turn to his advantage, if Lawrence would only keep the transparent screens of Egoth and Dartor out of it: the Mountains of Narnis were where Lawrence was looking—"that my feelings toward you, later that night as I lay awake in alcoholic overstimulation, tossing and turning in my narrow bed where you had so cavalierly dumped me and left, were rather like you have been avoiding describing your feelings toward that woman."

"I thought you passed out—" Bron's eyes went from the board to Lawrence's. "Pardon me?"

"I said, right after you so considerately put me to bed—I mean I suppose you could have left me lying on the hall floor; passed out? Ha!—I felt about *you* rather like you feel about *her.* I hated you, I thought you were hardhearted, insensitive, ungenerous and pignoli-brained; and quite the most beautiful, dashing, mysterious, and marvelous creature I'd ever laid eyes on."

"Just because you wanted to . . . ?" Bron frowned. "Are you suggesting that I want to—. . . with *her*?"

"I am simply noting a similarity of reactions. I would not presume to suggest *any* of my reactions might be used as a valid model for yours—though I'm sure they can."

Bron's frown dropped to the micro-mountains, the miniscule trees, the shore where tiny waves lapped the bright, barbaric sands. After seconds, he said: "She gave me one of the most marvelous experiences of my life. At first I only thought she'd led me to it. Then suddenly I found out she'd conceived, created, produced, and directed . . . She took my hand, you see. She took my hand and led me—"

Lawrence sighed. "And when you put your arm around my feeble, palsied shoulders—"

Bron looked up again, still frowning. "If we all *had* died this evening, Lawrence, I wouldn't have died the same person as I was if I'd died this morning."

"Which is what your initial comments about the whole thing seemed to suggest—before you began to intimate how cold, inhuman, heartless, and untrustworthy this sweet creature obviously was. I was only trying to remind you." Lawrence sighed again. "And I suppose I did, at least that night, love you in spite—"

Bron's frown became a scowl. "Hey, come on—"

Lawrence's wrinkled face (below the horseshoe of white furze surrounding his freckled pate) grew mockingly wry. "Wouldn't you know. Here I am, in another passionately platonic affair with an essential louse."

Seeing *her,* Bron said: "Lawrence, look, I do think of you as my friend. Really. But . . ." Lawrence's face came back, wryness still there. "But look, I'm not seventeen. I'm thirty-seven. I told you before, I did my experimenting when I was a kid—a good deal of it, too. And I'm content to stick by the results." The experiments' results, confirming him one with eighty percent of the population, according to those "quaint" statistics, was that he could function well enough with either sex; but only by brute, intellectualized fantasy could he make sex with men part of his actual life. The last brutal intellectualizing he'd done of any sort was his attendance at the Temple of the Poor Children of the Avestal Light and Changing Secret Name; brutality was just not what he was into. "I like you. I want to stay your friend. But, Lawrence, I'm *not* a kid and I've been here before."

"Not only are you a louse. You are a presumptuous louse. I am not thirty-seven. I am over seventy-three. I too have been here before. Probably more times than you have." Lawrence bent over and contemplated the board again, while Bron contemplated (again) the phenomenon by which, between some time he thought of as *then* (which contained his experiments with both sex and religion) and the time he thought of as *now* (which contained . . . well, all this), old people had metamorphosed from creatures three or four times his age to creatures who were only two up or less. Lawrence said: "I do believe it's your move. And don't worry, I intend to stay your friend."

"What do *you* think I should do, Lawrence?"

"Whatever you think you *should* do. You might try playing the game—hello, Sam!" who had come up to the table. "Say, why don't you two play together against me. Bron's gone quite mushy over some theatrical woman in the u-l and can't get up nerve to go back and find her, which is fine by me. But it's shot his concentration all to hell, which isn't. Come on, Sam. Sit down and give him a hand."

On the point of spluttering protest, Bron made room on the couch for the jovial, brilliant, powerful—should he just get up and *leave*? But Sam asked something about his meld strategy and, when Bron explained, gave a complimentary whistle. At least Bron *thought* it was complimentary.

They played. Tides turned. So did the score. By the time they adjourned for the evening (elementary players, Lawrence had explained, shouldn't even hope to play a game to completion for the first six months), Bron and Sam were pounding each other's shoulders and laughing and congratulating themselves and turning to congratulate Lawrence and, of course, they would all get together tomorrow evening and take up where they'd left off.

As Bron walked down the corridor toward his room, he decided warmly that the trouncing he had given the old pirate, even if it had taken Sam's help to do it, had made the evening worth it.

At his door, he stopped, frowned toward the door opposite.

He hadn't even asked Sam how Alfred was. Should he knock now and find out? A sudden memory of one of the few things like a personal conversation he'd ever had with Alfred returned: Once Alfred had actually taken Bron to a restaurant (recommended by Flossie, who had had it recommended to him by a friend of Freddie's) which turned out to cater almost entirely to well-heeled (and rather somber) nine- to thirteen-year-olds. (The younger ones were simply swathed in fur!) Only a handful of adolescents even near Alfred's age were present, and they all seemed to be overlooking the place with patent good will and palpable nostalgia. Bron was the single adult there. During dinner Bron had been rambling on about something or other when Alfred leaned across the table and hissed, "But I don't *want* relationships! I don't *want* friendships! I want sex—sometimes. *That's* what I'm doing at Serpent's House. Now get off my back!" Two sexually unidentifiable children, hands locked protectively around their after-dinner coffee bulbs, turned away small, bald, brown faces to muffle smiles in their luxuriant collars. Yet he still considered Alfred his friend, because Alfred, like all his others, had come to him, still came to him, asking that he do this, or could he lend him that, or would he mail this coupon to that advertiser, or this letter of protest about what some other had sent him, pick up this or that on the way home, or where should he throw that out and, yeah, sure you can have it if you *want* it. With varying amounts of belligerence, Bron complied to these requests (to keep peace, he told himself at first), only to discover that, in his compliance, he valued the relationship—friendship, he corrected himself (because he *was* thirty-seven, not seventeen). I suppose, Bron thought, standing in the hall, I understand him, which has something to do with it. I certainly understand him better than I understand Lawrence. Or Sam. (Or that woman . . . ? Again her face returned to him, turning in delightful laughter.) He turned to his door.

As far as knocking on Alfred's? If Alfred wasn't all right, Bron understood him enough to know that he wouldn't want to be caught at it. And if he was, he wouldn't want to be disturbed in it. (If he's all right, Bron thought, he's probably sleeping. That's what I'd do with my all-right time if I had as little of it as that poor kid.) Bron pushed open his own door and stepped into a dimly lighted room, with an oval bed (that could expand to hold three: despite Alfred's secretiveness, there was nothing in the co-op house rules that said you couldn't ball as many people as you liked as long as you did it in your own room), a reader, a microfiche file drawer, a television screen and two dials below it for the seventy-six public channels and his three private ones, two windows (one real, which looked out on the alley behind the building, the other a changeable, holographic diorama: blue curtains were drawn across both), clothes drawers, sink drawers, and toilet drawers in the wall, plastic collars here and there on the blue rug from which, at the push of a switch in the control drawer, inflatable chairs would balloon.

It was a room like Alfred's room, like Lawrence's, like Sam's, indeed like some dozen others he had lived in on one world and three moons: a comforting room: a room like ten thousand times ten thousand others.

At four twenty-seven in the morning, Bron woke suddenly, wondering why. After five minutes in the dark, an idea occurred—though he was not sure if it was the idea that had startled him from sleep. He got up, went out into the hall, and down to the console room.

Left over on the screen, from the last person to use it, were two lists. (Usually it was something from Freddie's—or Flossie's—home-study course.) Absently Bron ran his eye down the one on the right: After half a dozen entries, he realized he was reading down names of former presidents of Mars. His eye caught at Brian Sanders, the second of Mars's two (out of twenty-four male) women presidents. It was under Brian Sanders, the old firebrand and roaring-girl, that, fifty years ago, male prostitution had been made legal in Bellona; also, ran the story, she had single-handedly driven the term "man-made" from most languages of Earth (where her speeches had of course been televised) and Mars, by insistently referring to all objects of war, as well as most creations of Earth culture, as "boy-made."

The list on the left (male and female names mixed equally and at random) was—it was obvious just from the groupings into seven—names of the various governing boards of the Outer Satellite Federation. Yes, the last group were the ones in power now, during the War Alliance: Their names were all over the public channels. (Male and female names out here, of course, didn't mean too much. Anyone might have just about any name—like Freddie and Flossie—especially among second, third, and fourth generation citizens.) Bron wondered what political bet or argument the information had been summoned up to resolve; and, without even sitting, cleared the current program. A medical program was still set underneath it—but it wasn't Alfred's.

Bron punched out General Information.

He was expecting ten minutes of cross-reference and general General Info run-around when he dialed "The Spike: actress (occupation)"—how *would* you file information on someone like that? The screen flickered for a second, then blinked out:

"The Spike—working name of Gene Trimbell, producer, director, playwright, actress, general manager of a shifting personnel theatrical commune, which see. Confirm? : : biographical : : critical : : descriptive : : public record"

Bron frowned. He certainly wasn't interested in her biography. He pressed Biography anyway.

"Biography withheld on request."

That made him smile.

He knew what she looked like:

"Description" wasn't necessary.

He pressed Critical and the screen filled with print: "The Spike is the working name of Gene Trimbell, by common consensus the most striking of the young playwright/director/producers to emerge at the beginning of the current decade, many of whom were associated with the Circle (which see) at Lux on Iapetus. She attracted early attention with her stunning productions of such classics as *Britannicus, The Great God Brown, Vatzlav*, and *A.C./D.C.*, as well as a one-woman videotape production of *Les Paravents*, in which she took all ninety-eight roles. While still in her early twenties, she directed the now legendary (and still controversial) twenty-nine-hour opera cycle by George Otuola, *Eridani* (which see), that involved coordinating over three hundred actors, dancers, singers, two eagles, a camel, and the hundred-foot, flaming geyser of the title role. If her directorial work in traditional forms has tended toward the ambitious and monumental, her own creative pieces are characterized by great compression and brevity. She is, today, most widely known for her work in micro-theater, for which she formed her own fluid company three years ago. Frequently, her brief, elliptical, and intense works have been compared to the music of the twentieth-century composer Webern. Elsewhere, another critic has said: 'Her works do not so much begin and end; rather, they suddenly push familiar objects, emotions, and actions, for often as little as a minute or less, into dazzling, surreal luminescence, by means of a consortment of music, movement, speech, lights, drugs, dance, and decor.' Her articles on the theater (collected under the title *Primal Scenes* and represented as a series of exhaustive readings of the now famous epigraph from Lacan which heads each piece: 'The narration, in fact, doubles the drama with a commentary without which no *mise en scène* would be possible. Let us say that the action would remain, properly speaking, invisible from the pit—aside from the fact that the dialogue would be expressly and by dramatic necessity devoid of whatever meaning it might have for an audience: —in other words, nothing of the drama could be grasped, neither seen nor heard, without, dare we say, the twilighting which the narration in each scene casts on the point of view that one of the actors had while performing it?'), have given many people the impression that she is a very cerebral worker; yet the emotional power of her own work is what the most recent leg of her reputation stands on. Even so, many young actors and playwrights (most of whom have, admittedly, never seen, or seen little of, her work) have taken the *Scenes* as something of a manifesto, and her influence on the current and living art of drama has been compared with that of María Irene Fornés, Antonin Artaud, Malina, or Colton. Despite this, her company remains small, her performances intimate—though seldom confined in a formal theatrical space. Her pieces have been performed throughout the Satellites, dazzling many a passer-by who, a moment before, did not even know of their existence."

The index down the side of the screen listed a double-dozen more critical pieces. He read a random three and, in the middle of a fourth, switched the console off.

He pulled the door of the room to behind him—it wouldn't close all the way. Frowning, he turned to examine it. The lintel across the top had strained a millimeter or so from the wall. The evening's gravity 'wobble'? He looked at the console through the door's now permanent crack. How could you ask General Information about *that*?

Barefoot, he padded up the hall, suddenly tired.

Climbing naked into bed, he thought: Artists . . . ? Well, not quite so bad as craftsmen. Especially when they were successful. Still . . . of course he *would* go and fixate on someone practically famous; though, in spite of Lawrence, *he'd* never heard of her. Depressed, and wondering if he'd ever see her again, he fell asleep.

3. Avoiding Kangaroos

Philosophers who favor propositions have said that propositions are needed because truth is intelligible only of propositions, not of sentences. An unsympathetic answer is that we can explain the truth of sentences to the propositionalist in his own terms: sentences are true whose meanings are true propositions. Any failure of intelligibility here is already his own fault.   WILLARD VAN ORMAN QUINE, *Philosophy of Logic*

Audri, the boss he did like, put a hand on each of the cubicle's door-jambs and, standing at all sorts of Audri-like angles, said (with an expression he didn't like at all): "This is Miriamne—Bron, *do* something with her," then left.

The young woman, who, a moment back, had been behind her (Miriamne?), was dark, frizzy-haired, intelligent looking, and sullen.

"Hi." Bron smiled and thought: I'll have an affair with her. It came, patly, comfortably, definitively—a great release: That should get the crazed, blonde creature with the rough, gold-nailed hands (and the smooth, slow laugh) off his mind. He'd drifted to sleep thinking about her; he'd woken up thinking about her. He'd even contemplated (but decided, finally, no) walking to work through the u-l.

Miriamne, in the doorway, was wearing the same short cape in dove-gray the Spike had worn, was bare-breasted, as the Spike had been, and, more to the point, immediately recalled a job-form he had filled out seventeen years ago: "Describe the preferred, physical type you feel most assured of your performance with." His preferred description had been, patly: "Short, dark, small-boned, big-hipped." And Miriamne, short, dark, small-boned, and just a hair's breadth shy of callipygous, was looking somewhere about five inches to the left, and two inches above, his right ear.

At his eyebrow? No . . .

Bron rose from his chair, still smiling. She was the sort of woman he could be infinitely patient with in bed (if she needed patience), as it is often rather easier to be patient with those with whom you feel secure in your performance: He experienced a pleasant return of professional aplomb. Hopefully, he thought, she lives in a nice, friendly, mixed co-op so she doesn't lack for conversation (conversation in sexualizationships was not his strong point). Women who accepted this he had occasionally grown quite fond of. And there was something in her expression that assured him he could never, really, care. How much better could it be? Rewarding for the body, challenging to the intellect, and no strain on the emotions. He came around, sat on the corner of his desk—interposing himself between her and whatever she was now staring at behind him—and asked: "Have you any idea what exactly they expect me to do *with* you?" Two weeks, he decided, at minimum—at least it'll occupy my mind. It might even run three or four months—at maximum. Who knows, they might even eventually like each other.

She said, "Put me to work, I suppose," and frowned off at the memos shingling the bulletin board.

He asked: "What exactly *are* you into?"

She sighed, "Cybralogs," in a way (she was still looking at the board) that suggested she'd said it many times that morning.

Still, he smiled and, a flicker of bewilderment playing through his voice, asked: "Cybralogs . . . ?" and, when she still didn't look, asked also: "If your field is Cybralogs, why in the world did they send you to Metalogics?"

"I suspect—" Her glance caught his—"because they have five letters in common, four of them even in the same order. As all those war posters are constantly reminding us, we aren't *in* the world. We're on the last major moon of the Solar System, the only one that's managed to stay out of the stupidest and most expensive war in history—*just* managed. And after last night, one wonders how long *that'll* be for! Our economic outlets and inlets are so strained we've been leaning on the border of economic crisis for a year—and from the wrong side at that. Everyone in a position of authority is hysterical, and everyone else is pretending to be asleep: Have you known *any*thing to function as it should in the past six months? *Any*thing? I mean, after last *night*—"

Oh, he thought, she lives in the u-l. Well, that shouldn't be a problem; might even make things more interesting . . . And blinked away blonde laughter from the dove-gray shoulders.

"Yes, that business yesterday evening. That was pretty scary, wasn't it? A guy at the co-op I'm staying at is in the Intelligence Liaison Department. Afterward, he was trying to explain the whole thing away to a bunch of us. I don't think anyone was convinced." (That should show her he had some political consciousness. And now something for her ego . . . ?) "Really, I know Audri has to use whoever she gets, especially right through here, but what's the point of sending someone with your training to this department?" He twisted around on the desk corner, picked up the arc of wire from the com-rack, put the red bead to his ear and the blue one to his lips. "Personnel . . . ?" he said too gruffly; Miriamne glanced at him. "This is Bron Helstrom—" followed with the first ten of his twenty-two-digit identification number; for job purposes that was all anyone needed. "Get that down, please. I don't want to have to repeat it. You've sent us along, here in Metalogics, one Miriamne—I'm not going to ask her *her* number: *you* look it up. She's been bothered enough today already." He glanced at Miriamne, who *was* looking at him now, if a bit blankly. "She's a cybralogician and for some, bird-brained reason neither of us understands or appreciates, she's been sent to—"

"Whom do you wish to speak to in Personnel?" the voice answered with understandable testiness.

"You will do." (Miriamne could only hear his side of the conversation.) "This whole nonsense has grown up because responsibilities have been shuttled and shunted around for I'm sure a week or more. And I—that is, Bron Helstrom, in Metalogics—" Once more he rattled off his number: ". . . I'll assume you have that now, so that you know where this complaint is coming from—I *don't* intend to get lost in the shuffle. You've sent this woman into Metalogics, a department that can make full use of neither her training nor her talent. This is not the first time this has happened; it's the sixth. That is ridiculous, a waste of everybody's time, an interruption in everyone's work. Now *you* decide who ought to know, and *you* go tell them—" He heard the sharply drawn-in breath, then the click of the connection broken—"and if anyone wants to know where the complaints came from—now, get it this time:" Once more he gave his name and number to the dead, red bead. "Now, think about that, pignoli-brain, before you make the next person's life miserable by sending them to do a job they aren't trained for. Good-bye." He hung up, thinking: The "pignoli-brain" was for cutting him off. Still, he decided, he'd gotten his point across. He looked at Miriamne (with the ghost of belligerence playing through his smile): "Well, I guess we've made our point—for what little it'll do." He cocked his head.

The same ghost played through hers. She rubbed her neck with one finger. Her nails were short and chrome-colored. Her lips were full and brown. "I'm a cybralogist," she said. "As far as I know, there's no such thing as a cybralogician."

Bron laughed. "Oh. Well, I'll be honest with you. I've never even heard of a 'cybralog.'"

"I've *heard* of metalogics . . . ?"

While Bron laughed, inside the ghost momentarily became real. "Look," he said. "I can either tell you about metalogics and, by tomorrow, we can probably have you doing something that isn't too dull, if not useful." He turned his hands up. "Or we can have some coffee and just . . ." He shrugged—"talk about other things. I mean I know how exhausting these hurry-up-and-wait mornings can be. I had to go through my share before ending up here."

Her smile became a short (but with that sullen ghost still playing through) laugh. "Why don't we have the coffee and you can tell me about metalogics."

Bron nodded. "Fine. I'll just get—" getting up.

"May I sit in this—?"

"Sure. Make yourself comfortable. How do you take your—?"

"Black," she said from the sling chair, "as my old lady," and laughed again (while he reached into the drawer at his knee and dialed. One plastic bulb, sliding out, hit his knuckles and burned). "That's what my father always used to say." She put her hands on her knees. "My mother was from Earth—Kenya, actually; and I've been trying to live it down ever since."

Bron smiled back, put one coffee bulb on the desk, reached down for the other and thought: Typical u-l . . . always talking about where they come from, where their families started. His own parents had been large, blond, diligent, and (after years of working as computer operators on Mars, when their training on Earth, outmoded almost before their Martian immigration, had promised them glorious careers in design) fairly sullen. They were in their midforties when he'd come along, a final child of five. (He was pretty sure he was a final child.) Was that, he wondered again, why he liked sullen-looking women? His parents had been, like so many others it was embarrassing, laborers in a new world that needed such labor less and less. He had not lived with them since he was fifteen, had not seen them since he was twenty, thought about them (usually when someone was talking about theirs) seldom, talked about them (in concession to a code of politeness almost universal outside the u-l that, once he had realized it existed, he'd found immensely reassuring) never.

Bron handed Miriamne the second bulb. "All right. Metalogics . . ." Back behind the desk? No, better prop himself on the front again, for effect. "People—" He settled back on crumpling flimsies—"when they go about solving any real problem, don't use strict, formal logic, but some form of metalogic, for which the rules of formal logic can be considered—on off Thursdays—the generating parameters. You know the old one: If a hen-and-a-half lays an egg-and-a-half in a day-and-a-half . . . ?" He raised an eyebrow (the real one) and waited for her to sip:

Her plastic bulb wrinkled in miniscule collapse. She looked up.

"The question is: Then how many eggs does *one* hen lay in *one* day?"

"One?" she suggested.

"—is the quote logical unquote answer people have been giving off the top of their heads for over a hundred years. A little thought, however, will show you it's really two-thirds of an egg—"

Miriamne frowned. "Cybralogs are speech/thought representation components—I'm a hardware engineer: I don't know too much about logic, meta or otherwise. So go slow."

"If a hen-and-a-half lays an egg-and-a-half in a day-and-a-half, then *three* hens would lay *three* eggs in the *same* day-and-a-half, right? Therefore *one* hen would lay *one* egg in that day and a half. Therefore one hen lays—"

"Two thirds of an egg—" She nodded, sipped. The bubble collapsed more—"in one day."

"We get into metalogic," Bron explained (thinking: With the sullen, intelligent ones, that look of attention means we're getting further than we would if they were smiling), "when we ask why we called 'one' a 'logical' answer in the first place. You know the beginning tenet of practically every formal logic text ever written, 'To deny P is true is to affirm P is false'?"

"I vaguely remember something about denying the Taj Mahal is white—" Miriamne's bubble was all wrinkled plastic between bright nails—"is to affirm that it's not white . . . an idea that, just intuitively, I've never felt very comfortable with."

"You have good reason." Bron sipped his own and heard the plastic crackle. "The significance of 'white,' like the significance of any other word, is a *range* of possibilities. Like the color itself, the significance fades quite imperceptibly on one side through gray toward black, and on another through pink toward red, and so on, all the way around, toward every other color; and even toward some things that aren't colors at all. What the logician who says 'To deny the Taj Mahal is white is to affirm that it is not white' is really saying is: '*If* I put a boundary around part of the range of significance space whose center we all agree to call white, and *if* we then proceed to call everything within this artificial boundary "white" and everything outside this boundary "not white" (in the sense of "nonwhite"—now notice we've already introduced a distortion of what we said was really there), then any point in the total range of significance space must either be inside or outside this boundary—already a risky idea; because if this boundary is anything in the real universe, from a stone wall to a single wave pulse, there has to be something underneath it, so to speak, that's neither on one side nor the other. And it's also risky because if the Taj Mahal happens to be made of white tiles held to brown granite by tan grotte, there is nothing to prevent you from affirming that the Taj Mahal is white and the Taj Mahal is brown and the Taj Mahal is tan, and claiming both tan and brown to lie in the area of significance space we've marked as 'nonwhite'—"

"Wait a second: *Part* of the Taj Mahal is white, and *part* of the Taj Mahal is brown, and *part* of the Taj Mahal is—"

"The solution's even simpler than that. You see, just like 'white,' the words 'Taj Mahal' have a range of significance that extends, on one side, at least as far as the gates around the grounds, so that once you enter them you can say, truthfully, 'I am *at* the Taj Mahal,' and extend, on another side, at least down to the individual tiles on the wall, and even further to the grotte between them, so that, as you go through the Taj's door and touch only your fingernail to the strip of no-colored plaster between two tiles, you can say, equally truthfully, 'I have touched the Taj Mahal.' But notice also that the grounds of the Taj Mahal have faded (until they are one with) the area of significance of the 'surface of India,' much of which is not the grounds of the Taj at all. And the grotte between the tiles has faded into (until it is one with) Vriamin Grotte—grotte mined from the Vriamin Clay-pits thirty miles to the south, some of which went into the Taj and some of which went into other buildings entirely. Language is para-metal, not perimetal. Areas of significance space intermesh and fade into one another like color-clouds in a three-dimensional spectrum. They don't fit together like hard-edged bricks in a box. What makes 'logical' bounding so risky is that the assertion by the formal logician that a boundary *can* be placed around an area of significance space gives you, in such a cloudy situation, no way to say where to set the boundary, how to set it, or if, once set, it will turn out in the least useful. Nor does it allow any way for two people to be sure they have set their boundaries around the same area. Treating soft-edged inter-penetrating clouds as though they were hard-edged bricks does not offer much help if you want to build a real discussion of how to build a real house. Ordinary, informal, nonrigorous language overcomes all these problems, however, with a bravura, panache and elegance that leave the formal logician panting and applauding." Bron rocked on his desk once. "Visualize an area of significance space—which is hard to do at the best of times, because the simplest model we've come up with has to represent it in seven coordinates (one for each sense organ): and the one we use currently employs twenty-one, some of which are fractional—which isn't any harder than working with frac-tional exponents, really—and several of which are polar, because the resultant, nondefinable lines between bipolar coordinates nicely model some significance discontinuities we haven't yet been able to bridge coherently: things like the slippage between the denotative and the connotative, or the metonymic and the metaphoric. They take a smidge of catastrophe theory to get through—incidentally, did you know catastrophe theory was invented back in the twentieth century by the same twentieth-century topologist, René Thom, the neo-Thomists are always going on about?—but not as much as you might think . . ."

To outline the parametal model of language, he used the fanciful analogy of "meanings" like colored clouds filling up significance space, and words as homing balloons which, when strung together in a sentence, were tugged to various specific areas in their meaning clouds by the resultant syntax vectors but, when released, would drift back more or less to where, in their cloudy ranges, they'd started out. He wasn't sure whether he'd gotten the analogy from something he'd browsed over in the office library—perhaps one of the feyer passages in the second volume of Slade's *Summa?*—or if it were something from back in his training course. Possibly it had been both.

"I think I'm actually with you," Miriamne said at one point. "Only, a little while ago, you mentioned things-in-the-Universe. Okay:

Where in real space *is* this significance space? And what in real space are these seven-to-twenty-one dimensional fuzzy-edged meaning clouds, or ranges, made of?"

Bron smiled. "You've got to remember that all these visualizations, even n-dimensional ones, are in themselves just abstract models to— well, explain how what-there-is manages to accomplish what-it-does. What there is, in this case, is the highly complex organic matrix of the micro-circuitry of the human brain in interface with a lot of wave fronts distorted by objects and energies scattered about the cosmos. And what it does, in this case, is to help the brain to learn languages, produce arguments in those languages, and analyze those arguments in formal logical terms as well as metalogical ones. If you'll allow me to run some syntax vectors among some balloons that will shunt them all off over wildly metaphoric slippages: The space is in the brain circuitry, and the clouds are composed of the same thing the words are once they pass through the eardrum, the same thing the image of this coffee bulb is composed of once it passes the retina, the same thing the taste of a bar of Protyyn is composed of once it passes the taste buds, the same thing as the vectors that bind the balloons together, or the homing forces that anchor them within their clouds more or less where learning first set them: a series of routed, electrochemical wave fronts."

Miriamne smiled. "And I still think I'm with you."

"Good. Then throw out all the visualizations you've been forming up till now, first because there just *isn't* any way to visualize a directed wave-front mapping of seven-to-twenty-one dimensional space full of spectrally related meaning ranges that is less than—to put it mildly—oversimplified. And because, second, we're going to start all over with 'To affirm P is to deny not-P' and go running up a completely new set of stairs. Are you ready?"

"Off you go," Miriamne said. "Right behind you."

"All right: The two goals of metalogics are, one) the delimitation of the problem and, two) an exploration of the interpenetration among the problem elements in significance space. In old Boolean terms (Did you see the public-channel coverage about that stuff a few weeks back?), you might call it a rigorous mapping of the Universe of Discourse. Suppose we're constructing some argument or discussion about Farmer Jones's ice-fields, and we know the resolution will be in terms of some area on Farmer Jones's land; and most of the problem elements will be things already on the land or things that might be brought to the land. If we decide to call all of his land south of the Old Crevasse 'P,' then, depending on how and what things on the land affect the problem—that is, interpenetrate with it—, there *may* be no reason not to call all the land north of the Old Crevasse 'not-P.' Or, we might want to call all the land to the north *and* the things that are on all the land north and south, 'not-P.' Or, with a different type of problem, we may want to call all the land to the north and all the things on all the land north and south and all the things that might be brought to the land 'not-P.' Or, indeed, we might, depending on the problem, make some other division. Now remember, in formal logic, 'not-P' *had* to be taken in terms of 'non-P,' which (if P is Farmer Jones's south acres) includes not only the north acres but also the problem of the squared circle, the inner ring of Saturn, and grief—not to mention the Taj Mahal. But given what we know of the problem, it would be a little silly to expect any of these things to come into a real solution. Dismissing them from our consideration is a metalogical delimitation, resulting from an examination of the significance space around various syntax vectors connecting various words of the problem. This means our delimited area for P and not-P can be called metalogically, if not logically, valid. In other words: To deny *meaningfully* that the Taj Mahal is white, while it is certainly *not* to affirm, it is most certainly to suggest, that the Taj Mahal is *some* color, or a combination of colors; and it suggests it a lot more strongly than it suggests that the Taj Mahal is Brian Sanders, freedom, death, large, small, pi, a repeating decimal, or Halley's comet. Such suggestions hold significance space together and keep it in order. Such suggestions are what solve real problems. Getting technical again for a moment and returning to our n-dimensional nightmare . . ." From here he skirted into the various topological representations of metalogical interpenetrations of 'P' and 'not-P,' in whatever n-space volume the two were represented: ". . . not-P can cut off a small piece of P, or it can be a shape that pierces P like a finger through a ball of dough, sticking out both sides. It can be a shape that cuts through P and cleaves it in two—actually three, considering the result as two sides and a slice out of the middle. We have a very useful P/not-P relation where we say that, for whatever the space, not-P is completely contained by P, is tangent to it at an infinite number of points, and cleaves it into an infinite number of pieces—that's such a common one we have a special name for it: we say that not-P *shatters* P. That's the metalogical relation the hen-and-a-half wrongly suggests you use to get a quick answer of 'one.'" Bron took a large breath and found his own eyes wandering around the cubicle, pausing at the bulletin board, the wall and desk consoles, filing drawers, shelves, and readers. "And what we do here, in this department, is to take the programs for some very complicated problems, their verbal synopses and the specifications for answers—often the problems themselves contain millions of elements and millions of operations—and do a quick survey from which we try to map which one-space, two-space, or seventeen-space the problem/answer belongs to; and then suggest a proper topological interpenetration for the constituent P's, Q's, R's and S's that make up the thing, thus yielding a custom-tailored metalogic, that, when it goes into the computer, reduces the whole thing to manageable size and shape; however we do not send our results direct to the computer room, but shuttle them off to another department called, simply 70-E, which completely reworks our results into still another form and sends them on again to yet another department known as Howie's Studio (though I believe Howie has not been with us for over seven years) where still further arcane and mysterious things are done to them that need not concern us here. Getting back to what does . . ." and as his monologue slowly became a discussion once more, he discovered that many of the more technical aspects (". . . if we fail to generate a coherent problem-mapping onto a space of n coordinates, a cross-indexing of the mapping onto 3-space through a set of crossproduct matrices represented by ψ_1, ψ_2, ψ_3, . . . ψ_n can often suggest whether an approximation of coherence can be obtained on a space of $n + 1, n + 2, n + 3 \ldots n + r$ coordinates. Which is very nice, because all you have to do, for a given map, is take the volume

$$\int \int \int \left[\int\limits_{-\infty}^{\infty} \frac{\theta \Psi_n}{\theta z} \delta z \right] dx \; dy \; dz,$$

which only leaves you to figure out certain metalogical aspects of its translation which we can model as regressive acceleration with respect to the specific products of the noncommutative matrix i, j, and $k \ldots$") she seemed familiar with from other applications. The easy analogies, ultimately full of holes (the incoherencies the technical tried to fill), she poked through in the proper places immediately. He was beginning to suspect that, in anticipation of the job, she had pulled a Sam. Now and then she listened extremely attentively when he found himself veering toward a muzzy eloquence. In the midst of one such veering, the thought struck: Somewhere in real space was the real Taj Mahal. He had never seen it: He had never been to Earth. It and rain and unshielded daylight . . . what with the current political situation, he probably never would. Then, rising to replace the whole discomforting notion (though *why* it discomforted he did not know) was: If I'm really out to start an affair with this woman, perhaps I've been going on a bit . . . ? His eyes came back to Miriamne's. He waited for her to say, to whatever last thing he'd said, that she understood, or that she didn't understand, or that the view from the top of these steps was a little heady (he always found it so), or ask a question about some part of it, or finally admit that her attention had wandered and that she'd missed some; and would he please repeat.

What she did say, after she had crumpled her coffee bulb in her fist, looked around for a disposal, not found one, so finally tossed it into a corner with a lot of other crumpled bulbs he himself had inelegantly dropped there over the past month, was: "You know, I think you met a friend of mine yesterday over in the u-l. She runs a theater commune . . . the Spike?"

What happened next was that his heart began to pound. (The Taj crumbled in a welter of granite, grotte, tile . . .) He kept his smile in place, and managed to say, hoarsely, "Oh, you mean you know . . . ? Now that's a coincidence!" The pounding rose so high it hurt his ears—". . . the Spike?"—then ebbed.

Over the next six hours, by some process logical, metalogical, or random, he learned that Miriamne lived at the u-l co-op (Three Fires) which had offered the Spike's company the empty set of rooms on the basement level; that Miriamne had struck up a friendship with the Spike about a week ago, that the Spike had mentioned to her, last night, that they'd done a performance for someone who probably worked in the big computer hegemony off the Plaza of Light—no, the Spike didn't know his name, but he was into metalogics and wore one metal eyebrow. During all this, Bron took erasable writing slates out of his drawer, erased some, put them in other drawers, realized he had put them in the wrong drawers, kept smiling, briefed her on the Day Star project (with an explanation that, by the time he was halfway through it he realized, she couldn't possibly follow because it was simply incoherent, finished it anyway, and discovered she'd followed a good deal more of it than he'd thought), learned that when she'd been hired, she'd been told pretty certainly that she would not end up in her own field but, with things in the economic state they were in, you had to make do with what you could get. When they'd told her they'd try her in Metalogics, why, she'd wondered if she'd run into the tall blonde with the gold eyebrow. Yes, she had been surprised when she realized that he was the person sitting behind the desk, whom she had been assigned to as an assistant. Yes, Tethys *was* a small city. In the middle of all this, lunch-time came and he told her where the cafeteria was in the building, sent her off up there, having decided to eat something wrapped in plastic by himself in the office. Five minutes after she left. he remembered he was trying to start an affair with the woman. Sending her to lunch alone wasn't very smart if that was his goal, so he hurried up after her.

Just inside the cafeteria's double doors stood the Seven Aged Sisters (four of them were women, anyway) in their green, beaded cloaks and silver kerchiefs. A year or so ago they had come to work at the hegemony; rumor had made them, for a few months, something of a hegemony myth. They were the last survivors of some sect they had all joined at three or four years of age, which, for the last eight decades or more, had shunned all literacy, bodily regeneration, and the acquisition of mathematical skills. (What the sect did do, Bron was not sure.) A few years back, however, under the necessity of token devaluation and rising credit demands, there had been a change of sect policy. Using only the General Information drills and instruction programs available through the console of any co-op computer, the seven octogenarians had, in a year and a half, mastered not only basic reading and writing and a grounding in mathematics, but several rather advanced para-math design techniques: They had applied for work, passed proficiency tests, and been hired. Their sect still forbade their partaking of food with nonbelievers, but, from some sense of social decorum, they came each lunch hour and stood along the wall, smiling, nodding, exchanging the odd pleasantry with their fellow workers coming in to eat.

Bron nodded to the nearest, then looked across the busy hall. A dozen people were gathered around (yes, of course it was) Tristan and Iseult, the twelve-year-old twin sisters who, six months back, had been promoted to managers of the entire Tethys wing of the hegemony (. . . more proficiency tests, more phenomenal scores). Tristan, naked, stood scratching her left foot with the big toes of her right, looking very uninterested in everything. Iseult, swathed in diaphanous scarlet from face to feet, was chatting animatedly with the dozen at once. After three months, the girls had asked to be relieved of the taxing executive positions. They said it interfered with their other interests. They were now, again, working as credit technique assayers. But, so the rumor went, they'd retained their quadruple-slot credit rise.

As Bron looked from the vegetarian counter on the left, across the busy room, to the special diet line on the right, he experienced, for the boring, hundred-thousandth time, that moment of discomfort and alienation: Most of these people, as reasonable and as happy as he was, lived in the mixed-sex co-ops he had once tried, but found too tedious and too annoying to bear. Most of them—though not necessarily the same most—lived in co-ops where sex was overt and encouraged and insistently integrated with all aspects of co-operative life . . . fine in theory, but in practice their most annoying and tedious aspect. (A very few [slightly less than one out of five] like Philip—who was standing on the other side of the hall, rubbing his beard on his wrist and talking to three, junior programmers, whose sex Bron could not even distinguish [though one of them was naked] for the men and women passing between—lived in complex family communes.) Philip was the boss Bron definitely did *not* like.

Where was Miriamne anyway?

During Bron's first year in the Satellites, in Lux, he'd thought he might like a physical job, working with his hands, with his body—after all, he'd come from a physical job on Mars. He'd trained, he'd studied, he'd tested; and had gotten work at a large light-metal refectory (heavy metals were rarer and rarer as you got further and further from the sun). He'd hated the job; he was totally frustrated by the people. From there, he'd spent three weeks at a training program at a Protyyn recycling combine—that was so unpleasant it had decided him to forsake the moons of Saturn for the moons of Neptune. (Jupiter was on the other side of the sun: They were discouraging immigration to Ganymede that year.) Then there'd been the public-channel job.

Still, just to stand around the cafeterias in any of the four places for an hour, watching the people come and go, overhearing snatches of conversation, reviewing the emblems of their quotidian concerns, really, save for the fact two were on Iapetus and this was Triton, you could hardly tell them apart.

Miriamne, with her tray, was coming off the vegetarian line.

He started for her, among the workers moving here and there.

"Hello," she said. "You changed your mind?" Then she looked over his shoulder.

Bron looked too.

Philip, barefoot as Tristan, in an antiseptically white jumpsuit, walked toward them. A red plastic V was pinned, with brass clips, to his chest.

"Oh, hey, Phil . . . ?" Bron turned. "This is Miriamne, the new assistant Audri brought me this morning. Philip's my *other* boss, which sort of makes him your boss, too . . . or did you two meet before already?"

"We met," Philip said. "As I told you before, if Bron treats you badly . . . I'm repeating this now because I don't like saying things behind people's backs—you kick him—" Philip raised his foot and swung his toe lightly against Bron's calf (Philip's ankle was incredibly hairy)—"right *here*. Bron sprained his knee earlier this year—" which was true—"and I don't believe he had it attended to properly. It should cause him a great deal of pain."

Bron laughed. "Philip is a real comic." No, he did not like Philip at all.

Miriamne said: "I overheard someone say those two kids over there were head of this whole operation a few months ago . . . ?"

"Yeah," Philip said. "And it ran a whole lot smoother than it does now. Of course, that could just be all the pressure from the war."

Miriamne glanced at the group still gathered around the twins, shook her head with a little smile. "I wonder what they'll be doing in ten years."

"I doubt they'll even stay in business," Philip said. "That kind never do. *If* they do, by the time they're twenty-five, they'll probably have started a family. Or a religion, if they don't. Speaking of families, some of our kids are downstairs and waiting for me. Will you excuse me?" Philip walked away. To his back was pinned, by brass clips, a red plastic N.

Frowning after him, Bron said: "Come on, I'll get some lunch. You go find a booth."

There were booths all around the hall: for eating and reading, for eating and talking, for eating and silent meditation, private booths for anything you wanted—if she'd chosen one of these, Bron, with that little gesture of the hand, would have made his intentions clear right then.

But she had chosen one for conversation.

So, for the rest of the lunch-hour (he realized what he'd been doing two minutes before it was time to go back to work), he asked her about the Spike, the theater commune, some more about the Spike—not really, he pondered as they rode down the escalator to the Metalogics Department in the second subbasement, the way to get things off on the proper foot. Well, he had the rest of the day.

The rest of the day continued in the same wise, till, when she asked could she leave ten minutes early because, after all, there wasn't really anything to do today and she would make up the time once she got more into the actual work, and he said sure, and she mentioned she was walking back to her co-op, and Bron, remembering that after all he *was* trying to start an affair with her, asked if she minded his walking with her and, no, it wasn't out of his way, he took a roundabout route through the u-l frequently: She frowned and, a bit sullenly, agreed. Fifteen minutes later, when they turned off the Plaza of Light, down the deserted alley toward the underpass, he remembered *again* that he was trying to start an affair with her and put his hand on the gray shoulder of her cape: Perhaps this was the time to openly signal his intentions—

Miriamne said: "Look, I know it's a lot of pressure on you, having to teach somebody to do a job they're not trained for or even very interested in, but I also get the feeling, about every half an hour, when you can get your mind back in it, that you're coming on to me."

"Me?" Bron leaned a little closer and smiled. "Now why ever should you think that?"

"I'd better explain," she said. "The co-op where I live is all women."

The Spike's laugh returned to him, pulsing with his heartbeat which, for the second time, began to pound. "Oh, hey . . ." He dropped his hand. "Hey, I'm sorry—it's gay?"

"*It's* not," she said. "But *I* am."

"Oh." Bron took a breath, his heart still mangling blood and air in his chest. "Hey, really, I wasn't . . . I mean, I didn't know."

"Sure," she said. "That's why I thought I ought to say something. I mean, I'm just not into men in *any* way, shape, or form right now. You understand?"

"Oh, sure, of course."

"And I don't feel like getting yelled at later for leading you on, because I'm not. I'm just trying to be pleasant with somebody I have to work with who looks like a fairly pleasant guy. That's all."

"Really," he said. "I understand. Most people who live in single-sex, nonspecific co-ops aren't into men *or* women that much. I know. *I* live in one."

"You got it." She smiled. "If you want to go back to the Plaza, now, and catch your transport—?"

"No. Honestly, I *do* walk home this way . . . a lot of times. That's how I met Spike—the Spike—yesterday."

Miriamne shrugged, walked on, but at a distance that, as they neared the arch, widened. It's not sullenness, he realized suddenly: She's as preoccupied as I am. With what? he wondered. And, heaving into his mind, oppressive as a iceberg and bright as a comet, was the Spike's face. No (he narrowed his eyes at Miriamne, who was a step ahead), she said the Spike was just her friend: Like me and Lawrence, he thought. Then, the sudden questioning: Does *she* feel about the Spike the way Lawrence is always saying he feels about . . . ? His eyes narrowed further at the gray-caped shoulders ahead. I'll kill her! he thought. I'll make her sorry she ever heard of metalogics! Miriamne, staggering, drunk, in the co-op corridor, grasping at the Spike, caught in her arms, falling down soused on the corridor floor . . . He thought: I'll—Miriamne glanced back. "You're looking preoccupied again."

"Huh?" he said. "Oh. I guess I am." He smiled: I *will* kill her. I'll kill her in some slow and lingering way that will hurt amazingly and unbelievably and continuously and will seem to have no source and take years.

But, with her own preoccupations, Miriamne looked away.

Out of the archway, papers blew across the asphalt—a dozen printed flyers swirled their shins.

One pasted itself to Miriamne's calf. She tried to sidestep it, couldn't, so finally bent and pulled it up. As they passed into the green light, she examined the paper. A quarter of the way through, with a wry smile, she passed it to Bron.

So as not to look at her, he read it:

THESE THINGS ARE HAPPENING IN YOUR CITY!!!

the broadside proclaimed in askew, headline letters.

Smaller letters beneath announced:

"Here are Thirteen Things *your* government does *not* want you to know."

Beneath that were a list of numbered paragraphs:

1) The gravity cut that threw a blanket of terror over the entire Tethys Keep last night is not the first to rock the city. A three-sheet area in the unlicensed sector near the outer ring, that included the C and D wings of the Para-med Hospital Wards, was hit by a two-and-a-half minute, total gravity failure, which, while it caused only a half-pound drop in atmosphere pressure because the area was comparatively small, produced gale force winds in the peripheral area of the u-l whose peak force was never measured, but which, five and three-quarters minutes later, was recorded to have *dropped* to a hundred and thirty miles an hour! Damage figures still have not been released. There are twenty-nine people known to be dead— among them four of the seven "political" patients (inmates? prisoners?) at the C Annex of the Para-med. We could go into this in more detail, but there are too many other things to list. For example:

2) We have a copy of a memo from the Liaison Department between the Diplomatic Department and Intelligence, with a 4:00 P. A. issue circulation stamp, that reads, in part: ". . . The crisis tonight will be brief. Most citizens will not even notice—

"Excuse me," a hoarse voice said. "You better let me have that, sir."

Bron looked up in the green light.

Miriamne had stopped too.

"You might as well hand it over . . . sir." The man was burly. Grizzled hair (and one diminutive nipple) pushed through the black web across his chest. He wore a black skullcap, black pants, shoes open in the front over hairy, hammered toes. (They would be open in the back too, Bron knew, over wide, horny heels.) He held a canvas sack in one hand (that arm was sleeved in black), and in the other (bare except for a complicated, black gauntlet, a-glitter with dials, knobs, small cases, and finned projections) he clutched crumpled flyers. "Some bunch in the u-l printed up about fifteen thousand of these and dumped a batch at every goddamn exit. So all the e-girls have to go and turn pollution controllers!" He looked at Miriamne, who, with folded arms, now leaned one shoulder against the green tiles. Her sullen, preoccupied look had gone: It had been replaced by one of muted, but clear, hostility. "I mean you can't have junk like this just blowing around in the streets." His eyes came back to Bron's. "So come on, let a girl do his job and hand it . . ." His expression faltered. "Look, if you want to *read* it, just put it in your pocket and take it with you. There's no restriction on having as many of 'em as you want in your own room—but we're supposed to get 'em cleaned up off all publicly licensed property. Look, *I* don't care if you read it. Just don't leave it around in your commons, that's all . . . this isn't some goddamn police state. Where do you think we are, Earth? *I* come from Earth. I used to be an enforcement-girl—well, we called 'em enforcement-boys, there—in Pittsburgh, before I came out here and got on the force. In Pittsburgh you could get hauled off for resocialization just for something like that—" He nodded toward the tiled wall where Miriamne was leaning. Someone had painted across it in dayglo red (which looked thoroughly unappetizing under the green light-strips):

PLANT YOUR FEET ON IT FIRMLY!
THIS ONE *AIN'T* GREEN CHEESE!

Below it clumsy arrows pointed to the ground.

(In black chalk, someone had scrawled across one side of the slogan: "that's a bit difficult if they keep cutting the gravity" with several black arrows pointing toward the last, day-glo exclamation point.)

"Believe me, in Pittsburgh, that's *just* how they do." (Enforcement-agents at Tethys had, fifteen years ago, been almost all women, hence the "e-girl" nickname. With changing standards, and the migrations of the recent decade and a half, by now the force was almost a third male. But the name persisted, and, as Chief Enforcement Officer Phyllis Freddy had once explained on a public-channel culture survey to a smiling interviewer, and thereby cooled the last humor out of a joke that had never been more than tepid: "Look, an e-girl is a girl, I don't care if she's a man *or* a woman!") "Really. I mean, I know what I'm talking about. Now put it away or give it here, huh?"

Bron glanced at Miriamne again (who was watching quietly), then handed over the flyer.

It followed the others into the sack.

"Thanks." The black-clad agent pushed the papers down further. "I mean, you come out here to the moons and you take a job as a girl because it's what you know how to do, it's what you've been trained for—and believe me, it's a lot easier here than it is in Pittsburgh . . . *or* Nangking. I know 'cause I've worked in both—I mean you take the job because you want to *be* a girl—" He stepped by Bron, bent down, and swept up another handful from the papers fluttering along the ground—"and what do you end up? A garbage man!"

Miriamne started walking again, arms still folded. Bron walked too.

Blowing paper (and papers crumpled and crushed) echoed in the underpass.

On the dark walk, beside the rail, Miriamne turned left.

Right, bright, melding colors caught Bron's eye:

An ego-booster stood by the gritty wall some dozen feet down. Something was wrong with it.

"Excuse me," Bron called. "Can you wait up a moment?"

He walked toward it.

Someone had defaced it—probably with the same aerosol spray that the "green cheese" slogan had been written with on the underpass tiles. Against the normally melting hues, it was hard to tell which was booth and which was defacement; the only thing that made him sure was the legend above the entrance (only "your" and half of "society" showed), splotched out with red splatter.

The canvas had been yanked loose from its runners at one end; he pushed it back.

Inside was streaked scarlet. Had some religious cultist chosen this booth in which to perform self-mutilation—?

It was only vandalism.

The screen was caved, the red too bright for blood. The token slot was plastered over with half-chewed Protyyn, or worse. The lips of the card slip were pried.

"I guess," Bron mused, "last night just made people a little more annoyed about these things . . ."

Miriamne, somewhere just behind his shoulder, said, "That's been like that four months. You just noticed it?" Then she said: "Look, I don't mean to be impolite. But one reason I wanted to leave a few minutes early is that I'd like to try and catch a friend of mine at the co-op—it's rather important to me." She smiled "An affair of the heart, if you will . . . ? If you don't mind, I'll just go on—"

"No—" Bron said, turning. "I mean, I don't mind. But I—"

Miriamne had already started walking.

Bron caught up. "I mean, I thought I might stop by and see if

Spike—the Spike was there. I'd wanted to . . . well, tell her how much I liked her theater piece—unless of course they're out somewhere performing . . . ?"

"No," Miriamne said. "Not tonight. They may be rehearsing though." She uncrossed her arms, hooked one chrome-nailed thumb on her chrome waist-cinch. "From a couple of things she said, I wouldn't be surprised if she was rather glad to see you," which, as he hurried on (sometimes silently beside her, sometimes silently behind), made him bubblingly happy.

Dark streets, here and there slashed by a sodium light-tube set upright in a wall-holder (the bottom few inches of most of them were completely grimed over), gave way to narrower alleys. The glowing red coordinate numbers and letters, in their little frames above him, by now had so many superscripts and subscripts you'd really need a wrist calculator to figure out exactly where you were.

They went up some ringing metal steps between two walls maybe twenty inches apart, into a tunnel that was dead black, cool, damp, and whose roof (Bron knew it was filthy) kept brushing his hair.

"This way—" Miriamne said, muffled by dark walls—"I know I'm taking you by a pretty grim shortcut. But I'm in a hurry."

He went 'this way,' bumped his shoulder on the corner of the turnoff—while he rubbed it, ahead a line of orange light opened beside Miriamne, sweeping her into broad-hipped silhouette.

"In here—" which was a circular room with a single light-pole in the center, floor to ceiling. "This is Three Fires' visitors' lounge. I know it's pretty bare—" Bunk beds against the wall with blue plastic sleeping pads; a few floor cushions; some low shelves, on which were books. (How quaint, he thought. How u-l.) There was a reader beside the bed, but nothing like a file drawer for a library. (Which was also, he reflected, very u-l. The books, of course, would all be poetry.) "We don't have many visitors," Miriamne explained. "I'll go send the Spike down—you'll excuse me if I don't come back. But I really do want to catch my friend . . . If she's still here. If the Spike's not in, someone will come up and tell you. I'll see you at work tomorrow." She nodded.

"Thanks." Bron nodded after her, sitting on the bottom bunk, only now realizing with certainty that "her friend" was not the Spike after all. The orange plastic door, clicking bearings, closed on an image of her rocking waist-cinch, wide hips below and bare flesh above. Behind Bron's smile, a haze of hostility, with him since they'd entered the underpass, broke up, and drifted away.

He let out his breath, sat back on the air-filled pad, considered it again now that it was gone, and thought: I can't have that crazed lesbian in my office. Look how she makes me feel even knowing she lives in the same *co-op* with her! Bron (like most people) thought of jealousy as an irrational emotion. But it was also a real one. And he felt it infrequently enough to respect it when he did. I'll ask Audri (or Philip? No, Audri) to get her transferred to another department . . . She catches on quick and I could use someone with a brain to get that Day Star-minus nonsense into shape. But that's not the point, he decided. A transfer. Yes. I'll—

"Hello!" a familiar voice said, directly above him.

He looked up. Inset in the ceiling was a speaker. "Eh . . . hello?"

"I'm on my way—"

"You don't have to rush for—" but, hearing clicks, he looked down as the bright orange door finished rolling into the dull orange wall.

"Oh . . ."

"Hi, there!" She walked into the room. "What a surprise." Loose, red pants flapped at her bare ankles. From her waist, black suspenders crossed between her breasts (there brass clips hooked a large, red, plastic R . . . he had no idea why) and went up over her shoulders. She stopped with her hands against her thighs, nails clean of gold now, slightly dirty and endearing, lips unrouged and charming. "You could have knocked me over with an eyelash when Miriamne told me you were here—I was all set to spend the evening going over forty-six micro-scenarios that I know, without looking, are not our kind of thing at all. People keep giving us things that are minute-long gimmicks, instead of minute-long theater . . . you know what I mean? That's why we end up creating most of our own works. But I always feel I have to consider unsolicited material, anyway, just in case. My mistake was telling the endowment people I would devote a certain amount of energy to it. Some weeks you just feel less like considering them than others. And this is one of them." She sat down on the bed beside him—"We've been rehearsing a new piece all afternoon that goes into production tomorrow. We just broke off half an hour ago—" and placed her hand affectionately on his leg, little and ring fingers together, middle and forefingers together, with a V between, which on Earth, and the Moon, and Mars, and Io, and Europa, and Ganymede, and Callisto, and Iapetus, and Galileo, and Neriad, and Triton, in co-op and commune, park, bar, public walk and private soiree, was the socially acceptable way for men, women, children, and several of the genetically engineered higher animals to indicate: I am sexually interested.

"Would you like to come back to my room?" she asked.

For the third time that day his heart started to thud. "Um . . ." he said. "I mean . . . yeah. I mean, if you . . . sure. Yeah. Please . . ."

She clapped her knees.

He almost grabbed her hand back.

"Come on, let's go." She stood up, smiling. "I share the room with Windy—our acrobat. And Charo—that's our guitar player. It probably wouldn't bother you, their being there. But it would me—I'm a bit peculiar. I asked them to brave the steely-eyed glances of the commons room for a couple of hours. These single-sex unspecified-preference co-ops are like living on top of an iceberg!"

"Yeah," he said, following her through the orange doorway, through halls, down staircases, along corridors. "I live in one too."

"I mean," she said, stopping by a room door, and glancing back at him, "it's awfully nice of Three Fires to take us in at all—the company's got men and women in it, of all persuasions. But wow! The psychic chill!" And then: "You do? Well!" She pressed her thumb against the circular I. D. plate on the door (which seemed as quaint as the books in the visitors' lounge). "I mean—" she said, in a tone that told him she was politely picking up another thread of thought—"if Windy and Charo just sat around and read, I suppose it wouldn't be so bad. But they're always practicing. Both of them. I just find it distracting."

The door opened.

She stepped in.

He followed.

The bed was triple-sized and rumpled.

"Really, when Miriamne told me that *you* were her boss . . ."

He laughed, completely delighted. "What did she say about me?"

She glanced back at him, considered—with her tongue a small knob in her cheek: "That you tried hard." She turned before the bed, unsnapped a suspender that flopped down against the red pants. "I took it as a recommendation."

Stepping toward her, he wondered fleetingly if something terrible might happen.

It didn't.

They made love.

Afterward, she made lazy suggestions about getting back to her scripts. But, with one thing and another, they made love again—after which, to his astonishment, he broke out crying. Tears still brimming, he tried to laugh them away, ultimately rather proud of himself

for the openness of his emotions—what*ever* the hell they were . . .
Obviously moved, she cradled his head in her lap, and asked, "What
is it? There, there, what's the matter?"

Still laughing, still crying, he said: "I don't know. I really don't.
This doesn't happen to me very often. Really." It had happened to
him exactly twice before, both times when he was twenty, both times
with short dark, small-boned, broad-hipped women at least fifteen
years older than he was.

They made love again

"You know," she said at last, stretching in his arms, "You really are
quite lovely. Where—" and one arm went out over the side of the
bed—"did you learn to do that?"

Bron turned over on his stomach (quite recovered from his crying
jag) smiling: "I told you once, actually. But you've probably forgotten."

"*Mmmm?*" She glanced at him.

"Now *you're* probably the type to hold it against me," he said, not
believing it a moment. These wholesome Outer Satelliters were desperately accepting of any World-bound decadence; it supplied some
sort of *frisson*, he suspected, ordinarily missing from their small-
world lives.

"Dear heart—" she rolled against him—"*every*one's a type."

Raising his eyebrow, Bron looked down at the hollow between her
neck's ligaments. "From the age of . . . well, on and off between the
ages of eighteen and—oh, about twenty-three, my sexual services
could be purchased at a place in Bellona called—I kid you not—the
Flesh Pit."

"By who?" She cocked her head. "Women?"

"Yes. Women—Oh, it was a fine, upstanding, highly-taxed,
government-approved job."

"Taxes," she said. "Yes. I've heard worlds are like that—" Suddenly
she threw an arm over his shoulder. "What was it like? I mean, did
you sit in a cage and get selected by prowling creatures with dilated
pupils, silver eyelids, and cutaway veils?"

"Not quite." Bron laughed. "Oh, we got a few of the cutaway-veil
set. But they're pretty much restricted to old movies and ancient
Annie-shows. Not all, though—my gold eyebrow used to really turn
some of them on. But then, they knew what it meant.

"What does it mean?"

"Nothing pleasant. Come on. Give us a snuggle."

She snuggled. "Living on a world always sounded so romantic to me. I grew up on the Gannymede icefields. I'm practically a provincial bumpkin compared to you. Was it awful—being a prostitute and paying taxes and things? Awful to your psyche, I mean?"

"No . . . Sexually, at any rate, after a couple of A-seventy-nine forms, you just got a pretty good idea of who you really were."

"Did you have to go with *any* woman who would pay?"

He began to suspect the idea turned her on and considered beginning an erotic monologue he had actually employed with various women out here that (actually) contained only a few fantasies of omission: It ended with his being mauled by a dozen women in a locked room, where he'd been unwittingly lured, and leaving bruised, exhausted, drained; it could usually be counted on to incite more lovemaking. But he was curious about her curiosity. "For all practical purposes I did. But the Pit was there for its customers, so they were pretty efficient about the guys they hired. When you apply for a job like that the first time . . . well, you fill out a lot of performance forms, take a lot of response tests and what have you. I mean, it wouldn't really do to send a woman to a guy who just couldn't get it up for her—assuming that's what she was into; and a good quarter of the clients weren't, really."

"So you *could* choose just to go to bed with attractive women if you wanted—"

He shook his head, wondering if she were kidding. "Look, if you were the kind of guy who could only get it on with the nubile nymphs on the daytime video romances, really, you just wouldn't be too likely to apply for the job. When I got hired, I was down for all women with physical deformities. For some reason, a scar or a withered arm or leg always gets me off; which made me quite useful. And older women, of course; and dark skin; and big hips; I was also down for what they called second-level sadism."

"My Lord," she said. "What's that? No, don't tell me! Did women prostitutes get the same, deluxe treatment—performance forms and the like?"

"Female prostitution is illegal on Mars—oh, of course there was a lot of it around. Probably as much of it as there was the male kind, just in numbers. But because it was pretty harried by the e-girls . . . eh, e-men, if any single-establishment got near the size of one of the male houses, it was raided, broken up, and closed down. So you just couldn't get things quite to the same level of organization. But I got special credit exemptions and preferred ratings on standard government loans for each uninterrupted six-month period I worked—of which, incidentally, in three and a half years there were only two. It's the kind of job you take vacations from a lot." He put his hand on the back of her neck, rubbed. "Now, on Earth, female prostitution is government-licensed in most places and male prostitution is illegal. The oddest thing: Some of the big men that ran the Flesh Pit—and about half the other houses in the Goebels—went to Earth and set up Earth-licensed houses of female prostitution in various cities there, using the same techniques they'd developed on Mars for the male houses—screening the prostitutes, getting their performance charts and preferences. Apparently, they've cleaned up! Earth's oldest profession was also one of its most shoddily run, until *they* came along—or so they tell you on Mars. I worked with a couple of guys who'd free-lanced various places on Earth, illegally." He sighed. "They had some peculiar stories."

"Worlds must be very peculiar places." She sighed. "Sometimes I wonder if that isn't really the only reason we're at war with them."

"Or about to be at war with them. Triton, anyway."

The Spike's head came up. Her hair feathered the edge of his hand. "Small dark women with big hips and withered arms—" She glanced at him. "Someday you must tell me what you see in a big-boned, scrawny blonde like me."

"They're mutually inclusive areas, not mutually exclusive. And they include quite a bit more . . ." He nuzzled her shoulder and wondered much the same thing she'd just asked; his mind, used to such meanderings, had only been able to come up with a sort of generalized incest, or even narcissism, the denial of which was the reason for those other tastes, now (interestingly) broken through.

"Of course," the Spike said, "the whole thing sounds terribly bizarre, being a prostitute and all." She looked at him again. "What did your parents think?"

He shrugged; she had broached an uncomfortable area; but he'd always thought honesty a good thing in matters of sex: "I never talked about it with them, really. They were both civic constructionist computer operators—light laborers to you folks out here. They were pretty glum about everything, and I guess that would have only been something else for them to be glum about."

"My parents—" she said, yawning, "all nine of them—are Ganymede ice-farmers. No cities for them. They're good people, you know? But they can't see further than the next methane thaw. Now they'd be quite happy if I'd gone into computers, like you—or Miriamne. But the theater, I'm afraid, is a little beyond them. It's not they *disapprove,* you know . . . it's just . . ." She shook her head.

"My parents—and they were only the two—didn't disapprove. We just didn't discuss it. That's all. But then, we didn't discuss much of anything."

She was still shaking her head. "Ice-sleds, checking vacuum seals on this piece of equipment, that piece, always looking at the world through polarized blinkers—good solid people. But . . . I don't know: limited."

Bron nodded, to end, rather than continue. These u-l folk *would* talk about their pasts, and, more unsettling, nudge you to talk. (The archetypal scene: The ice-farm Matriarch saying to the young Earth man with the dubious past [or Patriarch saying to the equally dubious young Mars woman]: "We don't care about what you done, just what you do—and even that, once you done it, we forget it.") In the licensed area of the city, this philosophy seemed—within reason—to hold. But then, what was the u-l for, if not to do things differently in? "Now you see," Bron said, "that seems romantic to me, growing up in the untamed, crystalline wilderness. I used to go to every ice-opera they'd run at the New Omoinoia; and when they'd rerun them on the public channels, a year or so later, I kept an awful lot of clients waiting downstairs while I found out how Bo Ninepins was going to get the settlers out from under another methane slide."

"Ha!" She flung herself on the bed. "You did? So did my folks. They loved them! You've probably seen part of our farm—the ice-opera companies were always using our south acres to do location shooting. It was the only farm within six hundred miles of G-city that had any place on it that looked like it *could* have been in an ice-opera! Maybe hanging around the shooting company was where I got my first prod toward the theater—who knows? Anyway, we must have burrowed down to the Diamond Palace once a month from the time I was twelve, the whole lot of us. Like going to a religious meeting, I swear. Then they'd stay up till one o'clock in the morning, drinking and complaining about the details that the picture people had gotten wrong *this* time. And be right there for the next one next month—now *that's* what my folks think of as theater: Noble old loner Lizzie Ninepins saving the settlers from the slide, or virile young Pick-Ax Pete with his five wives and four husbands carving a fortune out from a methane chasm . . ." She laughed. "It was a beautiful landscape to grow up in—at least the south acres was—even if you never saw it without a faceplate between you and the vacuum. Now if I ever directed an ice-opera, my folks would think I'd arrived! Government subsidized micro-theater, indeed! I suppose I've had a secret urge to, ever since my name day . . . I chose the name of a mother of mine I'd never known, who'd got killed in an ice-slide before I was born." The Spike laughed. "Now I bet you've seen *that* one in a dozen ice-operas! *I* certainly had." (Bron smiled. In the Satellites, children were given only a first name at birth—about half the time the last name of one of their genetic parents, government serial numbers doing for all official identification. Then, at some coming-of-age day, they took a last name for themselves, from the first name of someone famous, or in honor of some adult friend, workmate, or teacher. Naming age was twelve on the moons of Saturn, fourteen on the moons of Jupiter; he wasn't sure what it was here on Triton, but he suspected it was younger than either. On Earth last names still, by and large, passed down paternally. On Mars, they could pass either paternally or maternally. His father's last name was Helstrom; if, as by now he was sure was pretty unlikely, he ever joined a family out here, Helstrom would be the [first] name of his first son.) The Spike laughed again, this time muffling the sound in his armpit. Then her head came up. "Do you know what Miriamne really said about you?"

Bron rolled to his side. "She *didn't* say I was trying hard?"

"She said that you were a first-class louse *but* that you were trying hard. She told me this terrible story about how you—" She stopped. Her eyes widened. "Oh dear! I forgot . . . you're *her* boss—she's not yours. The last job she had, she was a production foreman for a cybralog manufacturing compound . . . Well, *now* I've done it!" She shook her head. "I've never worked in an office, and I . . . forgot."

Bron smiled. "What was the horrible story she told?"

"As she was running out of here, she blurted out something about you making some personnel receptionist's life miserable on the phone just to impress her as a first step to getting in her pants."

Bron laughed. "I guess she had *my* number!"

"If that's what you were doing, you mustn't hold it against her."

"Oh, I wouldn't." He nuzzled again, closing his arms around her. "You know about the prostitute's heart of gold, lying around underneath it all?"

"Ah, but gold can be a very cold, heavy metal." Her head turned on his shoulder. "Do you think being a prostitute was helpful?"

He shrugged, cradling her. "I think it makes you surer of yourself when you're actually *in* bed—not necessarily a better lover—but a more relaxed one."

"You have," she said toward the ceiling, "a certain pyrotechnical flair that, I admit, I admire the hell out of."

"On the other hand, I don't know if it does anything for the relationship part of a sexualizationship. Maybe it's having so much sex right there, and not having to walk further than downstairs to the client lounge to get it, and it's paying the bills to boot—I guess when you finally get out into the real world and find that people are as interested in you as they are in your technique—*and* expect you to be interested in them too—it takes some adjusting to. Maybe I never have. Lasting sexualizationships just aren't my strong point . . . *no!*" He looked down at the top of her head. "That isn't the way I feel at all. Isn't it funny how we always say the cliché thing, even if we don't believe it! No. I don't think it hurt me in any way, at all. Some of it was pleasant. Some of it was unpleasant. And it was all a long time ago. But I learned a hell of a lot, about myself, about people. Perhaps I never had much of a bent for relationships, even as a kid; which is why I went into prostitution in the first place. But it's certainly made me a lot more tolerant of a lot more different types of people than most ordinary Martians—say most of my clients. What I learned there is probably the only thing that made it possible for me to adjust—however badly I've done it—to immigrating out here to the Satellites . . . where you—how do they put it?—can't make a redressable contract across either a sexual or a sectarian subject."

"That's right," she mused. "Marriage is legal on Mars too. For some reason we only think of that in terms of Earth out here." She nodded thoughtfully. "Though if what you said about relationships not being your forte is true, the other thing you said still makes sense, even if it is a cliché. Well, what does *any* type of life really fit you for today? I'm damned if I know what life in the theater has done for—"

The door flew in, crashing against the wall.

Bron jerked up on his elbow to see two bare feet, with frayed cuffs fallen away from red-haired calves, waving in the air. The acrobat (Windy?) walked in on his hands. In the hall, somebody was playing the guitar.

Bron was about to say something about knocking first when a little girl (perhaps six? perhaps seven?) on very thick-soled shoes and draped in a trailing, tattered veil of sequins, ran into the room, leapt on the bed (her knee bruised his thigh), weeping, and flung herself into the Spike's arms; the Spike shrieked, "Oh, my goodness . . . !" and, to Bron's astonishment (he was sitting on the bed's edge now, both feet on the warm plastifoam floor), began to weep, herself, and cuddle the grubby-fingered creature.

"Hey, I was just wondering if you—" That was the hirsute, half-blind woman with the mastectomy, leaning in the door. Astonishment bloomed over her scarred face. "Oh, I'm sorry!" As she pulled back, two more women—one carrying a ladder, the other a tool case—pushed in.

"Look," the one with the case said, clanking it on the floor and pushing the catch up with one, very pointy-toed boot, "we've got to get this done now. Really. I'm sorry." The cover clacked open.

"Hey, what—" Bron said (he was standing, now, near the wall) to the knobby ankle waving near his shoulder—"I mean is this just one of your damn micro-theater pieces? Because if it is . . ."

"Man," the head said (which was down at about his knee, a waterfall of red hair all around it sweeping the floor, between splayed, hammy hands), "don't *ever* live in an *all* woman co-op unless they're *all* straight, or they're *all* gay, every last one. It just isn't worth it, you know what I mean?" The hair shook aside enough to see an ear. "I mean, really!" The hands shifted. The feet swung.

The little girl, sitting on top of the ladder now, sniffled.

The last two women who had come in were making marks across the wall with black crayons.

The Spike, on the edge of the bed, was pulling up her baggy red trousers, standing and turning (on her back, fastened with the same brass clips, was a red Z, as mysterious as the R in front) and pulling her black suspenders up over her shoulder. She turned back and, knuckling her tear-wet eyes, came over to Bron. "I'm sorry about this, really, I am . . . But I just tend to anthropomorphize *every*thing!"

One of the women swung a small sledge against the wall. Cracks zagged out from the blow. The little girl on top of the ladder burst out weeping afresh.

So did the Spike: ". . . Oh, go *on*! Please, go on. Really!" She gestured behind her with one hand. Tears ran, in three lines, down one cheek, in one down the other. Suddenly she hit at Windy's foot. "Oh, *stop* sulking and stand up!"

The acrobat's feet swayed wildly, kicked violently, regained balance. From knee level came a torrent of exotic and specialized profanity that brought back to Bron, with incredible clarity, the face of one particular earthie he had worked with in the Goebels: If Windy had *not* spent time on Earth as an extra-legal, male prostitute, he'd certainly spent a lot of time with men who had!

But the Spike had seized Bron's arm and was pushing him toward the door, in which the guitarist (Charo?) stood, her instrument high under her breasts, her head bent pensively, her left hand, far up the neck, clutching chord after chord; the outsized muscle between thumb and forefinger on her right hand pulsed as her nails rattled notes into the corridor.

"By eight o'clock—!" The Spike turned back to the room and called, tearily, with a sweep of one arm that sent her staggering against him, "I promise! Really! By eight o'clock, I *will* know what I'm doing!"

The hammer smashed against the wall.

The Spike pushed past the guitarist—"No, not that way—" which, Bron realized, was to him, not her. She made a great, head-clearing snuffle—"*This* way!"—grabbed Bron's arm again, and tugged him into the hall.

In rakish imitation of Sam (which he indulged about once a month) Bron had gone to work that day wearing nothing. Still, he would have liked a chance to wash, or, failing that at least to sleep for twenty minutes more, cuddled against her rather bony back. But he followed her around a corner, where the hallway went completely dark—and collided with her; she had turned to face him. Her arms closed around him. Her cheek, still wet, brushed his. "This isn't very hospitable, I know. Shall we just stand here and hold one another a few moments? Really, it's just that our company is the co-op's guests—noncredit guests, too; one has to put up."

He grunted something between annoyance and assent; and held her and was held by her; and, except for the plastic letter against his chest, felt more and more comfortable.

People, from time to time, passed.

After the fifth, she disengaged. "Let's go outside and take a walk. I feel I've been just dreadful."

He grunted again, took her hand; she squeezed, and (to the sound of her brushing pantaloons) they walked along the corridor. "I was going to ask you," he said, getting the idea the first time that moment, "if you took all your 'audiences' to bed with you—as a sort of encore?"

"I don't even take *most* of them to bed. Why?"

"Well, I . . . it's just that I have difficulty, with you, sometimes, deciding what's real and what's theater."

"Do you?" she asked; she sounded surprised; and intrigued. Then she laughed. "But all theater is reality. *And* all reality is . . . theater!"

Bron grunted again, annoyed at something other than the ironic triteness. After a silent minute's walking, he asked: "When do we get outside?"

"We are outside."

"Huh?" He looked at the walls (a dull, doorless brown), at the ceiling; there was no ceiling. The walls went up and up and disappeared in unlicensed blackness. He brought his eyes down; ahead, red, luminous letters of the street coordinates glowed. "Oh."

"I liked you," she said at last, in answer to the question he'd asked over a minute ago; "What you looked like, first. Then, the way you . . . well, responded to our work. I mean, *we* know it's good. We've done that one for perhaps a dozen people so far, and all of them have *liked* it. But your response was so open and . . . well, 'rich' is the way Dian—that's our set designer—put it when we talked about it later."

"I got talked about later?"

"Oh, we always discuss each performance afterward. That's just part of the backstage (as it were) work the audience never sees. Presumably, however, the next audience gets the benefit. I mean, basically we're concerned with leading people gently into a single moment of verbal and spatial disorientation—I *say* disorientation: What I mean, of course, is a freeing, to experience a greater order than the quotidian can provide. A moment of verbal, spatial, and spiritual energy in resolution. That's so necessary in a world that's as closed in as life in any satellite city must, of necessity, be. Especially—" She looked up the high, blank walls—"in someplace as claustric as the u-l sector. Maybe wanting to be able to break out, even through art, is my ice-farm heritage working again. Yes, I spent my childhood scooting up and down plastic corridors from bubble-hut to bubble-hut, or in ice-treaders that were a lot more cramped than this. Still, the point is, those corridors and huts *were* transparent. And beyond them—" She took a breath—"was the sky!"

From last night, Bron remembered the disappointing stars.

"But what I was saying: You'd be surprised how many people *do* fight that moment of freedom, even with the drug boost, for the whole minute and forty-nine seconds the piece takes to perform! *You* didn't fight it; you went with it. I liked that. We all did—then, of course, there was just something engaging about your personality: despite its rather blunt side. Most people, unless they follow the theater seriously, don't even remember my name—I don't even bother to tell most people; even when they ask . . . you can't imagine how surprised I was when Miriamne brought you back with her."

They reached a wider thoroughfare—tracks curved along the far side, two red glints pointing the rails where they neared a street sign.

"You're really in charge of the whole company?" he asked. "You write, produce, act, direct . . . the whole thing?"

"I've even been known to sew costumes."

"Oh." The discomfort made him rummage through the other discomforts of the day. The most accessible was: "Do you know, all the way over here, I had the craziest notion that you and Miriamne were involved. Sexually, that is."

"Why?"

"Guess I was projecting." He laughed. "I live in an all-male, unspecified co-op over on the other side of the Great Divide. There's a friend of mine there, see, who's this perfectly crazed, seventy-four-year-old, unregenerated character who, whenever he gets drunk, is always making futile attacks on my tired, pale bod; then he sort of revels in it when I reject him. I think it gives him some sort of masochistic solace. Actually, though, he's a pretty great guy—In fact, why don't we go to my place now and I'll get old Lawrence looped and he'll regale you with adventures from his long and checkered career? You're the type—I mean being in the theater and all—who'd probably really enjoy him."

"We are all—" she began. "But I said that before. I don't think I'd necessarily like him. I have very little sympathy with political homosexuals."

Bron laughed. "That's what Lawrence said to me first time I met him." Then he frowned. "Why do you call him a political homosexual?"

"I mean if, one) he isn't happy with it and, two) he keeps going around pushing his affections on people who don't reciprocate, I just wonder why he doesn't do something about it? I mean not only do we live in an age of regeneration treatments; there *are* refixation treatments too. He can have his sexuality refixed on someone, or thing, that can get it up for him. And, as they are always saying in the brochures, the older you are, the better they work."

"Oh, sure," Bron said. "But I think Lawrence is just trying to prove a point."

"Which is why I called it political. And why I don't have much sympathy for him. Sexual point-proving is such a waste of time. Especially if you're seventy-four. And the refixation treatments are very effective. I know. I've used them."

Bron frowned over his shoulder at her. "You used to be a gay and gave it up?"

"No. But there was a very marvelous woman once who was very fond of me, spiritually and sexually, and wanted me very badly—an 'actress of the old school,' as she used to call herself. You know, she'd actually directed a handful of ice-operas—some of the better ones too. Anyway, I had a refixation—it takes five minutes and you're asleep through it all. We were very happy together. And when it was over, I had another one that got me back to tall, curly-haired blonds with high cheekbones—" She cocked an eye at him. "I swear by them. Anybody who is concerned about sexualizationships who doesn't take advantage of them, from pure prejudice—and it's nothing more (Your Lawrence friend sounds like he's from Earth.)—is a fool."

"You *are* opinionated!"

She shrugged. "Only when I'm right. You can be opinionated too if you want. With your experience—" She looked, blinking—"I would imagine you should know more about refixations than I do!"

"You mean back when I was a working man—? Well, sure, some of the guys used them. I never did." Bron shrugged. "I never had to. I don't particularly enjoy sex with men. But, when I've done it, it hasn't been difficult. So I always figured I could perform if I ever had to."

"Ah," the Spike said, with raised forefinger. "But refixation is a matter of desire, not performance. And I assure you, as one who is also a fair performer, desire is something else again. No—" She shook her head once more—"I don't think I would really enjoy your Mr. Lawrence."

"He probably has his reasons . . . which is probably why he's living where he is—You're a pretty cold and inhuman type," he said, suddenly. "You think you've got everything figured out from the start."

The Spike laughed. "And who is it who has called me a type three times in ten minutes? You seem to have done your bit of figuring."

Bron grunted again: "Lawrence is always saying everyone's a type, too."

"It's conceivable," the Spike said with mock deliberation (Or was it deliberate mocking?), "that we *may* both be wrong. But I doubt it." Then, suddenly: "By the Dark Ring . . . !" which was an exclamation till now he had only heard in ice-operas, though he'd once expected it to litter the conversation of all Outer Satelliters: he could not tell if it was heritage or affectation. "It's five minutes to eight!" She released his hand, clutched her forehead. (With dim, yellow numerals and scrolled arms, a clock hung high above in the black.) "Do I know what I'm going to do . . . ? *Yes!*" She faced him with wide, beating eyes, clasped his cheeks between her palms. "I've got to run! The company's waiting for me. You've been a love, really. Good-bye!" She turned. And ran. Red pants fluttered into the dark.

Bron stood, naked and confused, on the empty, unlicensed street, where anything, *any*thing could happen.

He stood there quite a while, thinking about what had, looking down at himself, looking up at the clock, or off into the darkness where she'd gone.

Across the tracks, with shuffling steps, came two mumblers. One, eyes tight, head bent, swung a blue plastic bowl. She led the other, a much older man, by the hand: His eyes were bound with rag.

Their voices, dull and fluttery, wound and twisted, apart and to-gether. The woman's mantra was a lengthy one, of interlocking sayable and unsayable sounds. The man's, on a single note, in a rasping voice . . . Bron had to hear it through five times before he would let himself be sure: and, by then, they had nearly reached the opposite alleyway; and the woman's voice kept obscuring it, here at the third syllable, there at the seventeenth:

"*Mimimomomizolalilamialomuelamironoriminos* . . ."

Alfred's fingernails (and toenails) were long and dirty. So was Alfred's hair. He leaned forward from the conversation chair, a red plastic K clipped with brass to the black suspenders (What in the world . . . ? Bron wondered: What in two worlds and twenty worldlets could they *stand* for?) hung loosely on his bony chest. "I just don't know, I really don't." Alfred shook his head, his voice low, raspy, and intense. "I don't know. . . ." The suspenders held up scarlet bikini briefs, ludicrously too large for Alfred's bony hips—but in the type of places Alfred probably frequented, that was, probably, the point. "In a week, I pick up two, three, four women and it's fine. Then, the next night—I'm horny as hell and the woman I get is a real knockout. But we come back here . . . and I've got the limps! Can't raise it no *way!* And *that* goes on for sometimes, three, four, five weeks, till I can't even do anything with it by *myself*, you know? And

I'm *still* getting women and they're just being as cooperative as *hell*! Which makes it worse. Then, finally, when I *start* to get it back together, and score with another one, and get her to come back here . . . and this *always* happens with the one you really want and you really had to work your tail off to get—we get goin' and—Pow!" Alfred bounced nearly to his feet, then sagged back in the chair. He shook his head. "Three seconds, four seconds . . . *maybe* ten! If I'm lucky!" He blinked green eyes at Bron. "*Then* I gotta go through a week of *that,* before I can get it on for a decent two or three minutes, over the next couple of times. I mean, that's why I live here, you know? I bring a woman back here, if I mess up I can say, 'Thanks for comin' by, ma'am. Sorry I wasted your time. See you around,' and get her *out* of here! Those mixed co-ops, where the guys and girls live together, makin' it with each other all the time—? I tried *six* of those when I first got here (and they had some *nice* women there . . . Wow!), you mess up more'n a couple of times there and the first thing you know they want to *talk* about it! And then you got to talk about it some *more.* The next thing you know, you have to have a damn *encounter* with all the other men and women who messed up that week—When *I* mess, I don't wanna *talk.* I wanna go to *sleep*! If I talked about every time I messed up with some woman I wouldn't have time to pee! And that's another thing—you ever try to pee in the sink with some woman you just messed up with lying in the bed *staring* at you? I mean, even if she *ain't* looking!" Alfred sat forward again, leaned on his knees, shook his head. "I just about given up. On peeing, I mean." The green eyes came up again. "Hey. I ordered this ointment from one of those shops down at the Plaza of Light, one that sells them magazines—?" Alfred leaned closer, his tone suddenly confidential. "I checked it out with the computer and it said there wasn't anything *wrong* with using it . . . It's credited to me already. But they said they don't get much call for it so they don't keep it in stock. They're gonna have it in tomorrow—only tomorrow I have to start these vocational aptitude tests. My social worker says I have to—You pick it up for me, Bron. The shop's on the southeast corner—not the big one. The little one, two doors to the left." Alfred paused, blinked. "You pick it up for me, Bron . . . okay?"

"Okay." Bron nodded, smiled, and felt put upon.

Alfred had emigrated from some minor moon (Uranus's—but then, which of Uranus's weren't minor; not one of the five was over 900 k's in diameter) as a fourteen-year-old orphan; and didn't like to talk about his past, either. (Even this much information had come to Bron via Lawrence.) Bron figured that emigrating at fourteen took about ten year's more guts than emigrating at twenty-four, even if it *was* within the Satellite Federation. Hell, three years ago the situation had been so tense only Ganymede and Triton were accepting emigrants from Earth and Mars. Triton only took them from Mars. "Alfred, has it ever occurred to you that you might be gay?" He asked because he felt he had to say something. "I mean, emotionally." (Alfred, having gotten his favor, would sit silent the next hour if given his head.) Also, bits of the Spike's conversation kept returning to him. "What I'd do if I had problems like that is check out a refixation clinic. Get your thing switched over to men and see if it all falls into place."

"No," Alfred said, shaking his head. "No. . . ." But both the *no's* and the headshake were despair rather than negation. "No . . . I mean, I *did* that, once, you know? I mean that's what my social worker said, too. They fixed it up for me. At a clinic in the u-l. For six months I tried it."

"And?"

"It was awful. I mean I was horny for men all right. But as far as how it went when I got 'em in the sack, I mean it was just the same thing—up, down, in, out, and, 'What, you're finished already?'—only with complications—I mean, if *they* go in and *you* finish up in three seconds, then it *hurts,* you know? So you gotta ask them to take it out, and they still wanna go, and *nobody* likes *that*!"

"*Mmmmm,*" Bron said, because he couldn't think of anything else.

"Finally, I just went back to the clinic and said, hey, please, would you put it back together the way it was before? Let me at least like what I *like* liking—you know?—whether I mess up or not. I mean—" Alfred sat back—"they're supposed to be very common problems. It's not like they were *rare* or anything." Alfred frowned. "I mean it's not like I'm the only person who ever had problems like that—you'd think they could do something for a guy." He sat back a bit more. "Did you ever have problems like that?"

"Well . . ." Bron considered. Two of his first three (major) sexual experiences (all within the month before his fourteenth birthday) might, with definition stretched, have been said to have involved premature orgasm, i.e., the orgasms had surprised him. But not since. What problems he now had (if they *were* problems) veered in the other direction: and even those merely tended to herald a recurrent (and blessedly mild) prostate infection that had popped up every year or so since he was thirty. "If you're making it every other night," Bron offered, "you can't expect it to go perfect *every* time." During his first professional years, when, at two, three, and often four a day, he had actually balled (the first time he'd calculated it, the number had taken him aback, too) eight hundred or more women, he'd been attacked by the 'limps' somewhat under a dozen times; since then, the frequency had gone substantially down. The only way he could conceive of Alfred's problems was to assume that it was tantamount to being, basically, asexual. He was sure Alfred enjoyed roaming in the many meeting places with their loud music, their low lights, enjoyed being eyed by women, being engaged in conversation by them (or perhaps Alfred did the engaging. Bron knew he tended to project his most common experiences—rather than his preferences—on everybody), even enjoyed bringing them back to his eccentric address ("An all male co-op . . . ? And you mean it *isn't* gay?"). Perhaps Alfred even enjoyed ordering out-of-stock ointments at tiny shops. Sex, however (Bron was convinced), Alfred could not *possibly* enjoy. "Give it some time," Bron said. "And, well . . . I mean, when I was your age . . ." But Alfred was seventeen. And Bron was a politic enough thirty-seven to know *no* seventeen-year-old (especially a seventeen-year-old who had elected to live so completely away from his peers as Alfred) wanted to be reminded of it. So, politicly, he let it hang. "You know, last night, after the shield went off and you had your nosebleed, I almost knocked on your door to say hello, but I figured you—"

"I wish you had," Alfred said. "Oh, man, I *wish* you had! I was all alone, no girl with me, no nothing—and suddenly I thought I was gonna *die* and my ears nearly popped and my nose started bleeding and I could hear things falling over in the other rooms—they cut the damn gravity!" Alfred took a breath. "They got me back together, you know—that big nigger who's always tellin' everybody what to do and why? But I couldn't go to sleep for the rest of the night. I wish somebody had come in to see me. I really do." Alfred's green eyes came back to Bron's. "You gonna pick up that ointment for me, huh?" They held all the old suspicion, the old mistrust. "Okay . . . Good." Then Alfred stood, turned (where the black suspenders crossed between his pimply shoulder blades, there was a red plastic Q. Bron thought: Q?) and walked away.

Understanding? Only slightly guilty, Bron asked himself: *Where* is it? And got no answer. I call it friendship, but it's simpler than that. He uses me and I let him. Lord knows I'd prefer to spend any hour in either Lawrence's or the big nigger's company. Still . . . is it just a bond between two, hung-up heterosexual males? He's hung up in performance (and the hang-ups he has with it honestly make less sense to me than the propensities of a Lawrence, a Miriamne!)—And what am *I* hung up in . . . ?

At any rate, Bron wished either Sam or Lawrence would come down into the commons room, with or without vlet.

For work next morning he wore clothes.

Lots of them.

All black.

He finished going through the Day Star Minus folder, closed it, put it back in the bottom drawer, and decided it would just have to wait for another week before he could bother writing up a coherency validation. He was looking over a diptych of multiple-state evaluation programs which, for the life of him, he could not figure out in which of three directions the modular context was supposed to function, when Miriamne rapped on the jamb of the open door. "May I talk to you a minute?"

Bron sat back, pulled his cloak around him. "Certainly."

She stopped, just inside the doorway, looking uncomfortable, looked at the bulletin board, looked at the desk corner. "Audri told me you'd asked for me to be transferred to another department."

With a black-gloved forefinger, Bron pushed the mask higher on his nose; it had slipped a bit, which was fine for reading but not for talking to people standing up when you were sitting down. As he put his gloved palms on the gray graphpapers shingling his desk, it slipped again; which meant he would have to conduct this interview—he felt the clutch of embarrassment high in his chest (or low in his throat) and swallowed at it—with her head cut off by his eyehole's upper edge, muzzily, at the nose. "That's right. After a little thought, I just decided it was silly, with your training—cybralogs, or whatever—to waste your time and . . . well, my time too."

"*Mmmm*," she said. "And there I thought I was catching on pretty fast for someone who didn't know her way around at all."

"Oh," he said, "really, that *isn't* the point—"

"I'm afraid what the point *is,* is that I'm out of a job."

"*Mmmm?*" he asked, not sure what she meant. "Well, you mustn't worry. They'll find you a place eventually—it may take another day or two. But chances are it'll be closer to your field."

She shook her head. "I've been through five departments already. I've been transferred in each case. The Personnel receptionist told me, somewhat icily, this morning—that they—whoever 'they' are—just didn't have work for me in my own field and that since they've tried me in three related fields and—in two others where my aptitudes were high—one of those was this one—they would simply have to class me as unemployable."

"Oh, well, now—that *is* a little silly. I mean, in a company like this, with someone like you—But then, the whole last couple of months *have* seen a lot of confusion slipping by—" He brought his boots together beneath the desk, parted his gloves a little more. "Why did the other departments transfer you?"

"They had their reasons." She looked at the desk corner, the other desk corner, at his face.

Bron lowered his head (which completely cut off hers), raised his gloved fingers, meshed them, put his chin on his clothed-over knuckles—the dark veiling along the mask's bottom pulled back against his lips—"Well, I have my reasons too."

She said, "*Mmmm,*" again, in a different tone; and had laid one brown finger on the edge of the office console and was sort of pivoting her hand around on its chrome nail—a nervousness he found incredibly annoying.

I had to transfer her, he thought. (His own hands, nervously, were back on the desk.) I couldn't possibly expect to work in the same eight-by-eight space all day with someone who, from major proclivities to minor ticks, makes me, however irrationally, *that* uncomfortable.

She said: "I was just wondering if it had anything to do with that nonsense yesterday."

Bron raised a questioning eyebrow. But of course she couldn't see it behind the full-head mask. "How do you mean?"

"Well, all day long you were leaving your hands around on various desks and tabletops with your fingers in the age-old socially acceptable position—rather like now . . ."

He looked down. "Oh . . ." He closed his hands on the graphpaper; that was one of the unfortunate habits that was left over from his youthful profession; sometimes he signaled without even knowing it.

"—and I wasn't being too responsive. I just thought you'd pick up on it. Half the time, I thought you actually had. But then, we didn't get it really straightened out till we were halfway home. And I made that crack to the Spike—she told me she'd told you, when I got back, all terribly apologetic. I guess theater people aren't really known for their discretion." Her hand dropped to her side. "What I said was pretty much joking."

He laughed, leaned forward. The tunic pulled uncomfortably across his back. Cape folds, falling whispered to the floor. "And so was I. I hope you didn't take any of *that* seriously—I didn't."

Her smile was worried. "Well . . . I just thought I'd ask."

"I'm glad you did. I'd feel terrible if you left thinking it was because of a silly remark like that. Really, I may—what was it?—be ' . . . a louse who's trying. . .' but, honestly, I'm not a monster. If it makes you feel better, I'd decided to ask for your transfer before any of that even happened." He felt sorry for her, suddenly, through the annoyance of embarrassment. "Look, be honest with yourself. There I was, pawing all over you yesterday—I mean I *didn't* realize you weren't interested. But that's just the type I am. I find you very attractive. You certainly couldn't have been looking forward to working with me all *that* much, with my carrying on like that—"

"You don't mean," she said, and even without her face he could tell she was frowning, "that you had me transferred because I *wasn't* interested in you sexually . . . ? I'll be honest. *That* hadn't even occurred to me!"

"Oh, *no* . . . !" Inside the mask, he felt his face grow moist. "I just meant that you probably wouldn't—You don't *really* think that, do you? Because if you do, you're just wrong! You're *very* wrong!"

"Until Audri stopped me in the hall this morning, all I was thinking was that you'd made Metalogics sound like a fairly interesting subject. And I was rather looking forward to working in the department."

"Well, thank you—" Without straining preposterously back, he could not see above her dark, delicate collarbone. "I'm glad at least I—"

"What it comes down to is: Is there any chance you might change your mind and keep me on?"

A surge of embarrassment and annoyance closed out all sympathy. He took his gloved hands from the desk and put them on his thighs, let them drop from his thighs, so that the voluminous double sleeves fell down about his wrists. Should he? Could he let her intimidate

him like this? "No." He took a breath, let it out. "I'm afraid I can't."
He raised his head high enough to see her chin: It was moving a little
oddly. "You can't run a department that way. I'm sorry about the job,
but—well, anything I say would just be silly at this point. My reasons
have to do with a lot of things, which, since you aren't in this department now, aren't your concern. We have the Day Star program to re-
work where, yes, I could possibly use you. But I've just finished going
over it again not ten minutes ago, and for all sorts of reasons, having
to do with equally important projects, I just don't want to do it now.
It's very simple and very straightforward: I just don't need you, right
now, for the jobs I have to do." He took another breath and felt, to his
surprise, somewhat relieved by his explanation. "Actually, I'm glad
you came to see me. Because I wouldn't have wanted you to leave
thinking it was something personal." Hoping he would never again
have to set eyes on her, even so much of her as he could see now, he
said: "Maybe we'll run into one another at your co-op; someday we
may even be able to have a drink and a laugh over it."

"You said I should be honest," came from somewhere above her
shoulders. "Frankly, I hope I don't see you or anyone else from this
lame-brained funhouse for a good, long time. And that, I'm afraid, is
completely personal!"

Bron's jaw clamped. His mask slipped so that he could not see
above her broad, chromium-cinched hips: They turned (not sharply,
not angrily, but slowly and, if hips could look tired by themselves,
tiredly) in the doorway, moved off into the corridor.

His cheeks were warm. He blinked, growing furious with the discomfort. While he'd been talking to her, he'd been trying to recall exactly *why* he'd wanted her gone. But she'd thrown him off with that
incredible suggestion that it was because she hadn't responded to his
advances! Sometime yesterday—and, yes, it *was* before the Spike had
related that stupid and insulting crack about his being a louse—he'd
come to the decision. And as a decision made, he'd stored it. Coming
into the office that morning, in a swirl of black, he had gone straight
to Audri's office and laid it out.

Audri had said: "Oh . . . well, all right."

He'd gone to his own cubicle, gone to work; and had been feeling
rather good until minutes ago . . . It had *been* a logical decision. Still,
for the life of him, he could not reconstruct the logic, *or* metalogic,
that had generated it.

He thought: If you reach a conclusion validly, you don't store all the work notes and doodles you've amassed on the way. Those are *just* the things conclusions are there to dispense with! (He crumpled a piece of paper that, looking at its gray, graphed corner sticking from the black-gloved knot, he realized he probably *would* need again.) She doesn't like me and I don't like her. You can't work in an atmosphere like that. *That's* logical!

He put the graphpaper down, pulled off one glove and, with a plastic graph template, began to clean his thumbnail. A bad adolescent nail-biter, he had, at the advent of his ephebic profession, finally broken the habit. But all his nails were now wider edge-to-edge than from cuticle to crown, which still looked a little odd. He didn't like his hands and, with certain drugs, avoided looking at them at all. Well, today at least, his nails were filed, lacquered, and of even length.

For practical purposes, they looked ordinary enough.

He put the glove back on, pulled his cloak around his left shoulder, then his right and, at last able to use both hands, adjusted the head-mask.

His cheeks were still warm. On both, he knew, would be mottled, red blotches, just beginning to fade.

In the cafeteria, he was sitting at a just-plain-eating booth, pinching at the folds of a half-collapsed coffee bulb, when, glancing up, he saw Audri with her tray. "Hi, there," she said and slid in across from him. "Ah . . . !" She put her head, half masked on the left (clean and bright as a silver egg with an eye), against the padded back. "This has been a day!"

Bron grunted.

"My feelings exactly!" Silver covered the left side of Audri's neck, her shoulder, one breast, down (below the tabletop now) over one hip, in a tight plastic skin that would have been quite svelte on anyone with less corners than Audri.

Bron reached up, lifted off his head covering, placed it on the wooden (an artificial cellular fiber indistinguishable from wood on any but micrographic level) table, and looked at the puddle of dark veils, the shaded eye-holes, the black sequins that damasked the whole basketball-like affair. "Sorry about that transfer this morning. I hope she didn't give you as much trouble about it as she gave me."

Audri shrugged. "Yeah . . . well, you know—I told her you weren't the type to change your mind about something like that. It *has* happened before. She sighed, picked up something long and dark and sprinkled with nuts, looked at it disapprovingly. "She said that there might be extenuating circumstances, though, and she wanted to talk to you. I tried to suggest as politely as possible that she might as well not bother. But, finally, I couldn't very well say no. I felt sorry for her, you know? She's been shuttled all over the whole hegemony and it really wasn't her fault. It's just the general confusion."

Bron grunted again. "I didn't know this would be her last chance. It never occurred to me she was going to be out of a job entirely."

Audri grunted back. "That's why I asked you to see if you couldn't do *something* with her when I brought her in."

"Oh. Well, yeah . . ." *Had* Audri made some special request of him about the girl? Bron frowned. He certainly didn't remember it.

Audri sighed. "I held the green slip back until she'd come from talking with you about it—"

Bron looked up from the crumpled bulb. "You mean it *wasn't* final?" He let the frown deepen. "*I'd* thought the whole thing was already a closed matter . . . If I'd known that, maybe I would have . . ." No, he wasn't *really* lying. It hadn't occurred to him that the slip had *not* been sent. "She should have told me."

"Well—" Audri took a bite of the nut bar—"it's sent now. Besides, everything's so messed up right through here anyway with the situation between us and the worlds, I'm surprised we're still here at all. Our accounts are all *over* the moons—even Luna. And what's going to happen there? Everybody knows that there're going to be a lot of people out of work soon, and nobody knows who. Who even knows what you and I'll be doing in six months . . ." She nodded knowingly. Then said: "Don't worry, I'm not threatening you."

"No, I didn't think you were." He smiled. "You're not the threatening type."

"True," Audri said. "I'm not."

"Hey," Philip said above him, "when are we going to see some work on Day Star, huh? Audri sent you an assistant yesterday and you send her back today. Move over—"

"Hey, come on—!" Bron said.

Philip's tray clattered down next to Audri's. "Don't worry, I don't even *want* to sit next to you." Philip, today in tight pants, barechested (very hairy), and small, gray, shoulder cape, fell into the seat next to Audri. "Has this *ever* been a day—! Hurry up and wait; wait because I'm in a hurry." He frowned through his curly beard. "What was wrong with her?"

"Look," Bron said to the burly little Philip, "when are you going to get me an assistant I can *use*? *This* one was into . . . what was it? Cryogenics or something?" Bron *really* disliked Philip.

"Oh come on. You don't need a trained assistant for that—" Philip's fists (hairy as his chest) bunched on either side of his tray. "You know what I think—?" He looked down, considered, picked up something messy with his fingers, and ducked to catch it in his mouth before it fell apart—"I think he just doesn't like dykes." He nodded, chewing, toward Audri, sucking one finger after the other, loudly. "You know?"

"What do you mean?" Bron demanded. "I like Audri, and she's . . ." Then he felt ridiculous. By intentional tastelessness, Philip had maneuvered him into saying something unintentionally tasteless and was (no doubt) racking up points, behind that congenial leer. Bron looked at Audri (whom he *did* like); she was twisting open the spout of a coffee bulb.

"With friends like you . . ." Philip said, and nodded knowingly. "Look, we're all at loose ends around here right now. It's confusion from one side to the other." Philip's left nipple was very large. There was a bald ring around it. The hair follicles had been removed. The flesh over that pectoral was somewhat looser than that over the right. Periodically, when a new child was expected at Philip's commune, out on the Ring, the breast would enlarge (three pills every lunch-time: two little white ones and one large red), and Philip would take off two or three days a week wet-leave. Bron had been out to the last Sovereignty Day blow-out—

"Look," Philip said, sucking one thick finger then another (he was a head shorter than Bron), "I'm a very straightforward guy—you know that. I think it: I say it. If I say it, you know I'm not holding it against you—unless I say I am."

"Well, I'm pretty straightforward too." Bron ran his gloved thumb carefully over the last of the mashed lentils on his tray, put his thumb into his mouth, and pulled it, carefully, out. "At least about my emotions. I—"

One of the junior programmers, wearing a blue body-stocking with large, silver diamond-shapes, said, "Hi, Bron—" then realized a "discussion" was going on, ducked a diamond-eyed head, and hurried away.

"I didn't like her," Bron said. "She didn't like me. That's not a situation *I* can work in."

"Yeah, yeah . . ." Philip shoveled up more food. "The way the whole emotional atmosphere around here is getting with all this war scare, I'm surprised anybody can work, period."

"Bron is one of your better workers, too." Audri took another bite of the long thing with nuts. "So just get off his back, Phil." (There were times his liking for Audri almost approached a sort of platonic love.)

"I'm off. I'm off. Hey, you've been at your new place practically six months now. Frozen in yet?"

"It's okay," Bron said. "No problems."

"I *thought* that's where you'd end up feeling most at home." In one of those heart-to-hearts Philip was always initiating without your knowing it, back when Bron used to put up with them, Philip had actually given Bron the name of Serpent's House. "I just had a feeling you might find things easier there. I'm glad you have. Other than the Day Star business—no, I *haven't* forgotten it—" Phil waved a thick, hairy, wet forefinger—"*I* certainly don't have any complaints about your work. Don't worry, we'll get you an assistant. I told Audri, gay-male and normal or straight-female superwoman . . . to which Audri said, I'll have you know: 'Well, he likes *me!*'" Philip laughed. "We'll get you one; and with the proper training. That's the kind you can relate to—speaking of gay males . . ." Philip swallowed, his hand, on its hirsute forearm, dropped below the table; the forearm moved back and forth, and the hand emerged, somewhat drier. "Marny—you remember her from my commune, Marny? Small, dark—?" The other hand came up and together they described a near callipygous shape. (From the Sovereignty Day shindig Bron remembered her very well.) Philip nudged Audri, winked at Bron. "She's the one who's the ice-engineer—climbing up and down the cold-faces like something out of a damn ice-opera! The last two kids she had, I was the dad. Anyway, she's going to have another one. And you'll never guess who by—Danny!" He turned to Audri, then to Bron. "You remember Danny . . . ?" Philip frowned. (Bron remembered Danny, and with some distaste.) Philip's frown reversed. "Anyway, this is only the second kid he's ever had in his life—and the first in this commune." Philip's fist fell to the table, relaxing—like a spilled sack of potatoes. "You know how important kids can be to gay guys—I mean, most of the time they think they're just never going to have *any*, you know? Now I don't care about kids. I got six of my own here and—Lord, I must have kids all over the Solar System. Let's see, three on Io, one on Ganymede, even one back on Luna, and a couple out on Neriad—" He frowned, suddenly. "You got kids, Bron? I mean, I know about Audri's."

"A couple," Bron said. Back on Mars a woman had once announced to him she intended to get pregnant by him. In the first year of his emigration, a letter had even followed him out here, with a picture of a baby—a double-chinned infant suckling at a breast much larger than he remembered it. He had been singularly unmoved. "On Earth," Bron added finally. Conception had taken place on Mars; but the letter had come from Earth.

"*Mmmm,*" Philip said, with a licensed sectarian's discomfort at mention of things too far in the past. "I never had any on a world— anyway: I asked Danny if he was going to help nurse." (Unlicensed sector people, Bron reflected, went on about the families they'd come from. Licensed sector people went on about the families they had. For all the latter's commitment to the here and now, Bron sometimes found both equally objectionable.) "—I mean because Marny wants someone to switch off with. Anyway, you know what he told me? You know what he said? He's worried about his figure!" Philip shook his head, then repeated: "Worried about his *figure*! Well, you know what that means for me." His hand came up and made a suggestive curve before his looser pectoral; his heavily-lashed lids lowered as he regarded himself. "Two little white ones—"

"—and one big red one." Audri laughed. "Well, congratulations to you all."

"His figure!" Philip shook his head, smiled fondly. "I mean Danny's part of my damn commune and I love him. I really do—but, sometimes, I wonder why."

Bron decided to put his mask back on; but Philip suddenly pushed the red plastic button on his corner of the table.

Philip's tray, with its smeared remains, shook, shivered, dissolved, and was sucked through the grid below: *Whoooosh*! While it was *Whoooosh*ing, Philip rubbed his hands over the grid, first backs, then palms, and, satisfied, stood. The *Whoooosh* died. "Look, when I came over here, I figured I was interrupting a delicate situation. I thought it might need interrupting and took my chance. You know you got Audri pretty upset over getting that woman canned." To Audri he said: "I want to talk to you about what we tell the Day Star

Plus people about Day Star Minus when I have to explain to them why no metalogical reduction yet. And soon." He turned to Bron: "And that's an excuse for Audri to cut out on you if it gets too rough, understand? All open and aboveboard. And you—you want your chance to stomp my nuts? You get Day Star out of the way inside a month! I've been telling people for a week now there's no way possible we can have it ready inside three. You finish it under that, and my face will be red all over four departments. See you both around." He slipped from the table and lumbered (neither tall nor broad, just thick, Philip still gave the impression of lumbering everywhere) across the cafeteria.

Bron looked at Audri. The hair showing on the right of her head was a riot of green, gold, purple, and orange. The visible half of her face was set, sullen, and preoccupied.

"Hey," Bron said, "were you really that bothered because I . . . ?"

"Oh," Audri said. "Well, yeah," which were words they used frequently with one another, sometimes phatically, sometimes not.

"Well, if you'd—" The thought came obliquely, sat a moment on his mind's rim, threatening to fall either in or out like an absurd Humpty Dumpty; then, suddenly, it didn't seem absurd at all: "Hey, did you see Miriamne later, yesterday? I mean *you* didn't go meet her somewhere after work . . . ?"

Audri's eyes came back to his from somewhere behind him. "No. Why? I never saw her before Personnel sent her down yesterday morning."

"Oh, because for a moment I . . ." Bron frowned; suddenly he picked up the veiled and sequined head-covering and put it on. With the thought had come the sudden recollection of exactly when (in the gray, canyon-like alley leading to u-l!) and why (that fanciful, unfounded relation between Miriamne and the Spike!) he had decided on Miriamne's transfer. Now it seemed ridiculous, cruel (he *did* like Audri), and self-centered. If he could have, he *would* have kept her on now. But the green slip—"I don't suppose she's still . . ." His voice was hollowed by the dark shell.

"*Mmmm?*" Audri said, sipping; his own bubble rattled loudly, collapsed completely. If the thought had been a world, the one that came with it, circling it like a satellite, was: Miriamne was the Spike's friend. Some version of all this would in all likelihood get back to her. What would *she* think? "Audri?" he asked.

"Yeah?"

"What am I like? I mean, what do you think of me . . . ? If you had to describe me to somebody else, how would you do it?"

"Honest?"

He nodded.

"I'd say you were a very ordinary—or special, depending on how you look at it—combination of well-intentioned and emotionally lazy, perhaps a little too self-centered for some people's liking. But you also have an awful lot of talent at your job. Maybe the rest are just the necessary personality bugs that go along."

"Would you say I was a louse . . . but maybe a louse who was— never mind. Just a louse."

Audri laughed. "Oh, perhaps on off-Thursdays—or on every second Tuesday of the month—some version of that thought flickers through my addled brain—"

"Yeah." Bron nodded. "You know, that's the third time in three days someone's called me that."

"A louse?" Audri raised one multicolored eyebrow (and lowered one silver one). "Well, *I'm* certainly not one of the ones who did—"

"You mean *Philip,* sometime earlier today, he . . . ?"

Both Audri's eyebrows lowered now. "No, doll. *You* did—just now."

"Oh," Bron said. "Well, yeah."

Back in his office, Bron sat and ruminated and flung more collapsed coffee bulbs into the corner heap.

They don't understand, he thought; then thought it over. Philip and Audri and Sam and Miriamne and Lawrence—even Danny (whom he remembered) and Marny (whom he remembered with some affection) didn't understand. And Alfred probably understood least of all—though from another point of view, Alfred probably understood the best; that is, Alfred certainly didn't understand *him*— Bron—but Alfred certainly understood by first-hand experience the feeling of *having* nobody understand you; and—Bron could allow himself the self-flagellation—in a way Alfred's particular type of non-thinking was probably pretty close to his own. Yes, Alfred understood by experience, even if he had no articulate awareness of that experience as a possible point of agony for any other human being but himself. And didn't (Bron was still thinking, five minutes after closing, as he walked, with rustling sleeves and cloak, out of the lobby and onto the Plaza) Alfred's complete refusal to offer anyone else any interpretation—speculative, appeasing, damning, or helpful—of their own psychological state represent a kind of respect, or at least a behavior that was indistinguishable from it? Alfred just assumed (but then, didn't everybody assume, till you gave them cause to do otherwise) that you knew what you were about . . .

Miriamne!

And Alfred's drawn, adolescent face was blotted out. He'd wanted to start an affair with her! She was his type. And now his own, involved, counterespionage against himself had lost her a job. His own responses that he should have used as flexible parameters he had taken as rigid, fixed perimeters.

Miriamne!

Of course she didn't understand either.

Poor Miriamne!

How could she know the how or the why behind any of what had happened to her?

Suffering the wound of having wounded, he thought: Help me. He made his way through the crowded Plaza. The upper edge of the eyeholes completely cut away the sensory shield with a darkness complete as the u-l's roof. Swathed and black, he made his way across the bustling concourse, thinking: Somebody help me . . .

Just like Alfred (he thought), alone in his room, his nosebleed already diagnosed, Sam and the others gone, wishing desperately, now that the catastrophe had abated, that someone, anyone, would stop by and say hello.

Bron's jaw tightened.

The mask slipped further down, so that—the thought came brutally as pain, and, with it, he swung his cloak across his shoulder and hurried on—had anyone tried to meet his eyes, with gaze friendly, provocative, hostile, or indifferent, he would not have been able to tell, since all but the very shortest in the crowd were now, muzzily, decapitated.

But if you want help that badly (bitterly he ground his teeth as someone brushed his shoulder; he jerked away, knocking into someone else's) and you still can't get it, the only thing to take your mind off the need is to help someone else:—which revelation, since it was one of the rare times he'd ever had it, brought him up short in the middle of the Plaza.

He stood, blinking: two people in succession bumped his left shoulder; one person stumbled against his right. When he stumbled, someone else hit him on the rebound and said: "Hey, watch, will you? Where do you think you are?"

And he still stood, still blinking, in the half-veiled dark.

Somebody else stumbled against him.

And somebody else.

The green slip was already in. There *was* nothing he could do for Miriamne . . .

Five minutes later, he found the smaller of the sex shops on the southeast corner and, well-muffled in his cloak, asked for the reserved package of ointment that had already been credited. There! The sense of moral obligations already slipping from his encumbered soul (and the tubular package in one of his cloak's numerous, secret pockets), he walked out onto the (almost deserted now) Plaza of Light.

Ten minutes after that, with his heart thudding slowly, he entered the greenlit tiles of the underpass, passing unheeded the admonitions from chalk, paint, and poster, scrawled left and right.

High and dim on the dark, one scrolled, archaic hand pointed to six, the other to seven. (Decimal clocks, he thought. Quaint.) He crossed the tracks, the gritty paving. He passed the high supports of an overhead walkway. Through the rails above, lights cast down a web of shadow.

At the next steps—on a whim—he turned up, pulling all his rustling clothes about him.

Bron gained the top.

They stood at the opposite rail, backs to him, looking out at a darkness that could have been a wall ten feet beyond or a night stripped of stars light years away.

He recognized her by the blonde, feathery hair, the high shoulders (no cloak now), the long curves of her back going down to a skirt, low on her hips: a ground-length swath, where brown and red and orange splotched one another like something from a postcard of an autumn hillside on another world.

Bron slowed, halfway across the walk. The cloaks and veils and sleeves and cuffs that had billowed behind him collapsed around his gloves and boots.

The other—?

Matted hair held a hint of blue (or green?).

Except for fur strips bound around one thick, upper arm, and one stocky thigh, he was still naked.

He was still filthy.

Bron stopped, ten feet away, frowning inside his mask (which, somewhere just beyond the underpass, he'd finally gotten to sit right), wondering at their quiet conversation.

Suddenly she looked back.

So did the man. Within the scarred and swollen flesh the sunken spot (even this close he was not sure if it could or could not see) glistened.

"Bron . . . ?" she said, turning fully to face him. Then: "That is you behind that mask . . . ? Tethys *is* a small city! Fred here—" (Fred turned too; the chain necklaces hung down the grimed, overmuscled chest with its sunken, central pit.) "—and I were just talking about you, would you believe?"

The nails visible on Fred's black-ringed and fouled fingers were quick-bitten. How, Bron wondered, could you bring yourself to bite them if your hands were that filthy—for which answer Fred raised one hand and began to gnaw absently, his visible, bloodshot eye blinking.

"Fred was just saying to me that he'd lived for a while on Mars. And on Earth too. You even spent some time on Luna, weren't you saying?" (Fred gnawed on, regarding Bron from under shaggy brows and over blackened knuckles.) "Fred was saying he knew the Goebels—wasn't that what you said the red-light district in Bellona was called, Fred? Fred was telling me what your gold eyebrow meant: That's really amazing!—Well . . . not only is it a small city. It's a small universe!"

Fred gnawed. Fred blinked.

And Bron thought: The things people will do to their bodies. Just as those outsized muscles were conscientiously clinic-grown (no profession in light-gravity labor gave you those ballooning thighs and biceps, those shoulders, that stomach, with all heads evenly ridged), so the filth, the scars, the sores, the boils that speckled the grimed arms and hips were from conscientious neglect.

And no one had genitals *that* size, other than by disease or (surgical) design.

The Spike said: " . . . it really is odd, just standing here, talking about you and suddenly there you are, right behind—" Then Fred, still gnawing, suddenly stepped forward (behind the mask, Bron flinched), crossed in front of the Spike, and started down the walkway: a gentle thud of footsteps, a jangling of chains.

Bron said: "Your friend isn't very communicative."

"It's his sect," the Spike said. "He was telling me the Beasts are having quite a bit of trouble, recently. They've just reformed, you know, from an older sect that dissolved; and now it looked like they may dissolve again. Dian—do you remember her; she's in our company—used to belong to the Beasts. She dropped out from them last month. Perhaps I'm biased, but I do believe she's happier with us. The whole problem, I suppose, is that any time some piece of communication strikes poor Fred, or any of the remaining Beasts, for that matter, as possibly meaningful—or is it meaningless? It's been explained to me a dozen times and I still can't get it right—anyway, his religious convictions say he has to either stop it or—barring that—refuse to be a party to it. You can imagine how difficult this must make ecumenical decisions during a religious council. Shall we take a walk . . . ?" She held out her hand, then frowned. "Or am I being presumptuous presuming you came to see *me*?"

"I . . . came to see you."

"Well, thank you." Her hand closed on his. "Then come."

They walked by the railing.

He asked: "Was Fred part of your theater piece too? That whole, opening gambit when you first froze me in—" which was ice farmer slang that had passed, by way of the ice opera, into general use: but, a moment out, as he recalled her origin, it seemed an affectation, and he wished the phrase back.

"Ah . . . !" She smiled at him. "And who's to say where life ceases and theater begins—"

"Come on," he said roughly, his own hesitation gone before her mild mocking.

So she said: "Fred?" And shrugged. "Before that afternoon, I'd never seen him before in my life."

"Then why were you talking to him here?"

"Well, because . . ." She led him down some steps. "—he was there. And I mean, since he'd punched me in the jaw once, and at that most delicate moment in the production, when initial contact with the audience is being established, I thought that might stand in place of a formal introduction. Apparently, he'd observed some of our pieces already—he told me he liked them, too. I was trying to discover how he fit that in with the mission laid on him by his sect. That led, of course, into Bestial politics, and thence into his life story . . . you know how it goes. I'd known something about it before from Dian, so I could make some intelligent comments; that naturally prejudiced him toward me; we started talking. As you might imagine, people with such commitments aren't the most socially sought-after individuals. I think he misses civilized conversation. I really found him quite an astute fellow. The metaphysical trouble with Fred's position, of course, is that communication involves minimum two people—more or less. Now," as they reached the ground, "two people may be talking, intensely, eloquently, or anywhere in between. But at any point, what's meaningful for one of them may become empty chatter for the other. Or the situation may reverse. Or the two situations may overlap. And all of these may happen a dozen times in any given five minutes."

"Poor Fred," Bron said dryly. (They turned into a narrow alleyway. The red street sign slid its miniaturized letters, dots, and dashes across her corneas watching him.) "Well, I'm glad he wasn't part of the whole circus."

"And I, as they say, am glad you're glad. I was thinking about asking him if he wanted to join the company. You have to admit he's colorful. And his performance, when I picked you up, certainly added a certain *je ne sais quoi*. If his sect *does* go bust, it would be tragic to let all that dedication just drift away! If I could only determine what his position was vis-à-vis theatrical communication itself—does he think it's meaningful or not? Whenever he—or Dian—talks about it, they get terribly abstract. Perhaps I just better wait until he's out of it. And you can tell he could use the job, just by looking at him." Bron was about to release her hand, but suddenly she smiled at him. "And what brings you here, interrupting my theoretical reveries on your person and personality with, as it were, the real thing?"

He wanted to say:

I came to tell you that no matter what that crazed lesbian says, I am *not* responsible for her losing her job—no matter *what* kind of louse she thinks I am! "I came to find out about you, who you were and what you were."

The Spike smiled up from under lowered brows. "All masked and veiled and swathed about in shadowy cerements? That's romantic!" They entered an even narrower alley—were, he realized, actually inside. "Just a moment—" She stopped in front of what was, he recognized, her co-op room door—"and we'll see what I can come up with to aid you in your quest. Out in a minute," and she was gone inside: the door clicked closed.

Over the next six minutes, Bron listened to drawers sliding, cupboard doors clacking—something overturned; a man's voice (Windy's?) protested gruffly; a guitar tinkled; the same man laughed; more drawers; then her own voice saying in the midst of a giggle (that made him sway back from the door, then touch it, then let his gloved fingers fall again, still moving), "Come on now, come on! Cut it out! Cut it out now—don't spoil my entrance . . . !" Then silence for a dozen breaths.

The door opened; she slipped out; the door clicked to behind.

She wore white gloves.

She wore white boots.

Her long skirt and high-necked bodice were white. Full white sleeves draped her wrists. She reached up and pulled the white cloak around her shoulders. Its paler than ivory folds swept around.

Over her head was a full-head mask: White veils hung below the eyes; the icy globe was a-glitter with white sequins. White plumes rose above it, as from some albino peacock.

"Now—" The veil fluttered with her breath—"we can roam the labyrinths of honesty and deceit, searching out the illusive centers of our being by a detailed examination of the shift and glitter of our own, protean surfaces—" She turned back to the door and called: "Don't worry, I'll be back in time for the performance."

A girl's muffled voice: "You better be!"

The white mask turned to him, with a mumbled, "—really . . . !" A settling breath, and veils settled. "Now, proofed in light and light's absence, we can begin our wonderings—" Her gloved fingers fell from her white-scarved throat, came toward his.

He took them.

They walked along the corridor that, once more, became high, roofless street.

"Now. What do you want to know about me?"

"I . . ."

After moments, she said: "Go on. Any way you can."

Moments later, he said: "I'm . . . not happy in the world I live in."

"This world—" She moved a white glove across the darkness before them—"that is not a world, but a moon?"

"It'll do. They . . . they make it so easy for you—all you have to do is

know what you want: no twenty-first-century-style philosophical oppression; no twentieth-century-style sexual oppression; no nineteenth-
century-style economic oppression. No eighteenth-century-style—"

"There was philosophical oppression in the eighteenth century
and sexual oppression in the twenty-first. And they've all had their
share of economic oppression—"

"But we're talking about our world. This world. The best of all
possible—"

"An awful lot of people who live around here are wasting an awful
lot of chalk, paint, duplicating paper, and general political energy trying to convince people that it is nowhere *near* the best. Bron, there's a
war on—"

"And we're not in it—yet. Spike, there's a lot of people around
where I live—and the sky is a very different color over there—who
honestly believe if the people you're talking about would mind their
own business, it would put us all a little closer to that world."

Her grip on his hand loosened. "I live in the u-l sector. You don't.
We won't argue about that now." It tightened again.

"And what I'm talking about is the same both places. If you're gay,
you find a gay co-operative; if you're straight, you go find yourself
one of the male/female co-operatives where everything is all *Gemüt-
lichkeit* and community consciousness; and there's every combination
in between—"

"I've always thought the division we use out here of humanity
into forty or fifty basic sexes, falling loosely into nine categories, four
homophilic—"

"What?"

"You mean you never punched Sex on General Info when you were
ten? Then you were probably the only ten-year-old who didn't.—Oh,
but if you grew up on Mars . . . Homophilic means no matter who or
what you like to screw, you prefer to live and have friends primarily
from your own sex. The other five are heterophilic." (Of course, he
knew the terms; of course he'd punched sex; frankly, the whole theory
had struck him as clever first and then totally artificial.) "I mean, when
you have forty or fifty sexes, and twice as many religions, however you
arrange them, you're bound to have a place it's fairly easy to have a giggle at. But it's also a pretty pleasant place to live, at least on that level."

"Sure. If you want to manacle eighteen-year-old boys to the wall
and pierce their nipples with red-hot needles—"

"They better be red-hot." From veils and glitter, her voice projected a smile too intricately mysterious to picture. "Otherwise, you
might start an infection!"

"They could be ice-cold! The point is, after work, you can always
drop in to the place where the eighteen-year-old boys who happen to
be into that sort of thing—red-hot needles on the second floor, ice-
cold ones on the third—have all gotten together in a mutually benefi-
cial alliance where you and they, and your Labrador retriever, if she's
what it takes to get you off, can all meet one another on a footing of
cooperation, mutual benefit, and respect."

"And the kennel's on the first floor?"

"And there's one here in your unit, and one in mine, and probably
a dozen more throughout the city. And if you're just not satisfied with
the amount or quality of eighteen-year-old boys that week, you can
make an appointment to have your preferences switched. And while
you are at it, if you find your own body distasteful, you can have it
regenerated, dyed green or heliotrope, padded out here, slimmed
down there—" Another intersection put them on another elevated
walkway. "And if you're just too jaded for any of it, you can turn to
the solace of religion and let your body mortify any way it wants
while you concentrate on whatever your idea of Higher Things happens to be, in the sure knowledge that when you're tired of that,
there's a diagnostic computer waiting with soup and a snifter in the
wings to put you back together. One of my bosses, at the office, he
has a family commune . . . out on the Ring."

"Sounds elegant . . . Did you say *in* the Ring or *on* the Ring?" because the Ring (which was not a ring, but a sort of scalloped endocy-
cloid along the outer edge of the city) comprised the most lavish
communal complexes in Tethys. (Tethys's governing families, when
elected, traditionally moved to the Ring's London Point.) The venerable serial communes that had grown up with the city for nearly ninety
years were located on the Ring's outer edge—rather than *in* the Ring,
which was the amorphous neighborhood extending an urban-unit or
two inside, but still posh by proximity.

"On."

"Super-elegant!"

"And he's the type who wouldn't give a presovereignty franq for
all your slogan-writing, pamphleteering malcontents. There's a guy in
my co-op who's actually *in* the government, and on what I'm sure you
would consider the wrong side, too: he probably thinks more of the

malcontents than Philip does." Over the railing, to their right, far away in darkness, a transport trundled. "Last Sovereignty Day, Philip had a big party out at his place—"

"That was patriotic!"

"—with all his colleagues, and all the colleagues of all the others in his commune. You should have seen it—"

"A couple of times I've been blessed with friends *in* the Ring—which is only a street or so away and that was pretty stunning."

"There's thirteen in his commune—"

"A regular coven!"

"—not counting children. Three of the women and two of the men—one, a really obnoxious faggot named Danny—are *in* the absolutely highest credit slot."

"I'm surprised all thirteen of them aren't."

"Philip is three slots higher than I am and is always talking about what a bum the rest of the family thinks he is. They've got at least two dozen rooms, half of them great circular things, with sweeping stairways and transparent west walls looking in among the city's towers with the shield ablaze overhead, and transparent east walls looking out over the ice-crags, with real stars in the real sky—"

"Shades of the place I called home—"

"Duplex recreation rooms; garden rooms; swimming pools—"

"You did say *pools,* with an 's' . . . ?"

"Three that I remember. One with its own waterfall, splattering and splashing down from the pool upstairs. Their kids are so damned well-behaved and precocious—and a third of them so obviously Philip's you wonder if they have him around for anything else. And people drinking and swimming and eating all over the place and asking, 'Did you hire any cooking craftsmen to help you with all this?' and some very sleek lady of the commune in lots of pearls and very little else saying, 'Oh, no, that's not the way we do things on the Ring,' and, with this amazing smile, 'That's how they'd do it over *there* . . .' nodding *in* the Ring's direction. And a gaggle of seven- and eight-year-olds being herded around by a little buck-naked oriental and someone says, 'Oh, are you their nurse?' and, with this big, oriental smile: 'No, I'm one of the fathers,' which, I suppose, if you'd looked twice would have been as obvious as Philip, and this one's into interstellar graviatrics—"

"The other top-slotter?"

"You guessed it. And just to try being rude, you ask another lady of the commune, who's been introduced to you as an Enforcement Commissioner in the Executive Department, if she's in the top slot too—"

"Two down from the top, I'd guess—"

"And she says, 'No, I'm two down from the top. What slot are *you* in—'"

"What slot *are* you in?"

"I've never been any higher than fifteenth from the top, and I don't see any reason to be higher. Only she's already asking me if I wouldn't like to go for a swim with her? The heated pool's *up*stairs; and if we want a chilly plunge we can just fall in right here. And is the music hired? No, it's by their two oldest daughters, who're just terribly creative when it comes to things like music and cooking and automotive physics. Then you meet another beautiful woman with two children—one of them obviously Philip's—calling her 'Ma' and playing together in the sand so you ask, 'Are you part of the commune too?' and she laughs and says, 'Oh, no. I used to be, a few years ago, but I've separated. I'm out now, on Neriad. But we just came in for the party. I wouldn't have *missed* it! The kids were always so happy here!' It was all so healthy and accepting and wholesome and elegant you wanted to vomit—I did, actually, on about my tenth glass of something awfully strong; and all over some weird-looking art object I figured would be difficult to replace and the worse for it. And sure enough, there's Philip, a kid on his shoulders, with his saggy left tit and one of his women, Alice, with a kid on hers—she's the nigger with the tattoos—smiling and holding my head and saying, 'Here, take this pill. You'll feel better in a minute. Really. Oh, don't worry about *that*! You're not the only one.' I mean, after a while, you *want* to be the only one—some way, some form, some how . . . Tattoos? I had tattoos when I was a kid. And I had 'em removed, too. The hard way. Toward the end I guess I fell into the pool and about five people pulled me out and I suppose I was just angry—not to mention drunk again. Just to do something really outrageous—there was one woman there named Marny who was really nice—I started talking about how I'd fuck anybody there for five franqs; just five franqs, and I'll show any one of you here heaven—"

"*Mmmmm*," the Spike said.

"Only who should be there too but that Danny character; with a big grin, he says; 'Hey, *I'm* into that, from time to time. Five franqs? I'll take you up!' I just looked at him, you know, and I said, 'Not *you*, cocksucker. What about one of your women?' I mean I just wanted to break through, *some*how. You *know* what he says to me, with this very concerned look, like you've asked him to play one of his old thirty-three recordings, but he knows it's got a scratch? 'Well, I don't really think any of our women are into that, right now—except *possibly* Joan. If you'll just wait a moment, I'll run and ask,' and goes dashing up one of those incredible stairways with the incredible view of the ice outside. Of course Philip is already back by this time, and I'm trying to tell these women, I mean I *am* a good lay. A *really* good lay. Professional quality—I *was* a professional. You don't even *have* any professionals out here! I mean, I could make it *work* for me. And Philip, who must be almost as drunk as I am, is saying, 'Yeah, I was into hustling—Marny and I both were when we were kids and hitchhiking around. First time she was on the Earth and I was on Luna we did it for a few months. The illegal kind, I think. Only I can never remember on Earth which kinds *are* illegal. It's great for the body. But it's a little hard on the mind.' He said it was like it was playing tennis all the time and never getting a chance to talk to anybody except over the net! I mean, can you imagine that? From Philip? If I hadn't been so drunk, I probably would've been surprised. As it was, I guess I realized it was just one more annoyance I was going to have to live in the same world with, maybe chuckle at from time to time. No matter how much puking I did." The walkway led them around a gentle curve. "After that, I *had* to leave. No logic or metalogic could have made me stay. It was all perfect, beautiful, without a crack or a seam. Any blow you struck was absorbed and became one with the structure. Walking back from the Ring—Philip had asked didn't I want to wait for Joan and, when I said no, he made me take another pill; they work—I kept on wanting to cry."

"Why?"

"It was beautiful, whole, harmonious, radiant—it was a family I'd have given my left testicle—hell, both of them—to be a daughter or a son to. What a place to have grown up in, secure that you are loved whatever you do, whatever you are, and with all the knowledge and self-assurance it would give you while you decided what that was. But the great lie those people hold out, whether they're in a commune or a co-op—and this, I suppose, when all is said and done, is why I hate them—even the ones I like, like Audri (who's my other boss), is: Anyone can have it, be a part of it, bask in its radiance, and be one with the radiating element itself—oh, perhaps not everyone can have it at an address within shoulder-rubbing distance of London Point, but somewhere, someplace, it's waiting for you . . . if not in a family commune, then in a work commune like your theater company, if not in a commune, then at a . . . well, a heterophilic co-op; if not at a heterophilic co-op, then at a homophilic one. Somewhere, in your sector or in mine, in this unit or in that one, there it is: pleasure, community, respect—all you have to do is know the kind, and how much of it, and to what extent you want it. That's all." He had almost cried coming back to his licensed sector co-op that morning. He almost cried now. "But what happens to those of us who *don't* know? What happens to those of us who have problems and don't know *why* we have the problems we do? What happens to the ones of us in whom even the part that wants has lost, through atrophy, all connection with articulate reason. Decide what you like and go get it? Well, what about the ones of us who only know what we *don't* like? I know I didn't like your Miriamne friend! I know I didn't want to work with her. I got her kicked out of her job this morning. I don't know how *any* of those things came about. And I don't want to know. But I don't regret it, one bit! I maybe have—for a minute—but I don't now. And I don't want to."

"Ah ha!" the Spike said. "I think we have just gotten down to a gritty—or at least a nitty."

He looked at her white mask sharply. "Why?"

"Your whole tone of voice changed. Your body carriage shifted. Even with your mask, you could see your head jutting forward so, and your shoulders pulled back into position—in the theater, you have to learn a lot about what the body has to say concerning the movements of the emotions—"

"Only I'm not into theater. I'm into metalogics. What about those of us who don't know what the body has to say about the emotions? Or the paths of the comets? Put it in terms that *I* know!"

"Well, *I'm* not into metalogics. But you seem to be using some sort of logical system where, when you get near any explanation, you say: 'By definition my problem is insoluble. Now that explanation over there would solve it. But since I've defined my problem as insoluble, then by definition that solution doesn't apply.' I mean, really, if you . . . No. Wait. You want me to say what happens in your terms? Well, you *hurt,* for one thing. Yes, people like me can sit down and map out how you are managing to inflict a good deal of that hurt on yourself. I suspect, at your better moments, you can too—"

"In *your* terms they're my better moments. In *my* terms they're my worst—because that's when the hurt seems to be the most hopeless. The rest of the time I can at least come up with a hope, however false, that things will just get better."

"In your terms, then, you just hurt. And—" She sighed—"from time to time—I mean I know how much Miriamne wanted that job; she's probably a good number of credit slots below you *and* me—you hurt other people."

They were silent for a dozen, rustling steps.

"You were asking me before if being a prostitute had done me any harm. I was just thinking. Your friend Miriamne thought the reason I'd gotten her fired was because she hadn't been interested when I'd made a pass at her. Well, maybe that's one bad thing hustling *did* do to me. You see, the one, degrading thing that happens to you again and again and again in that kind of job is people—the men who employ you as much as the women you're there to service—is people constantly give everything you do, just because you're selling it, some sort of sexual motivation. When you're in the business, you learn to live with it. But it's the difference between *them* and you—you get it in jokes, you get it in tips, you get it in jobs you're shuttled away from. And it never has anything to do with any real reason you might do anything real at all. Ask your friend Windy, he'll tell you what I mean: When I came out here, I'd heard all about the satellites' sexual freedom—it's the golden myth of two worlds. When I left Mars, I promised myself that was something I'd never do to any other person, as long as I lived; it had just been done to me too many times. Well, maybe being a prostitute made me oversensitive, but when Miriamne seriously said that, to me, this morning—that I'd gotten her canned because she wouldn't put out—well, it just threw me! It *isn't* something you find out here all that frequently, and, yes, that represents an improvement in my life. But when it *is* done, it doesn't make it any more pleasant. It's not something I could possibly do to anyone else. It's not something I like having done to me . . . As much as I dislike her, all the way over here I've been feeling sorry for her. But if she *is* the type who would do that to another person . . . hell, do it to *me,* I wonder if I have the *right* to feel sorry for her . . . You know?"

"On one level," the Spike said, her voice projecting an expression of seriousness as intricate as the former, projected smile, "everything you say makes perfect sense. On another, very profound one, I do not understand a single word. Really, I don't think I've ever met anyone like you before; and I've known a few. Your recounting of everything, from Philip to Miriamne—*his* women? *her* men? In fact you didn't even *say* the second one; I wonder if that's significant?—just sounds like a vision from another world!"

"I am from another world—a world you're at war with. And yes, we did things differently there."

"A world I hope very much we're not at war with."

"All right, a world we're not at war with *yet*. Do you think my inability to hold on to the fine points is just another example of my Martian confusion?"

"I think your confusion hurts other people."

He scowled behind the mask. "Then people like me should be exterminated!"

Her masked eyes glittered. "That would be a solution; I thought we were discounting those from the start."

He kept scowling and was silent.

After a few more steps, the Spike said: "So, now that you know all about me, what will you do with this precious information?"

"Huh? Oh, just because I've been carrying on about myself? Well, we're *in* the unlicensed sector, aren't we—"

"I would have called it complaining about your subordinates and bragging about your boss, but never mind."

"But I *do* know all about you," he said. "At least, a lot—you're the brat of nine Ganymede ice-farmers; probably as healthy and wholesome an upbringing as you could get in Philip's crowd—"

"Oh, more wholesome in some ways. Far more neurotic, I'm sure, in others—in *my* terms."

"—and now you're living the romantic life as a theatrical producer in the swinging, unlicensed sector of the big city, where you've gained fame and, if not fortune, at least a government endowment. What else is there to know?"

The white, plumed skull let a single syllable of laughter, almost a bark (he found it intensely ugly): a string of smooth ones followed it. "Well, you know at least *one* other thing about me."

"What?"

"I have fair tolerance as a listener. Tell me, do you think people who spend time, for whatever reason, in the Goebels, run to a particular personality type? I ask, because I must admit I find, here and there, similarities between your personality and Fred's. Oh, nothing specific, but just a general approach to life."

"I don't think I'm flattered."

"Oh, but of course! You must know everything about Fred too . . . I mean I don't think it has anything to do with prostitution itself. *He* wasn't one. And anyway, neither of you is the least like Windy. He was—but then, like you said, Earth is a different matter."

"You just don't understand." Bron sighed. "Help me. Take me. Make me whole."

"I'd have to learn something about *you* first." Her gaze was all white satin and sequins. "And I pay *you* the compliment of assuming I haven't even begun."

"I bet you think you could—what did you say?—sit down and map out how I'm managing to inflict a good deal of the hurt on myself."

"Your presumptions about what I think are so monumental as to be touching." Still holding his hand, she moved ahead. Suddenly, she looked back, and whispered: "Let me help you! Let me take you! Let me make you whole!"

"Huh?"

She raised a gloved forefinger against the veils before her lips. "Come with me. Follow close. Do what I do. Exactly. But on no account speak!"

"What do you . . . ?"

But she *shhhhed* him again, released his hand, and, in waves of white, darted down the steps beside them.

In waves of black, he followed her.

She crossed a cindery stretch and, immediately, hurried up a badly repaired stairway between walls scarcely wide enough for his shoulders.

She stopped at the top.

He stopped behind her. One sequin lapping the edge of his right eye-hole deviled his vision with scarlet glitter.

And her white plumes and satin headpiece had gone flickering red, brighter than any faulty coordinate sign could dye them.

Beyond the alley entrance, half a dozen people—among them the little girl he'd seen in the Spike's room last night, also the massive and mastectomized Dian—carried above their shoulders scarlet torches, a-hiss and a-drizzle with sparks. Windy, on a large contraption like a rodent's exercise wheel, bells fixed on his wrists and ankles, rotated head down, head up, head down: A target was painted around his belly button, rings of red, blue, and yellow extending far as circling nipples and knees. The guitar started. As though it were a signal, two men began unrolling an immense carpet across the ground—another mural: This one of some ancient fair with archaic costumes, barkers, and revelers.

Verbal disorientation, he thought, listening to the surreal catalogue of the lyrics: The melody was minor, this time rhythmic, more chant than song.

Who (Bron gazed about the spectators clapping to the intense, insistent rhythm) was the audience this time?

"Here!" the Spike whispered, picking up a pole leaning against the wall, thrust another into Bron's gloves and, carrying hers high, ran out over the spread carnival, into the circle of torchbearers (who fell back for her) waving her pole over her head.

Bron ran out behind her, waving his.

From the corner of his eye, he saw that Windy had left the wheel and was turning slow cartwheels (his fingernails and toenails were iridescent and multihued) through the milling torchbearers.

The top of the Spike's pole had erupted in blue sparks. He looked up: his own was a crackle of gold.

Then, beyond gold, he saw the trapeze arc down toward them. (Just how high *was* the ceiling here?) Two figures rode it. One was the woman, now in an ordinary cutaway street sack, who, when he'd last seen her, had worn mirrors on her toes. The other was younger, taller, with dark hair (they dropped within six feet of the glittering pole tops, then swung off and up); her features, from somewhere in Earth's Oceana, were set in astonishment as she craned back, rising away in the dark.

. . . and came swinging back, trouser cuffs and hair whipping. The singing changed key and timbre.

First he thought the song was breaking into polyphony. But everyone was just going off on their own. Above, the two women swung.

The music was complete cacophony.

The Spike raised her pole high and swirled it, with fluttering sleeves, in a wide circle (he raised his own, swung it; he was sweating inside his head-mask), then suddenly hurled it to the ground (his own pole clattered down a moment later). Immediately, the singers silenced.

Bron looked up, as did everyone else.

The swing's arc dipped, backward and forward, slowing

Someone to his left began a note. Someone to the right took up another, a third away. Others added to it; the chord grew, consonant and minor, like the waters of some alien ocean breaking about his ears. Suddenly it opened up into major—which made him catch his breath.

The swing came to an unsteady halt. The tall, young woman was clutching one of the ropes with both hands and staring down in amazement.

The chord died. Torches guttered on the ground, red, and blue, and gold, and red . . .

The younger woman said: "Oh . . . Oh, that was—Oh, *thank* you!"

The other woman on the swing said: "Thank *you* . . ." She released her rope and, balancing there with crossed ankles, began to clap.

So did the rest of the company.

The Spike had taken off her mask and, with it tucked under one arm, bowed, white plumes doffing, among the other, raggedly-bowing performers. Bron finished his own embarrassed bow, took off his own mask. Moist behind his ears and across the bridge of his nose, skin cooled.

"That was marvelous!" the young woman said, looking down among them. "Are you some sort of theatrical company?"

"A commune," explained the other woman on the trapeze. "We're working on a government endowment to do micro-theater for unique audiences. Oh, I hope you don't mind—we used some drugs—cellusin?"

"Oh, of course not!" the young woman said, glancing back and then down again. "Really . . . it was just—"

"So were you!" called up one of the men, picking up torches.

Everyone laughed.

Something tapped Bron's ankle. He looked down. Three people were rolling up the mural. Bron stepped over it. Barkers and revelers and amusement rides disappeared in the canvas bolt.

" . . . the song was written by our guitarist, Charo . . ." (whose guitar face flashed in Bron's eyes as it went into its case; Charo grinned at the swingers). " . . . props and murals are by Dian and Hatti, with help from our tumbler, Windy. This production was conceived, produced, and directed by our company manager, the Spike,"—who nodded, waved, and went to help Windy tear down the wheel—". . . with special appearances from Tyre, Millicent, Bron, and Joey—all of whom were our audience too, at one time."

"Oh . . . !" the young woman said, and looked down at Bron and the others indicated.

Bron looked around, surprised, remembered to smile up at the swing.

"Thank you again for being our audience. We really appreciate a responsive one. That was our final performance on Triton. Shortly, our endowment will be taking us on. We've been on Triton eight weeks now, in which we've given over two hundred and twenty-five performances of ten works—three of them never performed before— to almost three hundred people—" Someone picked up the pole Bron had thrown down, took it away—"Thank you again."

"Oh, thank *you!*" the tall young woman cried. "Thank *you* . . . !" The swing began to rise into the dark, by creaks and starts, wound up on a rackety pulley. "Thank you all! I mean, I had no idea, when you just suggested that we sit *down* on this thing that, suddenly, we would . . . Oh, it was just marvelous!"

Heads, hands, and knees, they jerked up into the shadow, away from the decimal clock, dim and distant on the dark.

Head-mask still under her arm, the Spike was talking to the woman who held the little girl now in her arms. All three were laughing loudly.

Still laughing, the Spike turned toward Bron.

He pulled off one of his gloves and tucked it under his arm with his own mask, just to do something. He was trying to think of something to say, and already the anger at not finding it was battling his initial pleasure.

"You did wonderfully! I always like to use as many new people in the performance as possible. In this kind of thing, their concentration and spontaneity lend something to it no amount of careful rehearsal can give. Oh, how marvelous!" suddenly taking his hand and looking at it (his nails, newly lacquered that morning when he'd decided on the dark attire, were, like Windy's, multihued and iridescent): "I do love color on a man! I make Windy wear it whenever I can." She looked down at his mask, at hers. "The only trouble with these things is that unless you break your neck, you can't see anything more than five feet off the ground!"

"What's this about your final performance?"

"That's right. Next stop—" Her eyes rose to the ceiling dark— "Neriad, I believe. And after that—" She shrugged.

Bron felt it through their joined hands. "Why didn't you tell me?"

"Well—you were so busy finding out about *me* I didn't get a chance." A few syllables of laughter surfaced over her smile. "Besides,

I was so busy trying to figure out how to get you here in time to go on, I wasn't really thinking about *anything* else. Did you enjoy it?"

"Yes."

"I'd hate to think what you'd have said if you hadn't! You just sounded like you were agreeing to supervise your own execution—" at which point painted arms, with iridescent multihued nails, flapped around her shoulder. Long red hair fell forward over her satin tunic; a bass voice growled from under it: "Come on, honey, let's go make this a night to remember!"

She shrugged Windy away (Bron unclenched his teeth) with: "I remember too many nights with you already. Cut it out, huh?"

The head nuzzling in her neck came up, shook back the red hair (it was the first time he had seen it right side up for more than a second at a time: good-natured, pockmarked, scraggy-bearded) and grinned at Bron: "I'm trying to make you jealous."

You're succeeding, Bron didn't say: "Look, that's all right. I mean, your friends are probably having some sort of cast party to celebrate—" Somehow one handful of multihued nails were now hooked over Bron's shoulder, the other still on the Spike's:

Windy stood between them: "Look, I'll leave you guys alone. Back at the co-op, they've said we can party in the commons room as late as we like." He shook his red head. "Those women want us out of there in the *worst* way!"

Both hands rose and fell at once. Bron thought: That's politic.

"See you back at the place—"

"We won't be using the room for the whole—"

"Sweetheart," Windy said, "even if you *were,* I got invites to *several* others." And Windy turned and bounded off to help someone carry away what the exercise wheel had collapsed into.

The Spike's other hand came up to take Bron's; his eyes came back to them, one bare with colored nails, three gloved (two in white, one in black). "Come," she said, softly. "Let me take you . . ."

Later, whenever he reviewed those first three encounters, this was the one he remembered most clearly; and was the one that, in memory, most disappointed. Exactly why he was disappointed, however, he could never say.

They did return to the co-op; she had put her arm around his shoulder, their capes had rustled together; bending toward him, as they walked through the streets, she had said: "You know I've been thinking about those things you were saying to me, about your boss.

And everything—" (He'd wondered when she'd had *time* to think.) "All through the performance, actually I just couldn't get it out of my head. The things you seem to have confused to me seem so clear. The arrows you seem to be assuming run from B to A to me so obviously run from A to B that I tend to distrust my own perception—not of the Universe, but of what *in* the Universe you're actually referring to. You seem to have confused power with protection: If you want to create a group of people, join a commune. If you want to be protected by one, go to a co-op. If you want both, nothing stops you from dividing your time between the two. You seem to have making a family down as an economic right denied you which you envy, rather than an admirable but difficult economic undertaking. Just like Mars, we have antibody birth control for both women and men that makes procreation a normal-off system. You have free access to birth pills at a hundred clinics—"

"Yes," he said, to be shocking: "I've taken them once—for a fee."

And in typical satellite fashion she did not seem to register any shock at all. Well, they *were* in the u-l, where the shocking was commonplace, weren't they?

"You only *have* two decisions to make about a family," she was going on. "Somewhere around nameday, you decide if you want to have children by accident or by design; if by design—which well over ninety-nine percent do—you get your injection. Then, later, you have to decide that you *do* want them: and two of you go off and get the pill."

"I know all that—" he said; and she squeezed his shoulder—to halt him speaking, he realized. "That," he finished, "at least, is the same as in Bellona."

"Yes, yes. But I'm just trying to spell the whole thing out to see if I can figure out where you got off the track. With it set up this way, less than twenty percent of the population chooses to reproduce." (That was *not* the same as Bellona; but then, Mars was a world, not a moon.) "In a closed-atmosphere city, that's just under what we can tolerate. In the satellites we try to dissolve that hierarchical bond between children and economic status Earth is so famous for—education, upkeep, and social subsidy—so that you don't have the horrible situation where if you have *no* other status, there's *always* children. And no matter how well you perform, I haven't the faintest idea *what* you've got sex confused with. On the one hand, you tell your story in a perfectly coherent way—only I've been to parties at family communes in, if not on, the Ring. I've been to parties at nonfamily co-ops, where, among forty or fifty adults there were always two or three one-parent families. I've been to parties given by adolescent family communes who, for religious reasons, lived in the streets. They've all got the same basic education available; and basic food and shelter you can't be denied credit for at any co-op . . ." She had gone on like this, pulling him closer every time he began to wonder what she was trying to say, till he stopped listening—just tried to feel, instead. They were already at the party by now. One of the first things he did feel was the faint hostility (Windy, who was really a pretty nice guy he decided, and Dian, who by the end of the evening was *the* nicest person, as far as he was concerned, in the company—with none of the Spike's brittleness and a gentler way with her equally astute insights—pointed a few subtle examples of it out) between the women who lived at the co-op and the commune who were leaving the next morning. "Though I suppose," Dian said, leaning arms as hairy as Philip's on equally hairy knees, "it would try anybody's patience to have a bunch of strolling players parked in your cellar, carrying on till all hours, while rumors of plague are flying . . ." and she nodded toward a modest TRITON WITH THE ALLIANCE NOW poster on the wall.

He talked to some of the other "audience" who'd been frozen into the last production—various people whom the troupe had performed for, and with whom various members had made friends. Yes, they'd been as surprised by it as Bron had been. From this discussion he looked up to see Miriamne in the room. For ten minutes he desperately wanted to leave, but could think of no way to effect it smoothly. Then, to his embarrassment and astonishment, he was asking her, across a conversation group that somehow they'd both become part of, how her job situation was going. She explained, in a friendly enough way, that she was going to work as a transport mechanic at an ice-farm not too far from Tethys. It wasn't cybralogs, but at least it was working with her hands. He expressed his relief and felt something sink still further inside, something invalidated, something denied.

He turned away to listen to an intense, polysyllabic discussion of the vast difficulty of performing pre-twentieth-century theatrical works for a twenty-second-century audience:

"You mean because of the length?"

"There's that. Primarily, though, it results from the peripetia's invariably pivoting on sexual jealousy; that's just so hard for a contemporary audience to relate to."

"That's silly," Bron said. "I get jealous—oh, maybe not specifically sexually. I know you—" to the Spike, who was leaning, affectionately, against him, "and Windy, and that woman who plays the guitar, must have something going. I mean, I've seen the bed—"

"He's even slept in it," the Spike said, still leaning.

"It would be silly to be jealous of that; but as far as *attention* goes, I'm as possessive of that in people I'm having a thing with as it's possible to be . . . I guess."

"So we've noticed," said that woman who played the guitar, with a slightly mocking smile (reminiscent of the Spike's) that bothered him slightly because, till then, he hadn't noticed Charo was holding the Spike's other hand. And somewhere else in the room Windy was laughing.

The Spike *had* been paying amazing amounts of attention to him, of the silent and unveering sort (Had she been once out of physical contact with him since they'd entered the room . . . ?) that made him feel relaxed, secure and, also, practically oblivious to her presence. (The three of them had probably discussed it the previous night and decided he was "that type"—which, though it did not break the relaxed security's surface, drove the unsettling wedge beneath it deeper.) He wished there was overt reason to dislike the gathering. But there was none of the plastic good will that crusted a gathering at Philip's, that you wanted to break with a sledge. Parties this side of the license-line were simply going to be more relaxed, more informal, more at ease. There was nothing you could do.

Over the next half hour he mulled over plans of asking her (whom he could just see out of the corner of his eye, but whom he could feel, tucked warmly under his arm) to abandon her life with the commune and come away with him to—what? He *did* want to do something for her. Finally, he contented himself with evolving a sort of sexual cadenza, a series of caresses, acts, positions, of mounting intensity, to perform with her when they should return to her room—and in a lazy moment when no one was talking to her, he turned to mouth against her ear: "Come . . . let me take you."

"What—?" she murmured.

"Come with me. Follow close. Do what I do . . ." and led her into the hall.

The lovemaking was splendid—though only halfway through the list, she implored him to stop. "It's marvelous," she whispered. "It's wonderful. But you'll *kill* me!" He had, he realized, let his imagination run away. Minutes later, he too was exhausted. Wrapped around each other, the arms of each straining around each other's gasped breaths, Bron waited for sleep . . . floated up toward it, a bit jerkily (like that inane trapeze, rising into the dark), each gasp.

And still the disappointment—certainly they were both physically satisfied. Was it just that he hadn't completed his scenario? Was it all some silly, essentially aesthetic flaw, some missed cue, some flubbed entrance, some inessential malfunctioning prop no one in the audience could possibly be aware of? But the audience was only one— And what had she done that he was able to see her less and less clearly, while he thought of her more and more in terms from her work, in words his own tongue had tasted first in her mouth?

He took another breath and was engulfed in sleep, immobilizing as methane ice—and woke from it two hours later, manic with energy, incredibly anxious to leave (he had to get home to change; you couldn't wear a get-up like this to the office two days in a row), which was all right with her, she was explaining while he pulled on his gloves, put on his mask, pulled the cloak around his shoulders, because *she* wanted to get ready before—

But he was at the door, wishing her Good Luck on her trip. And she was still in bed, laughing her smooth laugh, and wishing him Good Luck on his.

Bron hurried through the quiet, unlicensed streets.

On the torn, rubber floor-mat of the vandalized booster booth (why had he stopped to look inside it again? He still wasn't sure) lay pieces of paper. Already knowing what was on their undersides (the print just showed through), he picked one up, let the curtain fall and stuffed the flyer into one of his secret pockets (where, through his glove, he felt the package he'd been carrying around for Alfred all evening), entered the green-lit, scrawled-over tile, and stepped out under green (for licensed) street coordinates, onto pink, licensed pavement.

Between the high roofs the sensory shield, dark blue, blushed here and there with silver. He tried to remember what they *had* said on parting and found it oddly fuzzy—which was when he realized how clearly he remembered everything else, starting from the performance and ending with that moment when, entwined, they had slept.

The Spike was going. Today. So it was stupid to mull on it.

But each incident of the night, with its disappointment still intact, as well as its security, its relaxation, its almost unbearable pleasure, came back with such clarity something caught in his throat at each image. (Only smells usually returned memories to him that vividly.) Three times, on his way to the all-night Transport Station in the Plaza of Light, he stopped still on the street. And four times, as he sat, staring out of the window at Tethys' galaxy of predawn stars, dropping behind into the blue (like some flight to Neriad, and then on . . .) he came near tears.

" . . . to bother you at this hour, but I just wanted to get you your stuff as soon as possible, while it was still on my mind, you know? In case you . . . well, you've got it now." Up the inch-wide door-crack ran a flesh colored ribbon. At the top of it was tousled hair and a single, green, red-rimmed eye. At the bottom, after various mottlings, modelings, and creases, were thick veins and dirty toenails. "Okay." The door clicked closed.

Bron turned in the quiet hallway, walked across to his own room, pulling off his gloves—for a moment he looked at his own, colorful, well-cared-for fingers—took off his mask, and shouldered inside.

4. La Geste d'Helstrom

The melancholy left after three more hour's sleep.

The energy (and vividness) remained all the way to work, till, by three o'clock (he'd skipped lunch), when he was going over the Day Star's preprogram specifications yet again, it hit him: P would have to intersect *less* than half of Not-P (as well as pieces of Q, R, and S, while cleaving T); also it must surround *more* than half of it, and be tangent to it at not less than seven (which had been self-evident) and not more than forty-four (which had been the bitch!) points. *That* was getting somewhere.

Immensely pleased, he marched to Audri's office with his find.

"Great," Audri said, looking up from her desk. "For a reward you get a two-week vacation."

Bron said, *"Mmmm?"*

Audri leaned back and put her hands behind her head. "I said you get two weeks off, starting tomorrow."

"I don't under—" Suddenly he remembered some vague thing she'd said yesterday about "threatening": "Hey, *look*, now! That girl *got* another job. I mean, I saw her, later, and she's all right!"

Audri frowned. "What girl are you—Oh, for crying out loud, Bron! Don't give me any of your hard-time crap." Her hands came down on the desk. "I can't take it today. People are being laid off all over the whole hegemony. If you'd been at lunch, you'd've heard!"

"Well, I didn't *want* lunch," he protested, automatically. "I wanted to work. That's how I got the—"

She stopped him with lightly closed lids. "Look." They opened. "You can either take a two-week vacation with eight percent reduction in credit for the duration—"

"Eight per*cent*!"

"—or quit. Half a dozen people have. I've got to take ten days off myself. And, I've got to think of something to do with the kids."

Although Bron liked Audri, he *didn't* like her three children. When, from time to time, they came to the office, he found them precocious, presumptuous, and obdurate. She lived with them in a gay, women's co-op (not a commune—room, food, and work arrangements were friendly but formal) in an unpretentious spiral tower a unit from Bron's own squat, blocky building. With none of the laminated ostentation of Philip's multisexed, on-the-Ring dwelling, nor the insistently tatty quaintness of a u-l sector domicile, it was the most comfortable home he had visited on Tethys. All three visits, in fact had left him strangely relaxed and, strangely, depressed—but it had taken him three visits to realize they *were* two reactions.

Bron swallowed (and forgot) his next protest.

"We don't have to get hysterical yet, I suppose," Audri said. "It's *only* eight percent—this time. And just for two weeks. They want to make everything look like it's working at full capacity, only that people just all happen to be off doing something else."

"What sort of logic—or metalogic—is that?"

"I have three degrees in this subject and am in the midst of getting another one—which is three more than you—and *I* don't have the foggiest idea." Audri leaned her palms on the desk edge. "Look. Just get out of here. If you come up with any more on Day Star this afternoon, shove it under Phil's or my door. But don't bother us. Okay? And don't come in tomorrow."

Wonderingly, he said (he hadn't meant it to, but it sounded a little belligerent): "Okay . . ." and returned to his office.

He thought many confused thoughts, and didn't even bother to open the Day Star folder again.

The energy was gone by the time he returned to Serpent's House. Sitting in the commons, alone in a conversation niche, he reread the flyer picked up that morning from the booster-booth's floor:

"THESE THINGS ARE HAPPENING IN YOUR CITY!!!"

But, as he absorbed each political atrocity, he kept thinking of other things not happening in the city: like the performances of the little micro-theater troupe; and its director, who was no longer a resident. In a way he would not have dared define, it made the atrocities worse.

"You want to continue from where we left off?" Sam put the case up on the table and sat. "Lawrence said to set up the pieces as best we remembered, and *he'd* come down in ten minutes and make corrections." Sam thumbed back brass claws, opened out the board.

Bron said: "Sam, how do you reconcile working for the government with the appalling political situation on Triton?"

Sam raised an eyebrow.

Between them micro-waves lapped, micro-breezes blew, micro-trees bent, and micro-torrents plashed and whispered down micro-rocks.

"I mean, there you are in the—what is it? Liaison Department? Political commitment isn't a perimeter, Sam; it's a parameter. Don't you ever wonder? Don't you ever doubt?"

"What great metaphysical crisis have *you* just been through that's suddenly gotten all your angst up?"

"We're not talking about *me*. I asked you a question." So as not to face the answer, Bron opened the case's side drawer, removed the transparent plates of the astral cube and began to assemble them on their brass stilts. When he did glance up, Sam was regarding him seriously, the cards in his dark fingers halted in midshuffle. A corner of the White Novice showed, curved against Sam's darkly pinkish palm.

"Yes." The White Novice fell. "I doubt." Fifty cards fell, riffling, after it. "Frequently." For a moment, a little laughter shook, silent, behind Sam's face; Sam's eyes went back to the cards. He parted the pack, shuffled again.

"Come on. *What* do you doubt?"

"I doubt if someone like you could really be asking me a question like that for purely autonomous reasons."

Bron pulled out the other side drawer of velvet-cradled ships, warriors, horsemen, herdsmen, and hunters. "There *are* no autonomous reasons. Whatever makes the question come up in my mind, the fact that it is in my mind is what makes it *my* question. It still stands." He picked up the screen showing the horned head of Aolyon (cheeks puffed with hurricane winds) and set it, on its tiny base, upon the waters—which immediately darkened about it; green troughs and frothing crowns rolled about the little stretch of sea.

Sam put down the pack, reached into the control drawer and

turned a survey knob. From the side-speaker came a crack and crackle over rushing wind, followed by a mumbling as of crumbled boulders. "That's quite a storm . . . were there any sea-monsters in there? I don't remember—"

"What do you doubt?" Bron picked up his own scarlet Beast and set it on the rocky ledge, where it lowered over at the narrow trail winding the chasm below.

"All right." Sam sat back to watch Bron set out tiny figures. "One thing I've been worrying about since the last evening we all played this game—"

"—the night of the gravity cut." Bron thought: The night of the day I met *her.* He picked up green pieces and set them by river, rock, and road.

"At the Department, we knew something was going to happen that night. The cut wasn't a surprise. I guess it was pretty clear to the rest of you, too, I wasn't surprised . . . But they told us only a few people would go out to see."

Bron glanced up: Sam was turning a transparent die between dark forefinger and thumb.

"They had it all figured—statistics, trends, tendencies, and a really bizarre predictive module called the 'hysteria index' all said that practically no one would want to go out to see the sky . . . As far as they can tell, eighty-six percent of Tethys' population was outside within a minute and ten seconds, one way or the other, of the cut."

"What's to doubt there?"

"They were wrong." Sam got an odd expression. "I don't suppose I have any illusions about our government's being a particularly moral institution. Though it's more moral than a good many others have been in the past. Nor do I think for a moment that any of the accusations in that piece of trash you were just reading—" He nodded toward the leaflet, which had fallen to the orange rug; somehow the table leg had worked onto (or the paper under) it at the corner— "are particularly exaggerated. The worst you can say is that they're out of context. The best you can say is that they *are* emblems of the political context that gives them what meaning they have. But up until now—and this probably strikes you as quite naive—it never occurred to me that the government could be *wrong* . . . about its facts and figures, its estimates and its predictions. Up until now, when a memo came down that said people, places, incidents would converge at set times and in given ways, they did. The last memo said less than two percent of the population would go out. They'd be too scared. Over *eighty* percent went out. That's more than a ninety-five percent error. You may say it wasn't an error about anything important. But when you're on the edge of a war, a ninety-five percent error about *anything* just doesn't bolster confidence in your side. So I've been doubting."

"Sam, Earth has committed major atrocities on Luna, and allied herself with Mars for the all but economic domination of Jupiter's and Saturn's moons, big and little alike. Neriad has already said she'll go with us; and Triton stands on the edge of the whole business, waiting to plunge into one of the most senseless and destructive conflicts in human history—we've been splattered with gore and filth in a hundred ways already: The night of the gravity cut may have been the most flamboyant splash—I doubt if any one of us, even you, can assess the damage compared to—"

"Well," Sam said, one sparse eyebrow lowered, one corner of his full mouth raised, "it's not as if anyone were using soldiers," and let his expression break into a mocking, voiceless laugh.

"Some of your best friends are probably Jewish too," Bron said. The cliché about soldiers had been devalued rather like (an eccentric elderly woman Bron used to visit in the u-l had once explained to him) "law and order" had been devalued two centuries before. "So this one is all buttons and spies and sabotage, and only civilians get killed—those that aren't thrown out of a job by the economic wangling, or don't fall off the roof during a gravity cut—because that's all there are."

"You know—" Sam came forward again, to set scarlet's caravan, one piece after the other, on the jungle trail—"one of the reasons I moved into this place was so I wouldn't have to put up with six hours a day of political interrogation."

Bron fished out the last cargo ship from the drawer and positioned it at the edge of the storm—immediately it began to dip and roll. "Yeah? The government told you that you had a ninety nine point nine nine nine percent chance of only finding nonpolitical types in this type co-op? Well, maybe I'm just that odd and inexplicable point oh oh oh oh oh one percent they call an individual—"

"No. You're a type like the rest of us."

"—or maybe the government's just—" Bron turned up his hands and shrugged—"wrong again . . . ?" He meant it to be annoying.

But Sam was apparently finished with being annoyed. He laughed out loud. "Maybe—" and began to place the screens.

"Hello, Alfred." Lawrence's voice came loudly and cheerfully from the middle of the room.

Bron and Sam looked up.

Across the commons, Alfred hurried toward the balcony stairs.

"I said, 'Hello, Alfred,'" Lawrence (who had apparently been on his way to join the game) repeated. One wrinkled fist rested on his parchment-pale hip.

Alfred, at the steps' foot, a hand on the banister, twisted around. On his black suspender straps large, red letters sagged, behind and before. "Um . . ." he said. "Oh . . . Ummm . . ." He half-nodded, then darted up, 'Q' scarlet between his shoulder blades.

Lawrence came over. "The horrible thing is, he's improving. I've been going through this every day now for—what is it? Four months? If you speak to him twice, now, loudly and distinctly, he'll actually *look* at you. Pauses even. Sometimes even grunts a little. And the general behavior syndrome is no longer that of com*plete* inarticulate terror. The first thirty times, by count, he just pointed his nose straight ahead and ran faster. At this rate, I estimate, he *may* reach the state of acceptable human animal—not outstanding, mind you: just acceptable—in, oh, perhaps two hundred and fifty years." Lawrence came around the table, regarding the board. "Even with re-generation treatments, he won't last that long. *Mmm* . . . I see there's a war on."

Bron sat back. "Why don't you just lay off him . . . leave him alone."

Lawrence grunted and sat next to Sam, who moved over for him. "Sam and I are the best friends *either* of you two ambient social disaster areas ever had. By the way, when are you going to break down and fuck me?"

"Do you proposition Alfred in the same, warmhearted, friendly manner, from time to time?"

"Heaven forbid!" Lawrence turned a switch; the grid flickered over the board. "That's at least *three* hundred years off. *I* may not last that long!" which cracked Sam up, though Bron didn't think it was so funny. Lawrence pulled at the wrinkled folds under his chin, then reached out and adjusted two Queens. "I think those were there, actually. Otherwise, the two of you seem to have done pretty well. All right, now—Get away from me! Get away—!" That was to Sam, who was still laughing. "You're both playing against me now—don't think by sidling up like that you'll get any advantages." Bron found himself remembering the Spike's comment on political homosexuals . . . Sam changed his seat.

Lawrence picked up the pack and dealt. "With all the girls Alfred is constantly sneaking into his room—and why he feels he has to sneak, *I* shall never know—he should give up that ridiculous computer course his social worker's had him training at for the last two months—I mean, he doesn't like it and won't finish it—and go to Earth, or someplace where it's legal, and become a prostitute." Lawrence nodded knowingly toward Bron. "Doing it on an accepted basis for a while might be exactly what he needs, don't you think?"

It was the first Bron had heard of the computer course, which was annoying. On the other hand, there were some things about Alfred Lawrence didn't know (if Lawrence thought Alfred could possibly go professional), which pleased him. Annoyance conflicting with pleasure produced a noncommittal grunt.

"You know," Sam said, fanning the cards, "you are a patronizing bastard, Lawrence."

Which increased Bron's pleasure.

"I guess Mars is the only place where it is legal on the scale *he'd* need," Lawrence went on, oblivious. "And of course he *can't* go to Mars or Earth or anywhere like that, because of the war."

Bron looked at their joint hand, reached over and reversed two of the cards.

Sam said: "Lawrence, I have to make an official trip to Earth; I'm leaving tomorrow. Do you want to come along? It's on government credit: You'd have to share my cabin."

"Lord!" Lawrence protested. "You mean be shut up in the same five-by-five with you while we fell into the sun, with the hope that a very small ocean on a very small world just *happened* to be in the way? No, thank you! I'd be crawling the walls!"

Sam shrugged and glanced at Bron. "You want to come?"

"Not with you." Bron was thinking about work, actually—when, with a sting, he remembered that, for the next two weeks, he didn't *have* any work. A trip away from this whole, mean, depressing moon? What better way to wipe *her* out of mind. "You could always take Alfred." He wished Sam would ask again.

"Ha!" Sam said, without humor. "Let Lawrence work on him for another two hundred and fifty years. No . . . the experience would be good for the kid. But I've got an entourage quota this trip—and there is the rest of the party coming along to consider. I need somebody fairly presentable, who can be at least vaguely sociable; and can also entertain themselves if they have to. You two, yes. Alfred, I'm afraid—" Sam shook his head.

"Why *don't* you go, Bron?" Lawrence asked.

"Why don't you?" Bron asked back, trying to sound sociable; it had a vaguely sullen ring.

"Me? Cooped up together with *that* body?" Lawrence studied the board. "It's bad enough just trying to keep my self-control watching it loll around here in the commons. No; masochism no longer interests me, I'm afraid."

"Well, it's not—" (Sam had separated three cards out, apparently having decided on the first meld)—"as if I were born with it."

"No, you go with him, Bron," Lawrence said. "I'm just too old for hopping around the Solar System. And in time of plague to boot."

"If I go, who'll play your silly game?"

"Lawrence can teach Alfred," Sam said.

"Perish the thought . . . there's as much chance of my teaching Alfred vlet as there is of Sam's taking him to Earth. I think our objections are about the same."

"We'll be leaving tomorrow morning," Sam said. "We'll be back in twelve days. You'll still have a couple of days back here to do nothing in, before you have to get back to work at—"

"How did you—?"

"Hey!" Lawrence said. "You *don't* have to knock the board onto the floor!" He reset two pieces that Bron, starting, had overturned.

Sam, still looking at the cards, had that mocking smile. "*Sometimes the government's right.*" His glance flicked up. "You coming?"

"Oh, all right." Bron reached over and pulled out the four-card meld in the high Flames Sam had overlooked; which, for the first half hour of play, at any rate, gave them a decided advantage—before Lawrence, by adroit manipulation of all the gods and astral powers, regained his customary edge.

It was as if someone suddenly turned off the sensory shield.

To the left, jagged methane faces made scenery wild as that of some thousand ice-operas.

To the right the gritty rubble, which made ninety-six percent of Triton one of the dullest landscapes in the Solar System, stretched to the horizon.

They sped between, inside the clear conveyer tunnel. London Point dragged away behind. Sharp stars pierced the black.

Settled in his seat, with the two curved canopies of clear plastic over them (the stationary one of the car, and the tunnel above rushing backward at one hundred seventy-five kilometers an hour), Bron turned to the left (Sam was also sitting there), thought about ice-farmers, and asked: "I still wonder why you decided to take *me*."

"To get you off my back," Sam said affably. "Maybe it'll lead you to some political argument that seriously challenges my own position. Right now, though, yours is so immature there's nothing I *can* say to you, except make polite noises—however much those noises might sound to you like ideas. This way you'll have a chance to see just the tiniest fraction of the government close up and check out what it's doing. The government usually *is* right. In my experience that 'usually' is ninety-nine percent with lots more nines after the decimal point. I don't know: Maybe seeing a bit of the real thing will waylay your fears and shut you up. Or it may send you off screaming. Scream or silence, either'll be more informed. Personally, with you, I'll find either a relief."

"But you have your educated opinion which direction I'm likely to go, don't you?"

"That's your *uneducated* guess."

Bron watched ice-crag pull away from ice-crag, kilometers beyond Sam's shoulder. "And the government really doesn't mind if you take me along? Suppose I find out some confidential top-secret information?"

"The category doesn't even exist any more," Sam said. "*Confidential* is the most restricted you can get; and you can see that in any ego-booster booth."

Bron frowned. "People have been smashing the booths," he said, pensively. "Did the government tell you that?"

"Probably would have if I'd asked."

Broken glass; torn rubber; his own face distorted in the bent chrome slip: The image returned, intense enough to startle "Sam, really—why *does* the government want someone like me along on a trip like this?"

"They don't want you. I want you. They just don't mind my taking you along."

"But—"

"Suppose you *do* find out something—though what that could be I don't even know. What could you *do* with it? Run shrieking through the streets of Tethys, rending your flesh and rubbing ashes in the wounds? I'm sure there's a sect that's into that already. We simply live in what the sociologists call a politically low-volatile society. And as I think I said: The political volatility of people who live in single-sex, nonspecified sexual-preference co-ops tends to be particularly low."

"In other words, given my particular category, my general psychological type, I've been declared safe."

"If you want to look at it that way. You might, however, prefer to express it a little more flatteringly to yourself: We trust most of our citizens in this day and age not to do anything *too* stupid."

"Both sets of words still model the same situation," Bron said. "Metalogics, remember? Hey, you know, before I left Mars and came to Triton to be a respectable metalogician for a giant computer hegemony, I was a male hustler in the bordellos of Bellona's Goebels. But then I got these papers, see . . . What does your government, out here where both prostitution and marriage are illegal, think about *that*?"

Sam pushed his soft-soled, knee-high boots out into the space between the empty seats. "Before I came to Triton, I was a rather unhappy, sallow-faced, blonde, blue-eyed (and terribly myopic) waitress at Lux on Iapetus, with a penchant for other sallow, blonde, blue-eyed waitresses, who, as far as the young and immature me could make out then, were all just gaga over the six-foot-plus Wallunda and Katanga emigrants who had absolutely infested the neighborhood; I had this very high, very useless IQ and was working in a very uninspiring grease-trough. But then I got this operation, see—?"

Bron tried not to look shocked.

Sam raised an eyebrow, gave a small nod.

"Did you find it a satisfactory transition?" Sex changes were common enough, but since (as Bron remembered some public channeler explaining) some of the "success" of the operation might be vitiated by admission, one did not hear about specific ones frequently.

Sam gave a dark, thick-lipped leer. "Very. Of course, I was much younger then. And one's tastes shift, if not exactly change. Still, I visit the old neighborhood . . ." (Bron thought: Family man, high-powered, big, black, and handsome Sam . . . ?) "The point is: The government," Sam went on, in a perfectly reasonable tone (in which Bron now found himself listening for the lighter overtones in that security-provoking bass), "is simply not interested in my rather common sexual history or your rather peculiar one. And you *had* told me about your whoring days. I admit, I was surprised the first time. But shock value diminishes with repetition."

"You hadn't told *me*," Bron said, sullenly.

Sam raised the other eyebrow. "Well . . . you never asked."

Bron suddenly didn't feel like talking any more, unsure why. But Sam, apparently comfortable with Bron's moody silences, settled back in his (her? No, "his." That's what the public channels suggested at any rate) seat and looked out the window.

They sped through the dim, glittering landscape of green ice, gray rock, and stars.

Perhaps a kilo away, Bron saw something he thought was the Space Port that Sam said wasn't. A minute later Sam pointed out at something he said was.

"Where?" Bron couldn't see.

"Over there. You can just catch a glimpse of the edge, right between those two whatyamacallits."

"I still can't tell where you're—" at which point they plunged into covered tunnel; lights came on in the car. The engine whine intruded on Bron's awareness by lowering pitch. They slowed. They stopped. Then it was green, pastel corridors and opulently-appointed waiting rooms that, while you had a drink and were introduced to people— the rest of Sam's entourage—trundled quietly along invisible tracks, were hauled up unseen lifts—people laughed and glanced down at the geometrically patterned carpet when, once, the floor shook—and you were guided to the proper door by the little colored lights and the people in the party who were obviously old hands at this sort of thing. (There was no one resembling a steward around; but Bron wasn't sure if that was "standard tourist" or just "government.") He was enthusiastically telling someone who appeared to be enthusiastically listening about his own emigration trip to the Outer Satellites twelve years back, which " . . . Let me tell you, was a different matter entirely. I mean, the whole three thousand of us were drugged to the gills through the whole thing: and what *is* in this drink, anyway—" when he realized, in the midst of laughing, that six months . . . six *weeks* from now, he probably would never think of any of these affable Georges and Angelas and Arouns and Enids and Hotais again. I mean, he thought, it's a political mission: Nobody's even *mentioned* politics! I haven't even asked Sam what the mission *is*! Is that, he wondered as they walked along another corridor (some of the group were riding smoothly on the moving strip down the corridor's side; others ambled beside it, chatting and laughing), what Sam meant by politically low-volatile?

In one of the larger, more opulent, mobile rooms, with luxurious reclining chairs on its several, carpeted levels, there were more drinks, more music, more conversation . . .

"This is all marvelous, Sam!" someone called out. "But when do we get on the ship?"

Someone else lifted their ankle to check a complex chronometer strapped there: "I believe we've been on it for the last two minutes and forty seconds," which drew a group *Ooooo!* and more laughter.

"Take off in seventeen minutes." Sam came down the scroll-railed steps. "This is my cabin. Just take any couch you want."

Over the next ten minutes Bron learned that the blonde, blue-eyed woman on the couch next to him was part of Sam's family commune, and that the tan, plump girl, going around saying, "Drugs? Drugs, everyone?" and clapping her hand to the side of the neck of anyone who smiled and nodded, was their daughter.

"You mean you really can do it *without* drugs?" someone asked.

"Well, Sam means for us to watch the take-off," the blonde woman said, lying back on her couch and craning around to see the speaker. "So I'd suggest you take them—it can be a little unsettling, otherwise."

"That's exactly why I asked," the other speaker said.

When the plump girl got to Bron's couch, on an impulse he smiled and shook his head. "No, thank you . . ." But her hand clapped him anyway; then she jerked it away and looked distressed:

"Oh, I'm dreadfully sorry—You said 'No'—!"

"Um . . . that's all right," Bron mumbled.

"Well, maybe you didn't get very *much*—" and she darted off to the next couch.

A buzzer sawed through the cabin. A lot of the more opulent things—lighting fixtures, wall sculptures, shelves, ornamental tables—folded up or down or sideways into walls, floor, and ceiling. Several of the couches swung around so that they were all facing the same way in the now rather institutional-looking space. The wall before them hummed apart. What had been a corridor before was now a wall-sized window on star-speckled night, cut with a few girders, the tops of a few buildings visible at its bottom.

From the ceiling a screen folded down, its face aflash with myriad numbers, grids, and graphs.

There has never been a spaceship accident more than three seconds past takeoff less than 100 percent fatal, Bron recalled—which probably meant he had *not* gotten much of the take-off drugs.

"I always find these trips so exciting—" someone said—"no matter where or how many times I go. I have no *idea* why . . ."

Blue numbers (which were becoming more and more prevalent across the screen) he knew were the final navigation check figures. Red numbers (and a whole bunch went from blue to red) meant those figures had been approved and fed into the take-off computer.

"There's no turning back now," someone said solemnly.

"I hope the swimming pool cover is on tight," someone else said (and everyone chuckled). "I'd hate to have to take a swim too early."

Bron settled against the padding. Something began to roar—rather far away—on his right; then something else—much closer—on his left. There were only two blue numbers now, amidst a full field of red: and they were flickering oddly, which made him suspect they were broken.

Someone said: "I don't think those blue numbers are right . . ."

Someone else said: "Sam, I told you, you should have gotten a government cabin. The government's never wrong."

People chuckled again.

Then the building tops and the girders were gone. And the stars were moving.

The cabin lurched.

"Whoopsy-daisy!" someone called.

People laughed again.

Down had suddenly and disconcertingly established itself in some direction near his feet. Bron felt himself slip on the pad. The stars jerked to the side on the panoramic window; a moment later they were wiped away by landscape, moving too fast for Bron to tell if they were ten meters or ten—*there*! A web of lights and more lights swept by: Tethys itself. Every one *Oooooed* again.

They were at least ten kilometers up.

Stars now. Now landscape . . . but moving more slowly—at least forty. When the pitted horizon passed again, Bron could make out a distant curve. Then the cabin rocked grandly backward . . . or rather, "down" reestablished itself under the floor.

The screen, its two, broken, blue numbers still flickering (all the others were out now), folded into the ceiling.

Was it the drug—or that he hadn't gotten enough of one of the several drugs, or too much of another? . . . he stayed on his couch for quite a while, gazing at the circling stars. Ancient Earth men had tried to pick out pictures on those blue-white points. He tried to superimpose her face; but neither the stars, nor his memory, stayed still enough.

When he finally got up, people were already walking around. On the upper level, at the top of the stairs, the pool-cover had retracted. A few people were already paddling about. Light fixtures, bar, sculptures, and tables were once more out; and a trap had opened up with steps down into the cabin's free-fall section: a drum as big as this one just "below" it, with "real" (that is, only when accelerating) gravity. ("Guests are requested not to take liquids from one level to the other," said the sign on the stand beside the ladder, in whose white plastic rings already stood four or five unfinished drinks.) Completing his circuit of the pool, Bron walked back down the carpeted steps, with a drink now, as three people came up, laughing hysterically about something inane.

His acceleration couch turned out to contain endless interlocked and interleaved cabinets, compartments, and crannies, which a bony, garrulous redhead, almost short enough to be a midget, took great delight in demonstrating to him. It was a bed, of course; just pull that handle there and a soundproof privacy-bubble—well, almost soundproof—will swing over the whole thing. You can have it opaque or clear with that switch there. And that's a timer, preadjusted to help you rearrange your sleeping schedule over the ninety-hour trip so that you won't suffer too hugely from space-lag—though nobody ever follows it on a junket like this, anyway. There's your reader, though the selections in the file drawer—mark my word—will be monumentally uninspiring. I wouldn't even look through it, unless you just want a good snicker. (Though I once found one just jammed with twentieth-century science fiction—ever read any? Fascinating stuff!) Swing that half of the sleeping-pad up and you'll find a place for ablutions; that half, for defecation. And under there—just a second; *there* you go!—is your luggage.

Which Bron had packed, at Sam's suggestion, in a small, plastic bag. Sam had said don't take much; they'd all be pretty informal. But, wandering around the cabin, catching an occasional glimpse into the other luggage compartments when one or another guest was hunting around for some personal effect, he saw that at least three people had brought huge numbers of sacks, packages, bags, practically overflowing their couches. It made him feel slightly apprehensive at first. But as the hours went on, no one seemed about to dress.

He spent a lot of time "down" in the dimly-fit free-fall chamber, looking through the window there at the stars.

"Hey," Sam called through the trap to him, sometime during the second day out. "Come up here a minute. You have to see this."

Bron unsnapped the lounge net he'd been floating in, pushed off toward the ladder, pulled up, emerged into the weighted chamber— an odd experience, having your head, then your shoulders, then your arms and chest go all heavy (like getting out of the swimming pool, only *very* different; he'd compared them a couple of times on this trip, just to see)—and came up by the pool.

"Come on, take a look at this." Sam doffed a drink in one hand, guiding Bron's shoulder with the other. "Come on."

By the poolside, at one of the wall tables, sat the bony, little red-head; across from him sat an equally diminutive oriental woman with irregularly-clipped, black hair. Between them was a vlet board. It was only a quarter the size of Lawrence's. (A small traveling version?) The landscape was simply a laminated 3-D photograph, not Lawrence's animated holographic surface. The pieces were not carefully carved and painted but merely raised symbols on red and green plastic markers. The astral cube did not have its own stand. But Bron could see, in the deployment of the gods, the detritus of a vicious astral battle that green (the redhead's side) had evidently won.

Five melds were already down.

The woman threw the dice and, in a rather surprising way (a rather clever one too, Bron thought as soon as the move was completed), managed to bring her Guards in from the right, just as green's caravan crossed the forge, to pull it out of the influence of the scarlet Magician, substantially multiplied by three reflecting screens.

The redhead tossed the dice, discarded a low Flame, dispersed the screens to the corners of the board in one move (which left Bron, among the game's half-dozen spectators, frowning) and turned to rearrange a matrix on the astral board. *That's* clever! Bron thought. The woman would have to answer it, pulling some of her powers from the Real World, which would leave some of her strongest pieces unprotected.

The edge of the playing board, the table, and the woman's cheek flickered with reflections off the pool.

Sam nudged Bron and grinned. "I was thinking we might challenge them to a game of doubles, you and me. But I guess they're a little out of our league."

The woman won the battle in three moves.

Some time later they did play a game of doubles—and were wiped off the board in twenty minutes. While Sam was saying, "Well, we may not have won, but I bet we've learned something! Lawrence better watch out when we get back, hey Bron?", Bron, smiling, nodding (*her* memory deviling him in every flicker on the mosaic ceiling above), retired down into the free-fall chamber, determined never to play that stupid game again, with anyone, on any world, or in between, in or out of any league!

He was going hundreds of millions of kilometers to forget her: He zipped himself into the lounge net and rolled himself up in the idea. The stars drifted by the darkened chamber.

"Do you want to try some of this?"

"Oh, no, I can never eat on these trips . . . I have no *idea* why . . ."

"You know I never mind synthetic food as long as they aren't trying to make it taste like something *else*—algae or seaweed or something."

"I think the reason the food is so terrible on these flights is because they expect you to drink yourself to death."

"Did you ever think of Sam as a drinking man before? Lord, is he putting it away!"

"Well, this *is* supposed to be a political mission. He's probably under a great deal of pressure."

"What are we supposed to do after we get there?"

"Oh, don't worry. The government takes care of its own—are we decelerating?"

"I think so."

"Isn't some light or something supposed to go on down here so that we know to get back upstairs when that happens? I'm surprised this whole cabin just doesn't fall apart. *Nothing* seems to be working right!"

"Well, there *is* a war on."

Over the ninety hours, Bron was on the edge of, or took part in, or overheard ninety-nine such conversations. He was in the free-fall chamber when the lights did come on. "I think that means we better go upstairs." Around him, people were unzipping their lounge nets. "We make Earthfall in about an hour."

"Why didn't they come on when we were doing those turns out by the Belt?" someone asked.

"I think they only come on when we're going to accelerate or decelerate over a certain amount."

"Oh."

The wall rolled closed across the window for landing (on the screen, descended once more, the two blue numbers still flickered), customary, everyone said, with atmospheric touch-downs.

He was swung from side to side on his couch, bumping and thumping in a way that would really have been unsettling if he hadn't taken his full compliment of drugs. But world landings were notoriously rough.

There was some not very serious joking about whether or not they were still in the air; or in the ship for that matter, as the trundling began.

Then the window-wall rolled back: no glass behind it now—And some of the company were visibly more relaxed, laughing and talking louder and louder: Some, unaccountably, were more subdued (which included Sam); they wandered out into another, green, pastel corridor. (Bron was wondering about the Taj Mahal—but then, this was a political mission.)

"Do we get any scenery on this trip?" someone asked.

"I doubt it. The government doesn't believe in scenery for moonies."

"Ah! But *which* government?"

Over the next few days, though they went to sumptuous restaurants, took long trips in mechanical conveyances through endless, dark tunnels, even went to several symphonic concerts, and spent one afternoon at a museum in which they were apparently the only visitors (the collection was a private one; they had come up from some deep level in an escalator; at night they returned down to their separate, sumptuous rooms by different escalators), Bron had the feeling that they had not really left the Earth space-port complex. They had seen no sky. And, outside concert audiences (their party always had a private box), or other diners (their tables were always grouped alone), no people—although, as the little redhead took evident delight in explaining, if you took the time they had spent on mechanical transportation and averaged it out at even a hundred fifty K's an hour, they could be as much as two thousand kilometers from their point of arrival—quite a distance on a moon, but not so long considering they were on Earth.

It was a sumptuously pleasant and totally edgeless time—indeed, its only edges were provided by those moments when he could reflect on *how* edgeless it was.

One morning (at least he thought it was morning), wondering if he could hunt up anyone else who had also overslept for a late breakfast, Bron came out of his room and was crossing between a lot of lush vegetation under a high, mirrored ceiling, when he saw Sam hurrying toward him, looking worried.

And two strangers in red and black uniforms were coming toward him from where they'd apparently been waiting by a thick-trunked tree. The woman grabbed Bron's shoulder. The man said: "You're a moonie, aren't you? Come on!"

And twenty feet away, Sam froze, with a perfectly shocked expression.

5. Idylls in Outer Mongolia

We may note that, in these experiments, the sign "=" may stand for the words "is confused with."   G. SPENCER-BROWN, *The Laws of Form*

He started to say: "I am *a* moonie. But I doubt if I'm *the* moonie you're—" But they led him, roughly, off through the imitation jungle.

Rusted metal showed through the door's gray paint: The amazing lock contraption actually had a hole for a key; bright red letters spelled out EXIT.

They pushed through into a cement stairwell. He protested once and got a shove for it; they hurried him up. The walls and steps and banisters were grimed to an extent for which neither youth on Mars nor maturity on Triton had prepared him. More apprehensive each flight, he kept thinking: Earth is an old world . . . an old, old world.

They pulled him, breathless with the climb, out on a narrow sidewalk as a good number of people hurried past (who, in the less than fifteen seconds he got to see them, must, he decided, have only three basic clothing styles the lot); only one glanced.

Above irregular building tops (he had never *seen* irregular building tops before), the air was a grainy gray-pink, like a sensory shield gone grubby (was that *sky*? With atmosphere in it . . .?). A warm, foul odor drifted in the street (equally astonishing). As they pushed him to the vehicle, a surprising breeze (it was the first breeze he'd ever felt not produced by blower convections from some ventilator grate within meters) carried with it a dozen, clashing, and unpleasant smells.

"In here!"

They opened the vehicle door and shoved him down into a seat; "sky"-colored ticking pushed from one open seam. The two uni-

135

formed strangers (some kind of e-girls) stalked around the other side, leaving him momentarily alone with clambering thoughts (I could *run*! I could run *now* . . . !), but the unfamiliarity of everything (and the conviction that there was some mistake) paralyzed him: Then they were inside too; the doors slammed: the vehicle dropped straight down, and was caught up by, and bounced into, a subterranean stream of traffic with the jerkiest acceleration and, save for the Earth-landing, the strongest, he'd ever felt.

Ten minutes later he was yanked ("All right! I'm not trying to resist! I'm coming. I'm—") and yanked again from the car and hauled past towering buildings and finally marched into one that might have been eighty, a hundred eighty, or eight hundred years old (the oldest extant structure in Bellona was a hundred and ten years old; in Tethys, no more than seventy-five). He had not even noticed this time if there were sky outside or not.

A lift with a grimy brass gate took them up three floors (which seemed silly, as they had just walked up at least eight in the hotel): he was led across a hallway and shoved (one of his sandals slipped and he went down on one bare knee; he was wearing only shorts and a light V-shirt) into a cement-floored room with paint-peeled plaster walls. The door shut behind him; as he stood up, rubbing his knee (yes, the one he'd sprained last year), there were loud clicks and clashes as bars and locks and catches were thrown. The window was too high to see out, even if you (which he didn't because his knee hurt) jumped. The metal door was dull-gray, with scuffs and scratches at . . . kicking level! The room was maybe ten feet by eight.

There was no furniture.

He stayed in it almost five hours.

Getting hungrier, getting thirstier, finally he had to go to the bathroom. Beside the door, set in the corner of the cement floor, was a green, metal drain. He urinated in it and wondered where he was supposed to do anything else.

He was sitting in the corner across from it, when the door, clattering its sunken locks, pushed open. Two red and black uniformed guards stepped in, yanked him to his feet, and held him flat against the wall, while a portly, bald man in the least comfortable-looking of the three basic styles came in and said: "All right. What do you know about these people?"

Bron really thought he meant the guards.

"The *moonie* delegation!"

" . . . nothing—?" Bron said, wonderingly.

"Tell us, or we'll fish it out of you—and the places in your brain we fish it out from won't *ever* be much good for anything again: because of the scar tissue—that's assuming you ever get a chance to *use* it again, where we'll be sending you for the rest of your life when we're finished."

Bron was suddenly angry and terrified. "What . . . what do you want to know?"

"Everything you know. Start at the beginning."

"I . . . I just know it's a political mission of . . . of some sort. I really don't *know* anything else about it. Sam is . . . Sam just asked me to come along as part of the . . . the entourage."

"It's funny," one of the guards said to nobody in particular. "The moonies always sit in the corner soon as you leave 'em alone. Marsies and Earthmen always sit at the center of the wall. I've always wondered why."

The portly man looked askance, muttered, "Shit . . ." and suddenly one of the guards punched Bron, hard, in the side, so that he crumpled down the wall, gasping and blinking—as they left.

The door slammed.

Locks clashed.

Both guards had been women.

Three hours later the locks clashed again.

As the two guards marched in, Bron struggled to his feet (from the spot in the center of the wall he'd finally, after much pacing, chosen to sit). They grabbed him, pulled him up the rest of the way, flattened his back against the wall. (The guards were both men this time.) Another man, less portly and with more hair, came in and asked Bron the identical questions—verbatim, he realized at the same time he realized (and began to worry that) his own answers were at least worded slightly different. At the end, the man took something out of his side pocket that looked like a watch with fangs. He came over and jabbed it against Bron's shoulder—Bron twisted against the pain, not that it did much good the way the guards held him.

"Don't wince!" the man said. "It's supposed to hurt." Ridiculous as the order and explanation was, Bron found himself trying to obey.

The man jerked the instrument away and looked at it. "Wouldn't you know. He's telling the truth. Come on."

Bron looked down to see twin blood-blots on his V-shirt. Inside, something dribbled down his chest.

"It's funny," one of the guards said to nobody in particular. "The moonies always sit in the center of the wall as soon as you leave them alone. Marsies and Earthmen always take the corners." And when Bron turned to protest, because that seemed just the last, absurd straw, the other guard punched him in the side: He crumpled down the wall, gasping, blinking.

The man opened the door, left; the guards followed. The one who had hit him paused, a hand on the door edge, and frowned at what time and fear and the pain in his gut had forced Bron to leave on the floor by the corner drain.

"Jesus Christ . . ." He looked back at Bron. "You moonies are really animals, aren't you?" Shaking his head, he slammed the door after himself.

Forty minutes later, the same guard came back alone. Bron's shoulders stiffened. He pushed back against the plaster.

The guard walked over, took Bron by the arm and pulled him up. "Friend of yours is down the hall waiting for you. It's all over, boy." Bron was a head taller than the guard, who looked, Bron realized now, like a somewhat orientalized and beardless Philip.

"What will they . . . ?" Bron began.

"Sorry we have to beat up on you guys like that every time we leave. It's just routine—to get out safe, you know? But then, if you were even *connected* with what we thought you might be in the middle of . . ." He shook his head, chuckled. "Let me tell *you!* Just two guards in here? I was one scared son of a bitch." He pulled at Bron again, who finally came away from the wall. "You were in the meat market on Mars for a while, weren't you?" The guard held Bron firmly as he got his legs going at last. "Me too—when I was too young to know better." He shook his head again. "I told them, us meat-men just aren't the type to end up in what they thought *you* were into. *I* told them not to even bother with you when the report first came in. But I'm a marsie. On Earth nobody listens to marsies. On Mars, nobody listens to earthies. Makes you wonder what we're doing fighting on the same side, don't it?" He looked at the feces beside the drain. "Really, you *are* animals. All you have to do is read the goddamn instructions, they're printed right inside the—Now I *know* you didn't behave like that on Mars. You just pull it up by the . . . but then, maybe moonies just aren't used to the same amenities we're used to here, huh?" They walked into the hall. The guard's voice was friendly, his grip firm. "Well, I've hosed worse than that off that goddamn floor and those goddamn walls. And that goddamn ceiling." He made a face. "And that goddamn ceiling is goddamn *high*." He guided Bron through another door, into a large, nondescript office, with several desks, several chairs, and some dozen men and women sitting, standing, walking about, some in red and black, some not.

Sam stood up from one of the chairs. His face seemed to be just recovering from the expression Bron had last seen on it thirteen hours ago.

"Here he is," the guard said, and to another guard: "Larry, let the nigger sign for him and get him out of here, huh?"

While Sam leaned on the desk to sign, Bron kept waiting for the proper moment to ask what was going to happen to him next. He and Sam were halfway down the hall when it dawned on Bron he'd been released in Sam's custody. There was relief, somewhere, yes. More immediate, the sensation of fear descended into the apprehensible from the numb heights it had risen to, to settle finally, like something poisonous, on the back of his tongue, hindering the hundred questions that tried to dart out. In Bron's brain a hundred broken blue lights flickered.

Pushing open the tiled lobby's glass door, Sam finally asked: "Are you all right?"

Out on the stone steps, Bron took a deep breath. "Do you know what they did to me! Sam, do you *know* what they—"

"I *don't* know," Sam said softly. "I don't want to know. And if you care about either my life, or your own freedom, you will *never* describe any of what's just happened, to me or anyone else, so long as this war is on. In fact, just make that a flat never."

The fear—some of it, anyway—curdled; and became anger. But there was still fear. Finally he got out, as poisonously as he could (they left the bottom of the steps and turned toward the corner): "I guess the government was just wrong again."

Sam glanced at him. "Our government was right. Theirs was wrong." At the corner, Sam paused, looked at him. "No, we didn't foresee that. I'm sorry."

Lights glittered in glistening darkness off in four directions.

The street was wet, Bron realized. Had he been incarcerated through one of the fabled rains various areas of the Earth still underwent from time to time?

Suddenly that seemed the most incredible aspect of the injustice.

He felt, through the weakness and the hunger and the thirst and the fear and the rage, that he might weep.

Rain . . . !

One hand on Bron's shoulder and leaning close, Sam was saying: "Look, even without knowing the details, I know it's been hard on you. But it's been hard on me too. There were forty-five reasons why they might have arrested you, for any one of which—if they'd turned out to be the case—you'd be dead now: simple, fast, perfectly illegal, and with no questions. I had to go running around from our people to their people and back, trying to find out how to get you out of each one of those forty-five situations while avoiding finding out if any of them actually happened to pertain. Or anything about how they might if they ever should. They're things I'm not supposed to know about. If I *should* learn about them, I become useless here and the whole mission is a failure. That's why I don't want to hear anything about what they did to you or said to you. Even if it didn't mean anything to you, it could very possibly mean something to *me*—in which case we might just as well throw in the towel and the bunch of us go home—assuming they let us. Your life, my life, the lives of everyone we brought with us, and a good many more, would be in grave danger from then on. Do you understand?"

"Sam," Bron said, because he had to say something, "they checked everything I said with . . . with some kind of *lie*-detector!" He did not know if he'd chosen that because it was the greatest outrage or the most minuscule. In memory, he clawed back over the hours, trying to fix exactly what the others were. His throat was hoarse. Something kept catching in it, nudging him to cough.

Sam closed his eyes, drew breath, and bent his rough-haired head still closer. "Bron, they check me with one about five times a day, just as a matter of routine. Look—" Sam opened his eyes—"Let's try and forget it happened, all right? As bad as it was for you; as bad as it was for me, from here on, we just *forget* it." Sam swallowed. "We'll go someplace—just take off from the group, you and me. I'll call Linda when we get there. Maybe she'll join us with Debby. Maybe she won't. There's no real need to stick around with the rest, anyway. We'll reconnoiter later."

Bron suddenly took hold of Sam's wrist. "Suppose they're listening to us now . . . !"

"If they are, so far we haven't said anything they don't already know I know. Let's keep it that way . . . Please?"

"Sam . . ." Bron swallowed again. "I . . . I have to go to the bathroom. I'm hungry. I can't walk too good because my right side still hurts . . . my knee, you remember where I sprained it last—But I'm not supposed to say . . . and my shoulder's sore . . ."

Sam frowned. Then the frown fell apart into some unnameable expression. Sam said softly, "Oh, my—"

They took care of the first in a doorway down an alley (like an animal, Bron thought, squatting in the half-dark, swiping at himself with a piece of discarded paper. But apparently there were no public facilities in this particular part of this particular city); the second they remedied at a cramped place whose grimed, unpainted walls reminded Bron of the stairwell he'd first been bustled into. The food was unrecognizable, primarily fat, and when Sam took out his tourist vouchers, the counterman gave him a look Bron was sure meant trouble; but the voucher was accepted.

Outside, they walked for a few blocks (Bron said he felt a little better), turned up some metal steps into what Bron had thought was a ceiling between the buildings; but it turned out to be the support for some archaic, public rail transport.

On the gray-black above them was a bright, white disk which, Sam explained, was the full moon.

Bron was amazed.

First rain.

Now a full moon. *And* rain . . . ? That would make a story! Coming out of the old building into the warm (or were they cool?), Earth rains. Then the moon above them . . .

They took the next transport, rode in it awhile, made several changes in stations so dirty the brightly-lit ones were more depressing than the ones in which the sodium elements were just purple flickers through the sooty glass. His impression of Earth as a nearly a-populous planet suddenly reversed (on one leg of the journey, they had to stand, holding to ceiling straps, pressed against dozens of earthies) to nothing but gray/green/blue/brown clothed crowds. Bron was exhausted. His last articulate thought was a sudden realization, in the drifting fatigue, that of the three basic styles, one was apparently reserved for women, the other for men, and the third for young people and/or anyone who seemed to be involved in physical work—most of which seemed to be men, and all of which seemed so arbitrary he just tried to turn his mind off and not consider any more aspects of this pushy, unpleasant world. Any time he could, he closed his eyes.

Once, standing, and three times, sitting, he slept. Then they were in another large, crowded lobby, and Sam, at a counter, was buying more tickets. He asked where they were going now.

Onto a plane.

Which turned out to be a far more frightening procedure than the space flight—possibly because it was so much smaller, or possibly because the only drug available was alcohol.

Even so, while he stared through the oval window at the near-stationary cloud layer below, with dawn a maroon smear out in the foggy blue, he fell asleep again. And did not fully revive until Sam had herded him into some racketing land vehicle with seats for two dozen: Besides the driver, they were the only passengers.

They got down by a shack, with a lot of grass and rock stretching to a seemingly infinite horizon. Kilometers away, a gray wave was breaking above the world's edge . . . mountains? Yes, and the white along their tips must be snow! Other than the shack, rock and grass and brush just went on forever under a white-streaked sky.

"You know," Sam said, "every time I come here—" (The bus rocked away, from gravel—crunching became hissing—to tarmac, rumbled down a road that dropped away into the landscape, rose, much thinner, further off, and dropped again.) "—I figure this place hasn't changed in a million years. Then I look around and realize everything that's different since the last time I was here six months or a year back. I know *that* path wasn't there last time I came . . ." Spiky grass flailed in the light wind at the shack's baseboards, at the edges of the double ruts winding away. "And those great, shaggy pines you can just see off there—" (Bron had thought they were bushes and much closer; but, as it had been doing here and there with each blink since they'd gotten off the bus, perspective righted.) "Well, the caretaker informed me that they're historically indigenous to the area—they're Dawn Redwoods—but they were brought in just last year."

Bron raised his eyes, squinted about the stuff that was nothing but sky. "Is it . . . morning?"

"It's evening here."

"Where are we?"

"Mongolia. Outer Mongolia, this particular section of it used to be called. But that doesn't mean too much unless you know which di-

rection Inner Mongolia is, now, does it?" Sam took his hands from
the pockets of his long, leather overvest, breathed deeply, stretching
the gold mesh beneath. "I suppose where you are doesn't matter unless you know where you've been."

"Where did we come from?"

With lowered eyebrows, Sam smiled. "From Tethy. On Triton."

Bron reached into his collar, rubbed his shoulder under the blood-
stains. "I'm tired, Sam." It wasn't very bloodstained.

"Come on inside," Sam said.

In the shack, they sat at a scarred wooden table and were served a
salty, brown, bitter broth in dented brass bowls.

The salty, brown, bitter man who served it (from a dented brass
pot) wore a torn shirt and frayed apron both of which were stained
and splattered with—*that* was blood! From some ritual slaughtering
or butchering of meat? Uncomfortably, with the warm bowl in both
his hands, Bron drank more broth.

"The archeological diggings are over there. The town center is that
way." The salty, brown forefinger pointed vaguely toward a window
missing an upper pane. You can find accommodations over there."
The angle between diggings, center, and dwelling seemed to Bron
less than a second of an arc; which was resolved by: "Just hike along
that road there a bit—" pointing in the same direction—"and it'll
take you past all three. There's not much to do here, but you probably
know that; that's why you came—at least that's what most of you
tourist types tell me."

Outside, they walked along the road's shoulder.

"There's so little here," Sam commented happily, "and yet it's so
loud!"

The grass gnashed around them. An insect yowled between them.
The breeze drummed at them and a covey of paper-winged things,
blue as steel in half-light, broke silent about their knees and fluttered
across the meadow—butterflies, he realized, from some childhood
picture-strip, some adolescent museum visit. There were as many
smells (and as strange ones) here as there were in the city. Most of
them seemed to be various types of mild decay—products of slow
burning, rather than the fast which he'd already learned to associate
with more densely populous areas of this world.

Any place they were going must be pretty far away, since in all this
open space, Bron couldn't see it. (He was still deadly tired.) But the
landscape contained dells and outcroppings and hillocks which, be-

cause he had never really walked among such before, he didn't really see until he was upon, or under, or skirting one.

Two people were coming up the center of the road. From braided hair to crusted boots, they were the dirtiest people Bron had seen since Fred.

One kept digging a middle finger under the lens of some goggle-like things perched on her nose. (The dirt, however, wasn't black or gray, but sort of brownish.) The other wore a hat, with a brim(!), pushed back on his head. "It was really funny," Bron overheard him saying in a very serious voice. "I thought it was going to be all brushing and shellac. That's what I'd heard about."

"I'm afraid—" She scowled and dug—"this just isn't that kind of dig." (Glasses, Bron realized.) "You'll be troweling till they close us down—" (Hadn't glasses disappeared before man even reached the moon? Somewhere on Earth, people still wore *glasses* . . . !) "—when you're not pick-axing."

"I guess if we turned up anything delicate enough for brushes, Brian would shoo *us* off anyway."

"Oh, Brian'd probably show you how. It's just at the strata we're down to, nobody was *doing* anything that delicate."

The diggers passed.

Bron, lagging steps behind Sam (the tiredness had gotten to his knee), came over a rise around a crop of furzy rock: What looked like a construction site stretched away some forty feet, after taking a good bite from the road itself. Striped posts had been set on yellow plastic bases, or driven into the dirt.

Some had cameras. Some had wheelbarrows. Many, mostly shirtless, wandered through carefully pegged trenches, examining the walls. Somewhere in all that sky, the gray had torn apart, showing great flakes of blue and letting down a wash of mustard light.

Sam paused at the ropes. Bron stopped beside him.

A woman carrying a carton came by. Bron glanced in—she stopped, grinned, and tilted the box to let him see: skulls and skull pieces stared this way and that. Bits of marked tape were stuck here and there.

"All," the woman confided, nodding to her right, "from that part there, just in, or just under, Dwelling M-3 . . . if it *was* a dwelling. Brian has been wrong, by his own admission, three times on that one." She hefted the carton. "Maybe we'll see you here tomorrow? Everyone's knocking off now." As she turned away, a clutch of diggers broke around her, stepping over the ropes, moving around Sam and Bron.

"Man," one said, "if you don't lay off me about that piece of tile, I'm going to small-find your *head!*"

Diggers ambled away down the bright, black road in the late, surprising sun, while Bron again mulled on images of the Taj.

On one of the heaps, a woman, bare back to them, sat on a crate playing a guitar. In the lulls between rushing grass and voices, the music reached them, slow and expert, lazily hauled from seventh to archaic seventh. Her singing voice sounded as familiar as the music sounded strange.

Bron frowned.

He started to say something. But it wouldn't mean anything to Sam anyway. Because he was so tired, it took him a full minute to decide, but suddenly he swung a leg over the ropes, started across the rubbly ground, almost collided with another group of diggers: One put a hand on his shoulder and, smiling through a dusty beard, said: "Come on . . . on *that* side of the chalk line if you're gonna walk around in here—which you shouldn't be doing anyway!"

"Sorry—" Bron hurried across the loose earth; dirt was in his sandals. He came around the pile.

Small-breasted Charo sang, dreamily, looking down at her fingers, under the white and gold sky:

> *Hear the city's singin' like a siren choir.*
> *Some fool's tried to set the sun on fire.*
> *TV preacher screamin', "Come on along!"*
> *I feel like Fay Wray face-to-face with King Kong.*
> *But Momma just wants to barrelhouse all night long . . .*

Charo looked up from the strings, frowned at Bron's frown, suddenly raised her head, laughed, nodded to him; and still played.

Behind him, a man said: "Is that you?"

Bron turned.

"That *is* you!" Scraggly-bearded Windy, dusty from labor, came up the pile, a pail with things in it held out from his thigh, his other arm waving for balance. "What in the world are *you* doing here?"

"I was . . . I was just walking by. And I . . . What are . . . ?"

"The last time I seen you is on some damn moon two hundred and fifty million kilometers away. And he's just walking *by,* he says!"

"What are *you* all doing?" Bron asked. "On Earth?"

"The usual. Micro-theater for small or unique audiences. Government endowment. Just what it says in the contract that brought us here."

Bron looked around. "Is *this* one of *her* . . . ?"

"Huh? Oh, Christ, no! A bunch of us from the company just decided to volunteer a hand with the diggings. They're into some very exciting things." Windy laughed. "Today's biggest find, would you believe it, is a whole set of ancient digging implements. Apparently someone in the immemorial past was *also* trying to excavate the place."

Behind Bron, Charo's tempo brightened, quickened.

Windy went on: "Brian's been trying to figure out if they found anything, or whether they just gave up and went away—not to mention just how long ago it was."

Charo sang:

> *I've been down to Parliament; I've been in school;*
> *I've been in jail and learned the Golden Rule;*
> *I've been in the workhouse—served my time in those*
>   *hallowed halls.*
> *The only thing I know is the blues got the world by the balls.*

"But what are you *doing* here?" Bron asked again. Because it suddenly all seemed too preposterous. Flickering at the edge of thought were all sorts of Sam-engineered, arcane, and mysterious schemes, of which this was some tiny fragment in a pattern whose range and scope he would never know—on threat of execution or incarceration.

"Very highbrow program, actually. Very classical: a series from the Jackson MacLow *Asymmetries*. The man wrote hundreds of the things. We're performing from the whole range, and the final cycle of seven. The Sixties—that's the Nineteen-Sixties—are very *in* around here. Given our head, you know, we're much more into the contemporary. But—" Windy glanced about—"really, this planet must have the most conservative audience in the system. It's incredible!"

Charo was singing:

> *I've been in the Tundra and the mountain too;*
> *I've been in Paris, doin' what the Frenchmen do.*
> *I've been in Boston where the buildings grow so tall.*
> *And everywhere you look the blues got the world by the balls.*

"Is the . . . the Spike here?" Bron asked, which seemed a very silly and, at once a desperately important, question. "I mean *here*?" meaning the dig, which was not what he meant at all: he hadn't seen her.

"On site? Oh, she puttered around for a couple of hours yesterday. But those MacLows are a bitch, man. Besides, I think she's working up another of her double-whammy-zowie-pow! specials—gotta show the locals what it's all about." Windy set his pail down. "That'll probably be a unique audience number." He smiled. "And you've had yours, I'm afraid. But if you're around for a few more hours, maybe you can catch us in the evening performance of the MacLows. That's open to whoever's wandering by. You know—" Windy looked around again, picked up his pail—"Brian says that a million years ago—I think it was a million—this place was all desert. Imagine, nothing but sand!"

> *You can catch 'em from the preacher, or from the pool shark,*
> *find 'em in the grammar of the socialite's remark;*
> *or down in the washroom you can read it on the walls:*
> *Everywhere you look the blues got the world by the balls.*

The tempo changed again, slowing to the melody he'd first heard:

> *Sometimes I wonder what I am.*
> *Feels like I'm living in a hologram.*
> *It doesn't seem to matter what's right or wrong.*
> *Everybody's grabbin' and comin' on strong.*
> *But Momma just wants to barrelhouse all night long.*

The playing stopped, Charo stood, crab-walked down toward Bron, holding the guitar by the neck. "Do you have any idea where Boston is?"

"I don't think there is a Boston anymore," Windy said. "I remember once, hitchhiking somewhere on this damn planet and someone saying, 'We're right near where Boston used to be.' At least I think it was Boston." Windy shrugged. "Hey, look. We've got to get going. We still have a performance to put on—" He did a little dance step; red hair and the pail swung; a breeze, and the hair blew; the pail rattled. "Sing a few songs, turn a few backflips: always happy and bright." He ducked his head, grinned, as Charo took his arm, the guitar swinging from her other hand. They walked away.

Bron returned, wonderingly, to the ropes. As he climbed over, Sam asked:

"People you know?"

"Yeah. I . . ." Momentarily Bron considered asking if Sam had any idea *why* the troupe was here. But that was silly, and ridiculous, and the paranoid detritus of his encounter with the earthie e-girls—or whatever they were called here.

"While you were talking to them, I struck up a conversation with someone named Brian, who was telling me, you know, about a million years ago, this place was all caves and quarries and canyons. Isn't that amazing?"

Bron took a breath. "Where's . . . Boston from here, Sam?"

"Boston?"

Among the ambling diggers, Bron turned, with Sam, down the road.

"Let me see. Boston—wait till I picture a globe, now . . . yeah, I guess it should be in about *that*—" Sam pointed toward the ground at an angle noticeably off plumb—"direction—maybe a couple or three thousand miles . . . if there still is a Boston."

The town was as sudden as the digs.

One small house was built into the rock-face; they walked around it to find houses on both sides of the road. They turned another corner. Somewhere near a public fountain the street developed paving.

And steps.

"It's up here a-ways . . . But the view is worth it. We share a double room—that's all they had."

"Okay. But I think I may take a nap as soon as we get there. I'll be up in a couple of hours. There's something I want to catch in town."

"Fine. We'll go out and get something to eat when you wake up." And (after they had mounted, and turned, and mounted again) entered a wooden door (in a white plaster wall) with painted green flowers on it, and real blue flowers growing beside it in a wooden box.

A woman who could have been the older sister of the man who'd served them at the shack led them up wooden stairs to a room where, at the foot of a bed with a blue cover, lay, next to Sam's, Bron's yellow plastic luggage sack.

He didn't really remember laying down.

He remembered wondering, half asleep, whether or not he should enlist Sam's help in searching out the company's whereabouts, and if he should do it before or after they ate.

Then he woke, something soft under his chin. He looked down—
at the rayon rim of a blue blanket, with white-gold light at the corner
of his vision. He turned his eyes toward it; and clamped them against
the brilliance.

He pushed the covers off and stood up, blinking. Through the
room's wide-swung shutters, behind the pulsing after-image, red-tiled
roofs stretched down the slope. At the horizon, a wedge of sun blazed
between two mountains.

Sunset?

He remembered they'd arrived late afternoon. Much less sore, he
felt as if he'd slept a good three hours.

Sam lay sprawled on the other side of the bed in a welter of twisted bedding, bare foot sticking over the end, bare arm hanging off the
side, mouth wide and breath growling.

"Sam . . . ?" Bron said, softly. "Sam . . . we'd better get started if
we're going to get any dinner. Sam—"

Sam said, "Huh—?" and pushed up to one elbow, squinting.

"The sun's going down . . . I don't know how long I slept, but you
said you wanted to get some dinner and I'd like to—"

"It's five o'clock in the morning!" Sam said and collapsed back on
the pillow, turning and tearing up more bedding.

"Oh." Bron looked out the window again.

The wedge of the sun's disk *was* getting higher.

" . . . Oh," he repeated, looked around the room, then got back
into bed, dragging some of the covers loose from the inert body beside him.

He lay there, feeling very alert, wondering if he should get up anyway and explore the dawning town on his own.

And fell asleep wondering.

"In *that* one!"

They had been looking fifteen minutes, now, for a place to have
late breakfast.

"Okay," Sam said, surprised.

But Bron was already pushing in the wooden doors. Sky flared on
the long panes. Sam followed him in.

At first Bron thought it was just because they were a theater company that, among the two dozen eating in the room, they seemed so
colorful. But he (in his silver shorts, black shirt, and red gloves) and

Sam (in his high boots and short blue toga) were quite as outstanding as the actors. Everyone else wore (of the three basic styles) the
one that was (basically) dull-colored pants that went down to the ankles and dull-colored shirts that went down to the wrists . . . though
some wore them rolled up. Still, everyone seemed animated, even
friendly. Most were workers from the archeological site.

The Spike was rearing back in her chair, her hands behind her neck,
laughing. Black suspenders crossed her bare shoulders clipped with
brass to the red Z. Abstracted from its environment, it was immediately
recognizable: a red plastic letter from a u-l street coordinate sign.

Bron said: "Hello . . ."

The Spike turned. "Hi!" And the smooth laugh. "Someone said they
saw you wandering around here yesterday. What'd you do? Follow
me all the way from Triton, braving border skirmishes and the danger of battle to reach my side? Come on, sit down—you *and* your
handsome friend—and have something to eat."

A young woman (the one with the glasses he'd seen rubbing her
eye on the road; face and hands were much cleaner, but her clothes
were just as dirty) cupped her tea in both hands, dusty nails arched
against the thick, white crock, and was saying to Charo, who bal-
anced her chin on her knuckles: "I think it's so wonderful that you
people can come and be with us, in spite of this war. It's an awful
war! Just awful!"

"Well, at least—" (From the voice, Bron thought for a moment it
was Windy: It was an earthie with a beard and lots of rings, in his
ears and on his fingers.) "—no one's fighting it with soldiers."

"Sit down," Sam urged Bron from behind. And, to the people on
the bench, when no one seemed about to make room, with his most
affable grin: "How about spreading out and letting us in here?"

Three people turned their heads sharply, as though astonished.
Hesitantly they looked at one another—one even tried to smile and,
finally, slid over on the bench: Two moved their chairs. It's as though,
Bron thought, their whole response, reaction, and delay times are different. Is that, he wondered, the seed of why they think we're bump-
tious barbarians and we think they're overrefined and mean-spirited?
Bron sat on the bench's end and felt very much an alien in an alien
world, while Sam dragged over a chair from somewhere, fell into it,
and reared back too.

"Are you going to be digging this morning?" someone asked the
Spike.

Who said: "Ha!" That was the rough part of her laugh. She tapped the forelegs of her chair on the floor. "Maybe in a couple of days. But the company organization takes up too much time right now."

"She's got to work so the rest of us can go off and dig," the hirsute Dian called from somewhere down the table.

The girl was saying to Charo: ". . . without *any* taxes at all? That just seems impossible to me."

Charo turned her chin on her fist: "Well, *we* were brought up to think of taxes as simply a matter of extortion by the biggest crooks who happen to live nearest to you. Even if they turn around and say, all right, we'll spend the money on things you can use, like an army or roads, that just turns it into glorified protection money, as far as we're concerned. I have to pay *you* money so *I* can live on *my* property; and you'll socially rehabilitate me if I don't . . . ? Sorry, no thanks. Even if you're going to use it to put a road by my door, or finance your social rehabilitation program, it's still extortion—"

"Wait a minute," the Spike said, leaning forward with both elbows on the table. "Now wait—we're *not* fighting this war with soldiers: There's no reason to start using actors and archeologists." She leaned around Charo: "We just have a far more condensed, and far more highly computerized system than you do here. All our social services, for instance, are run by subscription to a degree you just couldn't practice on Earth. Or even Mars—"

"But your subscriptions are sort of like our taxes—"

"They are not," Charo said. "For one, they're legal. Two, they're all charges for stated services received. If you don't use them, you don't get charged."

"You're supposed to have slightly less than one-fifth of your population in families producing children," the man with the beard and rings said, "and at the same time, slightly over a fifth of your population is frozen in on welfare . . ." Then he nodded and made a knowing sound with *m*'s that seemed so absurd Bron wondered, looking at the colored stones at his ears and knuckles, if he was mentally retarded.

"Well, first," Sam said from down the table, "there's *very* little overlap between those fifths—less than a percent. Second, because credit on basic food, basic shelter, and limited transport is automatic—if you don't have labor credit, your tokens automatically and immediately put it on the state bill—we don't support the huge, social service organizations of investigators, interviewers, office organizers, and administrators that are the main expense of your various welfare services here." (Bron noted even Sam's inexhaustible affability had developed a bright edge.) "Our very efficient system costs one-tenth per person to support as your cheapest, national, inefficient and totally inadequate system here. Our only costs for housing and feeding a person on welfare is the cost of the food and rent itself, which is kept track of against the state's credit by the same computer system that keeps track of everyone else's purchases against his or her own labor credit. In the Satellites, it actually costs minimally *less* to feed and house a person on welfare than it does to feed and house someone living at the same credit standard who's working, because the bookkeeping is minimally less complicated. Here, with all the hidden charges, it costs from three to ten times more. Also, we have a far higher rotation of people on welfare than Luna has, or either of the sovereign worlds. Our welfare isn't a social class who are born on it, live on it, and die on it, reproducing half the next welfare generation along the way. Practically *everyone* spends *some* time on it. And hardly anyone more than a few years. Our people on welfare live in the same co-ops as everyone else, not separate, economic ghettos. Practically nobody's going to have children while they're on it. The whole thing has such a different social value, weaves into the fabric of our society in such a different way, is essentially such a different process, you can't really call it the same thing as you have here."

"Oh, I can." The man fingered a gemmed ear. "Once I spent a month on Galileo; and I was on it!" But he laughed, which seemed like an efficient enough way to halt a subject made unpleasant by the demands of that insistent, earthie ignorance.

Another earthie Bron couldn't see laughed too:

"Different kinds of taxes. Different kinds of welfare: and both emblems of the general difference, grown up between each economy, that's gotten us into an economic deadlock that has made for—what did they used to call it in the papers? The hottest cold war in history . . . Until they broke down and just started calling it war."

"It's an awful war," the girl said again. "Awful. And *I* think it's wonderful that in spite of it you can be here, with us, like this. I think it's wonderful, your showing us your theater—I mean, MacLow, Hanson, Kaprow, McDowell, Jonas, they were all from Earth. And who's performing their work on Earth today? And I think it's wonderful that you're here helping us with the dig."

Bron wondered where you got food.

Sam, apparently, had asked, because he was coming back across the room with two trays, one of which he slipped in front of Bron with a grin, and one of which he clacked down at his own place.

Bron picked up a cup of what he thought was tea, sipped: broth. The rest of the breakfast was pieces of something that tasted halfway between meat and sponge cake . . . a sort of earthie Protyyn. He took another bite and said: "Excuse me, but—?"

The Spike turned.

" . . . I mean I realize you'll be busy with the company, but if you have a few minutes, perhaps I could see you . . . I mean we might go for a walk. Or something. If you had time."

She watched him, something unreadable transpiring deep in the muscles of her face. At last she said: "All right."

He remembered to breathe.

And turned back to his tray. "Good," he said, which sounded funny. So he said, "Thank you," which also wasn't quite right. So he said, "Good," again. He had smiled through all three.

The rest of breakfast was overridden by impatience for it to be over; the conversation, all tangential to the war, closed him round like the walls of the earthie's cell where he had spent—*but I can't tell her about that!*

The thought came, sudden and shocking.

Sam said I mustn't mention that to anyone!

Of course, that must mean her too . . . *especially* her, if she was here on a government invitation. From then on his thoughts were even more alien and apart. What *was* there, then, to talk to her about, tell her about, ask her support for, her sympathy in, her opinion of?

It was the most important thing that had happened to him since he had known her; and Sam's crazed paranoia had put it outside conversational bounds.

Wooden chair legs and bench cleats scraped the planks; diggers got up to go. Bron followed the Spike to the porch, wondering what he *would* say.

Sam was still inside, still talking, still eating, still explaining—*just* like in the co-op.

The door closed behind them. Bron said:

"I just can't get over the coincidence: running into you like this! What are there, now? Three billion people on Earth? I mean to have just met you in Tethys and then, on the other side of the Solar System, just on a side trip to—where are we? Mongolia! To run into you . . . just like that! The chances must be billions to one!"

The Spike breathed deeply, looked around the square, at the mountains beyond the housetops, at the cloud-smeared sky that, by day, was infinitely higher than the night's star-pocked roof.

"I mean," he said, "it could be a million billion to one! A *billion billion!*"

She started down the porch steps, glanced at him. "Look, you're supposed to be something of a mathematician." She smiled a faint smile, with faintly furrowed brows. "With the war, there're only a dozen—no, nine, actually—places on Earth a moonie *can* officially go—unless you're on one of those inane political missions you're always reading about in subversive flyers and never hearing mentioned on the channels. All of those nine places are as out of the way as this one, at least five hundred miles from any major population center. Our company's part of an exchange program between warring—or, in Triton's case, nearly warring—worlds so that *all* cultural contact isn't cut off: The first place they suggested we go was a cunning little village just on the south side of Drake's Passage—mean annual temperature minus seventeen degrees centigrade. Frankly, I doubt if more than three of the specified areas are even *livable* at any given time of Earth's year. None of the nine has a population of more than fifteen hundred. And in a town of fifteen hundred, it's hard for two strangers who come into it *not* to learn of each other's presence inside of six hours. Given the fact that both of us *are* on Earth at the same time, and that both of us *are* moonies of our particular temperament and type, I'd say the chances of our running into one another were—what? Fifty-fifty? Perhaps slightly higher?"

He wanted to say: But I'm *on* one of those political missions! And I have been taken prisoner, questioned, beaten, abused—

"What *are* you doing here, anyway?" she asked.

"Oh, I . . ." Confusion rose as he remembered Sam's injunction. "Well, I'm here . . . with Sam." More diggers came down the steps.

"What's Sam here for?"

"Well, he's . . . I . . ." He was oppressed with the thousand secrets he was not even sure he held, revelation of any of which might send worlds and moons toppling together in some disastrous, cosmic pinball. "Well, Sam's sort of . . ." What could he say about Sam that would not return them to the forbidden subject? Sam is a friend? A woman who's had a sex change? A liaison executive in the Outer Satellite Intelligence Department—

"—with the government?" the Spike suggested. "Well, then, I

won't go prying around anymore into that! Every time you ask a
question on this world—about *anything*—there's always someone at
your elbow to point out politely that, really, for your own good, you'd
rather not know. There's even part of Brian's work that's apparently
not supposed to pollute delicate little moonie minds. And from what
I can gather, it's nothing more insidious than that, a million years ago,
all this was under the edge of an inland sea. I like my first supposi-
tion better—that you followed me across the Solar System because
you simply couldn't bear to be without me. That's certainly more flat-
tering than that you're an official agent sent to keep tabs. The nicest
one, of course, is just that it really *is* a coincidence. I'll accept that."

Bron walked beside her, his head huge with phantom data, smiling
and unhappy. "Well, whether it's a billion to one or one to a billion,
I'm glad we met."

The Spike nodded. "I guess I am too. It *is* nice to see a familiar
face. How long have you been here?"

"Here? Just since last night. On Earth? I guess a few days. It's not
. . . well, a very friendly place."

She hunched her shoulders. "You've noticed? They all seem to be
trying so hard. To be friendly, I mean. But they just can't seem to figure out how." She sighed. "Or maybe it's just that coming from where
we do, we recognize and respond to different emblems of friendship.
Do you think that could be it?" But she was talking about something
different from what he meant: black and red uniforms, furnitureless
cells, small machines with fangs . . .

"Perhaps," he said.

"We've been here two days. We leave in a few days for Mars. Will I
run into you there, perhaps?"

"I . . ." He frowned. "I don't think we're going to Mars."

"Oh. You're from Bellona originally, aren't you?"

He nodded.

"What a shame. You could have shown us around for an
evening—though the clear areas are as out of the way on Mars as
they are here. We probably won't be allowed within seven leagues of
Bellona, or any place like it."

"Bellona's the only place on Mars I really know," he said. "When I
was growing up, I don't think I got out of it more than a dozen times."

She mumbled something conciliatory.

"But Mars is friendlier than Earth. At least it was when I left."

"That's understandable. I mean, even if the government's closer to

Earth's, the texture of life, just day to day, would have to be closer to life on the Satellites. The whole ratio, and type, of girl-made object to landscape must be nearer to what it is out on the moons." She laughed. "With all that *space* they have here getting in between people every time you turn around—you're going to be in for a small adventure when you try and find your friend again, by the way—I guess it's understandable why people don't know how to relate to other people here. Well, Earth's the place we all came from. Remember that. Remember that, I keep telling myself. Remember that. A few times, at home, I've met earthies, even become pretty friendly with a few, especially before the war—they always struck me as a little strange. But I racked it up to the fact that they were in a strange and unfamiliar place. I think the oddest thing I've noticed, in the two days I've been here, is that they're *all* so much *like* all the earthies I've known before! They pick up an object, and somehow they never seem to really *touch* it. They say something, and their words never completely wrap around their ideas. Do you know what I mean?"

He mumbled back appropriate *m*'s.

The Spike laughed. "I suppose this isn't the best way to promote interplanetary understanding and good will, is it? Maybe if everything comes out of the sea and the ground and the air as easily as it's supposed to here you just don't ever really *have* to think. How do you like life under an open sky? Do you feel you've come home, returned at last to the old racial spawning grounds? Or are you as anxious to get home as I am?"

"I guess I am pretty anxious." They turned a corner. "When will you be returning?"

She drew a breath. It was a comfortable, relaxed breath: He drew one too. All the tiny smells, he thought; if you like them, you probably liked life under the open sky. If you didn't, you couldn't. He doubted it was more complicated than that.

"Our trip to Mars," she explained, "is sort of open-ended. When push comes to shove, they're a good deal more liberal there, especially in things like cultural exchange. And, from reports, the audiences have slightly more catholic tastes. I admit, I'm looking forward to it."

"I wish I were going," he said.

They rounded another corner.

She said: "This is where we're staying." The building was low, large, and shoddily whitewashed. "The People's Cultural Co-Operative. The diggers have most of it but we have four rooms on the top floor."

"You're always getting stuck in someone's cellar or off in the attic." Memories of concert halls, transport compartments, a verdigrised drain in a fouled cement floor, crystal gaming pieces on boards that were neither go nor vlet. "I still just can't get over the coincidence, no matter how small or large it is, of—could I come in a while?" because she had stopped at the wooden door painted yellow and noticeably askew in its frame.

She smiled. "Really, I've got a lot of work to do this morning. Right after lunch I have to have interlocking part rehearsals planned out for the new work. It's one of our most ambitious, and at least four seconds of it are still pretty loose."

"I . . . I . . . wish I could see it!"

She smiled again. "It's too bad you didn't catch the last performance of the MacLow cycle last night. They were open to passers-by. It would be nice to do this one for you, but really it's more or less understood as part of the conditions of our being here that we do everything we possibly can for the locals. Except for the MacLows, we haven't even had any of the kids from the dig for audience. We're trying to keep it to the indigenous inhabitants."

Save the man at the shack and the woman at the guesthouse, Bron wasn't sure he'd seen any indigenous inhabitants. "Well, I guess that's . . ." He shrugged, smiled, and felt desperate.

She offered her hand. "Good-bye then. Even if I don't see you—"

"*Could* I see you again!" he blurted, taking her hand in both his. "I mean . . . maybe tonight. Later, after your performance. We'll go somewhere. We'll . . . do something! Something nice. Please. I . . . I *do* want to!"

She regarded him.

The desperation he felt was heady and violent. He started to release her hand, then squeezed it harder. Movement happened behind the skin of her face.

Was it pity for him?

He hated it.

Was she searching herself?

What did she have to search for!

Was she considering things to say?

Why didn't she just say, "yes"?

"All right," she said. "Yes. I'll go with you this evening. After our last performance."

He nearly dropped her hand. Why didn't she *just* say—

"Is that all right," she asked, with that slight, familiar smile, "with you?"

He nodded, abruptly wondering: Where *would* they go? Back to his guesthouse? To her place? No—he had to take her somewhere. First. And he was a hundred million kilometers from anywhere he knew.

"Meet me here," she said. "At nine. How's that? It should be just about half an hour after sunset, if I remember correctly."

"Yeah," he said.

"And we'll go out somewhere."

He nodded.

"Good." She pulled her hand away, glanced at him again, hesitated: "Till nine then?" She pushed open the door. "I'll meet you here."

"That's awfully nice of you . . ." he remembered to say.

"Not at all," she said. "It'll be fun," and closed the door.

He stood on the narrow sidewalk thinking something was very wrong.

It was not exactly an adventure finding Sam again. But in the hour and a quarter it took him, he decided that whoever had laid out the village must have been certifiably insane. And while there were some jobs that the certifiably insane could do quite well, and while metalogics, as Audri occasionally used to joke at him, was one, city planning was definitely not:

There was a living establishment—the People's Co-Op—and there, to its left, was some sort of shopping area; and around the corner from that was a small eating place. All fine. Wandering through the small streets, he found another collection of small shops: Was there an eating place around the corner to *its* right? No. Was there a living establishment—of *any* sort—to *its* left? No! He had been quite prepared to find the urban units arranged differently from those on Tethys, as Tethys's were different from the units of Lux, or Bellona. (Indeed, Tethys employed seven different types of urban units—though for practical purposes you only had to be familiar with two of them to find anything you wanted in most of the city—and Bellona reputedly, though only one was common, employed nine.) After half an hour it began to dawn that there *was* no arrangement to this city's urban units. Half an hour more, and he began to wonder if this city *had* urban units. The only logic he could impute to the layout at all— after having walked up some streets many times and been unable to find others at all that he knew he'd passed—was that most of the shops and eating places seemed to be in one area, within three or four streets of the central square. For the rest, it was catch-as-catch-can.

He found the street with the stone steps just by accident.

In the backyard of the guesthouse, Sam sat at a white enameled table, by his elbow a tall glass of something orange with a straw in it and green leaves sticking out the top. He was looking into a portable reader, his thumb again and again clicking the skimming lever.

"Sam, what is there to do around here at night?"

Click. "Look at the stars, smell the clear air, wander out along the wild hills and meadows." Click-click-click. "That's what I'm planning to do, anyway. If you're stuck in the far reaches of Outer Mongolia, even in this day and age, there isn't much *to* do, except figure out more and more interesting ways to relax." Click-click.

"Do *with* somebody. I have to take someone out tonight."

Click; Sam reached for his drink, missed it, got it, and maneuvered the straw into his mouth. Click-click. "The woman you went running after, after breakfast?" He put the drink back on the table (Click); the edge of the glass was just over the side.

Bron narrowed an eye, wondering if he should move it. "I said I would take her someplace exciting. Tonight."

"I can't think of anyplace you could—" Sam looked up, frowning. "Wait a second." He moved the glass back on the table.

Bron breathed.

Sam dug among the rack of pockets down the side of his toga, pulled out a square sheaf of colored paper, which he opened into a rectangle.

Knowing full well what it was, Bron said: "What's that?"

"Money." Sam said. "Ever use it?"

"Sure." There were quite a few places on Mars that still took it.

Sam counted through the sheaf. "There's a place I've been to a couple of times when I've passed through here—about seventy-five miles to the north." He flipped up more bills. "There, that should be enough to take you, your friend, and half her theater commune." While Sam separated the bills, Bron wondered how Sam knew she was in the theater. But then, maybe he'd found out at breakfast. And Sam was saying: "It's a restaurant—where they still take this stuff. *Some* people consider it mildly elegant. Maybe your friend would enjoy it. If nothing else, it's a giggle." Sam held out the bills.

"Oh." Bron took them.

"That'll cover it, if I remember things right. It's quite an old place. Dates all the way back to People's Capitalist China."

Bron frowned. "I thought that only lasted ten years or so?"

"Six. Anyway, it's something to take a gawk at, if you're in the neighborhood. It's called *Swan's Craw*—which I always wondered about. But that's Capitalist China for you."

"You say it's seventy-five miles? I don't remember quite how much a mile is, but I suspect it's too far to walk." Bron folded the bills again and wondered where to put them.

"By a bit. I'll tell the landlady to make you a reservation. They'll send a transport for you—you know about tipping and all that sort of thing?"

"In the circles I moved in as a youth, you picked up the etiquette of money along with your monthly checkup for arcane and sundry venereal diseases." The bill showing was a thousand something—which he knew was as likely to be very little as it was to be a lot. "What *is* the tipping rate here?" he thought to ask "Fifteen percent? Twenty?"

"Fifteen is what I was told the first time I went; nobody looked unhappy when I left."

"Fine." Bron had no pockets in this particular outfit so he folded the money again, put it in his other hand, then transferred it back. "You weren't planning to go there, were you? I mean, if you needed this for yourself . . . ?"

"I was planning definitely *not* to go," Sam said. "I've been half a dozen times before. I really do prefer the open rocks and grass, the night, the stars. I brought the scrip specifically to get you off my neck for at least one evening while we were here, hopefully at something you'd enjoy."

"Oh," Bron said. "Well . . . thanks." He looked for a pocket or purse again, again remembered he had none. "Eh . . . Where do we go to pick up the transport?"

"Don't worry," Sam smiled slightly. "They pick you up."

"Ah-ha!" Bron said, and felt knowing—"it's *that* kind of place—" because there were no such places in the satellites.

"Elegant," Sam repeated, putting his eyes back down to the reader. Click-click-click. "Hope you enjoy yourself." Click.

In the room, Bron sat on the bed and wondered what to do till nine o'clock. Minutes into his wonderings, the landlady came in, carrying a tray on which was a tall glass filled with something orange, a straw, and leaves.

"You are going to the *Craw* this evening, with a friend? It is very nice there. You will enjoy it. The reservations have all been made. Worry about nothing more. If you, or your friend, wish to go in period dress, just let me know . . . ? Many people enjoy that."

"Oh," Bron said. "Sure . . ." with a dozen memories returning from his Bellona youth (as the landlady retired): He knew exactly the dress for an expensive, male prostitute, going to a similar, money-establishment on Mars. Certainly *not* period (the precredit period when money was in use) dress. That marked you immediately as one of those appalling tourists who visited such a place once, twice, maybe three times in their lives, who moved through leaving gentle smiles and snide chuckles. You went in period dress if you owned your own and were known by the establishment; anything else consigned you to that category of velvet contempt for those who did things Not Done. Also, the Spike didn't *know* where they were going. Her own dress was likely to be something modern and informal. On the other hand, he didn't want to go looking like one of those oblivious yokels who wander into such places with no sense that they were, indeed, in a historical institution. No matter how inappropriate the Spike's dress, if his own, unthinkingly, merely emphasized it, even if she were not offended, she would certainly *not* be impressed.

And this was Earth—*not* Mars. His experience of such places was not only from another world: It was from fifteen years in the past. But, he found himself thinking, the essence of such places *was* anachronism. Even if styles themselves changed in such establishments, the structure of stylistic deployment remained constant. In fact, an elderly woman client (with silver eyelids and cutaway veils, who had once taken him to such a place, where she herself had been going for twenty years) had once said to him as much in Bellona. (Her veils and lids recalled, her name and face somehow escaped . . .) With such ponderings and reveries, he occupied the rest of the morning: His own clothes, he decided, the ones he had brought, would provide his outfit, whatever he wore. He drank his drink, went out into the garden, looking for Sam—who was gone.

He went back into his room. Well, his own clothes and Sam's; he was sure Sam wouldn't mind. And he *had* gone looking for him to ask.

During the afternoon he spent at least two hours sitting in the garden trying forceably to relax. Each time, the landlady appeared with a drink. He'd assumed it contained some drug or other—caffeine, alcohol, sugar? But, from all effects, it was metabolically neutral. (Vaguely he remembered something about an Earth law preventing the admin-

istration of drugs of any sort without prior and complicated an-
nouncement and consent.) By eight he had laid out his clothing:

One silver sleeve with floor-length fringe (Sam had two in his
bag, but *only* a prostitute would go to such a place so flamboyantly
symmetrical: Two would have been all right for breakfast, barely acceptable at lunch. But supper—?) and a silver harness (his own)
rather like a Tethys e-girl's, and the silver briefs that matched it: a
black waist-pouch (Sam's) for the money. No pouch at all (implying
secret pockets) would have marked him (again) as a prostitute. His
own pouch with its inset mirrors and flashing lights, in such a situation would have identified him as a prostitute's client. He agonized
over the footwear for half an hour, till suddenly he had a brilliant
idea: First his own, soft black boots—then he rummaged Sam's
makeup kit out of the bosom of Sam's bag and, with the plastic lac-
quer, carefully painted his gold eyebrow (occasionally stopping to
brush at the shaggy real one with his thumb) black.

He had the lacquer-remover out, sure that he would have to redo it
half a dozen times; he had never done it before (at least not in black)
and was sure he would get paint all over his face. Crane and squint as
he would at the magnifying mirror, however, he had done, with three
strokes, a perfect job.

There!

Balance, he thought; asymmetry, and coherence. All the ideals of
fashion bowed to, yet none groveled at.

And it was ten to nine.

He pulled on the chosen clothes, hurried downstairs, out the door,
into the deep-blue evening, and down the street's stone steps (fringe a
waterfall of light), thinking: Don't think in urban units. Don't. There
aren't any!

First he hoped to arrive a minute or two before she came out; then
that she would be already there so he would not have to wait.

As he rounded the corner of the People's Co-Operative, the yellow
door opened; three people came out. Two were diggers. The person
they said good-bye to, who waved after them, and who now leaned
against the doorjamb to wait, in something sleeveless and ankle-
length and black, her short hair silver now as Bron's (or rather Sam's)
sleeve fringe, was the Spike.

The diggers passed. One smiled. Bron nodded. The Spike, still leaning, with folded arms, called: "Hello! That's timing for you!" and laughed. Smoothly. On one forearm, she wore a silvery gauntlet, damasked with intricate symbols. As he approached, she stood up, held out her hands.

Left arm a-dangle with silver, he took her hands in his, and chuckled. "How good to see you again!"—feeling for a moment that he was twenty and she was thirty and this were some assignation on another world.

"I hope," she said, "that we're not going anyplace where I'll need my shoes . . . ? If we are, I'll dash up and get some—"

"We are going someplace where someone as stunning as you may wear—" There was a ritual completion to the line:—*anything you can afford, including my heart on your sleeve.* But he was not twenty: This was here, this was now—"anything you like." Their hands joined in a four-way knot. "Actually, I had a little place in mind about seventy-five miles to the north of here—the *Swan's Craw*?" He smiled. "No don't laugh. That's just Capitalist China for you. It wasn't very long-lived, so we have to be tolerant."

She wasn't laughing though; she was beaming. "You know—I had the *slightest* precognition that we just might be heading there." She leaned toward him conspiratorially. "I'm afraid I don't have any money, though. And wouldn't know what to do with it if I did. I've never been near anyplace that ever used it. Windy and Charo went the first night we came—I was busy with company matters—and though I've got plenty of credit, I'm afraid they used up the quota of scrip for the three of us."

He thought fondly: You'd make a lousy whore: That's the line you use afterwards. But she probably meant it, which made him, momentarily, even more fond. "The evening's on me—Sam, actually. He's government. Money? He's got a limitless supply, and he's invited us to enjoy ourselves."

"How very nice of him! Why isn't he coming with us?"

"Hates the stuff himself." Bron turned, took her arm. They started down the street. "Won't touch it. When he's on the old racial spawning grounds, it's all rocks and grass and stars for him."

"I see . . ."

"You haven't been there before, have you?" He halted. "I'll be honest, it's *my* first time . . ."

"No, I haven't. And Windy and Charo were tantalizingly vague in their descriptions."

"I *see* . . ." He frowned at her silvered hair. "How did you know where we'd be going, though?"

Her laugh (and she started him walking again by the gentlest pressure on their joined arms—as if he were twenty and she from another world) was silvery as her hair. "When you're in Outer Mongolia, even in this day and age, I suspect they're just not that many places to go."

A whispering, which, for seconds, had been on the edge of consciousness, suddenly centered his attention.

Bron looked up.

Something dark crossed the paler dark between the roofs and, humming even louder, returned to hover, then to settle, across the road.

It was sleek, unwinged, about the size of the vehicle he and Sam had ridden in for the last leg of their journey here.

The side opened—let down like a drawbridge on heavy, polished chain, its purple padding held with six-inch purple poms.

"Why," the Spike exclaimed, "that must be for us! How did they ever find us, I wonder?"

"I believe it *is* for us."—but, with a pressure just firmer than that with which she had started him walking, he held her back from bolting forward. "Someone once told me they worked by sense of smell, but I've never really understood it. How did your performance go tonight?" Nonchalantly, he maintained their ambling pace. "Was this evening's fortunate audience appreciative? I gather you've been working pretty hard on this one, both from what you said and what Windy—"

At which point the Spike whispered: "Oh—!" because four footmen had come out to stand at the four corners of the lowered platform—four naked, gilded, rather attractive young . . . women? Bron felt a moment of disorientation: On Mars, the footmen would have been male, usually themselves prostitutes (or one-time prostitutes), there for the delectation of the ladies paying the bill. But male prostitution was illegal on Earth. The women probably *were* prostitutes, or had been at one time or another; and were there for *his* delectation . . . Well, yes, he thought, he *was*, officially, paying—which did not upset him in itself. But the reversal of roles was odd. After all, it was the Spike's delectation *he* was concerned with this evening. And, Charo aside, she had made it clear her lesbian leanings were rather intellectual. He said: "I'd be interested to know what you thought of Earth audiences now that you've had another performance."

"Well, I . . . ." They reached the platform. "Um . . . good evening!" she blurted to the woman beside her, who smiled, nodded.

Bron smiled too, thinking: She's *talking* to them! Which again (he realized, as a whole part of his youth flickered and faded) would be all right if *she* were paying and had known the young . . . lady on a previous occasion . . .

They walked across the plush ramp, entered the chamber with its red and coppery cushions, its viewing windows, its several plush hangings, its scarlet-draped walls.

As he guided the Spike to one of the couches, she turned to him. "*Isn't* there someplace where you can find out what it all *costs*?"

Which made him laugh out loud. "Certainly," he said. "If you'd really like to know." Again, that youthful moment returned—the client who had first taken him to such a place; his own demand for the same importunate information. "Let me see—sit down. There. . . ." He sat beside her, on her left, took the arm of the couch and tugged. Nothing. (Is everything on this planet backward? he wondered.) "Excuse me . . ." He reached across her, tugged the arm on her right. It came up, revealing on its underside, in a neatly-glassed frame, a card printed in terribly small type, headed: *Explication de Tarif*.

"You can find out there," he explained, "about the salary of everyone we will have anything to do with this evening, either in person or by their services, the cost of all the objects we shall see or use, or that are used for us, the cost of their upkeep, and how the prices we shall be charged are computed—I wouldn't be surprised, considering this is Earth, if it even went into the taxes."

"*Ohhhh* . . ." she breathed, turning in the comfortable seat to read.

The ramp was hauling closed. The footmen, inside now, took their places.

He looked at her shoulders, hunched in concentration. He suppressed the next chuckle. There was nothing to do: For the duration she simply must be the prostitute, and he must play the client. She was the young, inexperienced hustler, committing all the vulgarities and gaucheries natural to the situation. He must be charmed, be indulgent, assured in his own knowledge of the proper. Otherwise, he thought, I shall never get through the evening without laughing at her outright.

She was, he realized, reading the *whole* thing—which, frankly, was more like a diligent tourist. The real pleasure, of course, was in the amounts, and those you could get at a glance: *they* were printed in boldface.

The footmen, at the four corners of the chamber, sat at little tables that folded from the wall. Tables? Sitting? That was bizarre. What, he reflected, was a footman for if he (or she) did not remain on foot?

The chamber rocked. Ripples rained the drapes. He touched the Spike's arm. "I think we're on our way. . . ."

She looked up, looked around, and laughed. They rocked, they jogged. On a view window a darkness, either clouds or mountains, moved. "This thing must date back from when they first got gravity under control!" she exclaimed. "I doubt if I've ever *been* in a piece of transportation as old as this before!" She put her hand on his, squeezed it.

Moments later, they locked course; the jogging stopped. On cue, one of the footmen rose, walked toward them, stepping gingerly among the cushions, stopped before them, and inclined her head: "Would you like a drink before dinner . . . ?"

And in one horrifying moment, Bron realized he could not remember the name of that most expensive of drinks! What leapt to his mind was the name of that one, indeed, tastier, but cheaper—and by which one always rated clients Definitely Second Rate (far and above the most usual type) if they ordered it, or even suggested it.

The Spike was reading the *Tarif* again.

Discomfort concealed—Bron was sure it was concealed—he touched her arm once more. "My dear, the footman would like to know if you wanted anything."

Her eyes came up. Smiling, she gave an embarrassed little shrug. "Oh, I don't—well . . . really . . ."

He'd hope the misremembered name had passed her eyes, that its huge price had caught them.

She blinked at him, still smiling, still confused.

It hadn't. (She would make a lousy whore, he thought, a trifle less fondly.) He said: "Do you have any . . . Gold Flower Nectar?" The small of his back moistened; but it *was* the only name he could remember. (His forehead moistened too.) "No—*No* . . . I think we'll have something more expensive. I mean, you must have something *more* expensive that . . . well, don't you . . . ?"

"We have Gold Flower Nectar," the young woman said, nodding. "Shall I bring two?"

A drop of sweat ran down his arm, inside Sam's borrowed sleeve. Seconds into the silence, the Spike said, glancing back and forth between the footmen and Bron, "Yes! That sounds marvelous."

The footman nodded, started to turn, then, with a quizzical expression, asked: "You're from Mars, aren't you?" Bron thought: She thinks I'm a cheap Bellona john and the Spike is a *really* dumb whore! A sweat drop ran out of his sideburn Ed down his jaw.

The Spike laughed again. "No. I'm afraid we're moonies. We're part of the cultural exchange program."

"Oh." The woman nodded, smiled. "We keep Gold Flower Nectar mostly for the Martian clients—it really *is* very good," which went directly to Bron, with a wink. "Earthies hardly ever even *know* about it!" She bowed again, turned, and went back between the curtains behind her table.

The Spike took Bron's arm now, leaned closer. "Isn't that marvelous! She thought we were from a *world!*" She giggled. For a moment her forehead touched his cheek. (He almost flinched.) "I know it's all play-acting, but it really *is* exciting . . . if only as theater."

"Well . . ." he said, trying to smile, "I'm glad you're enjoying yourself."

She squeezed his wrist. "And the way you seem to know exactly what's going on, you really *are* the perfect person to go with!"

"Well . . . thank you," he said. "Thank you," because he could think of nothing else to say.

"Tell me . . ." And once more she leaned. "Isn't 'footmen' a masculine word, though—I mean on Earth?"

Though he was no longer perspiring, he felt miserable. Her attempt at distraction merely goaded. Bron shrugged. "Oh, well . . . isn't 'e-girl' a feminine one?"

"Yes," she said, "but this *is* Earth, where such things traditionally— I've been led to understand—matter."

He shrugged again wishing that she would simply leave him alone. The footman returned, drinks on a mirrored tray.

He handed the Spike hers, took his. "Why don't you let me pay as we go along," he suggested.

"It would be just as convenient if you paid at the end," the footman said, still smiling, but a little less. "Though if you'd prefer . . . ?"

The Spike sipped. "From what we hear at home, convenience is supposed to be very important on Earth. Why don't we do it that way?" then she glanced at Bron; who nodded.

The footman nodded too—"Thank you"—and retired to her table.

Bron sipped the drink, whose flavor was all nostalgia, all memory, all of which announced so blaringly that it was not fifteen years ago (when he had last tasted it), that this was not Mars: that there were footwomen here instead of footmen; that convenience was the tradition (Then why, he wondered, momentarily angry, indulge an institution whose only purpose was inconvenient extravagance?), and that he was an uninitiate tourist.

No!

Play-acting it may be!

But *that* was a role he could not accept. Both temperament and experience, however inadequate and outdated, denied it. He turned to the beaming Spike. "You still haven't told me how the performance went this evening."

"Ah . . ." she said, leaning back and crossing her bare feet on the cushions before her, "the performance . . . !"

Three times (Bron sat, dreading each one) the other three footmen offered them (the Spike *liked* Gold Flower Nectar—well, he *liked* it too. But that wasn't the point) another drink, the second with the traditional nuts the third with small fruits—olives, which he remembered as the hallmark of the best places. They offered three kinds, too: black, green, and yellow. He was impressed, which depressed him more. The client's job was *to* impress, not *be* impressed. It was the client's job to supervise effects, to oversee, to direct the excellent performance. It was not, at this point anyway, her (or his) place to be carried away. With the next drink, they were offered a tray of small fish and meat delicacies, served on savory pastry bases. With the last, they were offered sweets which Bron refused. "Afterwards," he explained to her, "they'll probably have some quite incredible confections, so we can pass these up in all good faith."

She nodded appreciatively.

Then, there was light through the view window. Excitedly, the Spike leaned across him to look. The chamber began to jog and jerk. Abruptly the jerking ceased: They'd landed. The purple-pommed wall-ramp let down on its chains. Outside lights blazed in the distance and the darkness. The footmen rose to take their positions at the ramp's four corners.

As they were walking between the first two, Bron said (in his mind he had gone over just how to say it several times): "I think it was presumptuous to assume we were from Mars—*or* the Satellites. Or *any*place. How should they know, just from what we order, where we're from?" He didn't say it loudly. But he didn't say it softly, either.

By the end of his statement, his glance, which had gone with calculated leisure around the night, reached the Spike—who was frowning.

With folded arms, she slowed at the edge of the plush (by the last footman). "I suspect," she said, with one slightly raised eyebrow, "it was because you called them 'footmen.' On the *Explication de Tarif* they're called 'hostesses.' 'Footmen' is probably the Martian term."

Bron frowned, wondering why she chose *that* statement to slow down on. "Oh . . ." he said, stepping from the end of the ramp, his eyes again going around the rocks, the railing, the waterfall. "Oh, well . . . of course. Well, perhaps we'd better . . ."

But the Spike, walking too, moved on a step ahead.

Beyond the red velvet ropes that railed the curving walk, rocks broke away, broke away further. Floodlights, lighting this tree or that bush, made the sky black and close as a u-l ceiling.

"Isn't it odd," the Spike said, her statement oddly tangent to Bron's thoughts, "you can't tell whether it's endless or enclosed—the whole space, I mean."

Bron looked over another rail, where the torrents crashed. Above, was the moon. "I think . . ." he said (she turned to look too), "it's endless."

"Oh, I didn't even *see* that!" Her arm brushed his as she stepped around him to the rope. "Why it's—"

"Look," he said, not meaning the scenery. She looked back at him. "I think, convenience or no, I *must* pay them now—if only for the theater." And before she could comment, or protest, he went back to the purple platform.

Bron stopped before the nearest, gold-skinned footman, his hand on his purse. "You served us that last drink, didn't you?—and it was certainly a marvelous one, considering my thirst and the exhausting day I've had till now. Whatever it says on the menu . . . ten, eleven? Twelve . . . ?" (It had said eight-fifty.) He fingered into the drawn, leather neck—"Well, your smile alone made it worth half again that much."—and pulled out two bills, the top one the twenty he'd expected. "Do you want it—?"

The footman's gilded lids widened.

"Do you . . . ?"

Separating the twenty off from the other bill (which was a thirty), Bron stepped up on the platform, held the bill high overhead. "Here it is, then—jump for it! Jump!"

The footman hesitated a moment, bit at her golden, lower lip, eyes still up, then leaped, grabbing Bron's shoulder.

He let go of the bill. While it fluttered, he shrugged off her hand

and stepped toward the next footman, the next bill in his fingers. "But you, my dear—" He felt ridiculous engaging in such banter, however formalized, with women—"you provided the first one, the one that relieved the parching thirst we arrived with. That alone triples the price! Here, my energetic one—" He held the note down beside his knee. "Do you want it? There it is. Crawl for it! Crawl . . . !" He let the bill flutter to the ground, and turned again, as the woman dove after it. "And *you* two—" He pulled out two more bills, one in each hand—"don't think I've forgotten the services you rendered. Yet . . . somehow though I remember, I cannot quite distinguish them. Here is a twenty and a thirty. You may fight over which one of you deserves which." He tossed the two bills up in the air, and stepped over one of the women who was already down on her knees, scrabbling after one of the others. Behind him, he heard the second two start to go at it.

Bron stepped from the platform (cries; scufflings; more cries behind him) and walked toward the Spike. She stood with palms pressed together at her chin, eyes wide, mouth opened—suddenly she bent with laughter.

Bron glanced back to where, on the pommed purple, the four footmen scuffled, laughing and pummeling one another.

"That's . . ." the Spike began, but broke up again. "That's *marvelous!*"

Bron took her arm and turned her along the walkway.

Still laughing, she craned back to look. "If it wasn't so perfect in itself, I'd use it in a production!" Her eyes came back to his. "I'd never have thought money could *still* do that . . . ?"

"Well, considering the mythology behind it, and its rarity—"

The Spike laughed again. "I suppose so, but—"

"I spent a spell as a footman myself, once," Bron said, which wasn't exactly untrue: He had once shared a room in Bellona with two other prostitutes who had; and had even been offered a job . . . something had come up, though. "It gets to you."

"That's really incredible!" The Spike shook her head. "I'm surprised they don't tear it to pieces!"

"Oh, you learn," Bron said. "And of course, like all of this, it's all basically just a kind of . . . well, Annie-show." He gestured toward the rocks, the sky, the falls, which ran under the transparent section of path they walked over (moss, froth, and clear swirls of green passed beneath his black boots and her bare feet) toward fanning columns of green glass that were the *Craw's* entrance.

The Spike rubbed a finger on her gauntlet. "This—if you look closely—has logarithmic scales. The middle band turns, so you can use it as a sort of slide rule." She laughed. "From what I've always heard, you needed a computer to figure almost anything to do with money. But I guess somebody used to it gets by on pure flamboyance."

Bron laughed now. "Well, it helps to know what you're doing. It *is* dangerous. It's addictive, no question. But I think the Satellites' making it illegal is going too far. And you just couldn't set up anything on this scale in the u-l." The columns, seventy or eighty of them he could see, rose perhaps a hundred feet. "Besides, I doubt it would even catch on. We're—you're just the wrong temperament out there . . . I mean, I *like* living in a voluntaristic society. With money, though, I suppose getting your hands on a bit once or twice a year is enough."

"Oh, certainly . . ." The Spike folded her arms, glanced back between them again. Bron put his arm round her shoulder.

He glanced back too.

The ramp had closed; the footmen were gone.

There were other walkways, other craft, other people ambling among the rocks.

Another footman, breasts and hips and hair dull bronze, stood beside what looked like a green ego-booster booth, curtained with multicolored sequins. Bron pressed a small bill into the bronze palm. "Please . . . ?"

She turned, drew the curtain. The interior was white enamel. The man who stepped out wore the traditional black suit with black silk lapels, black cummerbund, and small black bow at the collar of his white, white shirt. "Good evening, Mr. Helstrom." He stepped forward, smiled, nodded—"Good evening, ma'am."—smiled, nodded to the Spike, who, somewhat taken aback, said:

"Uh . . . hello!"

"How nice to see you tonight. We're delighted that you decided to drop by this evening. Let's all just go this way—" They were already walking together among the first fanning pillars of marbled green— "and we'll see what we can do about finding you a table. What mood are you in tonight . . . water? fire? earth? air? . . . perhaps some combination? Which would you prefer?"

Bron turned, smiled at the Spike. "Your choice—?"

"Oh, well, I . . . I mean, I don't know what . . . well, could we have all four? Or would that be . . . ?" She looked questioningly at Bron.

"One *could* . . ." The majordomo smiled.

"But I think," Bron said, "it might be a bit distracting." (She was charming . . . *All* four? Really!) "We'll settle for earth, air, and water; and leave fire for another time." He looked at the Spike. "Does that suit you . . . ?"

"Oh, certainly," she said, quickly.

"Very well, then. Just come this way."

And they were beyond the columns. The domo, though pleasant, Bron decided, was getting away with only the bare necessities. Those little extras of personality and elan that individualized the job, the evening, the experience (" . . . that you can never pay for but, nevertheless, you *do*," as one rather witty client of his had once put it) were missing. Of course, they were something you got by revisiting such a place frequently—*not* by being a tourist. But Bron was sure he looked used to such places; and the Spike's evident newness to the whole thing should have elicited some more humane reaction. They certainly looked like they *might* come back.

"Just up here."

The domo led them onto the grass . . . Yes, they *were* inside. But the ceiling, something bright and black and multilayered and interleaved, was very far away.

"Excuse me . . . *this* way, sir."

"*Uh?*" Bron looked down. "Of course." It was, very simply, Bron realized, that he did not like the man.

"This grass . . . !" the Spike exclaimed. "It feels so wonderful to walk on!" She ran a few steps up the slope, turned and, with an ecstatic shrug, beamed back at them.

Bron smiled, and noticed that the domo's professional smile had softened a little. Which damped Bron's own a bit.

"We roll it once a day and trim it twice a week," the majordomo said. "It's nice when someone notices and actually bothers to comment."

The Spike held out her hand to Bron, who walked up, took it.

"It *is* a beautiful place!" she said; and to the domo: "Which way did you say . . . ?"

The domo, still smiling, and with a slight bow—"This way, then"—started up the slope, in a direction Bron noticed was *not* the one they'd begun in.

The waterfall crashing outside apparently began in here, several levels above. For almost ten minutes they could hear it. Between high rocks, they climbed—

"Oh, *my* . . ." the Spike whispered.

—and saw it.

"Will this do?" The domo pulled out one of the plush chairs, moved around the table on the grass, pulled out the other.

They were practically at the top of the immense enclosure. Water frothed beside them, rushing away down the rocks, both in front and in back of them. They had a view of tier after tier of the restaurant.

"What a breathtaking location . . . !" the Spike exclaimed.

"Some people don't like to walk this far," the domo explained. "But you seemed to be enjoying yourself. Personally, I think it's worth it."

Bron's hand was on his purse, prepared to offer the ritual bill and the ritual request for a better table. But it was a good location. Really, he thought, you shouldn't accept the first place they showed you— clients never did on Mars; besides, he wanted to make the man work.

"Sir . . . ?" The majordomo raised an attendant eyebrow.

"Well . . ." Bron mused. "I don't know. . . ."

"Oh *do* let's sit here! It was such a lovely walk, after such a lovely ride. I can't picture a happier destination!"

Bron smiled, shrugged, and for the second time felt the perspiration of embarrassment break on the small of his back. The Spike was overdoing it. They *should* have been shown some other place first and this one second. That would have been the proper way. Who *did* these people think they were? "This is fine," Bron said, shortly. "Oh . . . here." He pressed the bill on the domo—it would look ridiculous to hunt out a smaller one.

"Thank you, sir." The nod and the smile were brief. "Would you like another drink while I bring you the menu?"

"Yes," Bron said. "Please."

"You were drinking . . . ?"

And Bron remembered the name of that drink: *Chardoza.* "Gold Flower Nectar."

"It *is* delicious!" The Spike dropped into her chair, put her elbows on the high arms and locked both hands, inelegantly, beneath her chin, stretched both feet under the table and crossed her ankles.

The domo's laugh was, momentarily, almost sincere.

The metal leaves on the table's centerpiece fell open. The drinks rolled out on marbled, green-glass trays.

Bron frowned—but then, the domo would have known what they were drinking before Bron had even summoned him from his cabinet.

Bron sat in his own chair across from the Spike and thought: She is totally delightful and totally upsetting. Somehow, though, the realization had crystallized: Play the client as he might, there was no way he could fit her into the role of his younger self. Her gaucheries, enthusiasms, and eccentricities simply had nothing to do with his own early visits to the *Craw's* Bellona brothers—for one thing, she simply did not despise him the way he had despised those who had escorted him there, so that, in the game of dazzling and impressing in which he was busily racking up points, she was just not playing. What am I doing here? he thought, suddenly. Twice now he had been reduced to the sweat of mortification—and probably would be so reduced again before the evening ended. But at least (he thought on) I know *what* to be mortified about. Both discomforts and pleasures assured him this was his territory. The sweat dried. He picked up the cold glass, sipped. And realized that, for the duration of his thoughts, the Spike had been silent. "Is something the matter?"

She lifted her eyebrows, then her chin from her meshed knuckles. "No . . ."

Smiling, he said: "Are you sure? Are you positive? There's nothing about my manner, my bearing, my clothing that you disapprove of?"

"Don't be silly. You know your way around places like this—which makes it twice the fun. You've obviously taken a great deal of time with your clothes—which I thoroughly appreciate: That's why I didn't go with Windy and Charo. *They* insisted on going in their digging duds, right after work."

"Well, the joy of a place like this is that you *can* come as formal or as informal as you like."

"But if you're going to indulge an anachronism, you might as well indulge it all the way. Really," and she smiled, "if I were the type to get upset over *anyone's* clothes, Windy would have cured me long ago." Now she frowned. "I suppose the reason I didn't go with them is that I know, deep down, part of his reason for coming is to be scandalous, or at least to dare anyone to be scandalized. Which can be fun, if you're in the mood. But I have other things to do, right now— The two of you, in your youth, shared a profession."

"Yes. I know," Bron said, but could not, for the moment, remember how he knew. Had she alluded to it? Or had Windy?

"He has some very unpleasant memories associated with places like this."

"Then why does he come back?"

She shrugged. "I suppose . . . well, he wants to show off."

"And be scandalous?"

Her lower lip inside her mouth the Spike smiled. "Charo said she had a fine time. They said I should really try and come if I could."

"Then I hope you have an equally, or even finer, time."

She nodded. "Thank you."

The domo, at his shoulder, announced: "Your menu . . . ma'am?"

"Oh!" The Spike sat up, took the huge, velvet-backed and many-paged folder.

". . . sir?"

Bron took his, trying to recall if, on Mars, they gave the menu first to the man, then the woman; or was it first to the younger, then the older; or was it the client, then the—

"Perhaps you'd like a little more air than that?" The domo reached up, snapped his fingers. The interleaved mirrors (after their ten-minute, uphill hike, only a dozen feet above them now) began to rise, turn, and fold back from the stars.

A breeze touched them.

The tablecloth's edge brushed Bron's thigh.

"I'll just leave you for a minute to make your choices. When you reach your decision—" A smile, a nod—"I'll be back." And he was gone behind a rock.

The Spike shook her head, wonderingly. "What an amazing place!" She turned her chair (the seat swiveled) to look down the near slope. "I mean, I don't think I've ever *been* in an enclosed space this large before!" It was at least six hundred yards to the top of the slope across from them. Some of the intervening space was filled with great rocks, small mountains, hillocks of grass, artificial ramps, platforms and terraced surfaces where, here and there, another table stood, tiny with distance, with or without diners bending to their meals. They could see a dozen furnace-fires where, from the equipment ranged around, the more brutal cooking was done.

Other customers, singly or in groups, accompanied by their own, black-clad domos, ambled along the paths, over the ramps. The far rise, slashed in three places by falling water, looked like some battle-field, at night, lit by a hundred scattered campfires on the dark, green, and craggy slopes. The multimirrored ceiling, as soon as their eyes drifted away thirty feet, was endlessly a-flicker with a million times the stars in any normal sky.

"Out where we come from—" the Spike's voice brought him

back—"I guess we just never have this much space to waste. Well—"
She opened her menu—"what in the world" and glanced at him, up
from under lowered brows, with a half-smile that brought him the
political significance only seconds later, "shall we have to eat?"

And while he was trying to remember the name of that dish he'd
had on his first visit to this kind of establishment in Bellona, the
Spike began to read out various selections, their accompanying descriptions, the descriptions of traditional accompaniments, the small
essays on the organization of meals customary for various cuisines.
As Bron turned pages, " . . . Austrian sausage . . ." caught his eye; he
stared at it, trying to recall why it intrigued him. But then she said
something that struck him so funny he laughed out loud. (He let the
page fall over.) Then they were both laughing. He read out three selections—all of which were hysterical. Somehow, with much hilarity
(and another round of Gold Flower Nectar) they constructed a meal
that began with a clear suomono, followed by oysters Rockefeller,
grilled quail, *boeuf au saucisse en chemise*—sometime amidst all this,
a steam-boat of fresh vegetables arrived at one side of the table and an
ice-boat of *crudités* at the other; the wines began with a Champagnoise
for the oysters, then a Pommard with the quail, and a Macon with
the roast.

Bron paused with his fork in a piece of the tissuey crust that had
chemisée'd the *boeuf*. "I love you," he said. "Throw up the theater.
Join your life to mine. Become one with me. *Be* mine. Let me possess
you wholly."

"Mad, marvelous man—" Carefully, with chopsticks, she lifted a
broccoli spear from the top tier of bubbling broth: The coals through
the steam-boat's grill-work glowed in her gauntlet—"not on your life."

"*Why* not? I love you." He put down his fork. "Isn't that enough?"

Gingerly, she ate her broccoli.

"Is it," he asked, leaning forward, "that I'm just not your type? I
mean physically? You're only turned on by dwarfish little creatures
who can do backflips, is that it?"

"You're very *much* my type," she said. "That's why I'm here. On
the animal line—and I do think that's to be appreciated—you're really most spectacular. I think large, blond, Scandinavians are quite the
most gorgeous things in the world."

"But I'm still not a monkey who can swing through the trees by
his tail, or who comes to places like this in his digging duds." He'd
realized he'd been offended by her remark only halfway through his

own. "Or, for that matter, a longhaired young lady who sits around and tinkles folksongs." He hoped the smile he put on now mitigated some of what, to his ears, sounded a bit harsh. "Alas, what can I do about these minor failings?"

Her smile was slightly reproving. "You have your own charm. And your numerous rough points . . . But also charm."

"Charm enough for you to come away with me forever?"

"Now it's my turn to say, 'Alas.'" She took the last of her broccoli between her teeth, drew the ivory sticks away. "No."

He said: "You've never been in love, then. That's it. Your heart is all stone. You've never had the heat of true passion melt it to life. Otherwise, you'd know I speak the truth and you'd surrender."

"Damned if I do and damned if I don't, huh?" She put down the chopsticks, picked up her fork, and cut at her beef. "Actually, I *have* been in love."

"You mean with Windy and Charo?"

"No. With them I am merely happy—a state, by the way, I value very highly, 'mere' as it is."

"Do you mean the lady you got refixated for, then?"

"No. Not even that. This was just a matter of the old, ordinary chemistry I was born with." She ate another bite and, with foreknuckle, brushed away crumbs from her lower lip. "In fact, I think I'm going to tell you about it. I have, really, been in love. And what's more, it was really and truly and dramatically unrequited. Yes, I *am* going to tell you. So just listen—I haven't got it all rehearsed, now, so it's going to come out very clumsily—who knows, even uglily. And I haven't any idea if anything in it will mean anything to you. But I'm sure somewhere in it the right feeling, if not the right words, will be there. Like the *Book of the Dead,* or something: Just read it once, and when you need it—when you can use it—you have to trust the necessary information will come back to you, if you just let it all flow through your ears even once. I used to teach—or rather, for the past few years because the company has been doing so well, we've been doing a sort of solstice seminar at Lux University. In theater. And I—"

The story *was* unclear. And clumsy. It had something to do with walking into her seminar room on the first evening, three years or five years ago, and seeing one student who was wearing only a fur vest and a knife—strapped to his foot; then there was something about a lot of drugs. *He* was either selling them or buying them . . .

Oh, yes, she had been struck practically inarticulate by him the moment she had walked into the room.

"Well, how did you teach the class then?"

Oh, she explained (in the middle of explaining something else), she was very good at that. (At *what*? but she was going on. . . .) He and one of the other, older students, had asked her, after the class, to contribute a running credit draft to a beer fund. (They were making beer in someone's back room.) Then, somehow, she was staying at his place. Then more drugs. And he was taking her, with a group of friends who made candles, first to hear a singer at an intimate club, then to visit a commune out in the ice—on his skimmer, which she sounded like she was more impressed with than she was with him, and then to see some friends of hers way away—the class had finished by now—and he was apparently the nephew of some famous naturalist and explorer Bron had actually heard of in connection with the Callisto ice-fields where there was an ice "forest" and the ice "beach" named after him; but this story had taken place on Iapetus, not Callisto—and " . . . when obviously it wasn't going to work out, and I had spent two weeks—at least!—without being straight one minute, you'd think it was his *religion*!—really, it was like walking around with your skull all soft and your meninges stripped away and every impulse from every sensation in the Solar System detonating your entire brain—you understand, the sex had been absolutely great as far as I was concerned. But the physical thing just wasn't him (he was one of your mystic types)—well, there was nothing for me to do but leave. Because I loved him absolutely more than anything else in the world. I slept the last night in the same room with him, on a blanket on the floor. Once I tried to rape him, I believe. He said fuck off. So I did, and later he said I could *hold* him if it would make me feel better, and I realized that I *didn't* want that. So I said, thanks, no. Brünnhilde on her bed of flame could not have burned more than I! (He said I was too intense—!) I lay there, all night, on the floor beside him, completely alone with myself, waiting for a dawn I was perfectly *sure* would never come.

"And that morning, he *hugged* me; and then he took me to the shuttle. And he gave me a notebook—the cover was blue plastic with the most amazing designs running through. And I was so happy I almost died. And kept writing him letters till he wrote me back—you see, one of my friends had said: 'You know, you've destroyed his life. He's never met anyone like you before, who thought he was that important!' And that was years ago. I just got a letter from him last week; he calls me one of the people he *loves*! You see . . . ? If you *really* love someone, and it's obvious that it's impossible, you'll *do* that. *Even* that. You see?" He had no idea what *that* was, either. While he listened, he found himself again remembering the occurrences back in the earthie cell. Whatever *had* that actually been about? Would the Spike have any suggestions? He longed to interrupt her monologue to ask. But Sam had said the subject was verboten . . . a matter of life, death, and would be so forever. Still, it made him feel rather romantic . . . if he could just suppress the frustration. And somehow, she was back in what seemed like the *middle* of the story, explaining that, you see, he had been older than the other students, that she didn't even like children as a rule, though one had to make an exception for Charo—who was nineteen—because Charo was, in many ways, exceptional. Then there was something about a lot of pictures taken on an ice-ledge, naked, in the skimmer with the Catherine of Cleves *Book of Hours*—who, he wondered, was Catherine of Cleves, and where did the ice-ledge get into the whole thing? Really, he *was* trying to follow. But during the last moments of her recounting, he'd noticed, just to her left, another group passing below, their majordomo leading them along on the paths and ramps toward their secluded table.

As he watched the four men and three women walking, Bron suddenly frowned, sat slightly forward. "Do you know," he said "—excuse me—but do you know that out of all the customers I've seen here, there isn't *one* wearing shoes!"

The Spike frowned too. "Oh . . . Well, yes. That's the one concession Windy made to fashion, when he came here with Charo. In fact, just before I left, he reminded me to take mine off, in case this was where we were going—but really . . ." Suddenly she giggled, drawing her own feet back under her chair (in his boots, Bron's own toes began to tingle)—"they *are* terribly informal here. Windy said bare feet are . . . well, encouraged—to enjoy the grass—but they really don't *care* what you wear!"

"Oh." Bron settled back; the majordomo came to flambé the bananas Foster—one red-gowned waiter pushed up a burning brazier, another a cart on which were the fruit, the brandies, the iced *crème bruleé*. The various courses had actually been served by these high-coiffed and scarlet-gowned women. (They had women as waiters, too! And in a place like this!) During his first months on Triton, Bron had gotten used to people in positions of authority frequently of an unexpected sex. But people in positions of service were something else.

Butter frothed in the copper skillet. The domo ran his paring knife around a ring of orange rind, of lemon peel: in with the praline, the sugar; then the deft stripping of the white bananas, peel already baked black; and, after a sprinkling of brandies and a tilting of the pan, a *whooosh!* of flame.

"You see," the majordomo said, laughing, tilting the pan. "Madame ends up with fire, water, earth, and air nevertheless!"

The Spike beamed with wide eyes and clasped hands. "It's quite a production."

With his heels pressed tight together beneath his chair, Bron spooned among the tiny flames that now chased one another around his dessert plate and began to eat the most entrancing confection he had ever tasted, while the sweat rose again on his neck and back. What was *so* awful (the Spike was now blithely chatting to the black-clad domo and one of the scarlet-gowned waiters—of course "waitress" was the word, but it seemed so out of place in a place like this—who were evidently amused by whatever it was she was saying) was that *they* knew exactly (for a second he searched the domo's and the waiters' faces for some sign, look, or gesture to confirm their knowledge; but no confirmation was needed: It was obvious from the entire situation's play and interplay. Bron sank back into his chair), exactly what they were: That she was new to all this, which they found delightful; and that he was someone who, on another world, had probably been taken to some similar establishment a dozen-odd times under dubious circumstances but that he had not been near such a place for at least fifteen years. Miserably, he spooned up the tongue-staggering sweet.

There were cheeses to taper off. There was coffee. There were brandies. From somewhere he dredged up a reaction to the Spike's resumption of her story about the affair with her student. What she had been telling him was important to her, he realized. Probably very important. But it *had* been unclear. And, what's more, dull. There comes a point, Bron decided, where for your own safety you have to take that amount of dull for the same as dumb. Which, he found himself thinking, applied to most of the Universe.

"*Do* you see?" she asked. "Do you *see?*"

He said: "I think I do," sincerely as he could manage.

She sighed, disbelieving.

He sighed back. After all, *she* was the actor.

She said: "I *hope* so."

The bill was immense. But, true to his claim, Sam had given him enough to cover it several times over.

"I can see there won't be any dishwashing for you tonight," the woman waiter now attending the majordomo said cheerfully, as Bron counted out the money. Which the Spike didn't understand. So Bron had to explain the woman's hoary joke.

As they wandered down the grassy slope ("Can't we take a long way?" the Spike exclaimed; the majordomo bowed: "But of course.") the falls splashed the rocks to their left. To their right, at a stone-walled fire, another scarlet-gowned waiter turned a spit where a carcass hissed and spat and glistened.

The Spike peered, sniffed. "When I think of all the things we *didn't* try—"

The majordomo said: "You must bring madame back again, sir."

"But we won't *be* here long enough!" she cried. "We're leaving Earth in . . . well, much too soon!"

"Ah, that *is* sad."

Bron wished the domo would just lead them out. He considered giving him an absurdly small, final tip. At the edge of the great, fanning columns he gave him an absurdly large one. ("*Thank* you, sir!") The Spike had apparently thought the whole, excruciating evening wonderful. But hadn't that been the point?

Bron was very drunk, and very depressed. For one moment—he had stumbled at the edge of the purple ramp—he thought (but this *was* his territory) he might cry.

He didn't.

It was a quiet trip back.

The single footman who accompanied them sat silent at her little table.

The Spike said it was wonderful to be so relaxed. And suggested they land just outside the town.

"Really," the footman said, smiling at Bron's final gratuity, "that isn't necessary. You've been *more* than generous!"

"Oh, take it," Bron said.

"Yes, do!" the Spike insisted. "Please! It's so much fun!"

Again they walked down the ramp.

Dawn?

No; near-full moonlight.

The shuttle rose, dragging its shadow across the great bite in the road from the diggings.

"You know—" The Spike's arms were folded; she kicked at her hem as they walked—"there's something I've been trying to work into one of my productions since I got here . . . I saw it happen the first day I arrived. That was right at the tail-end of some packaged-holiday company's three-day tour, and the place was *crawling* with earthie tourists—be glad you missed them! Some of the kids on the dig had gotten together right there, by the road, and started working on a rock. I mean, it was just an old piece of rock, but the tourists didn't know that—they were always out there, in droves, watching. The kids were going at it with brushes, shellac, tape measures, and making sketches and taking photographs: You would have thought it was the Rosetta Stone or something. Anyway, the kids kept this up till they had a circle of twenty-five or thirty people standing around gawking and whispering. Then, on signal, everybody stepped very decorously back, and one of the tougher young ladies came forward and, with a single blow of the pickax, shattered it!

"And, without a word, they all went off to do other, more important things, leaving a bunch of very confused tourists." The Spike laughed. "Now that's *real* theater! Makes you wonder what we're wasting our time on." At the rope, she looked at him. "But then, how could we present the same thing? Actors playing at being archeological students playing at being actors—? No, it's one whirligig too many." She smiled, held out a hand. "Come. Wander with me awhile among the ruins." She stepped over the rope.

He did too.

Dirt rolled from his boots, ten feet down into some brick-lined, lustral basin.

"A scar on the earth," she said, "stripped down to show scars older still. I haven't been walking in here since the first morning. I really wanted to take a look at it once more before we left." She led him down a steep, crumbly slope. Sheets of polyethylene were pegged across the ground. Makeshift steps were shored up with board. "I love old things," she said, "old ruins, old restaurants, old people."

"We don't get too many of any of them out where we live, do we?"

"But we're here," she objected. "On Earth. In Mongolia."

He stepped over a pile of boards. "I think I could enjoy this world, if we just got rid of the earthies."

"On a moonlit night like this—" She ran a thumb over the dirt wall beside them—"you should be able to think of something more original to say—" and frowned.

She ran her thumb back.

More dirt sifted down.

" . . . what's this?" She tugged at something in the wall, peered at it, tugged again.

He said: "Shouldn't you leave that for . . . ?"

But was she scraping dirt and gravel loose with her fingers, tugging with her other hand. "I wonder what it could—" It came out in a shower of small stones (he saw them fall across her bare toes, saw her toes flex on the earth) leaving a niche larger than he expected for what she held:

A verdigrised metal disk, about three inches across.

Bron, beside her, touched it with a finger: "It looks like some sort of . . . astrolabe."

"A what?"

"Yes, that part there, with all the cutouts; that's the rhet. And that little plug in the middle is called the horse. Turn it over."

She did.

"And those are . . . I guess date scales."

She held it up in the moonlight. "What's it for—?" She tugged at part on the back, that, gratingly turned. "I'd better not force it."

"It's a combination star-map, calendar, surveying instrument, slide rule, and general all-purpose everything."

"Why, it must be millions of years old!"

Bron scowled. "No . . ."

"Thousands?"

"More likely two or three hundred."

"Brian said it was very alkaline soil here." The Spike turned the instrument, its delicate inscriptions caked with green rime. "Metal will keep for—well, an awfully long time. I once heard Brian say—" She looked up at the mounds and heaps around—"that *sometime* in the past all this was mountain and crag and rock . . . I've got an idea—!" She handed Bron the disk and began to work her gauntlet down over her hand. "This is a sort of all-purpose everything too, in the slide-rule/calendar line. I'm going to make a trade. Where did you learn all about . . . what did you call it?"

"Astrolabes?"

"Did you have them on Mars when you were a kid?"

"No, I just . . . I don't know. Shouldn't you—?"

The gauntlet, with its calibrated rings, just fit the niche. She packed three handfuls of dirt after it.

"That doesn't look very—"

"I should hope not!" She glanced back. "It wouldn't be any fun if they didn't find it." She reached down, picked up a trowel leaning on a pail by his foot, and poked a few stones further in. "There—" She turned back to him. The trowel clattered into the pail—"now come with me . . ." Once more she led him among the excavations. There was a conversation, far more complicated than the little labyrinth they wandered, in which she explained both that she'd had a marvelous time but that, no (when he put his arm around her shoulder), she wouldn't go to bed with him that night; apparently she meant it, too, which made him angry at first, then guilty, and then just confused—she kept evoking motivations he couldn't quite follow. He tried getting physical twice, but the second time (when he was really horny), she elbowed him in the ribs, hard, and left.

For three minutes he thought she was hiding. But she had really gone.

He walked back into town and up the narrow stone steps, blades of moonlight from between the small houses sweeping across him every twenty feet. The Taj Mahal, he kept thinking. And: sausages . . . ? The Taj Mahal—would he get to see it after all? He must ask Sam how far away it was—that was much more interesting than Boston. But though he knew all about the clay-pits to the south of it and the story of the queen who died in childbirth buried within it, he wasn't sure which continent it was on—one of them beginning with "A" . . . Asia? Africa? Australia? The Spike had said something, before they'd started to fight, about giving him the astrolabe . . . ?

Thinking he held it, he looked at his hands, but (all the way back he'd assumed the moist knot in his left fist was a crumpled bill he'd been meaning to spread out and put back in his purse) they were both empty.

6. Objective Knowledge

When a man who knows the game watches a game of chess, the experience he has when a move is made usually differs from that of someone else watching without understanding the game. But this experience is not the knowledge of the rules.

LUDWIG WITTGENSTEIN, *Philosophical Grammar*

"Did you have a good time last night?"

"Oh . . . yeah. Sure."

"Well, come on," Sam said. "We've only got five hours to get back. I just spoke to Linda. They'll be waiting for us."

"Where?" he said sleepily.

"Never mind. Just get dressed and come on. Remember, a world's a little bit bigger than a moon, so you have to allow a little more time to get from one side of it to the other."

Nevertheless, in the eating place near the town square, they spent a good half hour over breakfast; the single digger also eating there engaged them in a particularly inane conversation: "They're always telling on the news about all those hundreds of political parties you have on each satellite, out where you guys are from."

"There're not hundreds," Sam said, sipping his broth. "Only about thirty to thirty-seven, depending on which satellite you're on."

"And when you have an election, none of them ever wins?"

Bron watched Sam decide to laugh. "No. They all win. You're governed for the term by the governor of whichever party you vote for. They all serve office simultaneously. And you get the various benefits of the platform your party has been running on. It makes for competition between the parties which, in our sort of system, is both individuating and stabilizing."

"It sounds pretty confusing." The digger, who was very dirty and probably about fourteen, grinned.

The only reason Bron didn't say anything insulting was because he couldn't think of anything.

Sam said: "Well, it's nowhere near as confusing as some of the excuses for government you've got here." But he was still smiling.

Ten minutes later they were walking along the road. Bron frowned at the archeological excavation. Some dozen diggers were clustered around one section (the sun was not the yellow disk on the blue it was always pictured, but a boundaryless, white-gold blot you couldn't really look at), but not the place, Bron decided at last, where the Spike had hidden her gauntlet. In fact, there was a small earth-mover filling in that section.

Sun flared on the mover's bubble.

"I believe," Sam said, "this is going to be what is known, in earthly parlance, as a scorcher—a *very* hot day!"

"What's the point of having the sun so hot and close if you can't enjoy it?"

But Sam only laughed.

They walked up the rise.

Somewhere in last night's conversation among the ruins, there had been discussion about when he would see her again. The Spike had given several answers, all negative, all evasive, and most beyond his comprehension.

They walked awhile more.

Then they rode.

Then they flew.

Then they flew again; this flight did not quite end. Their compartment had been transferred to rail, now, and was speeding along underground.

Then they were instructed by a speaker to get into another compartment; and after speeding along for a while in that one, they were instructed to leave through door B, which put them into a long, low, green corridor, with a moving walkway along one side.

"I think that's our party." Sam nodded along the hall, where a group of some dozen ambled ahead. "We better hurry."

Walking quickly along the moving walkway, it still took them another two minutes to catch up.

"Oh, hi, Sam!" Linda said with a smile much more surprised than Bron thought the situation warranted. "We were getting worried . . ." She looked very tired.

So did most of the others. Some looked downright exhausted.

Was that why some of the people seemed so unfamiliar?

As they passed through the door into the opulent cabin, with its carpeted levels and reclining chairs, Bron realized that at least three people were, indeed, new.

Sam, looking pretty tired himself but, smiling, had an arm around plump Debby's shoulders. Someone handed him a drink, and Bron was left with the disconcerting question—since all the chairs were taken—*which* three people were missing.

Take-off was very rough. And it was a different cabin—or else the take-off screen's broken blue lights had been fixed. There was conversation, laughter, gossip, all sounding somewhat strained.

Bron wondered if they all had secrets like his. His stint in the earthies' cell had returned to him with pressing vividness the moment the doors to the room had rolled to. Ten hours out he found himself doubting if the people he'd spotted as new were new after all. Nobody had made particular reference to them, everyone seemed to know them. But five hours later, after checking down in the free-fall cabin, and then surveying the swimmers in the pool, he had definitely identified one of the missing persons.

After refilling his drink, Bron walked up to the redhead who had been so garrulous before.

The little man was sitting on his couch, his own drink hanging from his bony fingers.

Bron said: "By the way, whatever happened to that charming oriental woman you were playing vlet with on the trip out?"

The redhead looked up sharply. He frowned. Then his shoulder dropped, and the exhaustion Bron had become used to on the faces around him worked its way back among the features. "I suspect—" The little redhead looked down again, turned his drink—"the chances are overwhelming she's dead."

Which made Bron start. (Someone passing glanced at them, then glanced away.) Chills rolled up his back.

The redhead's eyes raised. "This *was* a political mission." His voice was strained and soft. "Many of us were in great danger. All of us were under pressure. And . . . well, we *are* at war." He took a breath, looked out at the stars, and then went on to talk about something else with entirely information-less anecdotes, a style that Bron had noticed twice before. This time Bron commented on it, a bit annoyed. The redhead laughed and explained that he had developed that style of small talk back when he'd been actually working for Intelligence—

"That's where everything you say *is* used against you."—and then slaughtered Bron three games running on his small-sized, traveling vlet board; mercifully, no game took more than forty minutes. "But I think," the redhead explained by way of appeasement, "the next time you play someone else, you'll find your own game much improved." Bron had already recognized the beginning of another of those annoying friendships he was so frequently falling into when he fell into any friendship at all. The pattern was only confirmed when the redhead, in one of his anecdotes, mentioned something peculiar about life in some male homosexual commune that had something peculiar about its particular history. And the redhead, Bron realized, was one of those guys who wouldn't even proposition you outright and give you the satisfaction of telling him to fuck off. Not that Bron ever *said* fuck off; he'd just say, as politely as the situation allowed, No. A couple of times, when he was a kid on Mars, someone had taken his politeness as an invitation to get physical, so that Bron once had to elbow someone in the ribs. (The image of the Spike, elbowing him that night, how many nights ago, in the ruins of Earth, came back to make him grin.) But the physical approach—especially if you were over six feet tall—gets rarer as you get older. (And somehow the obsessive feeling about her had begun to slip away . . .)

All these thoughts, of course, were not consecutive, but spread over the next seventy hours. Around them and in between them, Bron learned, from overhearing several other conversations and hovering about the edges of several more (trying to think of a leading question, terrified of asking a stupid one), that while Sam had been keeping him off out of harm's way in Mongolia, indescribable atrocities had occurred, unspeakable retaliations had been committed, and that, though no one could really be surprised, the "we" who were at war now was, yes, Triton.

Sam was explaining to Bron, among half a dozen other, simultaneous conversations, that no, he wouldn't be returning to the co-op today; he, Linda, and Debby were anxious to get back to the rest of the family in Lux. A voice chirped overhead, in astonishingly low fidelity: "Will Bron Helstrom please go to one of the blue courtesy phones. Will Bron Helstrom please . . ."

Bron excused himself.

"And say hello to the old pirate for me when you get home," Sam called after him. "Hope you beat the fuzz off his balding pate—"

On the phone ("Yes, what is it?") they told him there was a letter for him and—Oh, excuse me: Apparently it had been already sent on to his co-op. In fact, it had come from Earth with him on the same rocket in which he'd—

"From Earth?"

That's right, and they were terribly sorry; they were just trying to get it to him quickly, but apparently there'd been some mix-up—

"Well, then why call me all the way to the—?"

Was he on his way home now?

"Yes!"

Well, if it was an emergency and he was passing any postal outlet, if he would just present his identification card, he would be immediately presented with a government facsimile of—

"And what is the government doing with a facsimile of *my* private mail?" (The mail was a co-operative, not a government, enterprise.)

This *is* wartime, they explained testily. And besides, he had just returned from a High Surveillance Mission; as he no doubt knew, that surveillance would continue on High for at least seventy-two hours after his return, for his own protection. Now, would he like to take advantage of it and pick up his letter before he got home?

"Yes!" Bron said. "Thank you!" Hanging up, he turned, angrily, from the phone.

The little redhead (who'd made noises about sharing a transport compartment back into Tethys) was the only one waiting.

"Seems I just got a letter from my girlfriend," Bron explained, realizing as he did so that it might just as easily be (in fact he hoped it was) an official apology from the Earth enforcement-girls (or whatever the hell they called them there) about the way he had been treated. "But they seem to have sent it on ahead by accident." An apology from the Spike? He smiled. Well, it was to be expected. But really, he didn't feel she'd done that much to apologize for. "I'll have to stop off and pick up the letter. I really enjoyed those games. I guess we'll be running into each other again—Tethys isn't that big a city, and once you meet someone, you practically can't get away from them."

"We probably won't," the redhead said with a mischievous smile. "I don't live in Tethys."

"Oh," Bron said. "I thought you said you lived in a—oh, you mean your co-op isn't *in* the city."

"That's right." And the redhead began to talk animatedly about something else, till they reached the transport. "Oh, and may I ask you a mildly embarrassing favor: Could you pay my fare with one of your tokens. It's only half a franq on your credit; I know it seems silly but—"

"Oh, sure," Bron said, opening his purse and fingering around for his half-franq token. He pushed the coin-shape into one of the change slots beside the entrance. (There was still some leftover money; but Sam seemed to have forgotten about it.) The green light flashed, and the token rolled out again into Bron's palm.

"Thank you," the redhead said, and walked through the gate.

Bron put the token in again; the light flashed again; again the token was returned (and somewhere two fares were billed against his labor credits on some highly surveyed government tape); returning the token to his purse, he followed the redhead onto the transport platform, constructing schemes of paranoid complexity about why the redhead might not want his presence in the city known. After all, basic transportation was a nonrefusable (what the dumb earthies would call "welfare") credit service.

They rode a while together. Then the redhead said good-bye and got off. (Bron's fantasies had gone to the other extreme by now: The redhead was probably just a skinflint credit cadger. Ex-Intelligence indeed!) Bron realized as the doors closed that actually he had no idea at all *where* the man lived (in some other city? on some other moon?), he didn't even know his name. Had he actually said *he* was living in the homosexual co-op, or just that *someone* had been living there? It had all been too artfully ambiguous. Forget it! Bron thought: Oh, forget it; he stood up, while the floor swayed, and went to stand at the doors. If he was going to pick up his letter at a postal outlet, before he got home, he'd better do it here:

The transport pulled into the Plaza of Light Station.

He expected his letter to be flashed in the viewing screen above the card slot (since there *was* a viewing screen). Instead, a larger slot at knee-level slowly extruded the black and gold edging of a space-mail envelope. He pulled it out the last inch. (Inside, something *chunked!* reproachfully.) Across the gray flimsy, covering one corner of his identity number, large pink letters proclaimed:

GOVERNMENT FACSIMILE

In the lefthand corner it said: "Gene Trimbell (the Spike)" but instead of an identity number beneath it (which would contain her mail-routing code, wherever she was in the Solar System), there was an old-fashioned return address:

Lahesh, Mongolia 49–000-Bl-pz
Asia, Earth.

Bron picked up his card and crossed the lobby, mistily mosaicked with ornate light-shapes from the colored glass wall across from him. He went out the arch, onto the Plaza, found a bench and sat. Across from him sat two very nervous-looking women (one of whom was naked). The Plaza, as usual at this time in the afternoon, was almost deserted. He opened the envelope by small pinches, unfolded the letter (stamped across the top, in the same pink: GOVERNMENT FAC-SIMILE). He recognized the erratically punctuated, ill-capitalized print of a first draft from a voice-scripter. Given the badly-aligned, heavily serifed type, it was probably a very old voice-scripter, too. Leaning forward on his knees, he read:

Bron, and then I guess you better put a colon no a dash—the world is a small place italicize is. And moons are even smaller. Running into you like that out here made me realize how italics small. In a small world when you get that unpleasant choice of being blunt or well mannered, after you've tried manners and that doesn't seem to work I guess you have to be blunt period bluntly comma I don't want to have an affair with you semicolon I don't even particularly want to be your friend period paragraph.

If it were seven o'clock in the evening instead of two in the morning I would just sign it there and send it but it is two o'clock in the morning with real moonlight coming over the Lahesh mountains and doing marvelous things to the rain that's been falling against the window for the last three minutes dash wouldn't you know, it just stopped dash and real crickets somewhere in the eaves dash a time that lends itself to hopefully quiet and presumably rational explanations semicolon and perhaps the illusion that, however painful initially, those explanations might help.

What do I want to explain?

That I don't like the type of person you are. Or that the type of person I am won't like you. Or just: I italics don't. Do I have the colon in there? Yes.

And it isn't all that altruistic, by any means. I'm angry—at
the Universe for producing a person like you—and I want to
rake up coals. I want them to burn. What frustrates me is
that—and it became apparent tonight—is that you do *italics ad-*
here to some kind of code of good manners, proper behavior, or
the right thing to do, and yet you are so emotionally lazy that
you are incapable of implementing the only valid reason that
any such code ever came about: to put people at ease, to make
them feel better, to promote social communion. If you ever
achieve that, it's only to the credit of whoever designed the behavior code a hundred years back. The only way you seem to be
able to criticize your own conduct *parenthesis* at one point I
watched the thought march across your face; you aren't very
good at hiding your feelings; and people like that simply cannot
afford to count on appearances *close parenthesis* that your version of the code was ten years out of date. Which is to so monumentally miss the point I almost wanted to cry.

But again I am being hopelessly abstract.

I *paragraph.*

do not *paragraph.*

like *paragraph.*

you

because: I was offended at your assumption that just because
I was in the theater I would automatically like your homosexual
friend: I was amused/angered at your insistence in talking
about yourself all the time and at your amusement-to-anger
that I should ever want to talk about me. I thought your making
Miriamne lose her job was horrible. She finally decided there
must be mitigating circumstances. Of the three explanations I
could come up with, the most generous is that you thought she
was involved with me and it was some weird sort of jealousy. I
won't even explain the other two. All three make you an awful
person. Yes, I did enjoy going out with you to the restaurant
this evening and actually getting a chance to talk. But—the
least offense, still, maybe it's the fatal straw on the back of the
camel—having to fight somebody off physically who wants to
make out with you when you don't want to is something I had
a fair amount of tolerance for when I was twenty (and how
many times did it happen to me then? Three? Five? Five and a
half?). I'm thirty-four and I don't now. At least not from people

my own age! Yes, you are my type, which is why we got as far
as we did. I've only met one other person in my life even
vaguely like you dash not my type dash but another man from
Mars and into metalogics wouldn't you know. But that was so
long ago I'd almost forgotten.

Emotionally lazy?

What's the difference between that and emotionally injured?
Emotionally crippled? Emotionally atrophied? Maybe it isn't
your fault. Maybe you weren't cuddled enough as a baby.
Maybe you simply never had people around to set an example
of *how* to care. Maybe because you quote feel you love me unquote you feel I should take you on as a case. I'm not going to.
Because there are other people, some of whom I love and some
of whom I don't, who need help too and, when I give it, it
seems to accomplish something the results of which I can see.
Not to mention things I need help in. In terms of the emotional
energies I have, you look hopeless. You say you love me. And
yes, I have loved others and I know what it feels like: When
you love someone, you want to help them in any way you can.
Do you want to help me? Then just stay out of my life and
leave me alone and / / Hey what are you doing, huh? / / Writing
a letter, come on go back to sleep / / How was your evening out
at the Craw? / / It was okay, now goodnight, please / / Hey,
look—why don't you just get rid of him, just say get lost I
mean: For someone you keep insisting you like so much you've
spent more hours agonizing over all the things he's done that
tear you up than you have about your last three productions / /
That's what I was just doing now go back to sleep I said / / Tell
him it's over / / I said that's what I just did / / Oh, hey, now, hey,
I'm sorry. I didn't um your letter there looks pretty first-drafty,
I mean I'll put it through the corrector for you if you want and /
/ Is that damned thing still on oh for / / Look I'll run it through
and you can lie down and get some sleep / / No, don't bother,
I'm sending it like it is, I just don't have the

Which was all there was.

The first paragraph had produced a sort of stunning chill. He read
the rest numbly—not so much with a feeling of recognition, but as if
he were reading about something he'd overheard that had happened
to someone else. He finished the last paragraph wondering harder

and harder whether it was Charo or Windy she was talking to (somehow it seemed important to know); then the frustration suddenly
overturned. What the hell *had* she been saying to them about him
anyway? Not to mention the rest of the company? Anger welled. The
type of person *he* was? He knew *her* type! Where did she come off
presuming he'd had anything personal to do with that crazed lesbian's dismissal? Everyone was being laid off. Even *him*! Didn't she
realize *every*thing was coming apart? There was a war on! And taking
offense because he'd wanted to introduce her to a guy who was probably his best friend! And fighting him off physically? Well, then, he
thought: If you don't want somebody to proposition you, make it
clear in the first place! And that nonsense about "agonizing": Who
did *he* have to agonize to? He'd been arrested; and practically tortured—practically? He *had* been tortured! And had *he* agonized to
her about what had been done to *him*? (That crap about not being
able to hide his feelings! He'd certainly kept *that* to himself!) She was
some dumb actress who probably hadn't ever had a real emotion in
her life!

And he'd *loved* someone like that?

Now that *was* crazy! How could anyone sane love such a shallow,
and presumptuous, and worthless, and conceited . . .

Breathing harder, he launched into the letter again. The first part?
This time it just seemed crazy from the start. She *must* be crazy! First
off, if she really thought he had done all those things she accused him
of in the second part, why would she have spent any time with him
at all? Obviously she couldn't believe the things she'd said. Why *say*
them, then? Why even *suggest* them? She was crazy *and* vicious! That
simpering drivel about moonlight and helping others. (And then
she'd elbowed him off to go crawling up into bed with someone she
could tell how awful he was!) How could he possibly have gone all
gooey for someone so obviously deranged and sick as—

Which is when the woman in clothes on the bench across from his
stood up, staggered a step forward, grasped her throat, and made a
strangled sound.

Bron looked up, dragged a great breath in on top of his anger: It
did nothing to relieve him. And his ears were painfully stopped.

Somewhere across the Plaza, someone screamed.

Then he felt a breeze on his neck that grew. And grew. And grew.
And grew—Bron suddenly staggered erect. The *war*! he thought. It
must be the . . . ! The gale behind him pushed him three steps for-

ward. The letter was snatched away, chattering. It hurled, like a slab of gray slate, against the transport station's kiosk, which, as if from the letter's impact, sagged. A piece of the kiosk roofing came off and spun away, bouncing over the Plaza, hit one man, who went down on his knees clutching his head, and shattered a shop window. And the other kiosk walls were down, were tearing away, were skidding across the concourse.

And it was getting dark.

Staggering in the gale, Bron looked up. The shield's colors, in patches, were fading to black—a black that was suddenly emptier than any he'd ever seen. The date-lights around the Plaza had gone off too. And the stars—! (A quarter of the sky was dark; *more* than a quarter!) They looked like the bright tips of long needles, shoved down at him, inches close. And the roaring! Somewhere something was gathering and pulling itself up and then . . . it tore loose! Bron was shoved backward. His knees hit the bench; he fell, grabbing the seat, felt something strike the bench hard enough to rattle it. He threw himself down to clutch the ground. Something else hit the bench and shattered. Bron's eyes snapped open in the stinging wind.

Somewhere people ran and shouted. Then the wind's roar wedged between them and him; the bench shook above him. One end swung loose. And Bron stood; and ran. The gale growing on his left changed his course, in half a dozen steps, nearly ninety degrees, then sent him sprawling to his knees and palms. He pushed to his feet, took another step and—fell . . . in slow motion, while the air was yanked from his lungs. His face and eyes and ears burned. He flailed onto the ground that heaved, slowly, under him; and broke open (he felt it) not far off.

Then all the air dropped, roaring, back down. The pavement under his palm parted—just a little. Little things struck his cheeks, ears, legs, and hands. His eyes were slits. And he was up and running. Had something hit his hip? It hurt miserably. He ran, hurting.

Lights, here and there, in his streaming eyes, lit fragments of an unreal city. He stopped. The wind was raging but—he realized suddenly—not around him. Somewhere far away something immense fell and took a long time doing it.

Some dozen people suddenly ran around him—and he turned watching them—making for a doorway. He ran again. The street became rubble under his feet. At first he thought the ground had shattered. No, only the (he stumbled on lengths of plastistrut, broken styroplate, and crumbling foam) wall of the building beside him had fallen. He stepped on a piece of tilted styroplate, that shifted. He looked down. An arm stuck out from under it—which made him stop.

It must have been a design-house mannequin or possibly an—

The hand, palm up, suddenly, made a fist (with irridescent, multi-hued nails). Bron ran.

Twenty yards later he stopped, turned: Go back, he thought. I've got to go back . . .

He heard them first, then saw them, crossing at the corner—maybe twenty, maybe fifty. They broke around him.

Then one grabbed him, spun him: "You fool! You damned fool! You *can't* go that way!" she shouted in his face. "That's the direction the break is in," then lurched on. So did Bron, wondering exactly what had broken, and where it was. He was terrified, with a chill, blunt terror that made his throat and the backs of his knees ache.

Ahead, people were stopping.

Someone said loudly: "Not through here! I'm sorry! Not through here!"

People milled. Between them he saw the cordon of e-girls across the way. (The one calling was a woman.) People pressed behind him.

"You can't go into this area! It's too dangerous. Now get back!"

Some people, with looks of frustration, were starting to the right or left.

Bron started right—the street sign (here in the licensed part of the city, where the coordinate numbers were green) told him he was two units from his co-op which surprised him; he hadn't known he'd come that far.

Following the street he was on, however, would take him into the unlicensed sector—which suddenly seemed the most ridiculous thing imaginable: The middle of a military crisis was not the time to go wandering around the u-l! (The wind was up again, but at a steady pitch—which, when you thought about it, was scarier in its implications than a sudden gust that stopped.) No, it just wasn't the—

He heard them, nearing; people started to move back, but Bron edged forward. The idea was neither complete nor verbal. He experienced it merely as a yearning to go home, without intellection as to method or its goal.

Trying to unravel the web of sound into their syllabic chains, he gained the crowd's edge.

Ragged and bowed, the mumblers shuffled up in quarter light.

Anticipating embarrassment, he stepped forward, shouldered among them, closed his eyes (The smell! he thought, astonished. He'd forgotten the sour, unwashed smell!), bent his head, and began to shuffle with them. He commenced his *Mimimomomizolalil* . . . but, a dozen syllables in, got lost; so, in time to his shushing sandals, he rolled his tongue through whatever nonsense came. Once, between squeezed lids, he glanced to the side to see eyes in a scaly face close: the woman recommenced mumbling. So did Bron. And shuffled.

The feeling was of lightness, almost of joy, of reasons and responsibilities, explanations and expiations shrugged off, abandoned. Is this, he thought (knowing a true mumbler should not be thinking), what I ought to have been doing all this time? Was he simply the sort of fool for whom it took some bellicose catastrophe to bring him to enlightenment? He mumbled his nonsense, tried not to breathe through his nose, and thought: I *will* become a novice! I will study, I will renounce the sensory world for the blind trip toward eternity. Something else fell to the right.

A few people jogged against him.

His shoulders had started to ache—from the hunching. He shifted them about, tried to stand a little straighter, just his head forward—which sent a throb along the back of his neck, so that he had to rub it. A *real* mumble would, of course, give him something to concentrate on. If this was the death of Tethys, what better way to die with it than to have his mind cleared of all quotidian concern (though, despite the random sounds, like rubble of the city itself in his mouth, he felt his mind was anything but clear: He'd been repeating the same three syllables for minutes now, and went on to something else. (Blinking, he saw his own sandals, and the rag-bound, filthy feet of the woman beside him, taking their tiny steps.) How far *had* they gone?

Someone squeezed in behind him.

Another interloper? More probably someone had just relinquished the Divine Guide position for peeking. Bron shuffled on, losing his own voice on the thunderous web of sound, trying to judge their slow, headlong progress. He wouldn't be able to get the ache out of his neck without putting his head straight up and (he suspected) stopping. His calves were beginning to ache too. His hip, at any rate, felt better. And his *Mimimomomizo* . . . had (he realized) degenerated to *Blablablablabla* . . .

Someone on the other side of him tripped, stumbled against him;

eyes still tight (and in violation of some sect canon, he was sure), he grabbed the bony shoulders (Bron wasn't sure if they belonged to man or woman) to steady them. One was sticky, hot, and wet; as his hand hesitated on the swaying back, Bron wondered how anyone could have such knobby vertebrae.

Over the roar of mantras—how many *were* in the group? Thirty? Fifty? Seventy-five?—other voices were shouting.

He caught the shrieked phrase: " . . . mutilation of the mind! Mutilation of the body . . ." The words ". . . catastrophe . . ." and ". . . ultimate, seventh-stage catastrophe . . ." separated out. And ". . . but the mutilation of the mind! The mutilation of the body . . ."

Again mumblers jarred him

Suddenly Bron opened his eyes and raised his head.

The darkness surprised him. Had they wandered into the u-l? He looked up. No: It was just that the shield was still out. Green coordinate letters glowed high on a wall ahead. Another mumbler lurched against him. Outside the group, people were shouting and . . . *fighting* with the mumblers at the group's edge! And there was a chalky smell among the unwashed bodies. No, it wasn't burning. But it made his throat feel funny.

" . . . in the wake of the ultimate, seventh-stage catastrophe, we have no recourse but the mutilation of the mind, the mutilation of the body . . ." came loudly from beyond the mumblers. All Bron's well-being left. Fear replaced it. He pushed between the mumblers, away from where the shouting was loudest—though there was shouting at the other side too.

A dozen feet off, between two ragged mumblers, stumbling obliviously on, he saw the overmuscled, fouled, and hairy figure, crouching and jeering with mutilated face (a woman, from the ragged mastectomy scars), saw her strike one of the mumblers (who fell to his knees), then turn, chains swinging from her neck, and shout: " . . . only the mutilation of the body, the mutilation of the mind . . ."

Was this supposed to be meaningful . . . ? meaningless . . . ? He plunged out among them. A scabby fist glanced his jaw. Nobody else hit him directly, but he had to wedge between two sweating, naked creatures, who, he realized on his third push, were pressing together solely to keep him from passing. One growled, inches from Bron's face, with fouled teeth and a jaw wet with lymph and pus.

Then he was through. Behind, shouting and mumbling made one ugly roar. He looked up, saw a set of green coordinates—

He was in the same unit as Serpent's House! The e-girls, confronted with a sect who would not have responded to them anyway, not knowing what to do, had let them pass the cordon! Arriving as obliquely as fear was the sudden conviction that he had been incredibly clever. He couldn't have *thought* of a more ingenious way of getting through the blockade!

Someone staggered into his back. He heard somebody else grunting rhythmically, under blows.

He didn't even look but ran forward, turned the corner—to find the street wet, then wetter; finally he was splashing, in his sandals, through two inches of water.

As he crossed the intersection, wind shattered the black glaze along all five streets that converged here, obliterating his own widening ripples; momentarily, it threatened to grow strong enough to push him to his knees. Splashing and staggering, he gained the far side. But the gust had already begun to die.

The lights did not come on automatically when he stepped through the door, nor when he found the switch box—the cover swung open as though someone had already tried it—and played with the range of press-plates inside. There was junk all over the common room floor; and the glow of unshielded night above told him that the skylight opening was several times too big; and the wrong shape.

From across the room came a sound that might have been a moan. Bron stepped, stepped again, stepped again—and barked his shin, hard—blood trickled his ankle. He'd scraped himself on something he couldn't see. Something he could, large and black and shapeless, blocked him anyway. He stepped aside on the rubbly rug, felt the wall brush his shoulder. He heard the sound again—it could also have been some piece of junk, sliding; it didn't sound *much* like a moan . . . A sudden scrambling, then something dodged past. Bron whirled, terrified, in time to see somebody dart out the door—a hand hit the jamb, a-glitter with gems: then the ringed fingers were gone.

"Flossie . . . ?" Bron called, after count five. "Freddie . . . ?" He didn't call *that* loudly. After all (he took another breath and another step) whichever it had been was probably, by now, a unit away. He stepped forward again . . . On the fifth step his knee struck sharply on what (probably) was an overturned chair leg. He went back to the wall. That sound again . . . No, it wasn't a moan.

An orangeish glow, above—flickering? No. But it was the balcony door.

His foot hit the bottom step. He grasped the rail—which gave under his hand, much too loose. Bron started up. Something small rolled from his foot and fell, clicking, back down three steps. Under his wet sole, next step, something else equally small cracked.

He reached the balcony, looked through the door. Someone had hung a light cube just inside, which, for some reason, was burning dim orange instead of yellow. Ahead, the left corridor wall sagged incredibly.

On the floor, spraddling the door sill (the speaker on the side still gave up the micro-shouts of micro-armies a-clash on micro-mountain ledges), opened out and inlay up, lay the vlet case—stepped on at least once and cracked, drawers loose, screens, cards, men and dice scattered. The astral cube was now only broken plastic lying among bent, brass struts.

Bron stepped lightly (frowning heavily) across the sill. The sagging wall made him dubious about the floor.

Outside, he heard a rushing with a few whistles in it—the wind again! Halfway up the steps to the next floor he saw that those dark blots on the carpet were blood—which either trailed up the steps or down, depending if the bleeding had been getting better or worse. (His ankle was only scratched and had a scab forming.) Halfway along his own corridor, he suddenly wondered why, in the midst of this wreckage, he was returning to his room.

Across from Bron's door, Alfred's door was ajar.

From it, a blade of light lay on the orange hall-carpet, swinging.

Bron went to the door, hesitated, pushed it in—it grated on junk over the floor. One wall was down! and half the ceiling; the light fixture dangled from its wires, swaying, a good-sized piece of ceiling still attached. Two of the bed legs were broken, or had gone through the floor. The bed was lopsided.

There were two people in it. (Bron swallowed, opened his mouth, started to step back, didn't, started to step forward, didn't do that either, closed his mouth.) A section of wall, and crumbled powdery stuff, had fallen across them.

Bron's first thought: The woman, she's *my* age!

It didn't look that heavy!

It didn't look that heavy at all!

A very dark oriental lay naked on her back, one arm pinned. Her other had been trying to push the wall away. Her head had fallen to the side, her mouth and one eye wide.

Alfred lay on his stomach beside her, arms folded under his cheek. Bron stepped forward.

Under straggly hair, Alfred's ear was full of blood, mostly dried now. It had trickled his jaw, forked around his mouth, run across his wrist to make a rusty blotch on the sheet, the size of Bron's hand.

The edge of the falling wall had cracked the red Q. The top part lay on Alfred's left shoulder, black suspenders wrinkled around it. (*How*, Bron wondered, could a nine-foot slab of plastic walling— well, maybe twelve-foot—be heavy enough to do all *that*?) Alfred's legs were visible (heels up, toes in) from midthigh down, the woman's (toes up, both leaning left) just from the ankles. The bottom part of the sheet was completely blood-soaked, some still wet.

Suddenly Bron backed toward the door, hit his shoulder, spun out into the hall.

He did not cross the hall to his own room.

Lawrence's door was six down from his.

Bron reached it, pounding with both fists. He stepped back, wondering if he should try the doors right and left (Fifty-odd men lived in this co-op. Bron thought. Fifty!), then pounded again because he heard something inside.

The door opened. Lawrence, naked, with wrinkled chin and knees, grizzled hair, and watery eyes, said: "Yes, what can I . . . Bron?"

"Lawrence! Alfred's dead! And some girl!"

"Yes." Lawrence opened the door the rest of the way. "That's right. And so is Max. And so is Wang. And then there are two at the end of the hall I don't even know. I think they may be visitors. I don't know them at all. I've never seen them before in my—"

"What about Freddie and Flossie?"

"Nobody's seen them since this morning."

"Oh," Bron said. "Oh, because I thought I saw—No, that's okay. Never mind. How—?"

"Only on the left side of the corridor," Lawrence said, frowning again. "Isn't it strange? The gravity deflection that got us must have stopped halfway under the building. The public channels have been saying that some of the gravity deflections that have hit parts of the city have been as high as three hundred times Triton normal for as much as seven whole seconds. Seven seconds at three hundred gravities! That's really incredible. I'm surprised that side of the house is even standing."

"But what about everyone else?"

Lawrence blinked. "Oh, they've evacuated. That's what we were instructed to do over the public channels. The sabotage attempts have been incredibly effective. They still don't know whether they can get it under control. Evacuate . . ." The knuckly finger rubbed at the unshaven cheek. "Yes, that's what they—"

"Then what the hell are *you* doing here!"

"Oh . . . ?" Lawrence frowned, reached down to scratch his knee. "Well, I . . . I've been playing pieces from my subscription series of aleotoric compositions from the late twentieth century. I played the Bette Midler track of *Friends*, which lasts—" Lawrence looked up again, blinking wet eyes—"not quite two and three-quarter minutes. Then I put on the Stockhausen *Aus Den Siegen Tagen*, which lasts slightly more than five and three-quarter hours." (From inside the room came the familiar clicks, electric viola glissandi, and single piano notes, spaced with resonating silences.) "Of course, I've heard them before. Both of them. But I just thought I'd . . ." Lawrence began to cry. "Oh, Lord, I'm sorry . . . !" The bony hands grasped Bron's arms.

"Hey, come on . . . !" Bron said, trying to support him. "Look, you better . . .

"They're dead—Max and Wang and Alfred and . . ." The face rocked against Bron's shoulder, wet as a baby's. "And I'm an old man and I don't have any place to go!"

"Come on," Bron said, his arm around the loose, dry back. Annoyance contended with fear. "Come on, now. Come on . . ."

"I'm sorry. . . ." Rubbing his cheeks, Lawrence pulled away. "I'll be all right. But they're all dead. And I'm alive. And I'm an old man with no . . ." He took a breath, blinked his reddened eyes. "I'm sorry . . . just no place to go. I'm all right now. I'm . . . What are *you* doing here?"

"I just . . ." Bron rubbed his own shoulder, still slick with Lawrence's tears. "I wanted to come back and . . . well, make sure you were all right. See about my things; about you. And Alfred—" and then remembered Alfred; he decided he didn't want to go into his own room at all. If it looked like Alfred's (up to three hundred times normal gravity? That was almost as high as the surface of Saturn, Jupiter, the Sun . . . !), he just didn't want to see.

Lawrence thumbed his eyes. "I don't know why it should, but it makes an old body like me feel . . . well, it's nice of you to say it, even if it isn't true."

"If everybody's evacuated, we better evacuate too. There's a lot of debris around. You should put some shoes on."

"I haven't owned a pair of shoes since I was seventy," Lawrence said. "Don't like them. Never have."

"Well, I've got another pair. Maybe you can get into them. Look, put *something* on, just for protection—come on, now." He tugged Lawrence by his skinny arm down the hall.

Bron really didn't want to go into his own room.

He pushed the door in. The room was perfectly in order. It's waiting for someone to move in, he thought.

On the floor next to the wall sat his yellow plastic luggage sack, delivered by pneumatic tube from the spaceport.

On his desk, beside the reader, was a black- and gold-edged envelope—this one, presumably, *not* a facsimile.

"Here," Bron said, opening a cupboard. Crouching down, he pawed through the slippers, boots, and shoes on the floor. That green pair that were too small for him . . . ? No, he hadn't returned them to his design rental house. "Put these on."

"Socks?" Lawrence asked, wearily, sitting on one corner of the desk.

"In there." Bron stood, pushed around the clothes hanging from the circular rack. "Look, put this cape on too. Out there, things *fall* on you, now. Wrap that around you and it'll be some help."

"Bright yellow?" Lawrence, holding the cape up by the hood, brushed through its folds with his other hand. "Lined with iridescent red and blue stripes . . . naturally."

"It may not be the highest style but it'll do the job."

Lawrence dropped the cloak over one arm and went back to snapping closed the shoes. The socks he'd slipped on were knee-length and lavender. "I always did think clothes were an obscenity."

"On you, sweetheart, they look good." Bron closed the cabinet. "Come on. Move!"

"Well—" Lawrence stood, pulling the cape around his shoulders and frowning down where it brushed the rug—"I suppose, in time of war . . ." He pulled the hood up, frowned, then pushed it back again.

At the door, Bron said: "It *is* the war, isn't it . . . ?"

Lawrence's wrinkled face wrinkled more. "That's what the public channels have been saying for the last hour." Lawrence pulled the cloak around him. "Now that I'm properly attired, just *where* do you propose we go?"

"Well, first let's get out of here." Bron went into the hall. The drive that had returned him had been thrown into reverse by the disaster of Alfred's room.

"Where's Sam?" Lawrence thought to ask, behind him. "Did the two of you come back together?"

"Just as far as the spaceport. Then he went off somewhere else."

"How was your trip to Earth?"

Bron barked a single syllable of laughter. "Remind me to take a lot of cellusin and tell you about it someday. We got out just before war was officially declared."

"Well, that's something, I suppose," Lawrence said, hurrying on behind. "The first two days you wouldn't have known anything was different; then, suddenly, this!"

Downstairs, through the hall; and Bron stepped out of the orange light onto the dark balcony. Behind him, Lawrence said: "Oh, *dear* . . . !"

Bron looked back.

Lawrence, stooping in the doorway, turned over the gaming case. "I've had this for practically thirty years." He closed it, pressed down the brass claws. The miniature shoutings of men, women, and children, like distant mumbles, ran down and, in a stutter of static, stopped. Lawrence fingered the cracked wood. I wonder if it can be fixed?" He laid it against the wall and began to pick up pieces.

"Hey, come *on*!" Bron said.

"Just a moment. I want to put these aside so nobody will step on them." Lawrence picked up the dice, the dice-cup. "When everything started, I ran up here, and as I got to the top, there was some sort of shock. I guess I must have dropped it." He shook his head. "Thirty years. I was older than you are the first time I *saw* the game; but I feel like it's been mine all my life." He pushed a handful of figures to the wall beside the case. "Be careful when you go down the steps. Some of them may have rolled downstairs. They break easily."

Bron said, impatiently: "Sure." But the growing realization that, despite his desire to be somewhere else, he too had nowhere to go, made him wait for the old man.

"You don't remember where the others were *supposed* to go?" he asked Lawrence, who was looking up between the buildings. Across the intersection rose a decorative arch, which, with all its light off, looked like two charred ribs from some incinerated carcass. There were a few stars.

"I wish they would turn on the sky again," Lawrence said. "It's not really agoraphobia—or . . . what *would* you call it? Anauraphobia? Fear of losing one's atmosphere? It's just what with all the gravitational fol-de-rol it . . . well, it would be nice to have it back."

"I think we must have developed at least a couple of holes." Bron squinted down the walkway, darker now than the unlicensed sector. "The wind got pretty rough for a while . . . but it seems to have died down—is that fire along there?"

"If it is," Lawrence said, "let's go the other way."

Bron started along the street, and Lawrence caught up a moment later.

"Audri lives down here," Bron said.

"Who's Audri?" Lawrence asked.

"My boss—one of my bosses. The other is some credit-dripping bastard whose commune lounges in luxury out on the Ring."

"If she lives down this way, I doubt she's dripping much more credit than you are."

"Oh, *she's* not. Just him. She's got three really unbearable kids and lives with a bunch of dykes in a gay co-op."

"Oh," Lawrence said. And then, three steps later: "Going through all this nonsense is bad enough on your own. I can *imagine* what it must be like with children!"

Bron grunted.

"The instructions that came through for evacuation were so garbled," Lawrence said. "I wonder if they got theirs properly?"

Bron grunted again.

"If they had the same sort of interference around them that we had . . . and with children!" Lawrence shrugged his cloak around him. "Oh, dear. That would be just terrible."

Bron felt uncomfortable.

Lawrence was slowing down.

"Do you think we should go down and see if they're still there and need a hand?"

Lawrence said: "The instructions came in *so* garbled . . . I mean, Wang was the only person to figure out that we were supposed to evacuate in the first place."

"There was an enforcement cordon around the area when I came in," Bron said. "I had to break through it."

Lawrence said: "With gravity going up and down at random all over the place, it's pretty dangerous. I'm sure it's safer out in the open than it is inside. On the other hand, if even the *tiniest* fragment of cornice fell on your head at three hundred gravities, you might as well have the whole wall come down on top of you."

"What's a cornice?" Bron asked.

"To be sure," Lawrence said. "The child doesn't know what a cornice is. Which way does your boss live?"

"Right across the street from us, one unit over."

"That should be over there," Lawrence said. "What's that—"

At which point there was an explosion somewhere to the left.

Bron pulled in his shoulders. "I don't know—"

"Not that," Lawrence said. "That—" which was a man, shouting, somewhere at the end of the block, in Audri's direction.

Curious (and even more uncomfortable), Bron turned down the street: Lawrence, beside him, let his cloak swing open again.

They were on the same side of the street as Audri's co-op.

The man—Bron could see him now—shouted again. In the voice Bron heard edges both of hysteria and rage. (Why, Bron wondered, am I walking down a street toward a strange, angry, and possibly crazy man, in the midst of a war. It's neither a reasonable nor a happy situation.) But Lawrence hadn't stopped, so Bron didn't either.

He was a big man, in a maroon jumpsuit, with a slashed shoulder.

"Let me in!" he bawled. "Goddamn it, let me in! Or send *them* out!" His voice tore at things in his throat. "At least send the goddamn kids out if you're too stupid to—" He staggered. "Will you send out my damned kids or I swear—!" He staggered again. "I swear I'll tear the place down with my own hands, so help me Jesus!" He rubbed his stomach, bent unsteadily, then threw back his head. "You send them out here, or I swear I'll come in there and—" Suddenly he rushed forward, up the steps, and pounded on the door (yes, it was Audri's co-op) with both fists.

Bron had been about to whisper to Lawrence that they step into a doorway, to give them time to check this madman out, when the man—he was backing away from the door, his fists and his face raised—glanced at them, turned:

"Oh, Jesus Christ . . ." He shook his head. His face was dirty and tear-stained. What shocked Bron was that the slash in the shoulder of his jump-suit was *not* something put there by a design house. The skin beneath it was badly scratched . . . "Oh, for . . . Jesus Christ! The goddamn bitches just don't understand. They just don't under—" He shook his head again, then turned back to the building and bellowed: "You just give me my goddamn children! I don't care what you do with any of the others, but you just send *mine* out here! Now! I *mean* it! I—" From each cuff dangled a wire cage that apparently could swing up over his paint-flecked hands. Another cage (Bron realized he had seen him before, but couldn't remember for the life of him where, which added to the discomfort) bobbed at the man's shoulder. "The goddamn bitches just don't understand about a—" He coughed violently, backed away, his wrist at his mouth, his eyes tearing—"a man and his children!" Again he turned to shout at the building, but the shout failed. Suddenly he turned, lurched off, reached the middle of the street, stopped, swayed, lurched on. He reached the head of an alley and started down it.

Bron and Lawrence frowned at each other, then looked again.

The craftsman was twenty feet along the alley when a lot happened, very fast: First, he went down on his knees, then fell flat over on his face, but not like an ordinary fall. It was as if he had been metal, and a magnet, suddenly turned on under him, had snapped him flat. Also the entire right-hand wall of the alley, and some of the left, poured—or rather shot—down on top of him.

Bron squinted. His hair snapped at his head. Lawrence's cloak whipped back, then forward about his legs, tugging the old man a few steps with it. Bron had to lean against the wind to keep from moving.

After a second or so the dust, which till now had only made low, rounded waves, thick and fast as water suddenly shot up, swirling, as if—but not "as if," Bron realized: It *was* what had happened—it had become a hundred times as light; as light, again, as dust.

The alley was heaped with ten feet of debris.

Dust drifted.

Bron looked at Lawrence (who coughed), at Audri's building, at the alley, at the building, at Lawrence. "I guess no one's inside," Bron said as the dust passed. Then, because that had sounded so inane, he said: "Maybe we better check, though." He hoped Lawrence wouldn't suggest checking in the alleyway too. Alfred had been bad enough; this could only be worse.

"Can we get around the side?" Lawrence asked, and obviously (and blessedly) meant the co-op.

Between the co-op building and the building next to it, there was a narrow gate, which, when Bron reached through and lifted the hasp ("Now *I* never would have thought of that," Lawrence said), swung open.

"Maybe we can find a window or something and get a look inside." Bron's skin tingled with memories of the alley he had just watched collapse. But Lawrence came in right after him, so he had to keep going forward: There wasn't room to squeeze back around him. He was wondering who would have a window facing out on a two-foot-wide alley when he came to one, with two, astonished faces in it—which were suddenly pushed aside by three more.

While heated conferral began among the women behind the glass, another woman pushed between them to look: and that was Audri, who grinned, nodded at him quickly, then turned away to join the conference.

Bron made come-out gestures.

They made helpless gestures back.

Bron made open-the-window gestures.

They made more helpless.

Someone carefully mimed something Bron thought must mean the front door was locked.

Bron made stand-back motions, took off his sandal, then thought better and got Lawrence to give him one of the green shoes, and made to hurl it at the window. Some of the women inside looked distressed. Others laughed. They all stood back.

So Bron hurled it, heel first.

The glass shattered into an opaque web—that hung there. It was backed with plastic film so that he had to throw the shoe several times more, and then finally tear it away with his hand, nicking his fingers several places.

"Come on, you've got to get out!"

"What?"

"You've got to evacuate this area," he shouted into the shadowed room full of women. "Audri? Hey, Audri, you have to get out of here."

"I *told* you those were evacuation instructions," one of the women was saying loudly to a group at the back of the room, "before the public channels went dead."

"Audri, you better get your kids and—Audri?"

But she had left the room with several others.

Bron climbed through the window (a woman he hadn't seen helped him down), while Lawrence went around to the front, and Bron more or less figured out from overlapping snippets that they hadn't wanted to open the front door because of the man Bron and Lawrence had seen shouting. At which point a dozen children came into the room with several mothers, among them Audri (who was wearing a bright scarlet body-stocking with a lot of feathery things trailing from her head-band). "Hey!" He made his way to her side, took her shoulder. "You better get your kids together so we can get out of here—"

She blinked at him. "What do you think we're doing? You said we had to evacuate, didn't you? Everyone will be down in a second."

"Oh," Bron said. "Oh, yeah. Sure." More kids came in.

Two women were calling out instructions.

"Um . . ." Bron said. "Hey! They better all wear shoes. There's lots of junk in the street."

Three children dashed out of the room to get them.

A woman who seemed to be in charge turned to Bron. "It really was something, your coming to tell us. Nobody's quite known what was going on since the retaliation this afternoon. And then with Mad Mike outside—well, he seems to be gone now. But we didn't know whether he'd done something to interfere with our channel reception or whether it was just part of the general confusion. With gale-force winds going on and off, nobody wanted to go out anyway, especially with the kids." Freddie and Flossie were the only one-parent family at Serpent's House, but at a sexually specified co-op, straight or gay, you would expect a few more. Also, of course, this was a woman's co-op. And, as a public-channel survey had once put it: As long as women bore 70 percent of the children, you couldn't be surprised that nearly 60 percent of the one-parent families had a woman at their head.

As they were leaving the building (one of Audri's boys had glommed onto Lawrence, along with another kid Bron had never seen) Bron asked: "Who *was* that Mad Mike character?"

Audri glanced around, checking, then said, confidentially: "He used to live with John—" She nodded toward a woman, in something flimsy, cream-colored and diaphanous, who, till now, he'd just assumed was one of the older children.

"She had two children by him. He's some sort of very eccentric craftsman, but what kind I don't know."

"Why didn't you let him in?"

Audri humphed. "The last three times she did, as soon as he got her alone, he beat her up; then sat her down for the next hour and explained why it was all her fault he'd done it. Really, John's sweet, but she's *not* very bright. We were trying to get through to the e-girls, but communication was out both in and out of the place."

"Oh," Bron said. "Yeah . . . well. I guess, maybe because they were his children—"

Audri humphed again. "This sudden revitalization of interest only started a year back when he became a Christian. He apparently wasn't very interested in them back when she was having them, or in the two years right after." Audri scanned the group as it turned the corner. "I mean, if he wants kids of his own, there are ten ways he can go about getting them—here, that is. And at least twenty-five over in the u-l."

Bron followed the herd of women around the corner. "I *thought* he might have been a Christian." They were heading back toward the Plaza of Light. "From some of the expressions he used." He looked up at the unfamiliar and unsettling night. "You know, they're almost as much trouble as the Jews?"

Audri said: "Hey, come on, you kids. Stop horsing around. *This way*. Where *did* he go, anyway? He usually hangs around a good deal longer when he decides to make a nuisance of himself. He was getting to be quite a neighborhood character."

"Oh," Bron said, feeling uncomfortable again. "Well, he saw Lawrence and me and then he . . . went away."

Audri glanced at him. "You scared him off? You get a vote of thanks for that! Character or not, he was getting to be a pain."

A child came up to ask Audri about something Bron didn't understand, to which she returned a (to Bron) incomprehensible answer, while Bron wondered when he would tell Audri of Mad Mike's fate. No matter how uncomfortable it made him, he *had* to do that.

Audri said: "It was downright heroic of you to come around and give us a hand like this. We were all pretty scared. Some of the sounds coming in from outside—and I just don't mean Mike's carrying on . . . Well, they weren't the sort to encourage you to take to the streets."

Bron was preparing to say, Mike is probably dead, when the sky (or rather the shield) came on.

The children cheered—which brought some dozen e-girls charging from the next alley:

What did they think they were doing in a restricted area?

Trying as best they could to get out of it!

Didn't they know that there was serious gravity derangement all over this sector of the city? Over a hundred and six people had been reported dead already!

That was *just* why they were trying to leave! Which way should they go?

Well, actually, the sensory shield's going on was the official signal that it was all under control again. They could go back home if they wanted.

Which brought more cheers, and laughter from the women.

Already other people were appearing in the street.

Bron turned to say something to Audri, only to find Lawrence at his shoulder.

"Let's go home," Lawrence said. "Please? Let's go home now."

Bron didn't want to go back to Serpent's House. He wanted to go back to Audri's, and have the women give him coffee and a meal and talk and smile and laugh with him, joke about his breaking the window and make much about his coming to rescue them and his scaring off the crazy Christian. But there would be the kids. And already women were——

". . . at work next week!" Audri was calling across lots of heads and waving.

"Oh. yeah!" Bron waved back. "I'll see you. At work."

"Come on." Lawrence said. "Please?"

Bron started to say something angry. But it failed. "Sure." Bron sighed. And after they had walked through two and a half units: "This has been some vacation!"

The Spike's (nonfacsimile) letter was waiting for him on his table.

In his clean room (the cupboard door was still open, but he was too tired to close it), he sat on his bed and reread it. Then he read it once more. Halfway through he realized he wasn't even hearing it in the Spike's voice, but in the voice of the woman at Audri's co-op who had been calling instructions to the other women. He started again, this time hearing the accusations in the electronically strained tone of the hegemony's Personnel receptionist. He read it once more, finally in the voice of the e-girl who'd been hallooing that he could not pass the cordon, and whom he'd tricked by joining the mumblers.

"Hey," Lawrence said, shouldering through the door, once more naked, carrying his cracked vlet case in both hands. "I've found almost *all* the pieces! Only four of them got stepped on, and I'm sure I can get another astral board from——"

"Lawrence?" Bron looked up from the black- and gold-edged flimsy. "Lawrence, you know, he was right?"

"This isn't *too* bad, is it?" Lawrence ran a yellowish nail over the cracked inlay. "There used to be a marvelous craftsman over in the unlicensed sector who specialized in games. I'm sure she could fix this one good as new—if her place is still up. The public channels were saying that the u-l got hit the hardest. But then, isn't that typical?"

"Lawrence, he was right."

"Who?" Lawrence looked up.

"That Christian—the one we saw out in front of Audri's co-op. Mad Mike."

"Right about what?"

"About women." Bron suddenly crumpled the letter between cupped hands. "They don't understand."

"You mean they don't understand *you*? Some of us, my dear, get along smashingly with women. Even me, from time to time. No misunderstandings at all: Just pure sympathy and sympatico right down the line. Of course with me it doesn't last. But does it ever, all the time, with anyone?"

"They don't understand about *men*—Not you, Lawrence. I mean ordinary, heterosexual men. They can't. It's just a logical impossibility. I'm a logician and I know."

Lawrence laughed. "My *dear* boy! I have observed you intimately now for six months and you are a sweet and familiar creature—alas, far more familiar than six months should make you. Let me tell you a secret. There *is* a difference between men and women, a little, tiny one that, I'm afraid, has probably made most of your adult life miserable and will probably continue to make it so till you die. The difference is simply that women have only really been treated, by that bizarre, Durkheimian abstraction, 'society,' as human beings for the last—oh, say sixty-five years; and then, really, only on the moons; whereas men have had the luxury of such treatment for the last four thousand. The result of this historical anomaly is simply that, on a statistical basis, women are just a little less willing to put up with certain kinds of shit than men—simply because the concept of a certain kind of shit-free Universe is, in that equally bizarre Jungian abstraction, the female 'collective unconscious,' too new and too precious." Lawrence's brows knitted; he frowned at Bron's knotted fists. "Why, I *bet* that's a letter from a lady—I confess, when I was checking for corpses, I had a peek in here and saw the name and the return address. Your problem, you see, is that essentially you are a logical pervert, looking for a woman with a mutually compatible logical perversion. The fact is, the mutual perversion you are looking for is very, very rare—if not nonexistent. You're looking for someone who can enjoy a certain sort of logical masochism. If it were *just* sexual, you'd have no trouble finding a partner at all—as your worldly experience no doubt has already informed you. Hang them from the ceiling, burn their nipples with matches, stick pins in their buttocks and cane them bloody! There're gaggles of women, just as there are gaggles of men, who would be delighted to have a six-foot, blond iceberg like you around to play such games with. You can get a list of the places they frequent just by dialing Information. But, though she is a religious fanatic like Mad Mike, who believes that the children of her body are one with the objects of her hand, or a sociopath like poor Alfred, who doesn't quite have a model for anyone, correct or incorrect; be she nun or nymphomaniac, a loud political pamphleteer running around in the u-l sector, or a pillar of society living elegantly on the Ring, or anywhere in between, or any combination, the one thing she is *not* going to do is put up with your hurry-up-and-wait, your do-a-little-tap-dance-while-you-stand-on-your-head, your run-around-in-circles-while-you-walk-a-straight-line, especially when it's out of bed and simply has no hope of pleasurable feedback. Fortunately, your particular perversion today is extremely rare. Oh, I would say maybe one man out of fifty has it—quite amazing, considering that it once was about as common as the ability to grow a beard. Just compare it to some of the other major sexual types: homosexuality, one out of five; bisexuality, three out of five; sadism and masochism, one out of nine; the varieties of fetishism, one out of eight. So you see, at one out of *fifty,* you really are in a difficult situation. And what makes it more difficult—even tragic—is that the corresponding perversion you're searching for in women, thanks to that little historical anomaly, is more like one out of five thousand. Yes, I have a—believe me—platonic curiosity about both male and female victims of this deviation. Yes, I exploit the attendant loneliness of the unfulfilled by offering friendship. Psychic vampirism? Believe me, there's as much of the blood donor about me as there is of Vlad Tepes. I don't know anything about the woman responsible for that—" He nodded toward the crumpled letter—"other than her public reputation. But I've lived a long time. I can make a few speculations about her. Bron, in your terms, she simply doesn't exist. I mean, how can she? You're a logical sadist looking for a logical masochist. But you *are* a logician. If you redefine the relation between P and Not-P beyond a certain point—well, then you just aren't talking about logic any more. All you've done, really, is change the subject."

"I'm a metalogician," Bron said. "I define and redefine the relation between P and Not-P five hours a day, four days a week. Women don't understand. Faggots don't understand either."

Lawrence hefted up the vlet case, leaned against the wall, and raised an eyebrow. "*Do* explain."

Bron hunched his shoulders. "Look, I . . .." He straightened them. "It was something to do with, I don't know, maybe a kind of bravery—"

"Bravery is just making a big thing about doing what's best for the largest number of people. The only problem is that the same process by which we make a big thing out of it usually blinds us to seeing the number of people as large enough to be really worthwhile—"

"If you're just going to stand there and say stupid things intended to be clever—" Bron was angry.

"You're angry." Lawrence hefted the case once more. "I'm sorry. Go on."

Bron looked at his meshed fingers, the gold-and-black edging between them. "You know, Sam's trip to Earth was basically a political mission. You can be glad you didn't go. During it, some of us were captured. Some of us were killed. I got off easy. I was just tortured. They held me without food. I wasn't allowed to go to the bathroom. They stuck prongs in me. They beat me up, all the time asking the same questions again and again . . . I know, it could have been worse. No bones broken; and, hell, I'm alive. But some of us . . . aren't. It wasn't pleasant. The thing that really made it bad was that we weren't even allowed to talk about any of it—by our side, either—to each other or to anyone else. Anything we might have said could have gotten one or all of us killed, just like that! And that's when I ran into this—" He held up the crumpled letter, looked at his fist, let it drop—"woman. Of course, you're right. She didn't exist. The day after I got out, I took her out to dinner. It was so funny, sitting there in this incredibly expensive restaurant, where they still use money, that she'd wanted to go to—some friends of hers had been there already, and she was on her ear to try it out—and realize that a single word from me about any of what had just happened to me might have meant my death, or the death of a dozen others, or even hers, while all she was concerned with was that she'd bowed to the proper fashion—you'd have liked it; it's one of those places where bare feet are *de rigeur,* but, frankly, I couldn't be bothered—or that she was making the right impression on the waiters and the majordomo, as a charming and naive innocent—that's when she wasn't prattling on about how marvelous this or that love affair had been. I mean, not that I should have been surprised. You know, I'd met her a few times before, here in Tethys. We'd even had sex a few times, casually and— well, I thought very successfully. But just as an example: The first time I met her, I told her about you, said that she ought to meet you. She got very huffy about that; apparently she doesn't like homosexuals. Doesn't approve of them or something. She's still going on about that in here—" Bron held up the letter. "Took great offense that I should think she would have anything to do with anyone who was. I mean, can you imagine? In *this* day and age—? Not that she isn't above engaging in a little herself from time to time, and quite happily, or so she claims, when she lets her hair down. But, apparently, *that's* different. Really, a logically consistent position is just beyond her— though, like you, she talks about logic enough. Really, the only rea- son she gives for not wanting to know *you* is because I happened to mention you were gay! Take a look—" Bron held out the crumpled letter.

Lawrence raised his chin. "Really, you're succeeding in making her sound like someone in whom I could not have the least interest—and certainly not in her scurrilous correspondence."

Bron relocked his hands between his knees. "Well, that's the type she is. Anyway, there we were, at the restaurant. It had been really rough on me, with the arrest and the interrogation. And I just felt I needed something—not sex: something *more* than that, some sort of . . . I don't know: support, friendship, warmth, compassion—though, believe me—once she got the slightest inkling I *did* want something more than sex, she decided sex was out as well. From then on it was just a big flat nothing. I mean, I *couldn't* talk about what had hap- pened to me, what I'd been through; it was just too dangerous. But she didn't even have a clue that anything was even wrong. There was just no understanding at all . . . They don't understand. They can't understand. Men just have to go through it alone."

"You were saying something about bravery?" Lawrence hefted the case again.

"Well, yeah. I mean I don't want to make a big thing of it; but, well, when I wanted to come back here, to check out you, and Audri and the kids, first I had to break through an enforcement cordon. It wasn't really that hard; I just mixed in with a crowd of the Poor Chil- dren of the Avestal Light and Changing Secret Name. Years ago I used to attend their instruction, so I could fake a mantra—well enough to get by, anyway. And I got through like that. I'm not saying it took a *lot* of ingenuity; but it took some. And in a time of social crisis, *some-body's* got to have that kind of ingenuity, if just to protect the species, the women, the children—yes, even the aged. And that ingenuity comes out of the aloneness, that particular male aloneness. It's not even conscious. I mean I wasn't even trying that hard. But in time of crisis, some things just have to be done. Sometimes it's keeping your mouth shut, or not doing something you want to that'll endanger others. Sometimes it's doing something you wouldn't do normally, like breaking through an enforcement cordon, or a window, or even through somebody's really dumb ideas." Bron laughed. "I'm just trying to imagine that crazed bitch I was out to dinner with, with all that stuff about this lover or that—they included the two she had at the present—keeping her mouth shut about *anything!* A matter of life or death? That wouldn't have stopped her! Or picking her way through the debris in the street out there. She'd have to spend a day deciding whether or not she had on the proper hiking clothes. Oh, I'm not saying women can't be courageous. But it's a different sort of—Well, I just guess women, or people with large female components to their personalities, are too social to have that necessary aloneness to act outside society. But as long as we have social crises—whether they're man-made ones like this war, or even natural ones like an ice-quake—despite what it says in the ice-operas, we need that particularly *male* aloneness, if only for the ingenuity it breeds, so that the rest of the species can survive. I suppose, in one sense, women *are* society. I mean, they reproduce it, don't they? Or seventy percent of it, today, anyway. Not that I begrudge them what, like you say, in the last hundred and seventy-five years they've been given—"

The vlet case slipped from Lawrence's hands, crashed to the floor, and fell open. Two of the side drawers flew out, scattering over the rug cards, dice, and red and green figures.

Bron stood up.

Lawrence, with a small cry, fell to his knees, muttering, "Oh, really . . ." and, "For crying out . . .", and went scrabbling after the pieces, looking more and more upset.

"Hey," Bron said, after a moment, "don't get so . . . Here, I'll help you get—"

"You're a fool," Lawrence said, suddenly and hoarsely. "And I'm tired. I'm tired of it, that's all there is. I'm tired."

"Huh?"

Lawrence clacked two dice back in place, reached for a third—

"Hey . . ." Bron heard the hostility in the clack and tried to retrace what he'd said to that point where it had been generated. "Oh, hey; when I said faggots didn't understand, I was just being—I don't know: bitchy. Look, whatever you like to screw or get screwed by, *you're* still a man. You've been alone. After all, you live in *this* place, don't you? You did just as much as I did to make sure Audri and the kids were all right. I mean it was really *your* idea to—"

Lawrence sat back; pale, wrinkled hands dragged against dark, wrinkled genitals. "You're a fool! You're a fool! You're a fool! You're going to talk to me about bravery?" One hand snapped up and pointed out the door. "There's your bravery. There's your ingenuity. Right across the hall, in Alfred's room—no, they haven't cleaned them out yet. The people who did that to them, busily doing what must be done for the survival of the species, and so efficiently! Without the loss of a single soldier. On either side." Lawrence's hand fell back to the floor among the pieces. "What I *came* in here to tell you in the first place . . ." Lawrence took a breath, let it go. His shoulders fell. "The war is over. They just announced it over the public channels. Apparently, we've won it—whatever that means. Lux on Iapetus has no survivors. Five million people—all dead. Sabotage was completely effective there. They lost all gravity and atmosphere. Loss of life was under eight percent on Europa and Callisto. G-City's figures from Ganymede aren't in yet, which may be good or bad. Triton, the last in, apparently got off lightest. On the other hand, we've charred eighteen percent of Earth's land-surface area. Eighty-two hours after Triton joined the war, all stops were pulled out by both sides. Mars officially surrendered, with casualties under a million, mostly in smaller urban Holds outside Bellona." Lawrence picked up a red Witch, looked at it, let it drop from his fingers into his palm, let his fist fall again to the floor. "There's apparently no official communication from Earth, but we're taking that as surrender: Everybody who could do it officially is dead. They're already showing aerial pictures of some of the sections we hit: mostly in North and South Africa, Central America, and East Asia. Though they tried to stay away from major population centers, they estimate that sixty to seventy-five percent of the Earth's population is either dead already or—as they so quaintly put it—will be dead within the next seventy-two hours. Because of the resultant 'confusion'—they called it." Lawrence shook his head. "*Confusion* . . . ! Bravery in time of crisis!" He looked at Bron. "I was *born* in South Africa. I didn't like it. I left it. I had no intention of going back. But that doesn't give them the right to go and just burn it all up! Oh, I know one isn't supposed to talk about embarrassing things like where one comes from. I sound like some political crazy over in the u-l, talking about *my* origins. They *still* don't have the right!" He leaned forward and swiped about at scattered pieces. "They still don't . . . ! Seventy-five percent! *You* were just on Earth . . . Didn't you, sometime, somewhere, meet one—just *one* person there that you liked, that you had some feeling for—negative or positive, it doesn't matter. The chances are now three out of four that that person, in the next seventy-two hours, will die. In the confusion. And when they have died, they will be just as dead as those two children across the hall— No, don't *bother* with these! I can get them myself. You go across the hall and just check *how* dead they are!"

But Bron had not started to kneel. Looking at the crumpled letter still in his fist, an image of the Spike, on Earth, 'in the confusion,' had hit him as vividly as a scene returned by chance odor: he had staggered. His heart knocked back and forth around his ribs. The thoughts flooding into his mind were too violent to be called thinking (at least *that* thought was clear); he watched Lawrence pick among the pieces. Finally—was it a minute? Was it five?—he asked hoarsely:

"You really think it's one out of . . . five thousand?"

"What?" Lawrence looked up, frowning.

"About the . . . women?"

Lawrence took a breath and began to pick up more pieces. "I *could* be off by as much as a thousand—in *either* direction!"

Bron flung the letter on the floor ("Hey, where are you—?" Lawrence called) and bolted into the hall.

He didn't go into Alfred's room.

Downstairs at the computer room, half a dozen men waited outside and, when he barged past, tried to explain that there was at least a twenty-minute wait to get any medical diagnostic program.

"I don't *want* a diagnosis!" He shoved past. "I know what's wrong! I want Clinic Information!" He banged into the cubicle. He wasn't sure if he could get Clinic Information if there was a diagnosis tie-up. But when he punched his request, the address ticked across the screen immediately. He pressed the purple button, and it was typed out on a strip of purple-backed flimsy. He ripped it loose from the slit and charged out of the room.

There was a small crowd outside the transport kiosk. Delays? He turned the corner, deciding to walk. The address was in the unlicensed sector. Which was typical. Here and there he passed stretches of wreckage. Labor groups were already assembled at some sites. He found himself comparing the shiny yellow coveralls the men and women wore here to the soiled work-clothes of the earthie diggers. (Seventy-five percent . . . ?) But it left him with a numb feeling, another irrelevancy, before his destination. I should pray for them, he thought, and tried to recall his mumble, all that came back to him was the ranting of the Beasts—*the mutilation of the mind, the mutilation of the body*! He hunched his shoulders, squinched his eyes in the dust swirling in the green light—the left-hand lightstrip was dead—of the tiled underpass. Walking out onto the darker way, it became apparent that the u-l had, indeed, been harder hit. Which was, indeed, typical.

Would the clinic be open?

They were.

The blue reception room was empty, except for a woman in a complicated armchair in one corner, a complicated console on one of its arms. Eyes to a set of binocular readers, she tapped an occasional input on the console keys. Bron walked up to her. She swung the reader aside and smiled. "May I help you?"

Bron said: "I want to be a woman."

"Yes. And what sex are you now?"

Which was not the response he expected. "Well what do I look like?"

She made a small moue. "You could be a male who is partway through one of a number of possible sex-change processes. Or you could be a female who is much further along in a number of *other* sex change operations: In both those cases, you would be wanting us to complete work already begun. More to the point, you might have begun as a woman, been changed to male, and now want to be changed to—something else. *That* can be difficult." But because in a completely different context he had once used such a console for three months, he saw that she had already punched in 'Male.' "Or," she concluded, "you could be a woman in very good drag."

"I'm male."

She smiled. "Let's have your identity card—" which he handed her and she fed into the slot at the console's bottom. "Thank you."

Bron glanced around at the empty chairs that sat about the waiting room. "There isn't anyone else here . . . ?"

"Well," the woman said, dryly, "you know we've just had a war this afternoon. Things are rather slow. But we're carrying on . . . you just go right through there."

Bron went through the blue wall into a smaller room, intestinal pink.

The man behind the desk was just removing Bron's card from the slot on his console. He smiled at it, at Bron, at the pink chair across from him, at the card again. He stood up, extended his hand across the desk.

"Delighted to meet you, Ms. Helstrom—"

"I'm male," Bron said. "I just told your receptionist—"

"But you want to be female," the man said, took Bron's hand, shook it, dropped it, and coughed. "We believe in getting started right away, especially with the easy things. Do sit down."

Bron sat.

The man smiled, sat himself. "Now, once more, Ms. Helstrom, can you tell us what you'd like from us?"

Bron tried to relax. "I want you to make me a woman." Saying it the second time was nowhere as hard as the first.

"I see," the man said. "You're from Mars—or possibly Earth, right?"

Bron nodded. "Mars."

"Thought so. Most of our beneficiaries are. Terrible what happened there this afternoon. Just terrible. But I imagine that doesn't concern you." He sucked his teeth. "Still somehow life under our particular system doesn't generate that many serious sexually dissatisfied types. Though, if you've come here, I suspect you're the type who's pretty fed up with people telling you what type you aren't or are." The man raised an eyebrow and coughed again quizzically.

Bron was silent.

"So, you want to be a woman." The man cocked his head. "What kind of a woman do you want to be? Or rather, how much of a woman?"

Bron frowned.

"Do you simply want what essentially could be called cosmetic surgery—we can do quite a fine job; and quite a functional one. We can give you a functional vagina, functional clitoris, even a function-al womb in which you can bear a baby to term and deliver it, and functional breasts with which you can suckle the infant once it is born. More than that, however, and we have to leave the realm of the cosmetic and enter the radical."

Bron's frown deepened. "What is there beyond that you can do?"

"Well." The man lay his hands on the table. "In every one of your cells—Well, not all: notable exceptions are the red blood cells—there are forty-six chromosomes, long DNA chains, each of which can be considered two, giant, intertwined molecules, in which four nucleotides—adenine, thymine, cytosine, and guanine—are strung along, to be read sequentially in groups of three: the order of these groups determines the order of the amino acids along the polypeptide chains that make up the proteins and enzymes which, once formed, proceed to interact with each other and the environment in such a way that, after time and replenishment . . . Well, the process is far too complicated to subsume under a single verb: Let us simply say *there* they were, and *here* you are! I say forty-six: This would be completely true if you were a woman. But what made you a man is the half-length chromosome called Y, which is paired with a full-length chromosome called X. In women, there are two of these X's and no Y at all. And, oddly, as long as you have at least one Y in the cells, it usually doesn't matter how many X's you have—and occasionally they double up— the organism is male. Now, the question is, how did this Y chromosome make you a male, back when various cells were dividing and your little balloon of tissue was suffering various Thomian catastrophes and folding in and crumpling up into you?" The man smiled. "But I suppose I'm merely recapitulating what you already know . . . ? Most of our beneficiaries have done a fair amount of research on their own before they come to us."

"I haven't," Bron said. "I just made up my mind about . . . maybe an hour ago."

"Then again," the men went on, "some *do* make their decisions quickly. And it might interest you to know that many among these are our most successful cases—if they're the proper type." He smiled, nodded. "Now, as I was saying: How does the Y chromosome do it?"

"It has the blue prints on it of the amino acid order for the male sex hormones?" Bron asked.

"Now, you *must* get the whole idea of 'blue-printing' out of your mind. The chromosomes don't *describe* anything directly about the body. They *prescribe,* which is a different process entirely. Also, that Y chromosome is, for all practical purposes, just the tail end of an X chromosome. No, it's more complicated than that. One way that chromosomes work is that an enzyme created by one length will activate, so to speak, the protein created by another length, either on the same chromosome or on a different one entirely. Or, sometimes, they will inactivate another product from another length. If you want to use the rather clumsy concept of genes—and, really, the concept of gene is just an abstraction, because there are no marked-out genes, there are just strings of nucleotides; they're not framed at all, and starting to read the triplets at the proper point can be a real problem—we can say that certain genes turn on, or activate, other genes, while certain other genes inhibit the activity of others. There is a complicated inter-chain of turning-off's and turning-on's back and forth between the X and Y—for instance, a cell with multiple Y chromosomes and no X's can't do this and just dies—which leaves various genes on both the X and Y active which in turn activate genes all through the forty-six that prescribe male characteristics, while genes that would prescribe certain female characteristics are not activated (or in other cases specifically inactivated). The interchange that would occur between two X chromosomes would leave different genes activated all over the X chromosomes that would in turn activate those female pre-scription genes and inactivate the male ones throughout the rest of the forty-four. For instance, there's a gene that is activated on the Y that activates the production of androgen—actually parts of the an-drogen itself are designed along a section of the X chromosome—while another gene, which Y activates on the X, causes another gene, somewhere else entirely, to get the body up so it can respond to the androgen. If *this* gene, somehow, *isn't* activated, as occasionally hap-pens, then you get what's called testicular feminization. Male sex hor-mones are produced, but the body can't respond to them, so in that case you have a Y and a woman's body anyway. This situation be-tween the X and Y makes it logically moot whether we consider the man an incomplete woman or the woman an incomplete man. The arrangement in birds and lizards, for example, is such that the half-length chromosome is carried by the females and the full-length is carried by the males: The males are X-X and the females are X-Y. At any rate, one of the things we can do for a man is infect him with a special virus-like substance related to something called an episome, which will actually carry in an extra length of X and deposit it in all his cells so that the Y is, so to speak, completed and all those cells that were X-Y will now be, in effect, X-X."

"What will this accomplish?"

"Astonishingly little, actually. But it makes people feel better about it. Many of these things have to come into play at certain times in the development of the body to have noticeable effect. For instance the brain, left to its own devices, develops a monthly cyclic hormone discharge which then excites the ovaries, in a woman, at monthly intervals, to produce the female hormones which cause them to ovulate. The introduction of androgen, however, makes that part of the brain stem develop differently and the monthly cycle is damped way down. The brain stem is visibly different during dissection—in women, the brain stem is noticeably thicker than in men. But the point is, once this development *has* occurred and the monthly cycle is suppressed, even if the androgen is discontinued, the brain doesn't revert back. Things of this sort are very difficult to reverse. They take ten or twelve minutes of bubble-micro-surgery. But that's the way we do most of what we do. We try to use clones of your own tissue for whatever has to be enlarged—the *uterus masculinus* for your uterus; and we take actual germ plasm from your testes and grow-cum-sculpt ovaries from them—which is quite a feat. Have you ever considered the difference between your reproductive equipment and *hers*—? Hers is much more efficient. At birth she's already formed about five hundred thousand eggs, which, through a comparatively nonviolent absorption and generation process, reduces to about two hundred thousand by puberty, each waiting to proceed down into the womb—you know, practically ninety-nine percent of the data about what's going to happen to 'you,' once the father's genes meet up with the mother's, is contained in the *rest* of the egg that's nonchromosomal. That's why the egg, compared to the sperm, is so big. You, on the other hand, produce about three hundred million sperm every *day,* out of which, if you're prime breeding material, perhaps a hundred or so can actually fertilize anything. The other two hundred million, nine hundred ninety-nine thousand and nine hundred are lethal mutations, pure wasted effort, against which the female has an antibody system (fortunately) that weeds the bad ones out like germs. In fact, stimulating this antibody system further—you have it too—is the basis of our birth control system." He coughed. "Topologically, men and women are identical. Some things are just larger and more developed in one than the other and positioned differently. But we begin by completing your X chromosomes. I say completing—you mustn't think I'm catering to some supposed prejudice on your part where, because you want to be a woman, I'm assuming you think men inferior creatures and I'm buttering you up by downgrading—"

"I don't think men are inferior," Bron said. "I just want to be a woman. I suppose you'll tell me that's a type too."

The man's smile drew in just a little. "Yes, Ms. Helstrom, I'm afraid it is. But then, it's not my place to judge. I'm only here to inform and counsel. Childbirth is only one of the things that can make a woman's life more complicated than a man's—but of course four out of five women today choose not to have children; does childbirth particularly interest you?"

"No."

"Well, at least you'll know you're free to change your mind. Basically, however, you'll be getting a much better designed, more complicated body. Treat it well, and all will go well with it. Treat it poorly, and, I'm afraid, because it *is* more complicated, there are more things that can go wrong with it. This can be a problem, especially to an inexperienced woman, a woman like you, Ms. Helstrom, who is—how shall I put it? Not to the manner born."

Bron wondered how many times a day he put it exactly like that.

"But I hope you'll accept the help I can give you, if only the information about the purely biological possibilities." The man took a breath. "Of course, other methods have been devised for female-to-male transsexuals. But that probably doesn't interest you . . . ?"

"I had a friend," Bron said. "He . . . she . . . well, he used to be a woman. Now he's got a family, and at least one child. How did that come about?"

"Oh, there are quite a number of possibilities." The man touched fingertips and nodded. "The simplest one, of course, is adoption. Then, there is a complicated process in which the germ plasm is induced to form all-X sperm, similar to the male bird or lizard. Was the child a daughter?"

Bron nodded.

"Then it's quite possible. But we were talking about you. What would you like us to do?"

"The whole thing."

The man drew another breath. "I see." But he was smiling.

"I want to be genetically, hormonally, physically a woman . . ." He found his hands clutching each other. He released them and said, more softly: "Don't you want to know my reasons?"

If there were a scale of smiles, the one in front of Bron would have dropped a minor second. "Ms. Helstrom, we are counselors here—*not* judges. We assume you have your reasons, that you have worked them out logically to your own satisfaction. I only have information, most of it biological: If this fits with your reasons, fine. If it makes you uncertain about them, by all means take as much time to reconsider as you need; five minutes, five days, five years—If you think it's necessary." The man suddenly leaned forward. "Ms. Helstrom, it would be completely fatuous of me to pretend I was unaware that, even in this day and age, such a decision as you have made may cause some consternation among one's co-operative, if not communal, colleagues. It's hard not to find such consternation upsetting—not to mention those nameless social attitudes that one internalized during a less enlightened youth on a world with a different culture, that are, very often, the same attitudes the dissatisfaction with which prompted one to the decision confronting us now. And while we have our own emotional commitment to bolster us, these external prejudices assail us nevertheless, invariably presenting themselves in the guise of logic. Let me try and offer you some support, Ms. Helstrom. Are you by any chance familiar with a current area of computer mathematics called metalogic?"

Bron raised his real eyebrow. "As a matter of fact I am."

"Thought you might be." The man's smile rose a perfect fifth. "Logic can only tell us about the possible relations of elements that are already known. It gives us no tools to analyze any of those elements into more basic knowns or unknowns. It gives us no way to extrapolate about elements outside what we know. Analysis and extrapolation are both accomplished by reasoning—of which logic is only a very incomplete part. The point is, with life enclosed between two vast parentheses of nonbeing and straited on either side by inevitable suffering, there is no *logical* reason ever to try to improve any situation. There are, however, many reasons of *other* types for making as many improvements as you reasonably can. Any reasoning process, as it deviates from strict, deductive logic, is a metalogical one. There is no logical way that you can even *know* that I am sitting here on the other side of the desk from you, or even that . . . well, that there is your own hand. Both could be illusions: We have the technology—downstairs, in the west wing—to produce illusions, involving both belief and knowledge of those beliefs as true, far more complicated than either, by working directly on the brain. What are your social responsibilities when you have a technology like that available? The answer that the satellites seem to have come up with is to try and make the subjective reality of each of its citizens as politically inviolable as pos-

sible, to the point of destructive distress—and the destruction must
be complained about by another citizen; and *you* must complain
about the distress. Indeed, there are those who believe, down to the
bottom of their subjective hearts, that the war we just . . ." He
coughed: "—won this afternoon was fought to preserve that invio-
lability. Soldiers or not, I don't. But basically our culture allows,
supports, and encourages behavior that, simply in the streets of
both unlicensed and licensed sectors, would have produced some
encounter with some restraining institution if they were indulged in
on Earth a hundred years ago." He cocked an eyebrow, let it uncock.
"The situation of your life in the world is such that you think it
would be better if you were a woman."

"Yes," Bron said.

"Very well." The man sat back, pulling his hands to the edge of
the desk. "We can get started anytime you like."

"And the psychological part?"

The smile dropped an octave, which left it hovering at the threshold
of a frown. "I beg your pardon?"

"What about the psychological part?"

The man sat forward again, the smile recovering. "I don't quite
under . . . ? You want to be converted physically into a woman. And
you . . ." And fell again. "You don't mean in terms of . . . well—" He
coughed again. "Actually, Ms. Helstrom, you have just presented a
situation that really *is* unusual. Most of our . . . our male clients want
the physical operation because, in one way or another, they feel they
already *are,* in some sense, psychologically more suited to a female
body and the female situation, however they perceive it. But I gather
. . ." The eyebrows gathered—"you don't?"

"No." And after the man said nothing for practically half a minute,
Bron said: "You *do* do sexual refixations and things like that, here, in
this clinic, don't you?"

"Yes, we—" The man coughed again and Bron realized it was an
honest cold, not a purposefully snide punctuation (another religious
fanatic, more than likely. Bron sighed)—"Well, downstairs, in the
west wing. Yes, we do. But . . ." Now he laughed. "Well, so seldom do
the two departments have to work on the same case that—well, there
isn't even a door from our office to theirs. I mean, they deal with an
entirely different type of case: friends, of whatever sex, who want to
introduce a sexual element into their relationships because one, or
both of them, are having difficulty doing it naturally; various functional problems; people who just want to try something new; or people

who just want the sexual element completely suppressed, often for religious reasons." The laughter broke again. "I'm afraid to avail yourself of their services, you literally have to go outside and come in all over again. Here—it's been a slow day. Let me come with you." The man pushed back his chair, stood.

The room was mottled green, octagonal: Pastel lumias glowed in gilt frames around the walls. It was apparently a much larger and busier department: War or no, a dozen men and women were waiting to be seen.

But though it was a different department, there was enough connection so that, coming in with his "counselor," Bron was taken right away into an ivory cubicle with two technicians and several banks of equipment.

"Could you do a quick fixation grid of this gentleman's" (Bron noted the restoration of his gender) "sexual deployment template? Just for my own curiosity—dispense with the interview part. I just want to see the figures."

"For you, sweetheart," the younger woman technician said, "anything," and sat Bron in a chair, put a helmet over his head that covered his eyes with dark pads and (at a switch he heard click somewhere) grew, inside it, gentle but firm restraining clamps. "Try to relax and don't think of anything—if you've ever done any alpha-wave meditation, try to come as close to that state as you can . . . yes, there you go. Beautiful . . . beautiful . . . hold that mental state . . . yes, hold it. Don't think. There! Fine!" and when the helmet hummed up on its twin arms, he saw the two technicians and the counselor who had brought him looking at several large sheets of— Bron stood up, stepped up behind them—numbers, printed over large paper grids: The numbers were different hues, making clouds of color, here interpenetrating, there intermixing, like a numerically analyzed sensory shield. The console rolled out a final sheet from its plastic lips.

"Well, what do you think?"

"What do they mean?" Bron asked.

The younger woman, with pursed lips, flipped through the other four sheets. "Ignore the yellow numbers and the ones around the edge of the configurations; they map the connections of your sexuality with other areas of your person . . . which, indeed, looks rather stunningly ordinary. The basic blue, red, and violet configurations—

now this is just from an eye-check of the color overlap of one-place numbers over three-place numbers and a quick glance at the odd-versus-even deployment of three-place figures—but it looks as if you have performed quite adequately with partners of both genders, with an overwhelming preference for female partners—"

"—there's a node line," the other technician said, "running through from small, dark women with large hips to tall fair ones, rather chesty. And from this cross section—that's about four levels down in the cortex—" She turned up another page and placed a thumb on a muzzy patch of red and orange numbers with trails of decimals behind them—"I would suspect that you must, at one time, have had some quite statistically impressive experience with older women, that was on its way to developing into a preference but, I gather, fell off sharply about . . . ten, twelve years ago?" She looked up. "Were you a professional when you were younger?"

"That's right."

"Seems to have made you quite sure of yourself on that general score." She let the pages fall back.

"Just how does his basic configuration map up with the rest of the population?" the man asked. "It's the majority configuration, isn't it?"

"There *is* no majority configuration," the younger technician said, a little drily. "We live in the same co-op," she explained to Bron. "Sometimes you *still* have to remind them, or life can get very grim." She looked back at the pages. "It's the current male plurality configuration—that is, the base pattern. The preference nodes are entirely individual, and so is any experiential deployment within it. It's the one that, given our society, is probably still the easiest to adjust to—though practically every other person you meet will argue that the minimal added effort of adjusting to some of the others is more than paid for by the extra satisfaction of doing something minimally difficult. You're an ordinary, bisexual, female-oriented male—sexually, that is."

The man said to Bron, "And I am to understand that you would like this configuration changed to . . . say, the current plurality female configuration?"

"What is that?" Bron asked.

"Its mathematical interpretation is identical with this, with a reversal of the placement of two- and three-place numbers. In layman's terms: the ability to function sexually satisfactorily with partners of either sex, with an overwhelming propensity for males."

"Yes," Bron said, "then that's what I want."

The younger technician frowned. "The current plurality configuration, male or female, is the hardest to change. It's really extremely stable—"

"And of course preference nodes, once the basic pattern is set, we generally leave to form themselves," the older technician said, "unless you have a particular preference for the type you'd prefer to have a preference *for* . . . ? If you like, we can leave your desire for women as it is and just activate the desire for men—"

"No," said Bron. "That's not my preference."

"Also, though we can play with the results of past experiences, we can't expunge the actual experiences—without breaking the law. I mean, your professional experience, for instance, will be something you will still remember as you remember it now, and will still, hopefully, be of benefit. We can, however, imprint certain experientially *oriented* matrices. Did you have one in mind?"

"Can you make me a virgin?" Bron asked.

The two technicians smiled at one another.

The older one said: "I'm afraid, for your age and experience, that's just a contradiction in terms—at least within the female plurality configuration. We could make you a virgin, quite content and happy to remain one; or, we could make you a virgin, about ready to lose her virginity and go on developing as things came along. But it would be a little difficult for us to make you a virgin who has performed quite adequately with partners of both sexes but who prefers men— even for us."

"I'll take the female plurality configuration then—" Bron frowned. "You said it would be difficult though. Are you sure—"

"By difficult," the older technician said, "we mean that it will take approximately seventeen minutes, with perhaps three or four checkups and maybe another fixation session at three months, to make sure it takes—rather than the standard three minute and forty second session it takes to effect most changes."

"Excuse me, Ms. Helstrom," the man said, touching Bron's arm lightly, "but why don't we take care of your body first?"

The drugs they gave her made her feel like hell. "Walk back home," they'd suggested, "however uncomfortable it feels," in order to "freeze in" to her new body. As she ambled in the early morning, among the alleys of the unlicensed sector, Bron passed one, and another, and then another reclamation site. Yellow ropes fenced the damages. The maintenance wagons, the striped, portable toilets (like exotic ego-booster booths) waited for the morning workers. The wreckages kept sending her ill-focused memories of the Mongolian diggings; somehow the phrase "The horrors of war . . ." kept playing in her mind, like the chorus of a song whose verses were whatever bit of destruction her drug-dilated pupils managed to focus on behind the gauzy glare.

She went through the underpass—the light-strip had been fixed: the new length was brighter than the old—and came out to squint up at the sensory shield which, here and there across its violet, blushed orange, silver, and blue. The wall of the alley, a palimpsest of political posters and graffiti, had been gravity-damaged. Scaffolding had already been set up. Several workers, in their yellow coveralls, stood around sucking on coffee bulbs.

One looked at her and grinned (but it was a woman worker. You'd think *some*thing would have changed) as Bron hurried by. If she looked like she felt, she'd been lucky to get a smile.

The horrors of war passed through her mind for the millionth time. Her legs felt stiff. They had cheerfully assured her that as soon as the anesthetic wore off, she would be as sore as if she had had a moderately difficult natural childbirth. They had assured her about a lot of other things: that her hormones would take care of the fatty redistribution (as well as the bushy eyebrow) in a couple of weeks, all by themselves. She had wanted further cosmetic surgery to remove some of the muscle fiber in her arms; and could they make her wrists thinner? Yes, they could . . . but wait, they had told her. See how you feel in a week or so. The body had undergone enough trauma for one six-hour—or rather, one six-hour-and-seventeen-minute—session.

With one hand on the green and red, stained-glass door of Serpent's House, a conviction arrived, with drug-hazed joy which slid her toward tears: "I don't belong here," and which finished, like a couplet she expected to rhyme, "despite the horrors of war," but didn't.

Walking down the corridor, she realized, with a sort of secondary amusement, she didn't know *where* she belonged. All ahead was adventure—she awaited a small thrill of fear—like taking off from Mars for the Outer Satellites, among three thousand others; she had been afraid then . . . There *was* no fear, though. Only a general muzzy pleasure, along with the incipient physical discomfort, which kept getting mixed up with one another.

In the room, she took off all her clothes, opened out the bed, lay down on it, and collapsed into sleep—

"Hello, I saw your door open and the light on so I—" Lawrence, halfway through the door, stopped, frowned.

Bron pushed up on one elbow and squinted.

"Oh, I'm sorry. I thought . . . Bron?"

"What is it?"

"*Bron*, what in heavens have you . . . Oh, no—You *haven't* gone and . . ." Lawrence stepped all the way in. "What got into you? I mean, why—?"

Bron lay her head back on the pillow. "I had to, Lawrence. There are certain things that have to be done. And when you come to them, if you're a man . . ." The drugs were making her laugh—"you just have to do them."

"What things?" Lawrence asked. "Really, you're going to have to do some explaining, young . . . young lady!"

Bron's eyes closed. "I guess it was something you said, Lawrence—about only one woman in five thousand still being around. Well, if you were right about the percentages of men too, one woman in five thousand isn't enough." Bron closed her eyes tightly, then tried to relax. "I told you, that crazy Christian was right; at least about the woman not understanding. Well, I can. Because I'm—I *used* to be a man. So, you see, I can understand. The loneliness I was talking about, it's too important. I'll know how to leave it alone enough not to destroy it, and at the same time to know what I *can* do. I've had the first-hand experience, don't you see?"

"You're drugged," Lawrence said. "You must have some sort of *real* reasons for doing this. When you've slept off the anesthetic, perhaps you'll be so good as to explain."

Bron's eyes opened. "I have explained. I . . . the horrors of war. Lawrence, they brought home something to me. We call the race . . . what? Humanity. When we went to rescue the kids, at Audri's co-op . . . to save those children and their mothers? I really thought I was doing it to save humanity—I certainly *wasn't* doing it for myself. I was uncomfortable, I kept wanting to turn away, to leave them there, to quit—but I didn't . . . ! Humanity. They used to call it 'mankind.' And I remember reading once that some women objected to that as too exclusive. Basically, though, it wasn't exclusive enough! Lawrence, regardless of the human race, what gives the species the only value it has are men, and particularly those men who can do what I did."

"Change sex?"

"What I did *before* . . . before, when I was a man. I'm not a man anymore, so I don't need to be modest about it. What I've been through in the war, and the torture and terror leading up to it, the bravery demanded there, because of it. That showed me what real manhood was.

"And it's the most important thing the species has going for it. Oh, I know, to a lot of you, it's all silly. Yes, Alfred's dead. So is that crazy Christian. And that's terribly tragic—both of them. It's tragic when men die; it's that simple. But even in the face of such tragedy, though you can't think of any logical necessity to go out and save a house full of children and their mothers, there are metalogical ones: Reasons, they're called. I guess my doing that or keeping my mouth shut under torture probably looks very dumb to you. But I swear to you, Lawrence, I know the way I know that here is my own hand—with every subjective atom of my being—it *isn't* dumb; and it's the *only* thing that isn't. And in the same way, I know that only the people who know it like I know it, real men (because there's no other way to have it; that's part of what I know), really deserve more than second-class membership in the species . . ." Bron sighed. "And the species is dying out." Her mouth felt dry and the ghost of a cramp pulsed between her legs. "I also know that that kind of man can't be happy with an ordinary woman, the kind that's around today. When I was a man, I tried. It can't be done." She shook her head. "One out of five thousand isn't enough . . . Why did I do it?" Bron opened her eyes again and frowned at the frowning Lawrence. "I did it to preserve the species."

"Well, I must say, my dear, you have the courage of your convictions! But didn't it occur to you that—?"

"Lawrence, I'm tired. Go away. Shall I be cruel? All right. I'm just not interested in doddering, old homosexuals. I never was, and I'm *particularly* not interested in them now."

"That's not cruel. In your position, it's just silly. Well, I've never thought your sense of personal tact was anything but a disaster zone. *That* obviously hasn't changed. Nevertheless, I am still your friend. You know of course, you won't be able to stay here now. I mean, except as a guest. I'll register you as mine as soon as I leave. I'm sure they'll let you keep the room for a while, but if they get another application from some guy, you'll have to move out. If that happens and you haven't found a place by then, you can bunk in with me—till one or the other of us threatens murder. It's been a while since I slept chastely beside a fair young thing, but then, I've never—"

"Lawrence, please."

Lawrence ducked out the door, ducked back. "As I said, I'll be back in to talk to you again when you've slept it off."

Which was about seven o'clock that evening. Bron woke up feeling like her insides would fall out if she stood up.

Fifteen minutes later, Lawrence came in, announcing: "We're going to move you this evening. Now don't complain. I'll brook no protests. I've been running around all afternoon, and I've got a room for you in the women's house of detention—forgive me, that's my pet name for it—that's Cheetah, the women's co-op right behind us. Then I'm going to dip into my geriatric widow's mite and take you out to a quiet, calm dinner, on my credit. Now don't start putting up a fuss. I want you to know I have nursed three people through this operation before, and you all say the craziest things under the anesthetic—though Lord knows, their reasons seemed a lot more sensible than yours. Really, it's just like having a baby, only the baby—as one of my more articulate friends commented, when in your situation not twenty years ago—is you. You've got to get into walking and exercising as much as you can take as quickly as possible, or there'll be hell to pay. Come on, up and at 'em. Lean on me if you want to."

She didn't want to.

But protest was as painful as compliance. And besides—she figured this out only when they were seated in a dining-booth (two other places they'd tried were closed: because of the war) behind a stained-glass partition in a restaurant Bron had never known was thirty yards from the Snake Pit's door (but then, four-fifths of the patrons were Lawrence's age or over, and nudity seemed to be *de rigeur*)—despite his age and predilections, after all, Lawrence *was* a man. And a real woman had to relinquish certain rights. Wasn't that, she told herself silently, the one thing that, from her life before, she now honestly knew?

Dinner was simple, unpretentious, and vegetarian. And, despite the soreness, with Lawrence's gentle chatter it was pleasanter than any meal she'd had on Earth.

7. Tiresias Descending

Coming across it thus again, in the light of what we had to do to render it acceptable, we see that our journey was, in its preconception, unnecessary, although its formal course, once we had set out upon it, was inevitable.

G. SPENCER-BROWN, *The Laws of Form*

Her first minutes back at work, Bron was very nervous. She had considered the all-black outfit. But no, that would only be delaying things. The previous afternoon, she and Lawrence had gone to Lawrence's(!) design-rental house and spent an amusing two hours during which Lawrence had had the house make up (among other things) a pair of his-and-hers breast bangles, glittering crimson with dozens of tiny mirrors on wriggly antennae. "Lawrence," she had protested, "I'm just not the type to wear anything like this!" Lawrence had countered: "But I am, dear. At least in the privacy of my own room. They're cunning!" She had taken hers home and put them in the cupboard as a memento of the day. Save the short gray shoulder cloak, she had rented no new clothing with her new image in mind.

Bron wore the cloak to work.

She had been in her office about an hour when Audri came by to prop herself, with one elbow, on the doorjamb. "Hey, Bron, could you . . ." Audri stopped, frowned. "Bron . . . ?"

"Yes?" She looked up nervously.

Audri began to grin. "You *are* kidding me—?"

"About what?"

Audri laughed. "And it looks *good,* too! Hey—" She came in— "what I wanted to get was that information about Day Star Minus." She stepped around the corner of the desk, put a folder down. "Oh, did you

235

see that memo from the Art Department—?" which Bron finally found
on the floor beside her desk. Some sculptor had arrived in the cafeteria
that morning with a pile of large, thin, polished, metal plates, demand-
ing to build a sculpture, floor to ceiling, then and there. The Art Department had sent around its memo, which included an incomprehensible
statement by the artist, explaining how the plates would be moved
within the sculptural space on small motors, according to an arcane
series of mystical numbers. The whole was intended as some sort of
war memorial. And could you please let us have a *yes* or *no* response
before ten-thirty, as the artist wished to have the work completed by
lunch.

"I suppose I'm feeling positively disposed to change today,"
Bron told Audri, and sent the Art Department a *yes* on the console—though she had always felt a mild distrust of mystical art.
Back at the desk, with Audri, she ran over more logical/topological
specifications.

At the door, about to leave, Audri halted, looked back, grinned
again, and said: "Congratulations, I guess," winked and departed,
bumping her shoulder on the jamb.

Bron smiled, relieved. But then, she'd always liked Audri.

Lunch?

She debated whether or not to go, right up to the minute. Staying
away, of course, would only be putting things off. Just then, the console began to chatter and flash.

Another Art Department memo:

As the sculpture had been completed, three artists from a rival
school, masked in turquoise but otherwise nude, had rushed into the
cafeteria and, with flamers, destroyed the work, charring and melting
the plates. The memo contained a statement from the marauders
even more incomprehensible than the artist's had been. (Basically,
they seemed to be attacking the first artist's math.) The sculptor, who
was eighty-two, had suffered a psychotic episode (the memo went
on) and been hospitalized, where she might well remain for several
years, it appeared, from the initial diagnosis. Chances for her eventu-
al return to art, however, were hopeful. The remains of the work
would be on view through lunch, after which it would be removed to
the hegemony's museum, over the cafeteria, where it would stay on
permanent exhibit. The memo closed with a flurry of apologies and
was signed (typically) by Iseult, with a parenthetical note saying that
Tristan dissented from the proposed suggestion and if enough alter-

nates were put forward before closing, there would be a vote among them tomorrow.

An area of the cafeteria floor, blackened and strewn with burnt metal, was roped off. Every minute, one of the Seven Aged Sisters, in beaded green and silver, would leave her (or his) position by the cafeteria door, and come to walk, slowly, around the blistered enclosure (Bron stepped back from the taped rope to let the Sister pass), pausing every seventh step to make sacred and purifying signs, then, on completing his (or her) circuit, exchange serious words and nod dolefully with one or more of the spectators. (*Just* like the cafeteria of that Lux, Protyyn-recycling plant, Bron reflected. Absolutely *no* difference at all!) Some of the statue's motors, still working fitfully, now and then flapped a coruscated stub of aluminum around, twenty feet along the frame (which shook and clanked and tottered from floor to ceiling), while, somewhere else among the struts still standing, another metal plate tried to tug away from some twisted shape to which it had fused, the whole, charred horror attesting, perhaps more than the silvery creation intended, to the dark and terrible import of art.

Bron backed away, trying to envision the undamaged work, while others moved in to take her place at the rope. She had already decided that this lunch the meal would be a carnivorous one, and so was angling to the left, away from the vegetarian counter, when somebody put a hand on her shoulder.

She turned.

"Beautiful!" Philip exclaimed, a grin splitting his beard's knap. "Audri told me, but of course I wouldn't believe it till I saw—" Philip made a gesture with the backs of both hirsute hands toward Bron's breasts. "Gorgeous. . . . ! This is permanent, now?"

"Yes," Bron said, wishing they were not in the middle of the floor.

"Here," Philip said. "Let's get out of the middle of the floor," and put his hand on Bron's shoulder again, which Bron wished he wouldn't do, to guide her over to the booths. But then Philip was touch–ish with all the female employees, Bron had noted before, sometimes with envy, sometimes with annoyance. (He was touch–ish with the male employees too, which, before, had just been annoying.) "And this . . . um, goes all the way down?" Philip asked.

Bron did not quite sigh. "That's right."

"Just marvelous." Philip dropped his hand but craned around to stare. "I can't get over those tits! I'm green with jealousy!" He covered his slightly loose pectoral with spread fingers. (Philip had come in naked today.) "I have to make do with one; and then it's just up and down like a leaky balloon. Bron, I want you to know I'm *really* impressed. I think you've probably found yourself. Finally. I think you just may have. It's got that feeling about it, you know—"

Bron was about to say, *Shove it, Philip, will you?* when Audri said:

"Hey, there. Is Philip ragging you? Why don't you lay off Bron, and let her get her lunch, huh?"

"Yeah," Philip said. "Sure. Get your lunch. We're sitting right over there." He gestured at a booth somewhere beyond the blackened disaster. "See you when you get back."

As she moved through the line, Bron remembered her thought with Lawrence: *All men have some rights,* and considered it against her annoyance with Philip. Philip was certainly closer to the type of man she'd set herself to be interested in than, say, Lawrence. What, she wondered, would Philip be like in bed? The blusteriness would transform to firmness. The honesty would become consideration. Philip (she considered, with distaste) would never think of lying on top of someone lighter than he was without invitation. And he would have some particularly minor kink (like really getting off on licking your ear) which he'd expect you to cooperate with and be just annoyingly obliging about cooperating with any of yours. In short, what she knew from the information left over from that other life: Philip was as sexually sure of himself as Bron had been. She had recognized it before. She recognized it now. And Philip was still (with his hand on the shoulder and his unstoppable frankness) the most annoying person she knew—plurality female configuration or not, she thought grimly. It was not that she felt no attraction; but she could certainly understand how, with men like Philip around, you could get to not *like* the feeling.

"Excuse me . . . ?" someone said.

She said: "Oh, I'm so . . ." and took her tray and started around the cafeteria.

She saw their booth, went toward it

As she neared, she was sure she heard Philip say:

" . . . still doesn't like to be touched" and thought, as she took her place across from him? I *didn't* hear the pronoun, but if I had and it was 'he,' I'd kill him. But the conversation was on Day Star and how the war seemed to have improved the personalities of two of the representatives, and what had happened to the third? No, he wasn't a war casualty, that much had been established. (And wasn't Lux just terrifying? Five million people!) One of the junior programmers said morosely: "I used to *live* in Lux," which, even for a u-l'er, was incredibly gross. About the table, people's eyes caught one another's, then dropped to their trays, till someone picked up the conversation's thread: But he *had* disappeared . . . In the midst of these speculations, Philip leaned his elbows on the table and asked: "Say, where're you living now?"

Bron told him the name of the women's co-op.

"*Mmm*," Philip said, and nodded. "I was just thinking, back when I was married—my second marriage, actually—my second wife was a transsexual . . . ?"

"When were *you* married?" asked the junior programmer, who wore a silver body-stocking from head to toe, with large black circles all over, and sat wedged in by the wall. "You're not an earthie. They don't even do that too much on Mars, now."

The programmer, Bron realized. She was probably *from* Mars.

"Oh, I used to spend quite a bit of time in your u-l; you can make any kind of contract you want there: *that's* why we've got it . . . But that was back when I was a very dumb, and very idealistic kid. Like I was saying, my wife had started out as a man—"

"How'd she stack up to old Bron here?" the programmer asked.

"I pretend to be crude," Philip said, leaning forward and speaking around Audri, "but *you* really are! She was great—" He settled back. "The marriage, however, was three or four times as bad as absolutely any sociologist I'd ever read on the subject said it would be, back when I was a student at Lux. And you know, I still had to do it two more times before I learned my lesson? But I was young then—that was my religious phase. Anyway; after we broke up and she left the mixed co-op where we were living, she moved into a straight, women's co-op for a while—I mean, she was about as heterosexual as you can get, which may have been part of the problem, but nevertheless: Then she moved into another women's co-op that was nonspecific. I remember she said she thought it was a lot nicer—I mean, as far as she was concerned. They were a lot more accepting of general, nonsexual eccentricities and things like that, you know? It was a place called the Eagle, if I remember. It's still going. If you have any problems with your place, you might bear it in mind."

"I will," Bron said.

The next day another memo came down from the Art Department. It seemed that, independently, twenty-seven people had come up with the suggestion that the memorial, in its new version, be titled *The Horrors of War* and so displayed in the hegemony museum. This suggestion had been duly passed on to the sculptor, in the hospital, who was apparently in touch enough to make the following reply: "*No! No!* Flatly and bluntly *No!* Title too banal for words! Sorry, art just does not work that way! (If you *must* name it something, name it after the last head of your whole, ugly operation!) It is my job to *make* works that you may get anything out of you wish. It is *not* my job to *teach* you how to make them! Leave me alone. You have done enough to me already." And so *Tristan and Iseult: A War Memorial* was transferred upstairs, where from time to time Bron, on her way to the office library, stopped in to see it among the other dozens of works on exhibit. The burned and broken bits were all in a large carton near one base, where they gazed up at her like ashy skulls in which you could not quite find the eyes.

Bron kept the memo in her drawer. She cut the words of the old sculptor out of the flimsy to take home and hang on her wall. They had struck some chord; it was the first thing in her new life that seemed to indicate that there might be something to live for in the world besides being reasonable or happy. (Not that it was art—any more than it was religion!) And two weeks later, with Lawrence carrying the smaller packages, Bron moved from the straight Cheetah into the unspecified Eagle.

"Oh, this *is* much nicer," Lawrence said, when they finally got things organized in the room. "I mean everybody seems so much more relaxed here than back at the place I got for you."

"As long as they don't try to be so damned friendly," Bron said, "and stay out of my hair, it's got to be an improvement."

After Lawrence left, she looked for the piece of flimsy to tape to the inside of her door. But it had gotten misplaced or dropped somewhere; at any rate, she couldn't find it.

She had been living at the women's co-op (the Eagle) six months now. This one had been working out well. On the fourteenth day of the nineteenth paramonth of the second year$_N$, at four o'clock (announced the lights around the Plaza), she considered once more, as she came out of the office lobby onto the crowded Plaza of Light, walking home—and, once more, decided against it: Just after lunch Audri had stopped her in the hall with raised finger and lowered brows: "You, I'm afraid, have been falling down in your work, Bron. No, it's nothing serious, but I just thought I better mention it before it *got* serious. Your efficiency index blinks a little shakily on the charts. Look, we all know you've had a lot to adjust to—"

"Did Philip say something?" Bron had asked.

"Nope. And he won't for at least another two weeks—which is why *I'm* mentioning it now. Look, just give it a little thought, see if there's anything you can think of that would help you get it together. And let me know. Even if it's something outside of work. Okay?" Audri smiled.

Back in her office cubicle, Bron had pondered. Once or twice she had consciously thought that she must be ready for her work to mean less to her than before; but that was supposed to happen only at the materialization of the proper man—though nothing like that man had come anywhere near materializing.

Take stock, she'd decided. What, she wondered, would her clinic counselor say? Leave an hour early, perhaps; walk home. Only, while she'd been pondering, closing time had crept up.

She would be satisfied with the usual transport and just stock-taking.

She went into the transport-station kiosk and down to the third level, which was rumored to be (fractionally) warmer and therefore (rumored to be) fractionally less crowded; the transport hissed in and, as the door slid back, a sign unrolled across it (simultaneously, inside, people stretched signs across the windows:

LUNA
RELIEF
ASSOCIATION

red letters blared on blue tissue). The one across the door (orange on black on green on pink) said:

Bursting through the tissue, men and women began to distribute leaflets; the first passengers behind them were coming off, shoulders and heads brushing orange shreds.

"Really," a man, wearing several rubber-rimmed privacy disks about his head, arms, and legs, said, "you'd think they could confine that sort of thing to the unlicensed sector. I mean, that's why we've got it."

A woman on the other side of him (apparently not with him) said testily: "Just think of it as theater."

Bron looked. The disk the man wore around his forehead cut the woman's profile at the nose. The man stepped from between them; Bron suddenly stopped breathing, stared.

The Spike glanced at her, frowned, started to say something, looked away, looked back, frowned again; then a politely embarrassed smile: "I'm sorry, for a moment you reminded me of a man I . . ." She frowned again. "Bron . . . ?"

"Hello . . ." Bron said, softly, because her throat had gone dead dry; her heart knocked slow and hard enough to shake her in her sandals. "Hello, Spike . . . how are . . . ?"

"How are *you*?" the Spike countered. "Well, this certainly—" She blinked at Bron—"is a surprise!"

There was a rising hiss of escaping air. "Oh—" the Spike said. "There goes my transport!"

Arriving passengers surged around them.

Bron said, suddenly: "Spike, come on! You want to get out of here and walk for a stop or two?"

The Spike was obviously considering several answers. The one she chose was: "No. I don't want to, Bron . . . Did you get the letter I wrote you—"

"Oh, yes. Yes, I did! Thank you. Really, thank you for explaining things to me."

"I wrote it to take care of this when it happened, Bron. Because I knew it would. Oh, I don't mean . . . But really; No, I don't want to walk a few stops with you: Do you understand?"

"But I've changed!"

"So I've noticed." Then she smiled again.

"Your letter was part of that, too." Bron was trying to remember what exactly had *been* in the letter, other than its general crotchety tone. But that was part of her life which, day by day, had seemed less necessary to remember, easier to forget. "Please, Spike. I'm *not* the same person I was. And I . . . I just feel I have to . . . talk to you!"

The Spike hesitated; then the smile became a laugh, that had behind it, like a dozen echoes, some dozen other times she had laughed and Bron had thrilled. "Look . . . I guess you have been through some changes. All right, I'll walk you down another stop. Then we go on our ways, okay?"

As they reached the steps to the pedestrian corridor, a memory returned of another day when they had walked together, laughing, when suddenly the Spike had begun to complain that Bron was always talking about herself—Well, she *had* changed. She wondered what she might talk about to prove it.

At the side of the corridor, just before the street, stood a ("Know Your Place in Society") kaleidoscopically-colored booth. "Have you ever actually *been* in one of those?"

The Spike said: "What?"

"Every once in a while I go in just to see what the government's got on me, you know?" They passed the booth, walked on into the street, under the sensory shield's paler swirls. "A lot of people pride themselves on never going into one at all. But then, *I've* always sort of prided myself on being the type who does the things no one else would be caught dead doing. I guess the last time I went into one was about a month back—or maybe six weeks. I don't know whether they've done it on purpose or not; Brian—that's my counselor at the clinic—says it's more or less government policy though there have been exceptions which she thinks are just government slipups, which I sort of doubt. I mean, whether you approve of it or disapprove, the government is usually right. Anyway, they only show clips taken since my operation. Isn't that amazing? Perhaps this is their own, bizarre way of showing that they care—" Bron stopped, because the Spike was looking at another group of Luna-Reliefers: Across the street, "Luna Is a Moon Too!" waved on bright placards.

"You don't see any Terra Relief around," the Spike said, suddenly, with the same bitterness Bron had heard in her comment to the man back on the transport platform. "After all, that's where we did the damage."

"That's right, you don't," Bron said. And then: "You must have gotten out just in time." She frowned. "Or were you there through it?"

"I got out," the Spike said. "What did you want to talk about?"

"Well, I . . . I guess there wasn't anything specific but . . . well I just wanted . . ." And Bron realized there was nothing to say; nothing of any importance at all. "What are *you* doing, Spike? I guess the company's going pretty well now."

"Actually, we're sort of in hibernation. Maybe we'll get together again someday; but once the endowment ran out, we more or less disbanded."

"Oh."

"I'm teaching right now, in the rotation circuit for Lux."

"University?"

"That's right. You know the city was completely wiped out. But the University is practically a separate suburb, under a separate shield, with a separate atmosphere and separate gravity control. The sabotage was pretty well set up to pass it by. Maybe that was Earth's way of showing they cared?"

Bron couldn't really think of much to answer. "I guess because you're working for the University is why you're out here instead of your usual haunts in the u-l."

"*Mmm,*" the Spike said. "I'm doing a month of lectures on Jacque Lynn Colton. After I finish here and on to Neriad, I'll be going back to Io, Europa, Ganymede . . ." She shrugged. "It's the usual rotation. Somehow, though, under the University—even on the run—just isn't the place to do creative work. At least, not for me. They've promised me some direction as soon as I get back. I'm working on plans for simultaneous, integrated productions of *La Vida Es Sueño, Phédra,* and *The Tyrant*—one cast for all three, all on the same stage, with both cast and audience using the new concentration drugs. The University has already used them to allow people to listen to four or five lectures at once, but nobody's tried to use them for anything aesthetically interesting."

"I thought . . . um, macro-theater wasn't your field?" Bron said, wondering where the information came from, or if it was even right

The Spike laughed. "Macro-theater is just a lot of coordinated micro-theater productions done one right after another without a break."

"Oh," Bron said again. Three plays at once sounded too confusing even to ask about. "Are you still with Windy and what's-her-name?"

"Charo. No, not really. Charo's here on Triton; and we see each other, get drunk together, and reminisce about old times. She's a pretty spectacular kid."

"Where's Windy?"

The Spike shrugged.

"Well—" Bron smiled—"I must admit he struck me as the roving kind."

"He's probably dead," the Spike said. "The whole company left Lahesh the same day you did, but Windy was going to stay behind on Earth for another six days. Windy was born on Earth, you know. He'd planned to hitchhike somewhere or other to see one of his families, and then join us later. Only the war . . ." She looked about the street. "Eighty-eight percent of the population at last report . . . The confusion there is still supposed to be horrible. They've said not to expect any reliable information from the place for at least another year. Then there're those who say there'll never be anything there again to have any reliable information about."

"I saw a public-channel coverage of the cannibalism going on in both the Americas." Bron felt welling distress. "And that was only a month ago . . . ?"

The Spike took a deep breath. "So that means the chances are—what? Four out of five that he's dead? Or, by this time, nine out of ten."

The only response to come to Bron was a tasteless joke about the chances of Windy's having been eaten. "Then you're not really involved·with anybody anymore—" And the distress was still growing; her heart began to knock again. What *is* this? she wondered. It certainly couldn't be sex! Was it the terror, or the embarrassment, of death? But she'd hardly *known* Windy; and his death was a probability, not a certainty, anyway. Then, astonishing herself, Bron said: "Spike, let me come with you. All the rest is ridiculous." She looked at the pavement. "I'll give up everything I have, go wherever you like, do whatever you want. You've had women lovers. Love me. I'll have a refixation, tonight. I want you. I love you. I didn't even know it, but seeing you again—"

"Oh, *Bron* . . ." The Spike touched Bron's shoulder.

Bron felt something inside reel about her chest, staggering at the touch. "Feeling like this . . . I've never felt like this about . . . *any*one before. Do you believe me?"

"Yes," the Spike said. "I do."

"Then why can't you—?"

"First of all, I *am* involved with someone else. Second of all, I'm touched, I'm complimented . . . even now: But I'm not interested."

"Who are you . . . with . . . ?" Despair built behind Bron's face like a solid slab of metal that began to heat, to burn, to melt and run across her eyes. She wasn't crying. But water rolled down one cheek.

The Spike dropped her hand. "You've met him, actually—though you probably don't remember . . . Fred? I believe the first time you saw him, he'd just punched me in the jaw."

"*Him* . . . ?" Bron looked up, blinking. "I hope he's taken a *bath* since I . . . !"

The Spike laughed. "As a matter of fact, I don't think he has. I'm always on the verge of trouble with the University over him—another reason I'll be glad to get out of teaching and back to work. I took him to one of my lectures. . . . on a chain—I had some of the students throw raw meat—he likes that. It was just for the theater. But I'm afraid most of the University types have simply never encountered anything quite like Fred before. I mean up close. They don't know what to do with him. It's too bad you never got a chance to talk with him—though, of course, a lot of his ideas have developed since we first met."

"But what in the world do the two of you—?"

"Fred is into some rather strange things—sexually, that is. And no, I *haven't* decided whether they're really me, yet. Frankly, it's not exactly my concept of the ideal but it's the one I currently care about the most and—Look—let's not talk about it, all right?" She looked at Bron and sighed.

"Does he want another woman?" Bron asked. "I'll go with him. I'll do anything he wants, as long as you're with him too; and I can be near you, talk to you—"

"Bron, you *don't* get the point," the Spike said. "Whether he might want you or not has nothing to do with it. *I* don't want you. Now let's call it a day. The transport's up there. You go on. I've got other things to do."

"You don't *believe* you're the only person I've ever felt like this about?"

"I told you: I *do* believe it."

"I've felt this way about you from the moment I first saw you. I've felt this way about you all along. I know now that I'll always feel this way, no matter what."

"And I happen to believe you'll feel rather differently three minutes—if not thirty seconds—after I've left."

"But I—"

"Bron, there's a certain point in meaningless communication after which you just have to—" Suddenly the Spike stopped, made an angry face, started to turn away, then hesitated: "Look, there's the transport. Use it. I'm going down this way. And if you try to follow me, I'll kick you in the balls."

Which, as Bron watched the Spike stalk down the street, naked back moving away between other pedestrians, seemed so absurd she didn't even try to run after her.

The burning behind her face continued: Under its heat she could feel her eyes drying, almost painful. Suddenly she turned and started toward the station kiosk. Feel differently in thirty seconds! Shaking with rage and embarrassment, Bron thought: How could a woman like *that* know what *anyone* felt! About anything! I must be crazy (she passed a kiosk, stepped onto the moving ramp, and kept walking), completely crazy! What could possess me to want a woman like that? And it *hadn't* been sex! For all the fear, the heart pounding, the sickness unto death, there had been none of the muzzy warmth in the loins, or even the muzzy expectation of it that she had felt enough times just walking along the street, looking at some transport attendant, perhaps some worker from another office, or even the occasional e-girl. If anything, it was sex's certain absence that had made the whole thing more distressing. Crazy! she thought again. There I was, about to throw over all I believe in, my work, my ideals, everything I want, everything I've become, for some leftover reaction that doesn't even have the excuse of pleasure about it, unless it's just a memory of sex—and what else are emotions anyway? An idea that had haunted her for the whole half year returned: Somehow she was now more at the mercy of her emotions than she had been.

Where the hell am I? she suddenly thought, and stepped off at the corner. She was at another kiosk, but which station? She looked up at the green street coordinate, took a breath, and started down the ramp.

Brian, she thought. Yes, Brian, her counselor . . .

It would be her third counseling session, the first optional one. She wished desperately that this whole depressing encounter had not taken place just then. It made the whole counseling thing seem too necessary.

Bron's distressing reveries completely enclosed her till she reached her co-op.

Across the commons, two older women were bent over a game; younger ones stood silently, watching. Bron had been planning to go straight to her room, but now she looked toward the table.

Between the players, on a flat board checkered black and red, carved figures stood.

Years ago on Mars, Bron had read something about such a game . . . She'd even known its name, once. But that was the past; she didn't like to think about the past. Besides, it was much too abstract and complicated. As she recalled, each piece (unlike vlet) had a fixed and definite way to move: Why *hadn't* Lawrence come to visit her recently? (One player, her fingers full of bright-stoned rings, moved a piece and said, softly: "Check.") Bron turned away. She hadn't seen Lawrence in months. Of course, she could always visit him. Putting it that way, however, she realized she didn't want to see him. Which, after all, may have been why he hadn't come to see her.

Then Prynn, the really obnoxious fifteen-year-old who had taken to confiding (endlessly) to Bron (not so much because Bron encouraged her, but because she hadn't figured out yet how to discourage) stamped into the room and announced to everyone: "Do you know what my social worker did? Do you *know*? Do *you* know!" The last *you* went more or less to Bron, who looked around, surprised: Rough black hair in a stubbly braid stood out at one side of Prynn's head. Her face had not quite enough blotches to suggest anything cosmetic.

"Uh . . . no," Bron said. "What?"

And Prynn, almost quivering, turned and fled the room.

One of the other women looked up from her reader, caught Bron's eye, and shrugged.

Five minutes later, when Bron, after lingering in the commons to flip through the new tapes that had come in that afternoon—half of them (probably all the good ones) were already out on loan—came up into the corridor where her room was, she saw Prynn sitting on the floor beside the door, chin on her knees, one arm locked around the floppy cuffs of her patchy black pants (there was something very wrong with one of Prynn's toenails), the other hand lying limp beside her.

As Bron walked up, Prynn said, without looking: "You *said* you wanted to know:—you sure took your time getting here." Which was the beginning of an evening-long recount of fancied insults, misunderstandings and general abuse from the Social Guidance Department, which, since Prynn had left her remaining parent at Lux (on Titan) and come to Triton's Tethys, had been overseeing her education. The comparison with Alfred had been inevitable—and had, inevitably, broken down. Prynn's sexual pursuits had none of Alfred's hysterical futility; they went on, however, just as doggedly. Once a week she went to an establishment that catered to under-sixteen-year-old girls and fifty-five-year-plus men. Unfailingly Prynn would return with one, two or, on occasions, three such gentlemen, who would stay the night. But, from her unflinching accounts of their goings-on, the mechanics of these encounters usually went off to everyone's satisfaction. Alfred was from a moon of Uranus. Prynn was from a moon of Saturn. Alfred had been going on eighteen. Prynn was just fifteen . . . In the midst of one of these recountings, Bron had once let slip her own early profession, and then, to make it make sense, had had to reveal her previous sex. Both facts Prynn had found completely uninteresting—which was probably one reason why the relation continued. "But they never come back to see me here," Prynn had said (and was saying again now; somehow, while Bron's mind had wandered, so had Prynn's monologue). "I tell them to. But they won't. The fuckers!" It apparently made her quite miserable. Prynn began to explain just exactly how miserable. During her first months, Bron had said (to herself) that her sexual activity was about equal to what it had been before the operation, i.e., infrequent. But now, she had to admit (to Prynn) that it had been, actually, nil—plurality female sexual deployment or no; which Prynn interrupted her own recounting long enough to say was kinky, then launched into more monologues anent the unfeeling Universe: From time to time, images of Bron's encounter with the Spike that afternoon returned to blot out the harangue—which was suddenly over.

Prynn had just closed the door, loudly, after her.

It *is* too much, Bron thought. I *will* call for a social guidance appointment. Tomorrow. I've got to get some advice.

"Do you think it could be hormones?"

"Which," Brian asked, from her large, deep, green-plush chair, "of the various things you've just gone over do you mean?" Brian was slim, fiftyish, silver-coiffed and silver-nailed, and had told Bron in their first meeting that she was (yes, they *were* in the u-l) from Mars. Indeed, Brian was what many of the Martian ladies Bron had once hired out to, fifteen years before, had aspired to be, and what those who could afford to keep themselves in such good shape occasionally approached. (Bron remembered their endless, motherly advice. Now, of course, Bron was the client: but otherwise—and both Bron and Brian had commented on, and rather enjoyed, the irony for the first half hour of the first counseling session—little had changed.)

"I don't know," Bron said. "Perhaps it *is* psychological. But I just don't *feel* like a woman. I mean *all* the time, every minute, a complete and whole woman. Of course, when I think about it, or some guy makes a pass at me, then I remember. But most of the time I just feel like an ordinary, normal . . ." Bron shrugged, turned in her own chair, as large, as deep, as plush, but yellow.

Brian said: "When you were a man, were you aware of being a man every second of the day? What makes you think that most women *feel* like women every—"

"But I don't want to *be* like most women—" and then wished she hadn't said it because Brian's basic counseling technique was not to respond to things unrespondable to—which meant frequent silences. For a while Bron had tried to enjoy them, as she might have, once, if they had occurred in any ordinary conversation. But, somehow during the tenth or so such silence, she had realized that they betokened nobody's embarrassment but her own. "Maybe more hormones—" she said at last. "Or maybe they should have doctored up a few more X chromosomes in a few more cells. I mean, perhaps they didn't infect *enough* of them."

"I think in terms of the chromosome business," Brian said, "there are a few things you will just have to come to terms with. A hundred and fifty years ago, some geneticists found a terribly inbred town in the Appalachian mountains, where all the women had perfect teeth; there was all sorts of talk about having discovered an important, sex-linked gene for dental perfection. The point is, however, any little string of nucleotides they might isolate is really only a section of a very complicated interface, both internal and external. Consider: Having the proper set of nucleotides for perfect teeth isn't going to do you much good if you happen to be missing the set that prescribes, say, your jawbone. You may have the nucleotides that order the amino acids in the blue protein that colors the iris of your eyes, but if you don't happen to have the string that orders the amino acids of the white protein for the body of the eye itself, blue eyes you will not have. In other words, it's a little silly to say you have the string for blue eyes if you don't have the string for eyes at all. The external part of the interface, which goes on at the same time, also has to be borne in mind: the string that gives you perfect teeth, assuming all the other strings are properly arranged around it, *still* only gives you perfect teeth *within* a particular environment—that is, with certain elements plentifully available, and others fairly absent. The strings of nucleotides don't *make* the calcium that goes into your teeth; a good number of strings are involved in building various parts of the machinery by which that calcium is extracted from the environment and formed into the proper lattice crystalline structure in the proper place in your jawbone so that it extrudes upward and downward in a form we then *recognize* as perfect teeth. But no matter what the order of your nucleotides, those perfect teeth can be marred by anything from a lack of calcium in the diet to a high acid/bacteria ratio in the mouth to a lead pipe across the jaw. By the same token, *being* a woman is also a complicated genetic interface. It means having that body of yours from birth, and growing up in the world, learning to do whatever you do—psychological counseling in my case, or metalogics in yours—with and within that body. That body has to be yours, and yours all your life. In that sense, you never will be a 'complete' woman. We can do a lot here; we can make you a woman from a given time on. We cannot make you have been a woman for all the time you were a man."

"What about the . . . well, my work inefficiency."

"I don't think that's hormones—or would be helped by them."

"Why, then?"

"It's possible you just may be somebody who believes that women *are* less efficient. So you're just living up to your own image."

"But that's ridiculous." Bron sat up in her chair. "I don't think any such thing. And I never have."

"Inefficiency, like efficiency, is another interface." Brian moved one hand to her lap. "Let me put it this way. You think women are different in many 'subtle' ways—more emotional perhaps, probably less objective, possibly more self-centered. Frankly, it would just be very hard to *be* more emotional—"

"But I *don't* think women are necessarily more emotional than men—"

"—more emotional than *you* when you *were* a man, less objective than you, and more self-centered than you, *without* becoming less efficient at your work." Brian sighed. "I've looked over all your deployment grids, sexual and otherwise. It's all written out very clearly; and all so desperately Martian. You say you *don't* want to be like most other women. Don't worry: You aren't. It's putting it a little brutally; but, frankly, *that's* something you'll never have to worry about—unless you want to work rather hard at it. In one sense, though you are as real a woman as possible, in another sense you are a woman created *by* a man—specifically by the man you were."

When Bron was silent thirty seconds, Brian asked: "What are you thinking?"

"When I was a child—" Bron was thinking about the Spike—"I remember once I found an old book, full of old pictures. Of couples. In the pictures, the women were all shorter than the men. It looked very funny, to have all the women in all the pictures midgets. I said something about it to the tutor for my study-group aide. He told me that hundreds of years ago, on Earth, everybody used to think that women really were shorter than men, because all the men would only go around with women who were shorter than they were and all the women would only go around with men who were taller than they were. I remember I wondered about it even then, because I figured if that were really the case, there would be a lot of very unhappy tall women and a lot of very unhappy short men."

"From what we know," Brian said, "there were."

"Well, yes. Of course later I learned it was more complicated than that. But I've always wondered if perhaps, back then, women really *weren't* smaller; perhaps there's been some sort of evolutionary change in humanity since then that's increased women's size. I mean, if there *had* been, how would we know?"

"Frankly," Brian said, "we wouldn't. The human chromosomes weren't completely mapped until well into the twenty-first century. You know about the one-two-two-one dominant/hybrid/recessive ratio for inherited characteristics?"

Bron nodded.

"Well, something seldom considered in the natural selection theory of evolution, but that has a great deal to do with it is simply that: For a recessive trait to be bred permanently into the species, it has to give an extreme edge on survival to those who show it—a survival edge, that, at least over a period of time, must equal a three-to-one chance of reaching breeding age over those who lack it. But for a dominant trait, it's a rather different story. For a dominant trait *not* to spread throughout the population, it has to be extremely antisurvival—in fact, it must be antisurvival enough to give the bearer, over a given period of time, a three-to-one chance *against* reaching breeding age. And any dominant trait *less* antisurvival than that is still going to grow subtly and inexorably. And if a dominant trait is at all weighted *toward* survival, even the slightest bit, it will simply race through the species. You know, the human race has done more real, honest to goodness evolving since the beginning of the twentieth century than probably at any other time in the previous ten thousand years. There used to be a dental anomaly called Carabelli's cusp, that manifested itself as a tendency for the third-from-the-rear molars to have a vestigial lug on the inside. It was universal throughout the species at the beginning of the twentieth century, evident in Africans and Scandinavians and Asians—it was particularly pronounced among Malaysians, where it accounted for a good many tooth problems, because the extra lug was not well supplied with live tooth tissue. Apparently a dominant mutation began, sometime in the early part of the century, that obliterated Carabelli's cusp entirely and made the back molars completely regular. By the twenty-first century, Carabelli's cusp had gone the way of the Neanderthal brow ridge and the four-toed hoof of the eohippus. The human race no longer possesses it. The ability to fold the tongue muscles laterally as well as ventrally swept the species even faster, over the same period. And left-handedness, which is definitely a recessive inherited trait (and what survival trait it's linked to we still can't figure out), has grown from five percent of the population to an even fifty. For that matter, up until nineteen fifty-nine, all biology texts said that human beings had forty-eight chromosomes—whereupon someone counted again and discovered it was only forty-six. Traditionally, this has been explained away as simply a gross, scientific mistake—however, it's just possible that humanity was simply finishing up an evolutionary change from a forty-eight to a forty-six chromosome species, and some of the early counts just happened to have been done on the last of the vanishing forty-eight chromosome types. So it's certainly possible that some sex-linked mutation has occurred increasing the size of women. But the other factors, however, are so overwhelming, it isn't likely. We have studies done in the same decade in which two men first walked on the surface of the moon, which show that a female infant of that time, during her first year of life, could expect to get less than half the physical contact with her parents that a male infant would. We know from painful experience what the effect of physical contact in infancy has on everything from future strength to psychological autonomy. We have studies from those years that show the middle-class North American father spent, on average, less than twenty-five seconds a *day* playing with his less-than-year-old infant, and the middle-class European father even less— so that the cross-sexual identification necessary for what we consider social maturity, no matter what the adolescent sexual proclivities eventually fixate on, hardly ever occurred except by accident. Right after World War Two, there was a rampant superstition that children should only have one close adult attachment during their first three years. But statistics show this just produced some very jealous, possessive individuals—with schizoid mothers. Our current superstition—and it seems to work, out here—is that a child should have available at least five close adult attachments—that's living, loving, feeding, and diaper-changing attachments—preferably with five different sexes. Mutation is possible, but the evening out in the social valuation between men and women, once colonization of Luna and Mars really began, is certainly the easiest explanation of the fact that today men and women seem to be equals in size and physical strength; and with the records of the Interworld Olympics for the last sixty years, no one could really question it."

"They used to think the male sex hormones made your muscles stronger, didn't they?"

"Testosterone makes the membrane of the muscle cell less permeable," Brian said, "which means, given two muscles, developed to equal strength, the one without testosterone clogging it up, so to speak, can function at peak efficiency marginally longer because it can diffuse fatigue products out through the cell wall marginally faster."

Bron sighed. "It's so strange, the way we picture the past as a place full of injustice, inequity, disease, and confusion, yet still, somehow, things were . . . simpler. Sometimes I wish we *did* live in the past. Sometimes I wish men were all strong and women were all weak, even if you did it by not picking them up and cuddling them enough when they were babies, or not giving them strong female figures to identify with psychologically and socially; because, somehow, it would be simpler that way just to justify . . ." But she could not say what it would justify. Also, she could *not* remember ever thinking those thoughts before, even as a child. She wondered why she said she had. Thinking it now, it seemed bizarre, uncomfortable, unnatural.

"You know," Brian said suddenly, "the only reason we can even have this conversation is because we're both Martians—and not even Martian roaring girls with cutaway veils and silver eyelids, but Martian ladies at that! Anyone out here listening to this would think we were out of our minds, the both of us." Her eyelids (which *were* silver! . . . but it was just paint) had lowered, projecting faint anger in that typically Martian way. "I know it's the height of rudeness, but really, talking to you always makes me remember how glad I am I left Mars. I'm going to be blunt." Brian cocked her head. "I said before, you were a woman made *by* a man. You are also a woman made *for* a man.

Just considering who *you* are, I suspect you'd be a lot happier if you got a man. After all, you're an attractive and intelligent woman, with a normal woman's urges. There's certainly nothing *wrong* with having a man; in your own quiet way, you act as though there were."

The knees of Bron's slacks were pressed together. She slid her hands over them and felt very vulnerable before the older and wiser Brian. "Only . . ." she said at last, "the man I want wouldn't be very happy with me if I came looking for him."

"Well, then," Brian said, "you might consider making do with what's available until perfection comes along."

A month later (it took her that long to decide), Bron felt like a perfect fool asking Prynn to suggest a place to go. The possibility, however, of being recognized in the places she herself had visited before, from month to month, made her uncomfortable. After all, the Spike— someone practically a perfect stranger—had recognized her just standing on a transport platform. Not that she'd gone to such places so often that anyone would recognize her had she been male. Nevertheless . . .

And of course Prynn couldn't simply suggest a few names and let it go. No, Prynn had to spend the next week " . . . asking around . . ." Bron tried to picture the requests: "Hey, I know this kinky sex- change, see, who's about ready to—" I am too old, Bron decided, to be embarrassed: which basically meant forgetting about it, thinking of other things.

One of the things she thought about was why she had not told Brian about meeting the Spike. But it was only a counseling hour, not some tell-all, honesty-or-nothing, archaic-style therapy session. And hadn't Lawrence once said (how *was* Lawrence, she wondered; he had not been over to see her forever) the only way to deal with a woman like the Spike was to treat her as if she didn't exist? And any- way, Brian's suggestion (slightly modified: Bron would *not* make do; but she might put herself in the *way* of what she wanted) would an- swer there as well. If she was tempted to fling over everything just like that, it might be a bit more reasonable to make sure that the next person who asked her to was at least the proper sex.

Prynn opened the door without knocking and said: "Okay, I've fig- ured out where I'm going to take you." Then she looked up at the ceiling, made a very unpleasant sound (supposed to express the ultimate in sophisticated boredom), and fell back against the wall. The cabinet door joggled.

"Now what's the matter?" Bron pushed back the reader (but let her hand stay on the skimmer knob). A strip of light from the edge of the case lay across her wrist. "You know, you really don't have to go with me. I'd understand: You're into older men. I doubt whether there'll be too many at the sort of place you'd take me—"

"My social worker," Prynn said, "says that *anything*, to the exclusion of everything else, is a perversion. So, once every six weeks, I go do something different. Just to prove I'm normal. This place is just swarming with twenty-year-old and thirty-year-old and forty-year-old men. I'll feel like a damn child molester. But you'll love it. Come on, get your clothes on. I swear, you take longer to get dressed than any five people I've ever known put together."

"You get out of here," Bron said. "I'll see you down in the commons."

The place they arrived at was pleasantly plasticky (which meant there was no attempt to make the plastic look like either stone, ice, or wood), with a decent-enough-looking clientele, who, Bron decided, probably liked to get things settled early. (The places Bron had used back when she had been living at the men's co-op tended to be places where people drank long and lingered late.) It was a collection of reasonably happy men and women—

"This is the active side of the bar, i.e., if you want to check out the beauties languishing on *that* side, without being bothered," Prynn explained. "That side if you want to be approached by someone who's made up their mind from *this* side. And that there is free-range territory. Nobody's really hard and fast about any of the rules here—which is why I come. But I'm just telling you what it says in the monthly newsletter."

—happily reasonable men and women, Bron thought, as Prynn stalked off. Take any five of them . . . But she did not want to look too hard at anyone. Not just yet. There, a man in a skirt of brown/green/orange cloth; there a woman's naked hip, another's fur-mantled shoulder. And there, in a hint at coming styles, Bron saw, on someone's back moving off among those gathered at the bar, a green plastic Y snapped to blue suspenders . . . But she would *not* focus on any individual, which made it all giddily adventurous—though she was familiar enough with such places from another world, another time, another life. She started to move around toward the other side of the bar to wait for someone to approach her—and experienced the oddest reaction.

If someone had asked her, then, what is was, she would have answered, astonished, "Terror!" Ten seconds into the feeling, however, and she realized it was more subtle than that. It was more like an insistent annoyance, signaling from some place edging consciousness that something extremely dangerous was near. Then, it resolved: She was here to *be* approached. But she was not here to *invite* approach. Certainly, she could not linger on the active side of the bar where she was now. That was just *not* the sort of woman she was interested in being taken for. If the man she was looking for were here (Any five . . . ? She thought, irrelevantly. Now she dared not look anywhere except the baseboard on the counter, between the legs of the people standing beside it, six feet away.) even being seen on this side would spoil everything. She turned, heading for free-range, passing Prynn, who, elbows on the bar, had eyes only for the older of the two women working behind the counter—certainly the oldest person in the place, probably in Lawrence's league. (And probably, Bron thought, a sharer of Lawrence's tastes.) As Bron reached the free area, she thought: What they need here, of course, is *three* counters: One for the ones who want to approach; and then one for the people who want to be approached, then one for the people who wouldn't *mind* being approached—but no, that wasn't the answer. There wasn't any difference between not-minding-it, and wanting-it-but-just-wanting it-a-little-less. Well, then: four . . . ? With a vision of an infinite regression of counters, each with fewer and fewer people at it, until she, herself and alone, stood at the last, Bron took her place at the center of free-range, where, indeed, a plurality of the reasonable and happy women and men in the place had gathered. She moved as close to the bar as she could get, looking, she knew, like a woman who wasn't interested in anything sexual at all. And in a place like this (she knew), that probably meant she would get no advances at all because there were too many people there who were. Oh, there'd be a few who, tired of the chase, might just want to engage in some—

"Yeah," a pleasant-looking youngster standing next to her said, leaning his elbows on the bar. "There really are times when it's *just* like that." He cocked his head, smiled, nodded.

Bron said: "There are a hundred and fifty other people in here you could approach who would be more interested in it than I am. Now get lost. And if you don't, I'll kick you in the balls. And I *mean* it!"

The youngster frowned, then said: "Hey, *sorry* . . . !" and turned away, while somebody else wedged into his place. And Bron thought, a little hysterically: I am in the position where I am here to be approached and cannot acknowledge an approach of any sort: Otherwise, I will turn off the person I am here to be approached by. That's ridiculous! she thought, shaking her head for the third time to the younger of the two women bartenders, who'd just asked her again what she wanted to drink. What in the world does *that* get you? In another time, on another world (or, indeed, in another bar, with the rules carefully spelled out in the monthly newsletter), raped. And that wasn't the answer either, because once on Mars (it had been the night after his nineteenth birthday) he had *been* raped, by a gang of five women with hard, metallic eyelids as banal as the lyrics to all the thousand (orphan-) Annie-shows that had spawned them, hell raising through the dawn-dim alleys of the Goebels and enraged by the symbol above his right eye; and though, for a few months, he had actually fantasized sexually about the one of the five who hadn't (actually) taken part and (for the first few minutes) tried to stop the others, he'd known even then that was just a strategy for salvaging *some*thing from a thoroughly unpleasant experience that had left him with a sprained thigh, a dislocated shoulder, and a punctured eardrum which (in another world, at another time) might have made him deaf in one ear for life. Remembering, she ran a foreknuckle along her gold brow—completely meaningless on a woman, of course; but out here no one would know. No one would care.

I simply shouldn't be here, Bron thought. The fear that it was somehow the sex itself she was afraid of was what, she realized, had held her here this long. (And that, she suddenly realized, was pushing an hour!) But it was everything else that circled the sex, that kept it closed, locking it in, and—was this something to be thankful for?—somehow pure.

Bron took her hands from the counter, stepped back, turned—

He stood at the "active" side of the bar, among the men and women there, just turning from a conversation, his face settling, from its laughter, into the familiar dignity, the familiar strength. (Had she dreamed about it . . . yes!) His eyes swept the room—passing hers, but her belly tightened when they did—to the even more boisterous "passive" bar.

Go, she thought. Go!

Really, it *was* time to leave! But he was there, like all she could ever remember imagining, as new as now and familiar as desire. She watched, numbing, knowing she had known him laughing among his hard-drinking friends, dark brows a-furrow in concentration over a problem whose solution might roll worlds from their orbits, carelessly asleep on a bed they had shared for the night, his eyes meeting hers in an expression that encompassed all the indifference of now but backed by the compassion of the unspeakably strong, the ineffably wise, and the knowledge of half a year's companionship.

She pushed from the bar, started toward him, thinking: I *mustn't!* I—and shouldered quickly between two people, her throat drying with the fear that, while she was turning to excuse herself here, beg a pardon there, he might leave. She *couldn't* do this! This was all hopelessly and terribly wrong. But she was pushing between the last two, now, reaching to touch his naked shoulder.

He turned, frowned at her.

Bron whispered: "Hello, Sam . . ." and then (by dint of what, she didn't know) felt a smile quiver about her own mouth. "Need any new wives in your commune, Sam . . . Or am I sallow enough . . . ?"

For a moment Sam's full mouth compressed into a great, black prune, the expression almost shock, or pain. Then his eyes left her face to drop down her body; and came slowly back, with a smile that was almost mocking. "Bron . . . ?"

Let there be something besides derision in his smile, she whispered silently; her eyes closed lightly before it. "Sam, I . . . I shouldn't be here . . . I mean on this side of the . . . I mean . . ." Bron blinked.

Sam's hands came down on her shoulders, like black epaulets (in the half-light, Sam's skin really was black, with a dim bronze highlight under his jaw, a dark amber one coiling his ear), and she had the wild vision she had somehow just risen in rank (thinking: And not a single soldier . . .) and thinking at the same time: And it *still* isn't sex! I know what sex is too well to fool myself into thinking that.

Sam was saying: "Hey, there!" And, "Well!" and then: "I admit, I'm . . ." Then just nodded, with approval(!) and with (still) the smile. "How've you been, huh? The Old Pirate mentioned you'd suddenly decided to cross the great divide. You keeping well?"

And because she suddenly felt her heart would crack the cage of her ribs, shatter her joints gone brittle at hip, knee, and elbow, she lay her head against his neck, held on to him. Had he been a column of black metal one degree below white-heat, he would not have been harder to grasp.

"Hey," Sam said, softly. His hands slid across her back, held her.

"Sam . . ." she said. "Take me out of here. Take me to another world . . . anywhere . . . I don't care. I don't even know if I can *move* on my own anymore . . ."

One arm firmed across her back. One arm loosened. Sam said (and she heard his voice rumbling somewhere inside the great shape of him, as the smile retreated down inside): "Seems like I'm always taking you from some place or another . . . Come on, we'll have a stroll," and tugged her shoulder, his arm still tight around her, bringing her with him through the crowd. She thought once to look around for Prynn. But they were already through a door, onto a dark ramp between high walls. "Just remember," Sam went on, "the last world I took you to didn't turn out such a hot idea, before you go asking me again. I mean, you never know where you'll end up with old Sam—"

The ramp turned, and emptied them at the edge of a dim arena, with odd shapes set out here and there, and a glittering ceiling, here only seven or eight feet high, brushing the heads of some of the taller men and women strolling below the orange and blue light; at other places it rose up three or four stories: This was the bar's "run," where those who wanted to could move about, could wander over some sort of obstacle course in pursuit of their pleasure, could be pursued, or just walk.

"Sam, I'm sorry . . . I didn't mean to . . ."

Sam squeezed her shoulder affectionately. "Sometimes it can be a pretty rough trip from there to here. I know. I made it myself. How're you freezing in?"

"I'm . . ." Bron let a breath go, felt her back muscles, that had tightened almost to a cramp, relax a little. "Well, I . . . guess you *would* understand . . ."

A man ahead glanced back twice, then turned off around an immense sculptural shape, under red light, then was beyond it into shadow.

"Some of it," Sam said.

A woman, hands thrust deep in her pockets, walked into the darkness after him (Bron saw one bare elbow bend as a hand came out of her pocket, with three gold rings bright as steam-boat coals in the red light; then she was into darkness too). And they were past, too far to see.

"Have you ever been in one of these places during off-hours?" Bron asked.

"Who hasn't?"

"They're so sad when nobody's using them."

"So's an all-night cafeteria at the first-slot credit level." (Which were the social-service food places where, despite your credit level, you had to be served.) "There's one two blocks from here that gives as good—or almost as good—service in food as this place does in sex."

They passed a snaking bench where a number of women (and a scant handful of men) were seated. A man walking past hesitated, glanced, then sat near one of the women who, as if her motion were the completion of his, got up and walked away, to turn, seconds later, around the end of another bench where those seated were mostly men: Her pace slowed, and she began surveying the seated figures as, moments before, the man who had prompted her to move had surveyed the figures on the bench where she had been. Here and there was the sound of faint laughter, or faint converse. Most, however, were silent.

"Around and around and around we go," Sam said, and added his soft bass rumble to the drifting voices.

Coming toward them, hand in hand, wearing only a complex metallic vest and briefs, a woman laughed, and a man, naked except for a jeweled domino, pushed up on his forehead now, smiled.

The couple parted around Sam and Bron; the laughter drifted off behind them. "And suddenly," Sam said, "for them, it's all worth it." He glanced back, added his own laughter again. People on the bench smiled.

Bron tried not to look away; and failed.

"Didn't somebody advise you to stay away from places like this till after you got a little better acclimated?" Sam asked. "*Bad* counseling. It's like going into a four-wall jai-alai tournament a week after you've had a broken leg set. I mean, even if you were the greatest player in the world before, it still can be a bit depressing."

"It's been six months since I . . . I had my leg set. My counselor's been telling me it's well past time I got in there and gave it a try."

"Oh." Sam's arm had loosened around her shoulder. "I see."

The desperation had started again. "Sam, please. Let me come live with you and your family. I wouldn't be much bother. You've known me as a friend for almost a year; I'll take the chance on your getting to know me as a lover."

"I heard you the first time, sweetheart," Sam said. "If you ask me again, I'll have to give you a clear, firm, unambiguous answer. And that would only hurt your feelings. So do yourself a favor and cut it out."

"You won't . . ." and felt her feelings rend as if knives turned in her liver. "Oh, *why*, Sam?"

"My women would never hear of it. We trade off, see, bringing the next sweet young thing into my harem. I choose one, they choose one. It's their turn this week."

"Sam, you're playing with me!"

"That's all you leave open . . . You do *remember* where my commune was?—No, you don't. That's good. Because when you first spoke to me, I thought that was your idea of a joke."

"Oh, you don't . . . you *can't*—"

"Sweetheart, you're reasoning from the converse. The sad truth is that I *could*—but I won't. It's that hard and that nasty. I'm your friend, but I'm not *that* good a friend, right now, tonight. The only advice I can give you is that even if it's hard where you are now—and I know it can be—you're still changing, still moving. Eventually, even from here, you'll get to somewhere else. I know that too. Now come here—" and did not wait, but pulled her to him, and, in his arm's she felt herself start to cry, could not cry, felt herself start to scream, but could not do that either, felt herself start to collapse. But that was just silly. So she held onto him, thinking: Sam . . . ! Sam . . . !

An age later, Sam released her and, with his hands on her shoulders, moved her away. "All right. You're on your own, lady. Sam's just too big and black and lazy for all this rambling around. I'm going back downstairs, where it's crowded. I'm out to get laid tonight. And I happen to be one of those guys who makes out better in the crush." He smiled, patted her shoulder, turned. And was gone.

I *can't* move, she thought. But moved, walking fairly normally, to one of the single seats cut into the side of a large, ceramic free-form.

Sam, she thought again; and again; then again; till the word became mysterious, alien, ominous, a single-syllable mantra. Then: . . . *Sam*—? Somehow, on this hundredth, or hundred-thousandth repetition, it suddenly cleared her mind.

Why had she been approaching Sam?

Sam was no more a man than she was a . . . No. She had to stop that thought; it could lead nowhere. Still, again, she had been about to sacrifice all her ideals, her entire plan, just for an . . . emotional whim! Yet, while it had been happening, it had seemed those ideals were just what she had been pursuing . . .

Sam?

That was ridiculous as the embarrassment and anger she had subjected herself to with that theater woman! Think! she thought: At one point there had been something she had thought she could *do* better than other women—because she had *been* a man, known first-hand a man's strengths, a man's needs. So she had become a woman to do it. But the *doing,* as she had once suspected and now knew, was preeminently a matter of *being*; and *being* had turned out to be, more and more, specifically a matter of *not doing.* And from the restrictions, subterranean and powerful forces seemed to have run wild in her that, as a result, threatened to corrupt everything she *did* want to do. In her work at the hegemony, in her friendships—with Lawrence, with Prynn—the force was apathy, tangible and inexorable as the ice-cascade crashing down the slope at the climax of an ice-opera. Then, whenever she reached a situation even near one in which her woman-hood was at stake, all that had been suppressed welled up in such a torrent she could not tell desperation from resentment, desire from need, making her blurt stupidities and nonsense instead of what, a moment before or a moment later, she would have known was rational response.

What *was* she trying to do? Bron asked herself. And found the question as clearing as Sam's name a minute before. It had to do with saving the race . . . no, something to do with saving or protecting . . . men? But she was a woman. Then why . . . ? She stopped that thought as well. Not her thoughts, but her actions were pursuing some logical or metalogical concatenation to its end. To try and ask, much less answer, any one of those questions would pollute, destroy, shatter it into a lattice of contradictions that would crumble on expression. She knew that what she wanted was true and real and right by the act of wanting. Even if the wanting was all—

A man had stopped a few feet away, to lean on an outcrop of the ceramic. He wasn't looking at her, but she saw the position of his hand on the green-swirled glaze. The insult of it! she thought, with sadness and desperation. Why didn't they just come up and slap you across the mouth? Wouldn't it have been kinder, less damaging to what she was trying to protect? And he might *be* the one! she went on thinking. I simply have no way to guess, to ask, to find out. If I were to respond in any way, I would never know, because even if he was, *any* response from me would cause him to put that side of himself away forever as far as I'm concerned, become all pretended reason and rationality. *He* could come here, could sit and wait, could prowl and search, as she had once sat or prowled, searching for the woman who would know, who would understand. Men could do that. She had done it when she was a man, and had found, prowling or being prowled by, five hundred, five thousand women? But she had no way to show she knew, because any indication of knowledge denied that knowledge's existence in her. And there was no way to overcome the paradox, unless there were an infinite number of such bars, such arenas, such runs, unless she could somehow interpose an infinite distance, a million times that between Earth and Triton, between herself and him, then wait for him to cross it, carry her back over it, as easily as Sam had carried her to Mongolia and—No! No, *not* Sam—

Bron looked up, blinking, because the man had dropped his hand, was walking past her, was ambling off.

She watched him, tears suddenly banking her lids. The thought came, insistent as certain knowledge: What I want to do is just . . . She clamped her eyes and mind against it.

Two tears spilled one cheek.

She blinked.

A feeble kaleidoscope of dim lights and massive sculptures cleared and flashed; she blinked again; it cleared, it flashed. What she knew was that she just must never come to a place like this again. Yes, he may be here, he may even be searching for her, here; but there was just no way in which, here, he could find her, she could find him. She must never come here; she must not be here now. She must get up, she must get up now, and go.

Half a dozen more men (and two women; yes, the place did have informal rules) came and stood near her, signaled or did not signal, and walked away. Hours passed—had already passed. And far less people had stopped near her during the last few. Was the rumor of her indifference being whispered to all and sundry about the place? Or—she looked up, having momentarily drifted off—were there simply fewer people?

She could see less than a dozen about the whole arena. The cleaning crew had turned on harsh lights along the far side; coils of cable dragged the gold carpet, behind the humming machines . . .

Before she went home, she stopped in the all-night cafeteria two blocks away, which, while she was there, began to clean up too. Sitting in a back booth (after the little table-speaker had politely asked her to leave the front so they could mop), she drank two bulbs of coffee, the first with lots of sugar, the second black. Nobody bothered her at all.

On her desk, when she woke, was the red- and silver-edged envelope of an inter-satellite letter. The return box said *D. R. Lawrence*, be-

neath which was a twenty-two-digit number. Under that, in parentheses: *Neriad*. Bron frowned. Standing naked on the warming carpet—one of the balloon chairs beside her heel kept pulsing in its
collar, trying to decide if it should inflate—Bron fingered open the
flimsy:

> Bron better put a semicolon no a comma I've been meaning to
> come see you for months italicize months but then suddenly
> there was all this and as you no doubt have already noticed I'm
> not even at the old snake pit anymore or even on Triton but on
> Neriad and so I thought the least I could do was write. Guess
> what. Twenty-years' interest in aleotorics has paid off. Have
> been swept up by a traveling music commune and would you
> believe that all of us one night after how many hundreds of
> hours' meditation and rehearsal simultaneously had a religious
> revelation that it was time to bring our music to others and so
> now we are singing for real people practically every night can
> you imagine with my voice but they seem to like it. Mostly I'm
> A-and-R man really though I do half a dozen solos I'm desper-
> ately happy at it. I think we are bringing a lot of people joy. Last
> night's audience was twenty-six thousand. They went wild
> comma but I'm recovering nicely thank you this morning under
> the ministrations of a lovely friend who simply attached himself
> to me right out of the audience just like that and who has just
> this minute brought me breakfast in bed. It's so nice to learn at
> my age that there are even more complex and elegant games
> than vlet dash though I will warmly welcome a game with you
> should the music of the spheres once again suspend us in the
> same chord. We head off next to that nasty little moon of
> Pluto's parenthesis where there aren't even twenty-six thousand
> people all together but that's religion for you I guess parenthe-
> sis and anyway this is just a note to let you know there's life in
> the old boy yet as if you cared heartless beauty that you've be-
> come but I'm Wiffles what are you doing oh really now stop it
> Wiffles stop it I'm trying to dictate a letter oh that tickles oh
> come on you dear creature I simply won't let

That was all there was.

Smiling, she put the letter down. But there was also, wheedling at
the back of the smile, regret. As she looked through the cupboard for

clothes, it grew until the smile flaked away before it. She was already late anyway and still exhausted from the previous night; she closed the cupboard and decided to take the day off from work.

And the day after that, back at the hegemony, she threw herself into the three new accounts that had come in, with a vengeance. (What else was there to do while she waited?) For the next week she kept up the pace, occasionally wondering what this must be doing to her efficiency index but, at the least glimmer of pleasure, damping the thought—with more work. Work now was not for pleasure or pride or reward; all those had been abnegated. What was left was merely a frantic, nearly religious gesture of respect toward time; no more.

A week later, one morning when she had been in her office perhaps an hour, Philip paused at the door, looked in, stepped in: "Audri asked me to stop by and take a look in on you. About eight months ago you were making noises about needing an assistant—at which point, if I remember, we sent you about six in succession that, for one reason or another, were pretty poor: wrong field, wrong temperament—you name it, we sent it to you." Philip looked at the floor, looked at Bron. "Not that we have anyone on tap now, but I was just wondering—well, Audri was wond79ering; but since things have loosened up around here in the past few months, if you still wanted one . . . ?"

"Nope." Bron went rummaging through a drawer for another folder—and noticed that Philip had stopped to look through the flimsys she'd left on top of the wall-console. "Don't get those out of order please," Bron said. She found the folder.

"Oh, I'm sorry," Philip said. And then, to Bron's growing surprise and distress, hung around for the next quarter-hour, making the sort of pleasant small talk you couldn't really take exception to, especially from your boss.

He left.

She sighed with relief.

Ten minutes before lunch he was back: "Hey, let me take you out on my credit this afternoon—no, don't say you've got another appointment. I know it's not true. Look—" Philip's bearded smile brought back Sam's black one at the bar, a layer of it friendly, another layer of it mocking, and something that was totally Philip and wholly unpleasant, beaming through—"I know we grate on each other's nerves from time to time. But, really, I *would* like to talk to you this afternoon," which, from your boss, was another thing you didn't refuse.

Philip took her not to the company cafeteria, but to a place across the Plaza where they sat in an enclosed bubble of opalescent glass, the table between them rimmed with black and gold, for all the world like an interplanetary letter-form; and over a remarkably good, if somewhat lichenous, lunch, Philip launched into endless gossipy speculations about two of the junior programmers, about Audri, about himself—his commune was thinking of moving further along the Ring, which would leave their place opened; Audri was due for a credit reslotting, and really she was much better at this job than he was and, maybe, ought to think about taking their place over, if she could find some compatible people to get a family going again and to furnish the other necessary credit levels. When was his group vacating? Well, he wasn't really sure, but . . .

Then they were leaving, Philip was still talking, and by now Bron, having become tired of her own annoyance and exhausted with pretending it wasn't there, was morosely wondering if perhaps this wasn't all some ineffably gentle prologue to getting fired—or at least a serious reprimand. She remembered Audri's warning two weeks ago. In all her new zeal, she might have committed some really amazing blunder that had just come to light. *Was* that possible? In the general confusion of her current life, she found herself thinking she could have done *any*-thing. Well, then, she was ready—

And Philip, at her office door, was smiling, nodding, was turning to leave.

And an hour later was back, still smiling, asking if the new topo-form specifications she had delivered yesterday had given her any particular problems (no), if Audri had been by (also no), if lunch had been all right (it was very nice, thank you). He only stayed five minutes this time, but seconds after he left, it suddenly struck her—and made her put both hands flat on the desk, look up, open her mouth, close it again, then drop her hands to her lap: Philip was getting ready to make a pass!

The idea should have been horrifying.

But it was too funny!

The only really horrible thing was just how funny it was!

What's the matter with Philip, she thought. Then she remembered: Hadn't he once been indiscreet enough to mention he'd once married a transsexual; oh, I *am* dense! she thought. He probably has a "thing" for them! Wouldn't you know, all I've done is become his particular type! Dense . . . ? That was not the word for it if it had taken her *this* long to realize what was going on! And when he actually came out and propositioned her? I will do, she thought, absolutely *nothing*! If he signals me, I will not see! If he speaks, I will not hear him! If he falls down on his knees to me, I will leave the room! I am just not here for that kind of shit! she thought on the edge of anger. And, holding both anger and the laughter back, she plunged again into the work.

Twenty minutes before closing, Philip was in the door again. "Hey, Bron—" with the ingratiating smile, the velvet voice—"Audri wanted to talk to you. I think we can all kick off early today. So I'll just leave you two to hash it out—" He ducked his head, and was gone.

And Audri, looking very nervous, stood behind where Philip had been. "Bron," she said, "do you mind walking back with me. I mean toward my place. At least for a couple of stops. I want to talk to you," and she stood, looking not quite at Bron, hands moving at her hips of her dark slacks.

Surprised, Bron said, "All right," because she liked Audri, and Audri was her boss too, and because Philip's absence was such a relief. "Just a second." She pushed things into the drawer, closed it, stood up.

Together, they walked out of the building, Bron becoming more aware of the silence.

Halfway across the Plaza of Light, Audri said: "Philip thinks I'm out of my mind, but he also thinks that whether I'm out of my mind or not, I should just be straightforward and come out with it. Which is going to be pretty hard. But I guess I have to . . ." Audri took a breath, tightened her mouth, let the breath out slowly, then said, almost in a whisper:

"Come home with me. Make love with me. Live with me . . ." Then she glanced at Bron, with a flicker of a smile—"forever. Or a year. Or six hours. Or six months . . ." She took another breath. "Philip's right: that *is* the hard part."

"What?" Bron said.

"I said . . . well, you did hear me, didn't you . . . ?"

"Yes, but . . ." Bron laughed, only it didn't quite sound. "Well . . . I just don't—"

Audri smiled at the pink pavement as they walked. "There's an easy part too. My credit rating goes up in two weeks—more postwar boom. Philips says there's a good possibility I can get this co-op unit out on the Ring if I can get enough people together. There are about four other high-rate women I've talked to who said they were interested. Together we've got five kids between us. There'd be room for you if you . . ." She paused. "Well, you know what Philip's place looks like. It's pretty nice. Even if you just wanted to try it, to see how it might work out . . . does it sound too much like I'm trying to lure you into my bed with promises of material gain?"

"No, but—Well . . ."

"Bron, you know I've always liked you . . . been very fond of you—"

"And I've always been fond of you too—"

"But then there was—I mean, before—always the physical thing. It took me till I was twenty-three, with my first two kids, to realize that men just weren't where I was. Some people learn that lesson very easily. With me it came late and hard. Maybe that's why I was never particularly interested in unlearning it . . . But, well—really, there was always something about you that I felt sort of warm and protective toward. Then, the day of the war, when you broke through the enforcement barricade to come to our co-op and help us get out of the danger area. That was so . . ." She shook her head. "—incredibly *brave!* I mean I've always known you've *liked* me—it's always pretty easy to tell what you're feeling; in a nonverbal way, I suppose you're a very open person—but when you came in to get us, I realized maybe that your liking me had a strength to it I'd just never suspected before. That you would put your life in danger for mine and my family's—I mean, I never told you, but they found Mad Mike's body the next day. He'd been killed by a gravity dip, when a wall fell on him. So I *know* how dangerous it was out there. Really, when I thought about what you had done, I was just . . . stunned! Really. That's the only way I can put it. You know I used to—" She laughed, suddenly and softly, then glanced again at Bron. "I used to say to Philip, even before the war, that if you were only a woman, I could . . ." She laughed again. "I mean, it was a joke. But then, to come in the day *after* the war and find that you *were* a woman. . . . You are a woman . . ." Audri took another breath. "I'm not the kind of boss-lady who goes chasing her employees around the desk. But—well . . ." She let the breath out, slowly: the glance again, the smile—"the last six months has been a little rough."

Bron touched Audri's naked shoulder. And felt Audri shake, once, without breaking step; Audri was looking at the ground about five feet ahead of them. "Audri, look I—"

"I don't really expect you to say yes," Audri said, quickly and quietly. "And no matter what you decide, nothing's going to change at work or anything. I promise. I made up my mind about that before I even decided to open my mouth. I told myself I wasn't even going to mention refixation treatments; but I guess I just did . . . I mean—the thing is, I guess because I've been open about it, I . . . ." She was still looking at the ground, only three feet ahead of them now—"I do feel better . . . ."

"Audri, I *can't* say yes. It just wouldn't be fair. Really, I'm awfully flattered and . . . well, touched. I didn't know you felt that way and I . . . but well, I . . . you just don't understand." There *had* been a surge of fear at first; she recalled it, now, only seconds old. Then she had felt a surge of compassion; and then, wheedling between the two, annoyance. She didn't want to be annoyed, not with Audri. "I mean, you don't even know anything about why I became a . . ." Bron laughed, and tried to make it as warm as Audri's smile, but she heard the unintended edge. She dropped her hand. "Audri, one of the reasons I became a woman in the first place was to . . . well, get *away* from women." Bron frowned. "From one woman, anyway—Oh, that wasn't the only reason." She looked at Audri, who, head down, hands against her thighs, was just walking, just listening. "But it was certainly a big part of it . . . not that it did much good." Bron looked ahead too. "You remember, back when you warned me about my efficiency index slipping? It was around then. That's probably what I was so worried about that kept my mind off what I was doing in the office." Bron thought: But Audri had warned her *before* she'd run into the Spike, hadn't she . . . ? Well anyway—"She had me awfully upset. It's a wonder I even got into the office at all during that time. She was . . ." Bron glanced over; "Well, sort of like you. I mean a lesbian . . . gay. She just wouldn't leave me alone." Wait, Bron thought; wait . . . What am I talking about . . . ? Audri glanced over now. Bron said quickly: "She'd had a refixation, you see, so she could respond sexually to men. Of course she didn't tell me about this until after I'd changed myself. She was just completely dishonest. About everything. And of course the thing that makes it so terrible, now, is that her feelings for me *are* real, no matter how unpleasant or ugly or inconvenient they are. To me. Or anyone else, for that matter. She'll involve anyone else in the whole awful business as soon as talk to them. She's *not* the world's most considerate person, at the best of times." Bron glanced at Audri; who nodded, listening.

"I can't hate her," Bron said. "Anymore than I could hate you. I mean, I *like* her, you know, when I'm not just at the end of my tether. But she simply has no concept of what's real and what's fantasy—did I say? She's in the theater. Maybe you've heard of her. She had her own company—had a company. She's called the Spike?"

"Is *she* gay?" Audri asked.

Bron looked at her quickly. "Do you know her?—or know somebody who does? I mean, Tethys is such an awfully small city, I'd just hate for any of this to get back to her. I'm just telling you because you *are* my friend, Audri . . ."

"No," Audri said. "I don't know her. I saw one of her microproductions about a year ago, that's all. I was impressed."

"This fantasy/reality confusion," Bron went on, "it's just marvelous in her work. I mean, there, it's practically like what *we* do, the fantasy working as a sort of metalogic, with which she can solve real, aesthetic problems in the most incredible ways—I was actually *in* a few of her productions last year; a sort of ersatz member of the company. But finally I just had to get out. Because when that fantasy seeps into the reality, she just becomes an incredibly ugly person. She feels she can distort anything that occurs for whatever purpose she wants. Whatever she feels, that's what *is*, as far as she's concerned. But then, I suppose . . ." Bron laughed at the ground, then looked up: they'd just left the Plaza—"that's the right we just fought a war to defend. But Audri, when someone abuses that right, it can make it pretty awful for the rest of us. The last time I saw her—" Bron dropped her eyes again—"she'd disbanded the whole company—she's got a sort of pro-temp university job now. She told me that she'd even give *that* up if I'd only become her lover, take her with me, away from it all." Bron laughed. "As if I *had* somewhere to take her! And of course my being a woman now only makes it worse for her. Not to mention me . . . I mean if she only could have been honest with me at the beginning, all this could have been . . ." She looked again at Audri; who blinked at her. For a moment she was terrified Audri would say something to shatter the whole, amazing fiction that wove itself on and on. Audri blinked again. "Do you see," Bron said, "I just couldn't say yes to you, not when I'm still involved with her, in all this nonsense—and I am, I am, up to my ears." She started to touch Audri's arm again, didn't. "Do you understand . . . ?"

Audri nodded.

"I'm . . ." Bron let her eyes move away. "I'm sorry. It's just that I feel—Oh, look, I've already said much too much about it already. Any more, and I'll just feel like the complete fool I am—"

"Oh, *no* . . ." Audri said. "No—"

Which brought Bron up short. Because somehow Audri's belief in all this was something she had not even considered a possibility. "Well, it's . . ." Bron began. "It's like what you said about learning a lesson hard and late—what this woman has taught me. About the Universe, even about me in it. Audri, I couldn't say yes to you, any more than I could say yes to her." She looked unblinkingly at Audri who looked, unblinkingly back. Bron thought: I can't believe this is happening. "Don't hate me for that."

"I don't," Audri said. "It's just so hard to believe that this—" She blinked again. "Look, there won't . . . there won't be any change at the office. I mean that. It's just . . . well, Philip, in his role as big brother to the universe, thought I'd feel better if I at least asked. I guess I do. But I think . . . I think I better see you tomorrow. So long . . . I'll see you tomorrow!" and Audri turned quickly away, off along the street.

Bron felt the third drop of sweat pause, halfway down her back, then roll on. At the corner she thought: Where am I . . . ? Where— Involved in her explanation, she hadn't noticed the street they had turned on. She looked at the street sign, took a great breath, and walked all the way to the next corner before she stopped.

Why did I lie to that woman?

She stood there, frowning at the next set of green coordinate letters and numbers across from her, losing their meaning behind her concentration.

Why did I lie to Audri? I *like* Audri! Why invent that incredible concoction about the Spike giving up everything for *me*? Not (she started walking again) that she'd said anything about the Spike's character she wouldn't stick by. Still, why choose to illustrate it with such a silly fiction? Especially when the truth was so much simpler.

Tomorrow at work, Audri *would* probably be back to normal—or; if not tomorrow, then a week from tomorrow, a month from tomorrow. But what about *me* . . . ? Why *lie*, outright and unequivocally? She wanted to talk to somebody. Brian? But she'd carefully kept from her the fact that the Spike even existed! Lawrence—? No, he was too old; she didn't want his aged, caustic homilies. Besides, Lawrence was on another moon, another world. And Prynn of course was too young.

Who else did she *ever* talk to about things?

Audri, sometimes. But she certainly couldn't talk to Audri about this!

She crossed the street, found the transport station; all the way home, the annoyance wound her thoughts: Sometimes she was annoyed with Audri, sometimes with herself, sometimes with the villainous Spike.

At the Eagle, in her room, she locked the door and sat on the side of her bed—did not answer when Prynn came pounding at seven-thirty, did not answer when Prynn came pounding and shouting again at nine. At ten, she went to a cafeteria over in the next unit to avoid meeting any of the women from the co-op, got something to eat, came back, went into her room, and locked the door again.

Why did I lie to that woman?

She had been in bed over an hour. She had switched on the public channels, switched them off, switched them on and off again. She turned over on one side, then turned back. But by now all her thoughts on the subject had been rehearsed a hundred times, repeating when they would not develop. Over three hours ago she had, for the first time, remembered she had mentally concocted almost the same story during the first two weeks she had moved here, in expectation of a proposition from that odd blonde with the black streaks in her hair who lived on the second floor and who was definitely gay; she had been *so* insistently generous to Bron with dinner invitations, offers of clothes, tapes, pictures (it was as bad as the woman's heterosexual co-op she'd moved out of!), sex was the only explanation. All but the first of each Bron had refused. There'd been no pass; the woman had moved. The contemplated subterfuge had been forgotten.

But the point is, Bron thought, even though I was *thinking* of telling her something like that, if the woman had actually *said* anything to me, I certainly wouldn't have used it. I would have treated her the same way I treated Lawrence; honest, straightforward. I mean if I learned one thing hustling it's that, in matters of sex at any rate, it pays to be straight. I wouldn't have told such a story to a complete stranger! *Why* did I tell it to someone I actually like? Hadn't it *begun* as an attempt to spare Audri's feelings, in some strange way? How ridiculous, she thought. Other people's feelings, beyond maintaining general civility, had never been one of her major concerns. Nor did she think very highly of people for whom they were. People take care of their own feelings; I take care of mine. Besides, if I'd just said, "No," to Audri's request, it would have been far kinder than all those complicated theatrics! That was worthy of an actress like the Spike! —oh, come on: the Spike had nothing to do with that! Nothing! But what Bron also realized, and it was almost as annoying, is that some- how she'd gotten, in telling the lie, something she'd wanted: The first thing she'd felt (when it was just over, before this stupid and unstop- pable questioning had set in) was satisfied. Now that's the question: Why? Bron turned over again and thought: I can tell, this is just going to be another of those nights—

—and was dreaming about the bar, the place Prynn had taken her; but it was different, because there were only women present. What a strange dream, she thought. For one thing, most of the women were complete strangers. Over there, leaning against the wall, was the blonde lesbian who used to live on the second floor. Now why, Bron wondered, should I be dreaming about her? But then, I was just thinking about her, wasn't I? A girl not much older than Prynn was sitting on a table corner playing her guitar. Charo? Over there sat a sixty-year-old woman with blue nails, blue high-heeled shoes, blue lips, and blue breast bangles. Bron was sure that if she'd ever seen her before, it was just in passing on the street. Still, all these strange women made her uncomfortable. She looked around again for some- one more familiar and saw, to her astonishment, the Spike sitting at one of the tables busily writing on the gold- and black-edged sheet of an interplanetary letter-form. And there was Audri, sitting not far be- hind her, with Prynn next to her; just behind them stood a woman she didn't recognize at all: a very dark oriental . . . was it that Miriamne person she'd almost been lumbered with as an assistant? No; too young. More likely it was somebody she had once seen with Alfred. Were they all looking at her? Or looking past her? Bron turned, thinking how silly it was to be in a pickup bar with nothing but women. But the door was opening. A man in maroon coveralls backed through it. Apparently he was still talking to a bunch of friends outside. He kept lingering at the door, calling to them, laugh- ing at them.

Bron looked at the women. Some were definitely looking at her now. Charo was smiling, nodding in time to her strumming. The Spike had apparently covered several sheets. Indeed, the sheet she was writing on so busily now was much too large for a letter-form. Prynn and a black girl had stepped up behind the Spike and were leaning over her shoulder to read. Prynn reached down to point something out; the Spike immediately made a correction. She wasn't writing a letter at all! She must be making notes on a new production. Bron turned to look at the man (he was at the bar now, but still looking away) and thought: This must be where *my* part comes in. Do I know my lines? At any rate, I'm sure they'll come back to me, once I begin. Again she glanced: Several of the women, with large, colored markers, were reaching over the Spike's shoulder to add notes of their own. This is going to be quite a show, Bron thought. The woman with the blue lips and bangles looked up at her, smiled, nodded her on. Bron turned back to the man, who was leaning with one forearm on the counter, still looking away at the door—as if, Bron thought at once, he might go after his friends outside any moment and miss the whole production! Nervously, she walked toward him.

He turned to her.

Somehow, she had expected it to be Mad Mike the Christian. But the face, under pale, curly hair, was someone else's. One eyebrow was rough and rumpled. The other had been replaced with a gold arc in the skin.

When she recognized him, she thought: Oh, *no* . . . ! It was just too . . . well, *banal*! For dream *or* theater! With this, no *mise en scène* was possible! Meeting her old self like that . . . well, it was just too pat. It was as cliché as—well, "waiting for the dawn," or "the horrors of war." Wasn't theater involved with belief? How could *any*one believe such an absurd coincidence! Just running into herself like that, why the chances were fifty-to-one, fifty *billion* to one!—There had been some mistake! That's not the way the production could have possibly been planned! The action, properly speaking, would be invisible from the pit . . . She glanced at the Spike again.

Almost all the women were writing now, crowding each other, reaching over one another's shoulders. With bright-colored pens, they filled in bright-colored numbers on the large paper grids scattered on the table—from just a glance, she knew they were filling in the plurality female deployment configuration. How *hopelessly* banal! Was she really going to have to take part in this absurd drama? She turned again to Bron—he stood at the counter, smiling at her, pleasantly enough, if a little nervous, but completely unaware. She raised her hand tentatively toward his face, then shrieked:

"I shall destroy you!" She clawed at his gold brow, hissing: "I shall destroy you, destroy you, do you hear!" Her nails, she noticed, were not the carefully-filed, surgically-narrowed ones from her last bit of cosmetic surgery, or even the broad and cleaned ones she'd had before the operation, but the bitten ones of her adolescence. "I shall destroy *you*—as you destroyed *me*!" The words tore at her throat. She turned, gasping, away.

It was over!

Some of the women were clapping politely.

She gasped in another breath, overcome with emotion. A terrible script! Devoid of whatever meaning—or was it meaninglessness?—it might have for an audience! But I *did* give a brilliant performance. I must have gotten carried away with the part. Completely carried away. Her eyes were tearing. She reached for a chair to collapse into, but it was over there, behind the third bar. So she staggered on another few steps. Lord, how many bars *were* there? But somewhere behind them all there must be a chair. She staggered on, still wracked by the emotions the performance had evoked, one fragment of her mind still aloof and objective: As moved as I was by it, it's *still* a terrible part! I mean—she gasped another breath, as the emotions welled on; it was as if the whole production had been some tawdry, twilight melo-drama the intellect could not bear but the heart could not resist—I *may* have been that kind of man. But I am *not* that type of woman! Hot, buffeting, embarrassing, her emotions roiled and seethed. Oh, I must sit down, she thought, reached out for the chair again—

—and woke, suddenly, completely, and (annoyingly) with the same question she had drifted off with: Why did I lie to Audri?

The silly dream—its emotional detritus still falling away from the images—certainly didn't suggest any answer. She turned over once more, with two questions, now, equally puzzling. First: Where had the lie come from? Second: Why was she so obsessed with it?

Why did I lie?

What could possibly have prompted it?

She lay, coldly and clearly awake: I never lied when I was a man. But thinking, for the hundredth time, over what she had said to Audri, it seemed to have resonances that filtered back through her entire life, the whole of it, on Triton, on Mars, as a man, as a woman. And she could not articulate any of them. You should always tell the truth, she thought, not because one lie leads to another, but rather because one lie could so easily lead you to that terrifying position from which, with just the help of a random dream, you can see, both back and ahead, the morass where truth and falsity are simply, for you, indistinguishable.

Oh, this is crazy, Bron thought suddenly. Why am I lying here, flagellating myself with guilt? I never *used* to lie: with Audri, or Philip, or anyone. If a situation came up, I faced it! Well, if I could before, I can now. It's only one slip-up. There's no reason to start being a moral perfectionist now. That's not your job. Were women just less truthful than men? All right: Was *she* less truthful as a woman than she had been as a man? Very well, then that's just one more thing I need a man to do—to tell the truth for me! Now turn over and go back to sleep!

She turned on her side, then to her back again, one hand against her chin. She bit at a piece of dead skin on her lip; and felt terribly empty. Here I am, she thought, as she had done from time to time ever since she'd come from Mars: Here I am, on Triton, and again I am lost in some hopeless tangle of confusion, trouble, and distress—

But this is *so* silly!

She breathed deeply and turned to the other side. It was just life and there was nothing logical you could do about it; and if sleep were denied her for the night, then there was nothing to do about that either but wait for dawn, that—suddenly and shockingly!—she was sure, sure for thirty-seven entire seconds (each counted with a louder and louder heart-thud that finally blocked her throat with terror), sure in a way that implied volumes on the rotation of the planets, on the entropy of the chemistry in the sun itself (moving and churning somewhere in the real universe beyond the sensory shield), sure with a surety which, if it were this subjectively complete must *be* objectivity (and wasn't that the reason why, her scrambling mind careened on, unable to stop even for the terror, that, in these ice- and rock-bound moons, the subjective was held politically inviolable; and hadn't they just killed three out of four, or five out of six, to keep it so—? Then, as suddenly, sureness ceased; and she was left, on her side, shaken, with stuttering heart and breath, biting her bleeding lip, with a memory of something that now only *seemed*—But . . . no, *not* if she had felt like that about it; she *had* been sure!), sure would never come.

—*London, Nov. '73/July '74*

Appendix A
From The *Triton* Journal:

Work Notes and Omitted Pages

"You know," Sam said pensively, "that explanation of mine this evening—about the gravity business?" They stood in the warm semi-dark of the co-op's dining room. "If that were translated into some twentieth-century language, it would come out complete gobbledygook. Oh, perhaps an s-f reader might have understood it. But any scientist of the period would have giggled all the way to the bar."

"S-f?" Bron leaned against the bar.

"'Scientifiction?' 'Sci-fi?' 'Speculative fiction?' 'Science fiction?' 'S-f?'—that's the historical progression of terms, though various of them resurfaced from time to time."

"Wasn't there some public-channel coverage about . . . ?"

"That's right," Sam said. "It always fascinated me, that century when humanity first stepped onto the first moon."

"It's not that long ago," Bron said. "It's no longer from us to them than from them to when man first stepped onto the American shore."

Which left Sam's heavy-lipped frown so intense Bron felt his temples heat. But Sam suddenly laughed. "Next thing you'll be telling me is that Columbus discovered America; the bells off San Salvador; the son buried in the Dominican Republic . . ."

Bron laughed too, at ease and confused.

"What I mean—" Sam's hand, large, hot, and moist, landed on Bron's shoulder—"is that my explanation would have been nonsense two hundred years ago. It isn't today. The épistémé has changed so entirely, so completely, the words bear entirely different charges, even though the meanings are more or less what they would have been in—"

"What's an épistémé?" Bron asked.

"To be sure. You haven't been watching the proper public-channel coverages."

"You know me." Bron smiled. "Annie-shows and ice-operas—always in the intellectual forefront. Never in arrears."

"An épistème is an easy way to talk about the way to slice through the whole—"

"Sounds like the secondary hero in some ice-opera. Melony Épistème, costarring with Alona Liang." Bron grabbed his crotch, rubbed, laughed, and realized he was drunker than he'd thought.

"Ah," Sam said (Was Sam drunk too . . . ?), "but the épistème was *always* the secondary hero of the s-f novel—in exactly the same way that the landscape was always the primary one. If you'd just been watching the proper public channels, you'd know." But he had started laughing too.

II

Everything in a science-fiction novel should be mentioned at least twice (in at least two different contexts).

III

Text and *textus*? Text, of course, comes from the Latin *textus*, which means "web." In modern printing, the "web" is that great ribbon of paper which, in many presses, takes upwards of an hour to thread from roller to roller throughout the huge machine that embeds ranked rows of inked graphemes upon the "web," rendering it a text. All the uses of the words "web," "weave," "net," "matrix" and more, by this circular 'etymology' become entrance points into a *textus*, which is ordered from all language and language-functions, and upon which the text itself is embedded.

The technological innovations in printing at the beginning of the Sixties, which produced the present "paperback revolution," are probably the single most important factor contouring the modern science-fiction text. But the name "science fiction" in its various avatars—s-f, speculative fiction, sci-fi, scientifiction—goes back to those earlier technological advances in printing that resulted in the proliferation of "pulp magazines" during the Teens and Twenties.

Naming is always a metonymic process. Sometimes it is the pure metonymy* of associating an abstract group of letters (or numbers)

---

* *Metonymy* is, of course, the rhetorical figure by which one thing is called with the name of another thing associated with it. The historian who writes, "At last, the crown was safe at Hampton," is not concerned with the metallic tiara but the monarch who, from time to time, wore it. The dispatcher who reports to the truck-

with a person (or thing), so that it can be recalled (or listed in a metonymic order with other entity names). Frequently, however, it is a more complicated metonymy: Old words are drawn from the cultural lexicon to name the new entity (or to rename an old one), as well as to render it (whether old or new) part of the present culture. The relations between entities so named are woven together in patterns far more complicated than any alphabetic or numeric listing can suggest: and the encounter between objects-that-are-words (e.g., the name "science fiction," a critical text on science fiction, a science-fiction text) and processes-made-manifest-by-words (another science-fiction text, another critical text, another name) is as complex as the constantly dissolving interface between culture and language itself. But we can take a model of the naming process from another image:

Consider a child, on a streetcorner at night, in one of Earth's great cities, who hears for the first time the ululating sirens, who sees the red, enameled flanks heave around the far building edge, who watches the chrome-ended, rubber-coated, four-inch "suctions" ranked along those flanks, who sees the street-light glistening on glass-faced pressure-meters and stainless-steel discharge-valves on the red pump-housing, and the canvas hose heaped in the rear hopper, who watches the black-helmeted and rubber-coated men clinging to their ladders, boots lodged against the serrated running-board. The child might easily name this entity, as it careers into the night, a Red Squealer.

Later, the child brings this name to a group of children—who take it up easily and happily for their secret speech. These children grow; younger children join the group; older children leave. The name persists—indeed, for our purposes, the locus of which children use and which children do not use the name is how we read the boundary of the group itself.

The group persists—persists weeks, months, years after the child

---

boss, "Thirty drivers rolled in this weekend," is basically communicating about the arrival of trucks those drivers drove and cargoes those trucks hauled. *Metonymic* is a slightly strained, adjectival construction to label such associational processes. *Metonym* is a wholly-coined, nominative one, shored by a wholly spurious (etymologically speaking) resemblance to "synonymy/synonym" and "antinomy/antinym." Still, it avoids confusion. In a text practically opaque with precision, it distinguishes "metonymy"—the-thing-associated ("crown," "driver") from "metonymy"—the-process-of-association (crown to monarch; driver to cargo). The orthodox way of referring to both is with the single term.

who first gave it its secret term has outgrown both the group and its language. But one day a younger child asks an older (well after the name, within the group, has been hallowed by use): "But *why* is it a Red Squealer?" Let us assume the older child (who is of an analytical turn of mind) answers: "Well, Red Squealers must get to where they are going quickly; for this reason sirens are put on them which squeal loudly, so that people can hear them coming a long way off and pull their cars to the side. They are painted with that bright enamel color for much the same reason—so that people can see them coming and move out of their way. Also, by now, the red paint is traditional; it serves to identify that it is, indeed, a Red Squealer one sees through the interstices of traffic and not just any old truck."

Satisfying as this explanation is, it is still something of a fiction. We were there, that evening, on the corner. We know the first child called it a Red Squealer out of pure, metonymic apprehension: There were, that evening, among many perceived aspects, "redness" and "squealing," which, via a sort of morphological path-of-least-resistance, hooked up in an easily sayable/thinkable phrase. We know, from our privileged position before *this* text, that there is nothing explicit in our story to stop the child from having named it a Squealing Red, a Wah-Wah, a Blink-a-blink, or a Susan-Anne McDuffy—had certain nonspecified circumstances been other than the simplest reading of our fiction suggests. The adolescent explanation, as to why a Red Squealer *is* a Red Squealer, is as satisfying as it is because it takes the two metonyms that form the name and embeds them in a web of functional discourse—satisfying because of the functional nature of the adult épistèmé*, which both generates the discourse and of which, once the discourse is uttered, the explanation (as it is absorbed into the memory, of both querant and explicator, which is where the *textus* lies embedded) becomes a part.

Science Fiction was named in like manner to the Red Squealer; in like manner the metonyms which are its name can be functionally related:

Science fiction *is* science fiction because various bits of technological discourse (real, speculative, or pseudo)—that is to say the "science"—are used to redeem various other sentences from the merely metaphorical, or even the meaningless, for denotative description/pre-

---

* The épistèmé is the structure of knowledge read from the epistemological *textus* when it is sliced through (usually with the help of several texts) at a given, cultural moment.

sentation of incident. Sometimes, as with the sentence "The door dilated," from Heinlein's *Beyond This Horizon,* the technological discourse that redeems it—in this case, discourse on the engineering of large-size, iris apertures; and the sociological discourse on what such a technology would suggest about the entire culture—is not explicit in the text. Is it, then, implicit in the *textus*? All we can say for certain is that, embedded in the *textus* of anyone who can *read* the sentence properly, are those emblems by which they could recognize such discourse were it manifested to them in some explicit text.

In other cases, such as the sentences from Bester's *The Stars My Destination,* "The cold was the taste of lemons, and the vacuum was the rake of talons on his skin . . . Hot stone smelled like velvet caressing his skin. Smoke and ash were harsh tweeds rasping his skin, almost the feel of wet canvas. Molten metal smelled like water trickling through his fingers," the technological discourse that redeems them for the denotative description/presentation of incident *is* explicit in the text: "Sensation came to him, but filtered through a nervous system twisted and short-circuited by the PyrE explosion. He was suffering from Synaesthesia, that rare condition in which perception receives messages from the objective world and relays these messages to the brain, but there in the brain the sensory perceptions are confused with one another."

In science fiction, "science"—i.e., sentences displaying verbal emblems of scientific discourses—is used to literalize the meanings of other sentences for use in the construction of the fictional foreground. Such sentences as "His world exploded," or "She turned on her left side," as they subsume the proper technological discourse (of economics and cosmology in one; of switching circuitry and prosthetic surgery in the other), leave the banality of the emotionally muzzy metaphor, abandon the triviality of insomniac tossings, and, through the labyrinth of technical possibility, become possible images of the impossible. They join the repertoire of sentences which may propel *textus* into text.

This is the functional relation of the metonyms "science" and "fiction" that were chosen by Hugo Gernsbach to name his new pulp genre. He (and we) perceived that, in these genre texts, there existed an aspect of "science" and an aspect of "fiction," and because of the science, something *about* the fiction was different. I have located this difference specifically in a set of sentences which, with the particular way they are rendered denotatively meaningful by the existence of

other sentences not necessarily unique to science fiction, are themselves by and large unique to texts of the s-f genre.

The obvious point must be made here: This explanation of the relation of these two onomal metonyms Science/Fiction no more defines
(or exhausts) the science-fictional-enterprise than our adolescent explanation of the relation of the two onomal metonyms Red/Squealer
defines (or exhausts) the enterprise of the fire engine. Our functional
explanation of the Red Squealer, for example, because of the metonyms from which the explanation started, never quite gets around to
mentioning the Red Squealer's primary function: to put out fires.

And the "function" of science fiction is of such a far more complex
mode than that of the Red Squealer, one might hesitate to use such
metonyms—"function" and "primary"—to name it in the first place.
Whatever one chooses to name it, it can not be expressed, as the Red
Squealer's can, by a colon followed by a single infinitive-with-noun—
no more than one could thus express the "primary function" of the
poetic-enterprise, the mundane-fictional-, the cinematic-, the musical-,
or the critical-. Nor would anyone seriously demand such an expression for any of these other genres. For some concept of what, primarily, science fiction does, as with other genres, we must rely on further,
complex, functional explanation:

The hugely increased repertoire of sentences science fiction has
to draw on (thanks to this relation between the "science" and the
"fiction") leaves the structure of the fictional field of s-f notably different from the fictional field of those texts which, by eschewing
technological discourse in general, sacrifice this increased range of
nontechnological sentences—or at least sacrifice them in the particular, foreground mode. Because the added sentences in science fiction
are primarily foreground sentences, the relationship between foreground and background in science fiction differs from that of mundane fiction. The deposition of weight between landscape and
psychology shifts. The deployment of these new sentences within
the traditional s-f frame of "the future" not only generates the obviously new panoply of possible fictional incidents; it generates as well
an entirely new set of rhetorical stances: The future-views-the-pre-
sent forms one axis against which these stances may be plotted; the
alien-views-the-familiar forms the other. All stories would seem to
proceed as a progression of verbal data which through their relation
among themselves and their relation to data outside themselves, produce, in the reader, data expectations. New data arrive, satisfying

and/or frustrating these expectations, and, in turn and in concert with the old, produce new expectations—the process continuing till the story is complete. The new sentences available to s-f not only allow the author to present exceptional, dazzling, or hyperrational data, they also, through their interrelation among themselves and with other, more conventional sentences, create a *textus* within the text which allows whole panoplies of data to be generated at syntagmatically startling points. Thus Heinlein, in *Starship Troopers,* by a description of a mirror reflection and the mention of an ancestor's nationality, in the midst of a strophe on male makeup, generates the data that the first-person narrator, with whom we have been traveling now through two hundred and fifty-odd pages (of a three-hundred-and-fifty-page book), is black. Others have argued the surface inanities of this novel, decried its endless preachments on the glories of war, and its pitiful founderings on sublimated homosexual themes. But who, a year after reading the book, can remember the arguments for war—short of someone conscientiously collecting examples of human illogic? The arguments *are* inane; they do *not* relate to anything we know of war as a real interface of humanity with humanity: they do not stick in the mind. What remains with me, nearly ten years after my first reading of the book, is the knowledge that I have experienced a world in which the *placement* of the information about the narrator's face is *proof* that in such a world the "race problem," at least, has dissolved. The book as text—as object in the hand and under the eye—became, for a moment, the symbol of that world. In that moment, sign, symbol, image, and discourse collapse into one, nonverbal experience, catapulted from somewhere beyond the *textus* (*via* the text) at the peculiarly powerful trajectory only s-f can provide. But from here on, the description of what is unique to science fiction and how it works within the s-f *textus* that is, itself, embedded in the whole language—and language-like—*textus* of our culture becomes a list of specific passages or sets of passages: better let the reader compile her or his own.

I feel the science-fictional-enterprise is richer than the enterprise of mundane fiction. It is richer through its extended repertoire of sentences, its consequent greater range of possible incident, and through its more varied field of rhetorical and syntagmatic organization. I feel it is richer in much the same way atonal music is richer than tonal, or abstract painting is richer than realistic. No, the apparent "simple-mindedness" of science fiction is not the same as that surface effect through which individual abstract paintings or particular atonal pieces frequently appear "impoverished" when compared to "conventional" works, on first exposure (exposed to, and compared by, those people who have absorbed only the "conventional" *textus* with which to "read" their art or music). This "impoverishment" is the necessary simplicity of sophistication, mete for the far wider web of possibilities such works can set resonating. Nevertheless, I think the "simple-mindedness" of science fiction may, in the end, have the same aesthetic weight as the "impoverishment" of modern art. Both are manifestations of "most works in the genre"—not the "best works." Both, on repeated exposure *to* the best works, fall away—by the same process in which the best works charge the *textus*—the web of possibilities—with contour.

The web of possibilities is not simple—for either abstract painting, atonal music, or science fiction. It is the scatter pattern of elements from myriad individual forms in all three, that gives their respective webs their densities, their slopes, their austerities, their charms, their contiguities, their conventions, their clichés, their tropes of great originality here, their crushing banalities there: The map through them can only be learned, as any other language is learned, by exposure to myriad utterances, simple and complex, from out the language of each. The contours of the web control the reader's experience of any given s-f text; as the reading of a given s-f text re-contours, however slightly, the web itself, that text is absorbed into the genre, judged, remembered, or forgotten.

In wonder, awe, and delight, the child who, on that evening, saw the juggernaut howl into the dark, named it "Red Squealer." We know the name does not exhaust; it is only an entrance point into the *textus* in order to retrieve from it some text or other on the contours, formed and shaped of our experience of the entities named by, with, and organized around those onomal metonyms. The *textus* does not define; it is, however slightly, redefined with each new text embedded upon it, with each new text retrieved from it. We also know that the naming does not necessarily imply, in the child, an understanding of that *textus* which offers up its metonyms and in which those metonyms are embedded. The wonder, however, may initiate in the child that process which, resolved in the adult, reveals her, in helmet and rubber raincoat, clinging to the side-ladders, or hauling on the fore- or rear-steering wheel, as the Red Squealer rushes toward another blaze.

It may even find her an engineer, writing a text on why, from now on, Red Squealers had best be painted blue, or a bell replace that annoying siren—the awe and delight, caught pure in the web, charging each of her utterances (from words about, to blueprints of, to the new, blue, bonging object itself) with conviction, authenticity, and right.

IV

Everything in a science-fiction novel should be mentioned at least twice (in at least two different contexts), with the possible exception of science fiction.

V

Saturn's Titan had proved the hardest moon to colonize. Bigger than Neptune's Triton, smaller than Jupiter's Ganymede, it had seemed the ideal moon for humanity. Today, there were only research stations, the odd propane-mine, and Lux—whose major claim was that it bore the same name as the far larger city on far smaller Iapetus. The deployment of humanity's artifacts across Titan's surface more resembled the deployment across one of the gas giants' "captured moons"—the under-six-hundred-kilometer hunks of rock and ice (like Saturn's Phoebe, Neptune's Neriad, or a half-dozen-plus of Jupiter's smaller orbs) that one theory held to have drifted out from the asteroid belt before being caught in their present orbits. Titan! Its orangeish atmosphere was denser (and colder) than Mars's—though nowhere near as dense as Earth's. Its surface was marred with pits, rivers, and seas of methane and ammonia sludge. Its bizarre life-forms (the only other life in the Solar System) combined the most unsettling aspects of a very large virus, a very small lichen, and a slime mold. Some varieties, in their most organized modes, would form structures like blue, coral bushes with, for upwards of an hour at a time, the intelligence of an advanced octopus. An entire subgenre of ice-operas had grown up about the Titan landscape. Bron despised them. (And their fans.) For one thing, the Main Character of these affairs was always a man. Similarly, the One Trapped in the Blue, Coral-like Tentacles was always a woman (Lust Interest of the Main Character). This meant that the traditional ice-opera Masturbation Scene (in which the Main Character Masturbates while Thinking of the Lust Interest) was always, for Bron, a Bit of a Drag. And who wanted to watch another shindo expert pull up another ice-spar and beat her way out of another blue-coral bush, anyway? (There were other, experimental ice-operas around today in which the Main Character, identified by a small "MC" on the shoulder, was only on for five minutes out of the whole five-hour extravaganza, Masturbation Scene and All—an influence from the indigenously Martian Annie-show—while the rest was devoted to an incredible interlocking matrix of Minor Characters' adventures.) And the women who went to them tended to be strange—though a lot of very intelligent people, including Lawrence, swore Titan-opera was the only really select artform left to the culture. Real ice-opera—better-made, true-to-life and with more to say about it via a whole vocabulary of real and surreal conventions, including the three formal tropes of classical abstraction, which the classical ice-opera began with, ended with, and had to display once gratuitously in the middle—left Lawrence and his ilk (the ones who didn't go into ego-booster booths) yawning in the lobby.

Appendix B
Ashima Slade and the Harbin-Y Lectures:

Some Informal Remarks Toward the Modular Calculus,
Part Two

A Critical Fiction for Carol Jacobs & Henry Sussman

Utopias afford consolation: although they have no real locality there is nevertheless a fantastic, untroubled region in which they are able to unfold; they open up cities with vast avenues, superbly planted gardens, countries where life is easy, even though the road to them is chimerical. *Heterotopias* are disturbing, probably because they make it impossible to name this and that, because they shatter or tangle common names, because they destroy "syntax" in advance, and not only the syntax with which we construct sentences but also that less apparent syntax which causes words and things (next to and also opposite one another) to "hold together." This is why utopias permit fables and discourse: they run with the very grain of language and are part of the fundamental *fabula*; heterotopias . . . desiccate speech, stop words in their tracks, contest the very possibility of grammar at its source; they dissolve our myths and sterilize the lyricism of our sentences.

MICHEL FOUCAULT, The Order of Things

I

[Concerning Ashima Slade and his Harbin-y Lecture *Shadows,* first published in Lux University's philosophy journal *Foundation,* issue six and the double issue seven/eight.]

Just over a year ago, at Lux on Iapetus, five million people died. To single out one death among that five million as more tragic than another would be monumental presumption.

One of the many, many to die, when gravity and atmosphere shields were stripped away from the city by Earth Intelligence sabotage, was the philosopher and mathematician Ashima Slade.

Lux University, where Slade taught, was unaccountably spared by the Earth saboteurs. A keep and suburb to itself just to the south, with its own gravity controls and plasma shield, the University was able to seal itself off until help could arrive from the surrounding holds and ice-farms, and gravity and atmosphere could be restored once more to the city, which had, in minutes, become a charnelhouse and necropolis.

The University housed thirty-five thousand tutors and students. The war did not leave it undamaged. On the campus, a hundred and eighty-three died. Reports of what occurred there only pale beside the devastation of the city of which it was, officially, a part.

Ashima Slade did not live on campus but, rather, in a spare room at the back of a co-op run by the Sygn, a religious sect practicing silence and chastity, in Lux's sprawling unlicensed sector. Not a sect member, Slade lived there as the Sygn's guest. From time to time it was rumored Slade was a Sygn official, priest, or guru. This is untrue. Various Sygn members had been Slade's students, but Slade's co-op residency was simple sectarian generosity toward an eccentric, solitary philosopher during the last dozen years of Slade's (and the Sygn's) life.

Once a month Slade visited the University to conduct his Philosophy of Mind seminar. Once a week, from his room, he would hold, over a private channel, an hour session whose title was simply its university catalogue number: BPR-57-c. During these sessions, Slade would talk of his current work or, occasionally, do some of it aloud or on the blackboard he kept beside his desk. These sessions were observed in holographic simulation by some three hundred students living in the University or in the city, as well as special attendees registered in the University rotation program. These sessions were difficult, tentative, and often—depending on the extent of one's interest—tedious. There was no question or discussion period. All response was by mail and seldom acknowledged. Yet students claimed them, again and again, to be endlessly illuminating, if not to subject, then in method, if not to method, then in logical style.

II

The Harbin-Y Lectures were established forty years ago as an annual, honorary series " . . . to be given by a creative thinker in the conceptual arts or sciences who will present a view of her (or his) field." Seven years ago, Slade was first invited to give that year's Harbin-Y Lectures. He declined, saying (a bit overmodestly) that his view of his own field was far too idiosyncratic. Two years later, he was invited again. This time, tentatively, he accepted, on condition he could lecture from his room, by holographic simulation, rather as he conducted BPR-57-c.

Slade's monthly seminar (which he held in person) had only six attendees. The traditional presentation procedure of the Harbin-Y Lectures is a personal delivery from the stage of the K-Harbin Auditorium to an invited audience of several thousand.

Twenty years ago, Slade had recorded a superb programmed course called *The Elements of Reason: An Introduction to Metalogics* which is still on store, unrevised, in the Satellite General Information Computer Network (and is considered the best introduction to Slade's own, early, ovular work, the two-volume *Summa Metalogiae*). At ease before any sort of recording or mechanical device, Slade still felt he would be uncomfortable before such a large, live audience.

The academic confusion over Slade's not overly exceptional request escalated, however, out of all proportion. Slade was an eccentric figure in the University, whose personal rarity on campus had led to some extraordinary (and extraordinarily idiotic) myths. Many of his colleagues were, frankly, afraid he would simply conduct a BPR-57-c session, completely inaccessible to his audience. No one was sure how to ascertain tactfully if he would discuss his work at the level they felt was called for by the occasion. How all this was finally resolved is not our concern here. But once more Slade did not deliver that year's Harbin-Y Lectures.

Slade was not invited to give the next year's lectures; it is said he expressed great relief about this to some of his colleagues with whom he was in correspondence, as well as to his seminar students. The reports, however, of Slade's work in the Modular Calculus (growing out of his early work in metalogics) had percolated down from the devotees of BPR-57-c, making it inevitable that he be asked again; once more the invitation was extended. Slade consented. This time he discussed the outline of the three lectures he wished to present with the Harbin-Y trustees in a way that lead them to believe the talks would at least approach the comprehensible. A holographic simulation was arranged in the auditorium. The lecture titles were announced:

Some Informal Remarks Toward the Modular Calculus:
    1) Shadows
    2) Objectives
    3) Illuminations

The three lectures were scheduled for the usual evening times. The usual invitations were sent. Thanks to five years' confusion, there was a good deal more than the usual curiosity. Many people—far more than might be expected for such an abstruse affair—turned to Slade's early work, the serious in preparation, the curious for hints of what was to come.

A perusal of any dozen pages from the *Summa* reveals Slade's formal philosophical presentation falls into three, widely differing modes. There are the closely reasoned and crystallinely lucid arguments. There are the mathematical sections in which symbols predominate over words; and what words there are, are fairly restricted to: ". . . therefore we can see that . . . ," ". . . we can take this to stand for . . . ," ". . . from following these injunctions it is evident that . . . ," and the like. The third mode comprises those sections of richly condensed (if not impenetrable) metaphor, in language more reminiscent of the religious mystic than the philosopher of logic. For even the informed student, it is debatable which of these last modes, mathematical or metaphorical, is the more daunting.

One of the precepts of Slade's philosophy, for example, explicit in his early work and implicit in his later, is a belief in the absolute distinction between the expression of "process/relation/operation" on the one hand and the expression of "matter/material/substance" on the other for rational clarity, as established by the contemporary épistèmé; as well as a belief in their absolute and indeseverable interface, in the real Universe. About this, Slade has remarked: " . . . This interface will remain indeseverable as long as time is irreversible. Indeed, we can only model the elements on either side separably with those tools— memory, thought, language, art—by which we can also construct models of reversible time."* As one of Slade's commentators has remarked, in an issue of the *Journal of Speculative Studies*: "Put this way, it is either understood or it isn't. Explication here is, really, beside the point."

The confusion attendant on Slade's previous invitations to lecture was a vivid memory for many of that year's audience. The people who assembled in the K-Harbin Auditorium that evening came with curiosity, trepidation, and—many of them—excitement.

The auditorium doors were closed.

At the expected time, Slade (with his desk and his blackboard) materialized on stage—dark, small-boned, broad-hipped—in a slightly quavery holographic simulation. The audience quieted. Slade began—there was some difficulty with the sound. After a few adjustments by the student engineer, Slade good-naturedly repeated those opening sentences lost on a loose connection.

An hour and twenty minutes into Slade's presentation, the first gravity cut hit Lux's unlicensed sector. Two minutes after that, there was total gravity loss. The city was stripped of atmosphere. And (among five million others) Ashima Slade, still in holographic simulation on the K-Harbin Auditorium stage, was dead.

---

* All quotes attributed to Slade are from the notes of Slade's current and former students. Statements reported in indirect discourse are from personal reminiscences of both students and Slade's fellow tutors and—in one instance—from notes on a comment the precise wording of which the writer did not feel she could vouch for as the notes had been hastily jotted down seventeen years ago. To all who have helped in the preparation of this appendix, the editor extends her grateful thanks.

III

Ashima Slade was born in Mars's Bellona in 2051. Little is known of his childhood; part was apparently passed in Phoenix Keep, a suburb just outside the city, and part in the notorious Goebels (which some have compared to the unlicensed sectors of the major satellite cities; the comparison must suffice for those who have never been to Bellona, but it has been argued elsewhere, lengthily, and on both sides). At seventeen Slade emigrated to the satellites, arriving, in a shipload of twenty-five hundred, at Callisto Port. Two months after his arrival, he became a woman, moved again to Lux and for six months worked in one of the city's light-metal refineries: It was here she first met Blondel Audion, when the famous poet descended, among some dozen others, for a flyting, or ritual exchange of poetic insults, in the refinery cafeteria. At six months' end (four days after the flyting's) Slade entered Lux University. Two and a half years later, she published the first volume of her *Summa Metalogiae*, which brought her, academically, both prestige and notoriety; and which led, over the next few years (when the second volume of the *Summa* appeared), to the development of metalogical program analysis, giving Slade a permanent, top-slot credit rating. Slade's reaction to the commercial success of what had begun as purely abstract considerations was sometimes humorous and, sometimes, bitter. Undoubtedly this practical success prejudiced many of her colleagues in those early years—and in several directions. Some took it as a vindication of pure scholarship. Others took it as an unfortunate sullying of the same. Still others saw it as evidence that Slade's own work was, at most, clever, rather than fundamentally profound. Slade herself once said (in a seminar, after a morning spent reviewing some of the commercial work done in metalogical analysis that had been sent her to review): "The saddest thing to me is that, though we *are* working under the same principles and parameters, I find what they are doing with them trivial, while they would find what I am doing with them incomprehensible, or meaningless if they *could* comprehend it."

At about the time of the publication of the second volume of the *Summa*, Slade first became closely associated with the Circle (as it has come to be commonly known since the various studies in the first decade of this century), a collection of extremely talented artists and scientists, some of whom were also connected with the University, some of whom not, but all of whom lived and worked (sometimes together, sometimes in opposition) in Lux. Over twenty-odd years, it included George Otuola, whose twenty-nine-hour opera cycle *Eridani* is still, twelve years after its initial production, considered one of the greatest influences on contemporary art; it included the mathematicians Lift Zolenus and Saleema Slade (no relation), the poets Ron Barbara, Corinda, Blondel Audion, and Foyedor Huang-Ding, as well as the venerable actress Alona Liang and her then-protégé, Gene Trimbell, better known in the world of the theater today as the Spike, who at age twenty-two, directed that first, legendary production of *Eridani*.

Some commentators have expended great energy and ingenuity to show that all the work of these, and several other artists and (particularly) biologists, associated over the years with the Circle, revolved around the parameters of Slade's philosophy—so that Slade might be considered the Circle's center. If none has completely succeeded, one hindrance to their proof is the complexity of Slade's work. Also, Slade's thought for this time is only available through her students' report. The only thing Slade herself published in these years was her translation, from the twentieth-century American " . . . into this Magyar-Cantonese dialect, with its foggy distinctions between the genitive and the associative, personally or politically enforced, which serves us for language in the Satellites, on Mars, as well as over eighty percent of Earth . . ." (translator's introduction) of Susanne K. Langer's *Mind*. Her students through this period were allowed to make notes and were encouraged to ". . . construct alternate models from these ideas as widely deviant as possible." But her talks could not be recorded, as Slade considered her BPR-57-c sessions then ". . . merely sketches, full of inaccuracies . . ." which makes assessment of her actual ideas rather difficult—until the corpus of notes, rescued from that small, back, basement room two weeks after the war, is made available.

Other commentators, less successfully, have tried to show that all the work of the principle Circle members, including Slade's, hinges on the mystic precepts of the Sygn. As anyone knows who has read in the Circle's history, that history is intimately connected with the Sygn's: Barbara and Otuola were both members of the sect during their adolescence, only to break with it (in Barbara's case peacefully, in Otuola's rather violently) in their twenties. Barbara's first book, *Relearning the Language*, deals fairly directly with his religious struggles during his speechless youth. And the Sect of Silent Singers, who figure so prominently in the action of *Eridani's* fifth, seventh, and seventeenth acts, is a fairly direct, if unflattering, portrayal. Slade's final residence at the Sygn cooperative is only another example, among the myriad possible to cite. The difficulty of proof here, however, is the difficulty in learning more than superficial fragments of the Sygn dogma. Those who emerged from the sect, even those highly critical such as Otuola, were fairly respectful of its mysteries: The sect renounces speech, writing, all publicity, and sex. This makes ascertaining its fundamental tenets during these years only slightly more difficult than ascertaining the letter of Slade's philosophy.

The most probable verdict is, probably, the most conservative: A great deal of personal, social, and spiritual interplay occurred between members of the Circle and members (and exmembers) of the Sygn. But it is what these men and women brought to it, rather than what they took from it, that ultimately makes the Circle the fascinating moment in the intellectual life of the Satellite Federation that it is.

Slade was fifty-four. *Summa Metalogiae* was two dozen years in the past. The triumphant opening of *Eridani* (which to many represents the peak of Circle creativity) was two years by. Only three months before, Corinda's eighth collection of poems, *Printed Circuits,* had occasioned her receipt of the Nobel Prize for Literature, making her not only the youngest person so awarded (she was then thirty-six), but also the first person born on a moon to be so honored by Earth's Swedish Academy. (Many felt, with justification, that the award was really being given, in retrospect, for her magnificent *Eridani* libretto, written four years before. Even so, many took the award as a beacon whose light might hopefully banish some of the shadows which, day by day, were darkening relations between Earth and the Satellite Federation.) In the thirteenth paramonth of the second year$_s$, Ashima Slade, Gene Trimbell (then twenty-four), Ron Barbara (twenty-nine), with two men who had recently broken with the Sygn, Sven Holdanks (nineteen) and Pedar Haaviko (fifty-eight), decided to form a family commune. Otuola was, apparently, invited to join. For various reasons, however, she refused.

The commune lasted three months.

Exactly what happened during that time is not known and probably never will be—unless it is on record in some Government Information Retention Bank, available only to the participants. Its obviously painful character, however, is probably one reason biographies of all the survivors are not in General Information and are "withheld on request."

Because some of the members are still alive, speculation must be fairly circumspect.

At the end of the three months, at ten o'clock at night, the building near the center of the Lux u-1, housing the commune's sixteen rooms, went up in flames, gutted by a furious chemical fire. Holdanks, the commune's youngest member, had committed suicide the same afternoon in a music practice room on the University campus, hanging himself with piano wire. A day later, Ms. Trimbell was admitted to a rest clinic for extreme distress (hallucinations, exhaustion, and hysteria) where she remained several months. Ron Barbara simply disappeared: His whereabouts only became known three years ago when, in quick succession, five slim volumes of poems (*Syntax I, Syntax II, Rime, Themos,* and *Syntax III*) appeared from a small, experimental publishing house in Bellona, where he has apparently been living for some while, having immigrated there after wandering for nearly a decade about the ice of four moons. The poems are abstruse, nearly incomprehensible, contain more mathematical symbols than words, and are in vast discord with his earlier, extremely lucid, direct and, essentially, verbal style that brought both popularity and critical approbation to such Barbara works as *Katalysis* and *Ice/Flows*. The new poems are the more frustrating because they contain (so people associated with the Circle have claimed) many references to the events of those three months. On the day of the commune's breakup, Haaviko rejoined the Sygn and sank into its secret and silent rituals.

On the morning after the holocaust, Slade was found, unconscious, in an alley two units from the house, blinded, severely lacerated, and otherwise maimed—most of the injuries, apparently, self-inflicted. Sometime during the three-month interim, she had again become a man.

Slade was taken to a clinic, from which he emerged two months later, frail, blind, white-haired, prematurely aged, a round, two-inch silver photoplate set off-center above his scarred eye-sockets, which he now used to "see" with. (The photoplate was set off-center because Slade did not want to block his "third eye," or pineal gland, an eccentricity easily complied with by the visual clinicians—another thing that has led some critics to suspect Slade's connection with the Sygn to be greater than it was: the Sygn set heavy store by this traditional site of cosmic awareness. Slade himself, however, once said this decision was more in the nature of "Pascal's wager," which, on another occasion, when discussing Pascal [and not himself at all] he referred to as " . . . the archetype of moral irresponsibility to the self.") Whatever occurred in those three months, we can only assume that it shook Slade on every level a human being can be shaken. Slade left the clinic presumably cured, but many of his friends, who would occasionally meet him, walking barefoot, in his shabby, gray cloak, through the alleys of the Lux u-l, avoiding the main thoroughfares because they made him uncomfortable, felt he was not entirely responsible, especially during these first weeks.

Some of the younger members of the Sygn (Haaviko had been transferred to another city by the sect) invited Slade to live in the Sygn co-op, an invitation which he accepted, remaining, with their consent, however, apart from their rituals and practices.

Eventually Slade resumed teaching. He seldom left his room, except at night, or on his monthly visit to the University to hold his seminar.

The only people Slade really associated with now were a few of the other elderly eccentrics who gathered in the all-night cafeterias of Lux's u-l, among whose crabbed and, more often than not, complaining conversations, he would, from time to time, enter a comment. Most of these men and women never knew he was, not a bottom, nonrefusable credit-slotter like themselves, but one of the most respected minds in the Solar System.

Most of them died not knowing—among the five million.

IV

In issues six and seven/eight of *Foundation,* we published the extant fragment of *Shadows,* the first of the three Harbin-Y Lectures Ashima Slade was to deliver on the modular calculus—and our subscription order, never particularly large, tripled. This popular (if a jump from five to fifteen thousand can be taken as an emblem of popularity) interest has prompted the commentary in the issue at hand.

A difficulty with *Shadows,* besides its incompleteness, is that Slade chose to present his ideas not as a continuous argument, but rather as a series of separate, numbered notes, each more or less a complete idea—the whole a galaxy of ideas that interrelate and interilluminate each other, not necessarily in linear form. Consider, however, these three statements from the last dozen notes Slade delivered:

42) There is no entrance to contemporary philosophical thought save at the twin gates of madness and obsession.

45) The problem of the modular calculus, again, is: How can one relational system model another? This breaks down into two questions: (One) What must pass from system-B to system-A for us (system-C) to be able to say that system-A now contains some model of system-B? (Two) Granted the proper passage, what must the internal structure of system-A be for us (or it) to say it contains any model of system-B?

49) There is no class, race, nationality, or sex that it does not help to be only half.

While none of these statements offers much difficulty in itself, it is still reasonable to ask what the three are doing in the same "galaxy." A sympathetic critic might answer that together they suggest the range of Slade's concerns. An unsympathetic one could hold that they *only* suggest; they certainly do *not* demonstrate; the fragmentary nature of the presentation precludes real profundity; to be significantly meaningful, the concerns should have been presented more deeply and with greater focus: At best, we have only a few, more or less interesting aphorisms. A third critic might simply dismiss many of the notes as examples of Slade's notorious eccentricity and suggest we concern ourselves only with those notes, if any, that discuss the modular process head-on.

Our purpose in this article, however, is to explicate, not judge. And certainly the three threads from which the collection of remarks are braided, as these three notes suggest, are the psychological, the logical, and the political.

Slade took the title for his first lecture, *Shadows,* from a nonfiction piece written in the twentieth century by a writer of light, popular fictions; it employed the same galactic presentation and the term "modular calculus" appears (once) in it. There is little resemblance beyond that, however, and it would be a grave mistake to take this older piece as a model for Slade's. Once Slade paraphrases it, in his note seventeen, " . . . I distrust separating facts too far from the landscape that produced them . . ."; but for Slade the concept of *landscape* is far more political than it was for the author of the older work. Consider Slade's thirty-first note: "Our society in the Satellites extends to its Earth and Mars emigrants, at the same time it extends instruction on how to conform, the materials with which to destroy themselves, both psychologically and physically—all under the same label: Freedom. To the extent they will not conform to our ways, there is a subtle swing: The materials of instruction are pulled further away and the materials of destruction are pushed correspondingly closer. Since the ways of instruction and the ways of destruction are *not* the same, but only subtly and secretly tied by language, we have simply, here, overdetermined yet another way for the rest of us to remain oblivious to other peoples' pain. In a net of tiny worlds like ours, that professes an ideal of the primacy of the subjective reality of all its citizens, this is an appalling political crime. And, in this appalling war, we may well be destroyed for it, if not by it."

Though Slade's major concern was logic, and his major contributions were made through the explorations of the micro-theater of single logical connections, Slade valued the role of Philosopher as Social Critic. How do the two concerns, politics and logic, fit together? Because the lecture is incomplete, we have no real way to know if Slade would have given us some statement on his concept of the relation between the two. Perhaps, however, his idea of the relation is suggested by the warning he gives in note nine of the lecture:

Suppose we have a mold that produces faulty bricks, and the flaw in single bricks can be modeled with the words *tends to crumble on the left;* if we then build a wall with these flawed bricks, that wall may or may not be flawed; also, the flaw may or may not be modelable with the words *tends to crumble on the left;* but even if it is, it is still not the *same* flaw as the flaw in any given brick; or the flaw in the mold. Keeping all these states clear and unentailed, despite the accidental redundancies of the language we can use to talk about them with, is the way out of most antinomies.

What Slade is suggesting, besides what he has to say of antinomies, is that even if we have discovered the form of a micro-flaw common to every element of our thinking, to think we have necessarily discovered the form of a macro-flaw in our larger mental structures—say our politics—is simply to fall victim to a micro-flaw again. This is not to say that macro-flaws may not relate to the micro-flaws—they usually do—but it is a mistake to assume that relation is direct and necessarily subsumed by the same verbal model.

Slade, as we have said, is also concerned with psychology—specifically the psychology of the philosopher. How does he relate this to his logical explorations? There is little in the extant text of *Shadows,* beyond the rather flamboyant note forty-two already cited, to tell us—though I might refer the interested reader to Chapter VI, Section 2 of Volume One of *Summa Metalogiae,* where Slade discusses mistakes in reasoning, under which he includes many that " . . . another generation would have simply called insanity."

Note twenty-two would seem to be the most accessible and detailed statement of Slade's modular concerns:

What must pass from system-B to system-A for system-A to model system-B? Turn to animate organisms and the senses. First we have what we can call *material models.* With the senses of Smell, Taste, and Touch, actual material must pass from one system to the other, or at least come into direct physical interface with it, for system-A to begin to construct a model of the situation from which the material came. In the case of the first two, nerve clusters respond to the actual shape of molecules to distinguish information about them; in the last, variations of pressure generate the information into the nervous system as to whether a surface that we run our hand across is smooth or rough, hard or soft. Next we have what we can call *reflected-wave models.* Sight is the prime example: A comparatively chaotic and undifferentiated wavefront originates in some relational system-Z (say the filament of a light bulb when current passes through it, or the fissioning gases near the surface of the sun) and scoots through the universe until it hits and interacts with relational system-B (say a collection of molecules that make up a hammer, a nail) and is then sent out, by this interaction, in other directions. The nature of this interaction is such that the wavefront has not only had its direction changed—or rather been scattered in precise directions by the surface of the molecule collection—, many of the undifferentiated frequencies have been completely absorbed. Others have been shunted up or down. Other changes have occurred as well. The distortion of the newly directed wavefront is so great, in fact, we can just as easily call the distortion at this point organization. As an extremely narrow section of this distorted/organized wavefront passes through the cornea, iris, and lens of the eye—part of relational system-A—it is distorted even more. At the retina, it is stopped completely; but the pattern it has been distorted/organized into, on the retina, excites the rods and cones there to

emit chemo-electric impulses that pass up the million-odd
fibers of the optic nerve toward the brain. Now the pattern on
the retina was not *in* the wavefront expanding through the air.
It resulted from a fraction of a second of an arc of that front
bent further in such a way that ninety-nine percent of it can-
celed itself out altogether, in much the way troughs and peaks
rippling over the surface of still water will, when they meet,
cancel one another even as they pass through. But once inside
the optic nerve, well before we get to the brain (the central or-
ganizer of relational system-A), we are not even dealing with
the original wavefront anymore. New photons are involved.
And the frequency of the impulse in the optic nerve fibers is
hugely below the frequency of the light that was our original
front, however distorted; these new frequencies are not even related as simple multiples of the original frequencies. At this
point, even before we reach the brain, we must ask ourselves
again: What has actually passed from system-B to system-A? If
we are honest, we must be prepared to answer, "Very little." Indeed no *thing* has passed from B to A . . . certainly not in the
sense that things (i.e., molecules) would have passed if system-
A were smelling system-B rather than seeing it. The waves did
not come *from* system-B, they simply bounced off it, trans-
formed by the encounter. What we can say, with reflected-wave
models, is that the original wavefront is at one order of randomness; the distortions system-B superimposes on that wavefront
are at another order of randomness so much lower that when
there is any change in that second order of randomness at all
(say system-A and system-B should move in relation to one
another; or they might both move in relation to the wave
source) the panoramic change in the order of randomness can
uniquely preserve the changes at the lower order through a series of simplifying operations that the eye and optic nerve (and
eventually the brain) of system-A impose. In other words, visual order is a record of the *changes* in random order (as opposed
to *either* the order *or* the randomness) of a series of wavefronts.
Or, to become slightly metaphorical, all order is at least the
fourth or fifth derivative of chaos. Now a third type of model
can be called a *generated-wave model*. Sound is our primary example. Here we are also working with wavefronts, but these
wavefronts have their origin *within* system-B, the system that

system-A is attempting to model, and bear their distortion/organization with them from their inception. Notice: Once we pass the eardrum into the aural nerve, much less distortion occurs than, say, with light, once it has stimulated impulses in the optic nerve. The impulses in the aural nerve are pretty much the same frequency as the waves passing through the air. Still, it is the *changes* in the order that allow us to distinguish between, say, the three notes of a chord struck only for a second. In that second, what has been simplified into three singable pitches is in the realm of fifteen hundred bits of information. And it is the redundancy and the differences among those bits that give us, finally, a primary mental model (i.e., an experience) of, say, an A-minor triad. Even the single note A, sounded for a second, involves eight hundred and eighty changes of pressure on the eardrum. Two points should be made here: (One) When speaking of wavefront models, the only difference between distortion and organization—between noise and information—is the ability of the receiving system to interpret. In terms of clinical psychology, the answers to this first question of the modular calculus proliferate endlessly and become the psychology/physiology of perception. We can leave this question to the psychophysiologists with our next point: (Two) Within the human organism—indeed, within any animal nervous system—once the proper passage has occurred between system-B and system-A, be it material or waves (reflected or generated), and we are dealing with the information that has gotten through the surface of the system, so to speak (i.e., past the sense organs), and into the nervous system itself, *all* of it has been translated into the form of *generated wave models*. In other words, sound is the *modular form* of *all* information *within* the nervous system itself, and that includes smell, taste, touch, and sight. The aesthetician Pater wrote: "All art aspires to the condition of music." Yes, and so does everything else. But our answer to the first question of the modular calculus has altered the second question so that it begins to be quantifiable, or at least topological: What is the necessary structure of a series of generated wave models within system-A which will allow it to know/experience aspects of the system-B which first excited these waves, either by reflected waves, as generated waves, or with material?

Answers to this rephrased question, some of which Slade lists, with all the attendant symbols and terminology, fill the next six notes; presumably these and like notes form the bulk of the calculus. How he arrived at some of these solutions would, presumably, have been discussed in the two undelivered lectures. Fortunately, Slade's students from BPR-57-c have been able to fill in much here, as this is exactly what Slade had been wrestling with during the original work sessions for three years. Some of their papers will appear in future issues.

Since Liebniz, or even Aristotle, the boundaries between mathematics and logic, and between logic and philosophy, have always been strangely fuzzy. Try to define them too carefully, and they disappear. Change your position only a fraction of a degree, and they seem clearly present once more. From this new angle we begin to define them again—and the process repeats. Is it, then, just the maverick statements that our third critic would claim Slade has simply scattered through his discussion of the logic of models that tempt us to take what seems essentially a discussion of the foundations of a limited, mathematical discipline and call it a philosophy? Your editor does not think so; we feel that for all its eccentricity of presentation, Slade's work is philosophically significant—though already (a situation which has existed about Slade's work since the publication of the *Summa*) articles have appeared which claim otherwise. The emblem of a philosophy is not that it contains a set of specific thoughts, but that it generates a way of thinking. Because a way of thinking is just that, it cannot be completely defined. And because Slade's lecture is incomplete, we cannot know if he would have attempted even a partial description. Your editor feels that the parameters for a way of thinking have, in the extant notes of *Shadows*, been at least partially generated. Rather than try to describe it, we think it is best to close this limited exegesis with an example of it from Slade's lecture. The note we end on—note seven—along with note twenty-two, completes the clearest nonmathematical explanation of the calculus Slade was trying to describe. (In note six, Slade talks about the efficiency of multiple modeling systems, or parallel models, over linear, or series models: his use of pictures, in note seven, to distinguish between words about reality and the real itself is a self-evident example of what he discusses in six. Slade drew the pictures hastily on his blackboard with blue chalk and pointed to them when they came up again in the flow of his talk.)

Here is note seven:

There are situations in the world. And there are words—which are, to put it circularly, what we use to talk about them with. What makes it circular is that the existence of words, and their relationship to meanings, and the interrelationships among them all, are also situations. When we talk about how words do what they do, we are apt to get into trouble because we are maneuvering through a complex house of mirrors, and there is almost no way to avoid that trouble, short of resorting to pictures—which I am not above doing.

Many situations in the world have aspects that can be talked of as directed binary relationships. Some examples of talk about these situations which highlight the directed binary relationship are:

"Vivian loves the Taj Mahal."

"Alicia built a house."

"Chang threw the ball."

"Sad means unhappy."

"The hammer hit a nail."

Let us take the last sentence, "The hammer hit a nail," and consider it and the situation it might commonly be used in, and explore the modeling process that is occurring in some detail. First, we have a thing, the phrase *the hammer,* standing for a thing, ⊨. In that phrase, we have a thing, the word *the,* standing for an attitude toward ⊨, and we have another thing, the word *hammer,* standing for the object ⊨ itself. Next, we have a thing, the verb *hit,* standing for a relationship, ⟨⇥⟩. After that, we have still another thing, the phrase *a nail,* standing for another thing, ⊤. As in the first phrase, in the second we have a thing, the word *a,* standing for an attitude toward the object ⊤ different from the attitude modeled by the word *the.* And, as in the phrase *the hammer,* we have a thing, the word *nail,* which stands for the object ⊤ itself. Also, we have a relationship, composed of which thing (i.e., word) is put before the verb and which thing (i.e., word) is put after it, that stands for an aspect of the relationship ⟨⇥⟩ not completely subsumed by the verb *hit* alone, i.e., which object is the comparatively active one and which is the comparatively receptive one—or what can be talked of as "the direction of the binary relationship." Now the direction of the relationship is, itself, a relationship; so here we have a relationship, between noun, verb, and noun, standing for an aspect of the relationship ⇥⇤ .

Now there are other notable relationships in the sentence "The hammer hit a nail," to attract our attention. In the phrase *the hammer,* for instance, which we have said consists of two things, the word *the* and the word *hammer,* it is necessary that the things appear in just that order. Likewise, the phrase *a nail* must preserve its order, if the sentence is to strike us as proper. What are these particular relationships necessary for? What would be wrong with the sentence "Hammer the hit nail a," or "Hammer hit nail a the," or "Hammer a the hit nail," or "The a hammer hit nail"? In all of these, we still have the things in the sentence which stand for the things in the situation, and in all of them the relation between *hammer, hit,* and *nail,* which models the direction of the relation in the situation, is preserved. Is the relation between *the* and *hammer,* or *a* and *nail,* modeling anything in the situation which is suddenly lost or obscured if these relations are lost?

To the extent that our attitudes toward the objects in a relationship are not in that relationship, the simple answer is no. The relationship between *the* and *hammer* and between *a* and *nail* are necessary to preserve the integrity of the model itself; they are necessary if we are to recognize the model as a proper thing for modeling in the first place. But these relationships, between *the* and *hammer* and *a* and *nail,* do not model anything in the situation talked about by the sentence. To destroy them, however, may prevent other relationships (that *may* be modeling something in the situation, *or* may be preserving the integrity of the model) from standing forth clearly. This simple answer is, however, rather oversimplified.

What shows the situation to be more complicated than our discussion so far is that the same thing may be said about the relationship between, say, the three *a*'s in the sentence. About their relationship we can accurately say: "In the sentence *The hammer hit a nail* there must be seven letters and two spaces between the first *a* and the second, and one letter and one space between the second and the third. Though there may well be a number of other sentences that also have this rela-

tionship between three *a*'s, if there is any *other* relationship between three *a*'s in a sentence, that sentence will *not* be the
proper sentence *The hammer hit a nail*." Using just letters, and
the number of spaces and letters between them, it is interesting to try and work out a minimum number of such relations
that will completely describe a given sentence. (One eventually has to resort to specifying distances between different letters.) Notice, however: If we consider the sentence *The hammer
hit a nail* to be made up of its letters and the relationships between them, then only a single *thing* among its elements, the
single letter *a*, is doing any modeling. The vast majority of the
things, as well as the vast majority of the relationships, that
make up and describe the sentence are nonmodular. Notice
also: How I decide to divide the sentence up into things is
going to determine what sort of relationships, whether modular or nonmodular, I must list to describe it, whether particularly or completely. If, for instance, instead of dividing the
sentence up into letters as a typewriter might type it, I were to
divide it into the single strokes that make up the letters on a
computer display flash-out, where each letter is made up of
lines in a matrix

each of which is given a number, then your minimum list of
things and relations (minimum because some letters can be
made in two forms:

is going to be very different from the list we talked about before.

But let us sum up what modeling is being done by the sentence *The hammer hit a nail*. We are modeling attitudes, objects,
and various aspects of a relation between them; to do this job,
we are using, among a large group of things and relations, various of those things and relations to stand for the objects, attitudes, and relations we wish to model.

A last point more or less separates the place where the modular calculus separates off from the modular algebra: Suppose,

by considering the sentence as a set of letters, we finally found a list of relationships that would completely describe it, such as:

1) Three *a*'s must be separated by, respectively, seven letters and two spaces, and one letter and one space.
2) Two *m*'s must be separated by no letters and no spaces.
3) One *m* must follow one *a*.
   Et cetera . . .

Even though, at the end, we have a list of relationships that completely describes the sentence (so that, say, a computer could translate our list into the matrix form of a flash-display, i.e., a list of numbers), still *no* relation, or even consecutive group of relations in our list, can be said to stand for any thing, attitude, or relation in the situation which the sentence models. Yet the sentence is completely described by this list.

Notice also: The list of numbers for the matrix display also completely describes the sentence. Yet here, some consecutive groups of numbers *can* be said to stand for things, attitudes, and relations in the situation—since certain groups of numbers stand for certain words and certain word groups. Notice as well that, while in this list there will be a consecutive group of numbers that stands for the relationship of *the* and *hammer,* and *a* and *nail,* there is no consecutive group that stands only for the relation of *hammer, hit,* and *nail:* because the numbers standing for the second *a* in the sentence will be in the way.

We can call the computer matrix display a *modular description* because it preserves *some* of the modular properties of the sentence in a list that describes the sentence.

We can call the list of letters in relation to each other a *nonmodular description* because it preserves *none* of the modular relations of the sentence in a list that describes the sentence.

As we have seen, with our computer example, complete descriptions of models can be translated from nonmodular descriptions into modular ones and back again and remain both complete and intact. The first useful thing the modular calculus yields us is the following information:

Consider language a list of relationships between sounds that model the various ways sounds may relate to one another—or, if you will, a list of sentences about how to put together sentences, i.e., a grammar. The modular calculus lets us know, in no uncertain terms, that even if such a list were complete, it would still be a nonmodular description. It has the same modular order (the proof is not difficult) as our description of the sentence *The hammer hit a nail* as a set of letters precisely spaced and divided.

The calculus also gives us tools to begin to translate such a list into a modular description.

Now the advantages of a modular description of either a modeling object, like a sentence, or a modeling process, like a language, are obvious vis-à-vis a nonmodular description. A modular description allows us reference routes back to the elements in the situation which is being modeled. A nonmodular description is nonmodular precisely because, complete or incomplete as it may be, it destroys those reference routes: it is, in effect, a cipher.

The problem that still remains to the calculus, despite my work, and that will be discussed in the later lectures, is the generation of formal algorithms for distinguishing incoherent modular descriptive systems from coherent modular descriptive systems. Indeed, the calculus has already given us partial descriptions of many such algorithms, as well as generating ones for determining completeness, partiality, coherence, and incoherence—processes which till now had to be considered, as in literature which so much of this at a distance resembles, matters of taste. But their discussion must be left for the last lecture.

About the Author

Samuel R. Delany is a professor of English at Temple University. His many books include the Return to Nevèrÿon series, *The Einstein Intersection, Dhalgren, Trouble on Triton,* and *Atlantis: Three Tales,* all reissued by Wesleyan University Press. His most recent books include *Shorter Views* (Wesleyan, 1999), *Times Square Red, Times Square Blue* (1999), and a graphic novel with artist Mia Wolff, *Bread & Wine* (1999).

Library of Congress Cataloging-in-Publication Data
Delany, Samuel R.
  [Triton]
  Trouble on Triton : an ambiguous heterotopia / Samuel R. Delany;
  foreword by Kathy Acker.
       p.   cm.
  Originally published: Triton. New York : Bantam Books, c1976.
  ISBN 0-8195-6298-X (pbk. : alk. paper)
  I. Title
PS3554.E437T75   1996
813'.54—dc20   95-46796